THE ENFORCER
LAKESIDE UNIVERSITY

AVERY KEELAN

AVERY KEELAN

PLAYLIST

1. Be Your Love – Bishop Briggs
2. Echo (feat. blackbear) – Maroon 5, blackbear
3. Will It Ever Feel The Same? - Bazzi
4. Feel – Fletcher
5. the 1 – Taylor Swift
6. <3 – Vi
7. Glycerine – Bush
8. exile (feat. Bon Iver) – Taylor Swift
9. Haunt You – Social House
10. What I Put You Through – Conor Maynard
11. Out of My Hands – SHY Martin
12. Perfectly Wrong – Shawn Mendes
13. Lost My Mind – Alice Kristiansen
14. Slow Down – Chase Atlantic
15. Trust Me – 4ever Falling
16. Tribulation (feat. VÉRITÉ) – Matt Maeson
17. Like That – JP Saxe
18. September – James Arthur
19. Butterflies (feat. FLETCHER) – MAX

PROLOGUE

SEPTEMBER - FRESHMAN YEAR

Nash

I SHOULD KICK VAUGHN'S ass for dragging me to this party. It's not even nine p.m., the keg is tapped, and the rest of the beer is room temperature.

A cheesy pop song tumbles out of the speakers in the center of the Alpha Gamma Nu living room while several scantily clad girls gyrate on a wooden coffee table dangerously close to collapsing. People clutching red plastic cups watch from the periphery, but all I see are people I either don't know or don't want to talk to. I'm flying solo because my teammate fucked off upstairs with some chick from the soccer team a minute ago. I can't exactly complain, since I did the same thing to him last weekend.

My phone chimes, letting me know the rest of the team is in the basement playing beer pong. Time to school them—again—but first, I need a refill. Yanking open the glass patio door, I step outside in search of another beer because someone had the bright idea to store all the drinks outside amid a ninety-degree September heatwave. That, combined with some of the things I've witnessed tonight, leads me to seriously question how some of these people got into college.

When I flip open the top of the blue-and-white cooler, I discover why the last beer Vaughn gave me was piss warm—no ice. I rifle through its contents, trying to see if any cans are at least semi-cold, but it's full of girly shit like peach-flavored spiked seltzer and light lime-flavored beer. Did a sorority do the alcohol run tonight, or what? Who drinks this crap?

Footsteps sound on the wooden deck behind me as someone approaches. I glance over my shoulder, expecting to find someone from the team, but I'm pleasantly surprised to see it's a chick. A hot chick. Light blonde hair falls around her shoulders in loose waves, accenting one of the nicest racks I've ever seen. Her black tank top is slightly cropped, exposing a sliver of her creamy midriff, and her ripped jeans hug every curve of her lower half. But when I glance back up, it's her features that pull me in; big, doe-like eyes, a full, pouty mouth, and a perfect ski-jump nose.

I've found the rare total package: a banging body with a gorgeous face to match.

She's easily a ten, and I hardly ever say that. She's also petite, probably not much taller than five-three. In her left hand is a peach-flavored spiked seltzer, which answers my previous question. Hot chicks drink that crap, that's who.

I snatch a can at random and slam the cooler shut, pushing to stand while trying to place her face. Do I know her? Pretty sure I don't, but I want to.

"Hi." Her candy-pink lips tug into a tentative smile as she takes a step closer, regarding me with the bluest eyes I've ever seen. They're a piercing shade of blue like…fuck, I don't know. The sky? It's a deep, endless sort of color that I've never seen before.

On some level, I know I'm staring, but it's hard not to.

"Hey." Tearing away my focus from her, I look down at the can I'm holding to see what I grabbed. Room temperature lime beer it'll be, I guess.

She closes the distance between us and touches my upper arm, her cold fingertips landing on my bare skin. Electricity passes between us with the contact, and the intensity of the effect it has on my body catches me by surprise. I've been touched by plenty of girls in my time, and this interaction is downright G-rated.

"Could you do me a favor?" Her voice is so quiet, it's nearly inaudible over the din of the partygoers outside. Between the background noise and the height differential between us, I have to duck my head closer to hear her. It puts us within intimately close range and her perfume drifts over to me; something sweet with a bit of spice. Vanilla and cinnamon, maybe. Something edible, anyway, which isn't helping me keep my mind out of the gutter.

"For you?" I flash her a cocky grin. "Anything."

Her eyes dart off to the left, then back over to me. "See that guy over there?"

I follow her line of sight across the deck to where a stout, ruddy-faced guy in a gray varsity athletics t-shirt is glaring at us. Not at us, actually. At me. He looks like he wants to strangle me with his meaty red hands.

When my gaze swings back to her, there's tension across her pretty face that triggers a cascade of corresponding tension within me. My grip on the unopened can I'm holding tightens. That sweaty asshole is nearly three times her size. If he groped her, we're about to have a chat. Fist to face.

"What about him?" I ask, fighting to keep the edge out of my voice. "Is he giving you a hard time?"

She winces, tucking a lock of golden hair behind her ear. "You could say that. He's been following me around since I got here, and he won't take no for an answer. I can't find my girlfriends that I came here with, either." Pausing, she draws in a breath, and the words that follow come out in a rush of air. "Could you pretend to be my boyfriend for a while? Because I sort of made one up, and now I'm in a bind."

Cracking my beer, I steal another glance at the dude to assess the situation. The heathered gray cotton of his shirt is plastered to his torso, fabric straining against his broad frame. Probably a football player, if I had to guess. He's not as tall as I am but he's twice as thick. Built like a fucking tank, and appears equally as smart as one, too.

Judging by his hostile expression and even more hostile body language, there's a decent chance I'm signing up for a brawl by agreeing to her request, but another glance at her confirms that's a risk I'm more than willing to take. I'm not one to back down from a fight, especially not when I have an opening with the hottest chick at this party.

Her teeth sink into her lush bottom lip while she watches me, waiting for a response. I try not to let my mind go down a rabbit hole thinking about where I would like to have those lips, and only partially succeed.

"Sure." With a wink, I slide my arm around her narrow waist, and she leans into me, nestling her small frame beneath my shoulder. Another surprise? As a rule, I hate public displays of affection, but I don't hate this. At all.

"Thank you." She lets out a sigh of relief, palpably relaxing. While I'm not in the habit of doing favors for people, I think I'd have said yes even if I didn't want to hit on her. But I'd be lying if I said that wasn't a bonus.

"I think I'll need your name to sell this, though."

A rosy hue tints her cheeks. "Violet."

"Nice to meet you, Violet. I'm Nash." I take a sip of beer, trying to figure out what to do next. I'm not overly keen to stay out here with that lurking linebacker watching our every move, but I don't want to seem pushy like him, either. "So, Violet. What would your pretend boyfriend do next in this scenario?"

The patio door flies open, and Marcus pokes out his head, frantically scanning the crowd until he spots me. "What the hell, Richards? We've been waiting for you so we can begin the game." He barrels toward us, raking a hand through his black hair in exasperation, so pressed that you'd think I was delaying a playoff game and not a basement round of beer pong.

"Little busy with other things," I tell him, narrowly resisting the urge to trip him as he approaches. "As you can probably see."

Way to read the fucking room, man.

He gestures, his silver can of beer gleaming beneath the porch light. "Don't blame me. You said you'd kick our asses if we didn't wait, and now Hendricks is too scared to start without you."

Next to me, Violet stifles a giggle. I glance up at the indigo evening sky, channeling what little patience I have, then back down at Violet, giving her an apologetic look. She offers me a tiny smile in return that tells me maybe, just maybe, Marcus didn't fuck this up completely.

"Want to play a round of beer pong with us?" I ask her. "I can introduce you to the team."

She gives me a deer-in-headlights look that's cuter than it should be. "I would, but I've never played before. I'm probably going to be awful."

"Nah, it's easy. I can teach you."

———

Violet

I'm not sure I ended up holding hands with a hockey player.

It started with trying to avoid Ted or Tad or whoever was following me around, breathing down my neck after I lost Claire and Phoebe—mental note to never pee alone again at a party, by the way. While dodging my wannabe stalker, I stumbled across a hot potential knight in shining armor and spent the last few hours learning how to play beer pong with him and his friends. Or trying to learn, because I'm about as terrible as I'd expected. Once Claire and Phoebe resurfaced, they joined the game and I resigned myself to spectator status for everyone's sake.

Did I mention that said knight in shining armor is incredibly funny, smells like heaven and sin combined, and has a smile that could make you forget your own name? I've never crushed so hard, so fast.

With a final plunk of the ping-pong ball into a red solo cup, the tournament wraps up, leaving two of Nash's friends as victors.

"Refills!" A blond guy shouts, and the basement clears out as they stampede upstairs in a blur of drunken testosterone.

On the couch across from where Nash and I are standing, my dormmate Claire is perched with Sawyer, a senior on Nash's team, while she eyes Nash and me uncertainly. Probably because out of our three friends, I am by far the least experienced. Claire had an older boyfriend in high school, and Phoebe already disappeared about fifteen minutes ago with one of Nash's other teammates. Everything I know about sex, on the other hand, I learned from pages of Cosmopolitan magazine, and I suspect it may not translate perfectly.

"Want to get some air?" Sawyer asks Claire, flipping his white Grizzlies cap backward.

"You good, Violet?" Claire asks, looking torn. I can tell she wants to go with him, but she's trying to look out for me. "Want to come upstairs with us, or...?"

"No, that's okay," I tell her. "We'll catch up with you in a few."

They disappear up the staircase, leaving me alone with Nash. While this was my goal, I suspect I'm in a little over my head because he is definitely way more experienced than I am. Don't ask me how I know. I can just tell. Call it virgin's intuition.

Nash sets down his beer and nods to the basement bar beside us, motioning to indicate our nearly comical height difference. In addition to his broad, athletic frame, he's approximately six-foot-infinity.

"Can I set you up here so we're more eye to eye?" he asks.

Set me up there...as in, he's going to touch me? Holy mother of God.

"Yeah, sure." I try to sound confident, but it comes out breathy. Probably because I suspect he's going to kiss me, and while I want that, I'm nervous. My kissing practice to date consists of one sloppy, underwhelming encounter with Jordan Peltzer at my friend Maria's graduation party. Which means, for all I know, I might be a sloppy, underwhelming kisser, too. I don't have any data points to draw on for comparison's sake. Something tells me that's not the case for Nash.

Enormous hands wrap around my waist, interrupting my thought spiral and sending a thrill through my entire body. My feet leave the floor and I become momentarily weightless until Nash gently places me on the cool laminate counter, allowing me to take in his features up close. Square jaw, a slightly downturned mouth, and deep-set green eyes that I could lose myself in. Something about him looks serious—broody, like the bad-boy love interest in a romance novel. The one the heroine doesn't end up with because she decides the light-haired good guy is a more sensible choice.

"So, this is what it's like to be all the way up here. Nice view." I set down my nearly empty cooler, sliding it out of the way. Why, I'm not sure. It seems like having my hands free might be a good idea, even though they're trembling.

His lips tug. "You are pretty short."

"Or you're really tall, depending how you look at it." There's that stupid breathlessness again. Why do I sound like this? I don't think I've ever been so nervous in my life.

"Bit of both, really." His broad hands land on my knees and slide up to my hips, moving with a confidence that makes my breath catch. His thumbs gently caress the bare sliver of skin between my shirt and my jeans, kickstarting a flutter between my thighs. It occurs to me that this is probably the part where I should do something with my hands, too, but I don't know what. I settle for placing them on his shoulders, which are shockingly firm and built beneath the cotton fabric of his black t-shirt.

Everything about him feels like night and day compared to all the guys I knew in high school just months ago.

Nash tilts his head. "I have to ask. Why'd you come up to me?"

Leaning over, I grab my peach cooler and take another sip, emptying the last of it. Half-hiding my face, I look at him over the rim. "What do you mean?"

"This party is packed with guys." His expression is tinged with amusement, like he knows I'm trying to dodge the question.

"Are you fishing, Nash?"

He shrugs, playfulness shining in his forest green eyes. "Maybe a little. But when the hottest girl at the party comes up to you, it's a fair question."

All I know about him so far is that he plays hockey and he's a freshman, like me. Now I can add to the list: he's a flirt. Setting aside my empty drink, I draw in a breath and silently summon the Goddess of Flirting. Whoever she is. I could really use some divine inspiration right now.

When our gazes meet again, I get a rush of courage and opt to go with the only answer I have: the truth but make it flirty. Somehow.

I hold out a hand, ticking off my finger. "Well, you're one of the biggest guys here."

"Ah."

Ticking off a second finger, I add, "I had a hunch you weren't a creep."

This, while fully true, is another thing I can't explain. He arguably looks the least approachable and possibly the most dangerous out of every guy at this party, and paradoxically, that's what made him feel like the safest choice.

"Solid reasoning." He nods, taking a sip of his beer as he waits for me to continue.

"And I thought you were cute. Win-win." As soon as the words leave my mouth, heat floods my face; it's the most forward thing I've ever said to a guy. This night is full of firsts, apparently.

The reaction it garners me is fully worth the risk. Nash's expression darkens and he sets aside his beer, his warm palm gently cupping my face. "Oh, it's definitely a win for me."

My heart drums against my chest as our noses brush, our breaths mingling. His scent envelops me from all angles, delicious spicy cologne blended with notes of lime beer and an undertone of masculinity, and my fingertips dig into his shoulders a little more, urging him on.

Finally, his lips brush against mine, gently coaxing them apart. My eyelids flutter shut as his tongue sweeps into my mouth, tasting of citrus and beer, untold risks and rewards. It's softer than I expected, at first, but as I kiss him back, he draws in a breath and dials up the intensity. Every nerve in my body comes alive, burning brighter with each passing second.

This is no sloppy high school kiss. This is everything.

Everything in the world fades out except for his mouth moving against mine. He caresses my face, angling it against his to deepen the kiss, and gently parts my knees, coming to stand between them. His other hand slides up my ribcage, stopping shy of my breasts, and my body silently cries out for him to continue. Again, it makes no sense—I'm kissing a near stranger, but he doesn't feel like a stranger.

"We've been drinking," Nash says against my lips, kissing me softly again. "I like you, Vi, and I don't want to fuck this up."

He's not wrong. I'm tipsy. Not enough to regret what I'm doing, I don't think, but enough that I have a little extra courage coursing in my veins, for sure.

"I like you, too."

He pulls back, giving me a boyish grin. "Maybe you can come to our next game, and we can hang out after. You know, not drinking."

"Yeah?" A smile pulls at my cheeks. "I'd like that."

CHAPTER 1
THE ONE THAT GOT AWAY
NASH

SEPTEMBER - SENIOR YEAR

"RICHARDS?" Drew's voice brings me plummeting back to reality. My gaze falls to where he's standing on the other side of my black Infiniti QX60, waiting for me to unlock the passenger side door. I glance over his shoulder again, but it's too late. The blonde I was staring at has already disappeared into Dalton Hall.

Drew smacks the roof with the palm of his hand to get my attention again, raising his eyebrows. "Earth to Richards."

"Sorry. Thought I saw someone." I press the button on the chrome door handle twice to unlock the SUV, sliding into the driver's seat. A wave of thick, suffocatingly hot air assaults me, black leather upholstery scorching the backs of my thighs. Tension winds through my shoulders as I turn the air-conditioning to full blast and let the engine idle, trying to push the thoughts of her aside.

In the passenger seat, Drew buckles his seatbelt and reaches for his phone, entering his passcode. He turns it to face me, its lit-up screen displaying a breakout play diagram for this weekend's game. "Where did I lose you?" he asks. "Do you need me to go over the whole strategy again from the start?"

While our team captain, Marcus Grant, is a deadbeat in the leadership department, Drew more than compensates for that in his role as alternate captain. Thanks to Drew and our Head Coach, former professional centerman, Dallas Ward, we're excessively prepared for each game, including contingency plans to cover scenarios like losing multiple players due to injury or both of our goalies shitting the bed. They probably have a backup plan in case of alien invasion, too.

Despite his apparent concerns, I've already memorized all of the plays. I cram more before games than I do before my engineering exams. I know what will be paying the bills after college, and it sure as hell isn't my degree.

"No, I just missed the last thing you said." Shifting the ignition into reverse, I check the backup camera before easing out of the parking stall. Another glimpse back at Dalton Hall reveals the mystery blonde is still MIA. Probably wasn't her, anyway. Somehow, I've gone more than two years without bumping into her on campus even once. It's a little strange, actually; Lakeside University might be big, but it's not *that* big.

Then again, if I did run into her, what would I even say?

Drew clears his throat. "I said, are you ready to face Eriksen again on Saturday? The guy has it out for you."

That he does. Sleep with an opposing player's ex-girlfriend one time over the summer, and suddenly the whole team wants your head on a hockey stick. Not that Michigan State University needs a reason to hate us; Lakeside University and MSU have battled for conference titles, divisional championships, and rankings since the schools were founded. Our rivalry runs deeper than the Dead Sea. This is merely another excuse to fuel that animosity.

Besides, how was I supposed to know that Penelope chick just dumped him? I had no idea who she was. Am I supposed to be doing reference checks at the door to my bedroom?

"Do I look like I'm scared of Eriksen?" I ask. "Come the fuck on."

"He was out for blood last week," Drew points out, slipping his phone into the pocket of his varsity jacket. "And that was a preseason game."

"And? Who's the one who walked away from that with a black eye?"

Aaron Eriksen talks a big game, but when the gloves come off, he can't fight worth shit. Not to mention, he has a ridiculous name. At any rate, the guy is overreacting. He and Penelope weren't even together when it happened. Though I can't say it would have stopped me if they were.

He barks a laugh, half-amused and half-exasperated. "You're lucky they didn't toss you from the game."

"Not my fault the refs didn't get there in time after he threw the first punch. That was self-defense." Signaling, I shoulder-check and exit the parking lot, merging onto the main road. My aching biceps protest as I maneuver the steering wheel—a bad sign in terms of how I'll be feeling later. At least the drive home is short. I can collapse on the couch until I have to go back out for practice later.

"Just watch out for them this weekend," he says. "We don't need anyone getting injured this early in the season."

"I'm not the one who should be worried." Sure, I could crush Eriksen like the insect he is. And if that cheap fucker tries to trip me again, I might. But there are certain advantages to being in his head, too. He's one of MSU's scoring leaders, and if our last pre-season game against them is any indication, his game has been completely thrown off by this ex-girlfriend situation. He couldn't get the puck to the net, let alone in it.

Drew pops a stick of gum in his mouth, offering the pack to me. "On another note, student trainer evaluations start tomorrow."

My jaw clamps down on the cinnamint gum at his reminder. More evaluations? Great. I'm sore as hell—in the kind of way that won't be resolved within 24 hours—and I'm about to be run through the gauntlet by the athletic training team for a second time this month.

Fitness testing won't be an issue, but the biomechanical and injury assessment might be a different story. Somehow, I skated by the first time, and I'm not sure I'll be so lucky again. I'm nursing a few chronic issues that I'd rather hide the full extent of from Coach Ward. Nothing dire, but he'll be up my ass about resting and rehab if he finds out, which is why I'd rather he didn't. I can push through with a couple of painkillers and some mental grit, like always.

"Heard two of the interns this year are chicks," he adds.

Unease settles in the pit of my stomach. My ex-girlfriend, Violet, is in the athletic training program. What if she's one of them? Then again, she probably has some say in where she does her internship. There's no way she would want to work with our team after the way things ended between us. With the way I ended things, specifically.

The unease in my gut morphs into something far more troubling, and a glimmer of regret rises to the surface. I swallow hard, fighting to repress the unwelcome feelings stirring in the back of my mind.

The only thing worse than having a 'one that got away' is knowing you're the one who pushed her to leave.

"Coach give you any names?" I ask, trying to sound casual.

Drew glances over at me. "No, why?"

"No reason."

———

Drew jogs upstairs to take a shower while I ease down onto the black leather couch in our living room. Or try to, at least. Suppressing a wince, I move in slow motion while every muscle in my lower body protests. Even after maintaining a strenuous training schedule over the summer, getting back into shape for the season has been a bitch. Mostly because I'm still playing catch-up with my conditioning after a shoulder injury sidelined me last January.

In the adjacent kitchen, Vaughn rummages through the freezer, emerging with a handful of blue jelly ice packs. Without warning, he lobs one across the room, sending it sailing straight for my head. I narrowly catch it in time to avoid being smacked in the face.

"Heads up." He smirks, sauntering into the living room holding a cold compress for himself.

"Thanks, bro," I say sarcastically. But the truth is, I need it; that much is obvious based on how I'm shuffling around like the Tin Man. I've never been worked so hard this early in the season.

Someone must have pissed off Coach Ward before he got to practice this morning.

Vaughn sinks onto the other couch and props his feet up on the black leather ottoman, resting the ice pack on his left knee. Grabbing the remote, he turns on the flat-screen TV and flips through the guide, landing on a football game. His gaze cuts over to me. "Detroit game? It just started."

"Sure." I shrug, placing the blue compress where the top of my shoulder meets my collarbone. Soothing cold seeps into my skin, calming the pain that's been nagging at me since practice.

Both exhausted, we lapse into a comfortable silence while we zone out in front of the TV. One of the things I like most about Vaughn is that he doesn't feel the need to run his mouth constantly —and when he does speak up, you know he's going to say something important. Sometimes I just want to exist in peace without having to make small talk about the weather, the news, or who's banging who at school. Okay, fine. I never want to make small talk about any of that shit. If you ask me, most people talk at least twice as much as necessary.

Near the end of the first half, one of our other roommates, Connor, strolls in from his late afternoon class. Speaking of people who like to talk: Exhibit A. Connor is like a brother to me, but sometimes the dude does not shut up. Especially when it comes to his hookup play-by-plays. They're so detailed, they could give Penthouse letters a run for their money.

"Sup." Connor tosses his leather bag on the ground, carelessly abandoning it, and I clamp down on the urge to throw my ice pack at his head. No matter how many times I nag him to put away his stuff, it's always everywhere.

I've had several near-death experiences tripping on his stray personal belongings in all kinds of unexpected and bizarre places. Who leaves a magazine on the fucking stairs? I blame the fact that he was raised by a rotation of overly lenient nannies. If I'd done stuff like that growing up, my dad would have beat my ass. Literally.

Connor flops down beside Vaughn, nimbly crossing his legs at the ankle. He's far more limber than I am, currently. A second later, Drew comes down the stairs and hops onto the opposite end of the couch from me, turning his black Grizzlies baseball cap backward. For some reason, I seem to be the only one who feels like a creaky eighty-year-old trapped in a twenty-one-year-old's body. Weaker people might blame it on overtraining, but I'm writing it off as a fluke.

A tsunami of fatigue crashes over me and I close my eyes, leaning against the couch. The guys begin to go over drills for tonight's practice while I half-listen. We have two hours until we have to leave and I'm strongly considering going upstairs for a power nap, except that would require getting up. My limbs are unbearably heavy, like the force of gravity is ten times stronger than usual.

"What's the word on our trainers this year?" Connor's voice brings me crashing back to reality. "Drew said a few of them were chicks. I wonder if they're hot."

My eyelids pop back open at the unwelcome reminder, and any trace of drowsiness vanishes into thin air.

I shift the cold compress to my aching lateral delt, shaking my head. "Can't hit it and quit it with the trainers, dumbass. You have to see them every day."

"Right," Drew agrees. "Use your head, man."

Vaughn gestures to Connor with the Granny Smith apple he's holding. "Who's to say Haas could even land one of the trainers? They're obviously smart, which means they'd know better than to fall for his shit."

"Ha ha, fucker." Connor makes a face. "Not all of us are celibate like you."

Vaughn's dark eyebrows lift. "I'm not celibate, I just don't fuck anything that—"

"Chill, you two." Drew holds up his hand, cutting them off. As the level-headed mediator of our group, he puts our dysfunctional little family back on track whenever things go sideways, which is fairly often with four competitive athletes living under one roof.

Out of all of us, Vaughn and Connor clash the most, probably because their personalities and backgrounds could not be more different. Vaughn grew up below the poverty line and relies on his full-ride scholarship to survive, whereas Connor was handed a platinum AmEx and his own Benz at sixteen. But Vaughn isn't literally celibate, he's just picky as hell—unlike Connor, as Vaughn so eloquently began to explain.

On a scale from abstinent to player, Drew and I fall somewhere in the middle. While I haven't had a relationship since freshman year, I'm not exactly hurting for hookups. I have zero interest in anything more serious than that. Relationships only complicate things, especially when you have faulty emotional wiring like me.

"House rules," Drew reminds them. "Next one to start chirping gets dish duty for a week."

Connor rolls his eyes. "Yes, Dad."

They quit sniping, and we return our attention to the football game—which is for the best because none of us want Connor on dish duty. He does a terrible job.

A few minutes later, Drew's phone vibrates on the coffee table next to him and he unlocks the screen, scanning the text that came through. Glancing back up at us, he slides off the couch, reaching for his black team hoodie. "Gotta pick up Savi from work. See you guys at the rink."

"Have fun with your girlfriend," Connor calls.

Drew flips us off over his shoulder as he disappears down the hallway, and Connor snickers, reaching for his stainless Grizzlies water bottle. The garage door slams, followed by the sound of Drew's truck engine revving as he pulls away from the house.

"But seriously, what's up with those two?" Connor asks, idly flipping through the stations in search of something to watch while the football game is in halftime. He settles on a re-run of Hockey's Greatest Plays. "Savannah slept in his bed last weekend, and he said nothing happened. It's weird."

"They've been friends for years." Vaughn gives him a 'duh' look, taking another bite of his green apple. He's perpetually short on patience when it comes to gossip, probably because he's often the target of it himself. "I know it's an unfamiliar concept to you, but not everything is about sex."

Connor pretends to think. "Nah, that sounds like a myth. Like Narnia."

Leaning forward, I reach for my water bottle, a replica of Connor's with my number emblazoned on the side instead of his. Searing pain shoots up my shoulder joint, and an involuntary grunt escapes my lips. Note to self: do not extend arm. Should be easy enough, except for the part where I have to wield a hockey stick four to five days per week on the ice.

"How's your shoulder?" Vaughn glances over at me.

"It's fine." My shoulder is not fine, nor is it the only problem plaguing me. I have some nagging issue with my knee that refuses to fully heal. It doesn't hurt, per se, but it doesn't feel right.

Connor narrows his eyes. "Uh-huh..."

You know things are dire when Connor Haas is judging you. That's when it's really time to question your life choices, starting from the beginning.

On the other hand, there's no one better to get wasted and forget your problems with. You're just liable to create some new problems in the process.

"You should do some rehab for that," Vaughn suggests. "Talk to Christina."

"Yeah, maybe." He's right, but raising red flags for injuries and having the athletic training team bench me again is the last thing I need. Getting drafted was only half the battle. If I want to make it to the league after graduation, I have to crush it on the ice this year or risk losing my entry-level contract with Chicago.

Connor's phone chimes at an ear-piercing volume, nearly giving me a goddamned heart attack. He glances over at it with his brow furrowed, and then he scoffs, shaking his head. "Coach sent a follow-up email about the training interns. Some kind of 'behavior contract.' It says we have to respond after reading it, letting him know that we understand and agree. What is this, fucking pee-wee hockey?"

"What's this about?" I mutter, grabbing my cell. At the top of my inbox, sent three minutes ago, is a new message from Coach Ward.

Subject: Team Update – Athletic Trainers

Athletes,

Because this is the first year that we've had female students working closely with the Grizzlies, I would like to issue a reminder that you must adhere to the Lakeside University Athletics' Code of Conduct at all times, both on- and off the ice. Specifically, you are expected to maintain a friendly and __professional__ working relationship with the athletic training interns. Any complaints regarding inappropriate behavior or comments will be dealt with swiftly and severely.

In advance of training, the fourth-year student interns that will be joining our team for the semester are:

Julianna Anderson

Violet Dahl

Preston Lowell

I don't move an inch but inwardly, my brain explodes.

This is bad.

This is really, really bad.

Beneath the list of names is another wall of text reiterating tonight's practice plan, but I can't stop staring at the middle name. My pulse jumps, grip on my phone tightening. This can't be right. Working with the team? What the hell is she thinking?

"Oh, shit," Vaughn murmurs, staring at his screen. Having witnessed me go off the rails firsthand after our breakup, he's the only other person who understands how disastrous this development is.

I have very few regrets in life, and all of them involve her.

"Fuck my life." I toss my phone aside. It bounces off the couch cushion, landing on the hardwood floor with a clatter. Its heavy-duty, military-grade case spares it from damage—unlike my mental stability, which was just obliterated.

In addition to the obvious problems associated with seeing my ex-girlfriend multiple times per week, all of the guys on the team are going to be thirsting over her because a) she's gorgeous, and b) that's how they are. Coach Ward's warning won't deter them for a single second. That'll be short-lived, though. She's off-limits, and I'll make that crystal fucking clear by any means necessary.

Connor gives me a funny look. "What's the problem, Richards? Did you bang one of the interns or something?"

I scrub my jaw with my hand, debating how to respond. Puck bunnies throw themselves at the team constantly, both at home and on the road, and it's true that I have been known to indulge a little. That said, this situation would be infinitely less complicated if it involved a casual hook-up or one-night stand.

"It was a little more serious than that. Violet is my ex."

His jaw nearly unhinges. "As in, ex-girlfriend? When the hell did *you* have a girlfriend?"

"It was before you started here. We met September of my freshman year and broke up the following spring. And now I'm fucked because I'm going to have to see her every day."

"Maybe it'll be okay." Vaughn shifts to face me on the couch, placing his heavily tattooed forearms on his thighs. "Violet's always been pretty chill, and it was a long time ago."

Connor waves off my concern, flipping the channel back to the football game. "Exactly. It'll be fine."

Stellar insight from the guy whose idea of a relationship is hooking up with the same girl twice. Maybe he could start an advice column.

"I'm not so sure about that." I lean back against the couch with a groan, staring at the popcorn-textured ceiling. A lone neon orange suction cup dart hangs in the corner. I have no idea how it got there. "Violet hates me."

CHAPTER 2
RED VELVET AND REGRETS
VIOLET

I'VE ALWAYS LOVED SURPRISES. Getting stuck with my ex-boyfriend's hockey team for my senior-year athletic training internship, however, is a surprise that I could have done without. Clutching a double-strength gin and tonic in one hand, I re-load the Lakeside University Student Portal for the umpteenth time. Much to my despair, no amount of prayer or denial has changed what it says.

Dahl, Violet – LSU Student no. 124668337
Bachelor of Science, Athletic Training
Senior Internship Placement
Team: Grizzlies
Supervisor: Christina Hamilton

I stare at the words until they jumble together, and my stomach curls into a fist. This is what I get after weeks of making inspiration boards and writing daily affirmations? After all my time spent on visualization and meditation? According to the countless crunchy-granola podcasts and the stack of self-help books I devoured over the summer, if you simply align your energy with the universe, you're supposed to manifest what you want. Something clearly backfired because I sure didn't want this.

Mental note to burn those books.

"What the hell happened?" Sighing, I slam my laptop shut and flop back into a pile of decorative cushions. Ice cubes clink as the drink in my glass spills over the edges, dripping onto my purple pajama pants and the tan-colored microfiber couch.

Julianna leans over, plucking the cocktail from my hand. "Okay, Violet. You're cut off."

Swaying slightly, I reach over and take back my gin and tonic, downing two hearty gulps. Julianna doesn't protest, though she probably should because this is drink number three of the evening. If I make it to number four, there's a solid chance I'll end up rapping freestyle karaoke. Or vomiting. Possibly both.

"It's my birthday and I'll drink if I want to."

"Your birthday is in March," Julianna points out, tucking an unruly lock of auburn hair behind her ear.

"Close enough," I mumble into my half-empty glass. The ice-to-alcohol ratio is way off. There is entirely too much ice, and not nearly enough gin.

"Let's soak some of that booze up, kay?" Ever the mother hen, she gives me a wry smile and pushes a bowl of rippled potato chips across the coffee table to me.

Food. Brilliant idea. After the day I've had, I deserve some carbohydrates. I grab a handful of the plain chips, cramming them into my mouth. We should order delivery. Pizza maybe, or Chinese. Heck, why not both? Even better: a dozen cupcakes from Crave Bakery so I can drown my sorrows in red velvet and cream cheese frosting.

This is a two-cupcake emergency, easily. Probably more like three.

Except I don't have a phone to order food with because Julianna confiscated it. To prevent me from "doing something regrettable," she claims. Too bad that dates back to freshman year, and it can't be undone.

I blink away the memories, channeling every ounce of strength I have to keep my voice level. "I don't get it, Jules. I requested the women's hockey team as my first choice."

In addition to our men's team, LSU is home to a highly renowned Division II women's hockey team that I'd hoped to work with. My second and third internship choices were our men's and women's basketball teams, respectively. Our men's hockey team, the Grizzlies, wasn't even on my list. For good reason.

Julianna gives me a sympathetic smile laced with more than a little pity. "At least we're together. Besides, you like hockey, right?"

Hockey is practically a religion in my family. Growing up, my older sister Grace and I watched games on TV with our parents every weekend, complete with matching team jerseys. When our father got promoted to partner back in elementary school, the first thing he did was purchase season tickets to the local professional team, the Blades. Grace and I always used to fight over who got to attend which game, especially during the playoffs. Actually, we still fight over tickets to the playoff games.

I do not, however, share the same degree of fondness for the LSU men's hockey team.

In my former life, I used to religiously attend their games. Then my ex-who-shall-not-be-named—the Grizzlies' top defensive enforcer—cross-checked my heart into the boards at the end of freshman year, and I've made a second job of avoiding him ever since.

It's a task that requires herculean effort at our school because social life on campus revolves around hockey: pre-gaming, attending the games, and partying after the games. The recently built, twelve-thousand-person capacity arena sells out on a regular basis. Our hockey players are local celebrities, complete with hordes of fans—and the egos to show for it.

"I love hockey," I concede. "But not under these circumstances."

She shifts on the couch, tucking her athletic legs beneath her. "What happened with your ex, anyway? You've never told me."

Julianna didn't transfer to LSU until sophomore year, and I wasn't exactly offering up a detailed play-by-play of how he turned my heart into roadkill to all my new friends. I give a half-hearted shrug, scooping up an obscene amount of sour cream and onion dip with my potato chip and shoving it into my mouth instead of replying. At this rate, I'll gain five pounds before the internship even starts.

"Do we hate him? Because I'll hate him if you tell me to. I'll glare at him all semester long." Julianna narrows her hazel eyes, trying to look mean, but she's too baby-faced for it to be credible.

"We should absolutely hate him." He went from being the perfect boyfriend at the beginning to someone I didn't recognize by the end. From being sweet and thoughtful to a study in emotional unavailability, with a heart colder than the ice coating a rink. After one especially shitty deed, I ended things with him and moved on without looking back.

Well... I moved on. There was more looking back than I care to admit.

Julianna waves me on with a ruffled potato chip. "But?"

"I don't know. When I think of him, I feel lots of things. Hurt. Regret. Sadness. Maybe resentment. But hate? Not really." I almost wish I did; it would be easier that way. "Long story short, we dated for almost all of freshman year. Rumor has it, he turned into a complete fuckboy after that. I guess I broke him."

"Ugly breakup?" She grimaces behind her glass.

I slide down the arm of the couch and lay on my back, staring up at the ceiling. "Hideous."

While I know she means well, I'd rather not elaborate on the slow, painful decline of our relationship, nor the rocky parts in between. If I'm being honest, it was a pretty equal mix of good and bad, and not in the 'evens out' kind of way. In the rollercoaster way. The highs were through the stratosphere, but the lows were deeper than the Mariana Trench.

"Maybe you should talk to Professor Rempel," she suggests.

"I don't know," I mutter, flinging a fleece-covered arm over my eyes, peeking out at her beneath it. "I mean, have you *met* Rempel? She's not exactly the type of person who encourages you to open up to her about your love life."

"Fair. Rempel is a little terrifying."

"A little?" Rolling onto my side, I arch a brow. "She made Professor Citas cry in the middle of Sports Nutrition last year."

Julianna holds up a hand, squinting at her phone beside her. "Hold on. Rempel sent an email about the placements."

A jolt of nerves shoots through me, and I scramble to sit upright. Super. What more could possibly go wrong?

She furrows her brow, reading aloud, "Congratulations on being awarded the top honor of being selected to work with the Grizzlies for your senior internship placement. As you know, the Grizzlies are a pivotal part of the Lakeside University community, and after their championship run last season, university administration has decided to devote our most valuable resources to support the team. In this case, that support includes extending our best students in the athletic training faculty for internship placements."

"I see." My head bobs in a nod, but it feels weightless, like it's detached from my body.

While I hate to admit it, there is some merit to Professor Rempel's explanation. As a Division I hockey school in the Midwest, our program is a massive draw for funding and donations. Between sold-out games, corporate sponsorships, media licensing fees, merchandise, and other revenue streams the team brings in, it's said that hockey single-handedly keeps the LSU budget in the black.

Like the email states, the two of us have some of the highest GPAs in the program. Top ten, if not top five. Still, it feels a little like Jules and I are being punished for that by having our ranked choices completely ignored. Why did they even ask what we wanted if they didn't care? I suspect the choice was driven by political will from a higher pay grade than Professor Rempel.

"Christina is supposed to be amazing," Julianna points out.

"So I've heard," I murmur, mentally cataloging the pros and cons. Christina Hamilton's resume is a mile long, full of impressive accomplishments and extensive experience working with athletes at both the collegiate and professional levels. She's known as "the injury whisperer" thanks to her knack for identifying and correcting maladaptive movement patterns. But my objection doesn't lie with the internship supervisor.

Over in the entry, the front door creaks open and slams shut. Our other roommate, Claire, strolls in, eyes widening when they land on me. While Julianna is ready to go out like we'd planned, I am not nearly as presentable, in purple plaid pajamas with my ratty old bathrobe thrown on top, smudged remnants of the day's makeup, and my hair in a messy bun. Not a cute messy bun, either. I'm rocking a rat's nest.

I rarely pull out the bathrobe, but when I do, my roommates know it means business.

"When you said you were pre-gaming with some drinks, I thought…" Claire trails off, her mouth tugging into a frown as she takes in the disarray. She shrugs out of her camel peacoat and unwinds her plaid Burberry scarf, smoothing her glossy brown hair. "What's going on?"

I cut off Julianna before she can reply. "We got our placements today."

The words slur together but Claire seems to understand, and her expression brightens. "That's great. Did you get what you wanted? Women's hockey team, right? Are we celebrating?"

"No." I chuckle darkly and raise my drink to drain the last of it, ice cubes rattling. "We most definitely are not. I got placed with the men's hockey team."

Claire freezes, ruby lips in a tiny 'o' as she processes what I said. Her eyes widen the instant it clicks. "The Grizzlies? With— with *him*?"

"Yup."

I've lived with Claire since freshman year. As the one who had to sweep up all the pieces of the wreckage he left behind, coaxing me out of bed with food and bribing me to leave our dorm in the weeks that followed our breakup, she is not exactly his number one fan. She's also one of those people who makes their strong opinions known—loudly. I'm certain to receive a lecture from her about how I should ask for a different internship placement.

Realization stretches across her face. "So we're not celebrating. We're stress drinking."

"Exactly. And stress eating." I hold up the bowl of chips to illustrate. "Can we order from Gino's?"

"Guess we're not going to train for our 10K tomorrow like we'd planned, huh?" Claire bustles into the kitchen, glasses clinking as she pours herself a gin and tonic.

"Not unless you want me to die," I call out.

Two orders of delivery later, I've drowned my sorrows in garlic breadsticks and red velvet cupcakes, reluctantly told Julianna all the gory breakup details, and effectively switched back into denial mode. I've also switched to drinking water at the suggestion of Claire and Jules, and by "suggestion," I mean they took away the gin. Probably for the best. I'm going to hate my life when I wake up tomorrow enough as it is.

"You're not going to ask to be moved?" Claire asks slowly, setting down her slice of half-eaten thin-crust vegetarian pizza. The subtext in her tone makes her opinion all too clear. And maybe she has a point, but it's hard enough being a woman in a male-dominated field like sports; the last thing I need is to seem like I'm whining over a man.

Avoiding her gaze, I lick the last remnants of cream cheese frosting off my index finger. "No. Two years is a long time. I've given it some more thought, and I'm sure it won't be a problem."

It's a lie. There's a huge problem. Seventy-six inches of problem. Two hundred and twenty sculpted pounds of problem.

A four-letter problem.

Nash.

CHAPTER 3
LOGIC OVER EMOTION
VIOLET

THE REST of the week flies by at an unnaturally fast pace. Before I know it, it's Thursday morning and we're due to report for the first day of our internship with Christina at ten-thirty a.m. But first, our entire cohort attends a special Athletic Training Professional Practice Seminar where we are treated to a lengthy lecture from Professor Rempel that does nothing to assuage my fears.

She prattles on about internship rules, protocols, and expectations while I nod and smile, having a silent meltdown at my desk. Gnawing my bottom lip, I weigh whether to request a reassignment. If I do, I risk ruining my reputation within the entire department. Being unable to set personal issues aside could reflect poorly on me. Not to mention, this is the first year they've allowed undergraduate female athletic trainers to work with the men's hockey team. Do I really want to hand them a reason to never do it again? Maybe I'm experiencing some delusions of grandeur, but I feel like I would be singlehandedly setting back the feminist cause.

Professor Rempel wraps up her speech, raising her voice to emphasize her last point. "…And as I'm sure you're already aware, internships are a professional environment, and you will be expected to adhere to departmental standards of behavior. Amorous or sexual relationships are strictly prohibited between student trainers and their athletes."

A sliver of hope creeps in. Technically, Nash and I aren't involved in either of those. We're practically strangers now. It's almost like we never happened. Or at least, that's what I'm going to tell myself.

After our seminar wraps up, Julianna and I walk one building over to LSU's sprawling, state-of-the-art hockey facility. It's a veritable shrine to the sport, sleek and modern, finished in monochromatic shades of gray with stainless steel accents. An oversized Griswold the Grizzly statue sits in the center of the vaulted atrium, backed by a massive glass wall filled with framed championship photos and gleaming trophies from past seasons.

We reach the tiled corridor that leads to the Hockey Conditioning Center, dodging idle students milling about, and a queasy feeling floods the pit of my stomach. What if Nash has a girlfriend? It's a given that he's moved on—I have, too. But knowing that and seeing it are two very different things. I've spent the last two years intentionally avoiding that very kind of information. What if I have to see Nash with someone else at their games all semester?

My steps slow to a crawl, verging on immobile. I know I need to keep moving forward, but my feet don't want to cooperate. Under different circumstances, I would be excited; in this case, it feels more like marching to my own execution. It'll be the death of my sanity, at the very least.

Worst part is, I bet Nash won't even blink.

Julianna touches my arm, bringing my thought spiral to a screeching halt. "Nervous?"

"First-day jitters, you know how it is." I take another sip of my vanilla latte, even though a stimulant is the last thing I need. Between the caffeine and my nerves, I'm vibrating.

Our destination comes into view, and I toss my half-full coffee cup in the trash before I follow Julianna into the training room. I'm greeted by fluorescent lighting, the rubber smell of gym flooring, and an entire team's worth of hockey players scattered haphazardly around the room. A dream come true for many sports fans and puck bunnies alike, but my worst nightmare.

Our friend and classmate, Preston, is already standing at the front of the room, evidently far more prepared than I am for what's about to transpire. He looks like a textbook athletic trainer with his sandy blond hair neatly styled, dark gray athletic pants, and a black Grizzlies zip-up jacket that he must have recently picked up from the campus store. He nods at us, and I follow Julianna to join him.

When Preston's gaze settles on me, his mouth pulls into a concerned frown. "You look a little pale. Are you feeling okay?"

"Yeah, I'm good." But the rasp in my voice says otherwise.

"Right," he says, unconvinced. "Now that we've got that lie out of the way, how are you actually doing?"

"A little nervous," I admit.

His eyes linger on me for another beat and it's clear he's about to push the issue. Before he can, Julianna strikes up a conversation with him about a biomechanics quiz next week. Mental note to buy her drinks tonight as a thank you for rescuing me from that line of questioning.

Trying to appear relaxed, I clasp my hands to stop myself from fidgeting and scan the room, spotting a handful of semi-familiar faces. Between the roster that Christina sent out, the players I was acquainted with through Nash, and the various promotional campaigns around campus, I can identify over half of the team.

Then my eyes land on Nash in the middle of the crowd, and the air in my lungs turns to cement.

He's sitting next to his best friend, Vaughn, with his long legs sprawled out in front of him and a bored expression on his handsome face. His sun-kissed brown hair is trimmed shorter on the sides, his jawline is sharper, and his broad frame boasts significantly more muscle, but it's him. Heartbreak in human form, sitting right in front of me.

Of course, in the way life tends to mess with you, he's hotter than ever. A lingering summer glow warms his skin, charcoal athletic shorts displaying his powerful calves and thighs. A new—or perhaps not-so-new, just new to me—sleeve of dark tattoos adorns the entire length of his right arm, disappearing beneath the sleeve of his black athletic shirt. My focus lingers on him while I fight to draw in a breath, obstructed by invisible chains wrapping around my ribcage.

Nash's attention swivels over to me, and my heart slams into my chest.

I've spent twenty-eight months convincing myself it was better this way, rationalizing my way out of feeling things for him. Logic over emotion. Brain over heart. Convincing myself what we had was never real.

And the moment our eyes lock, all those lies I've told myself shatter at my feet.

His expression remains impassive as he holds my gaze for a heartbeat longer than casual eye contact should entail. Somehow, looking at him makes two years feel like yesterday and decades ago all at once. My pulse accelerates with every passing moment until he breaks away and returns his attention to his teammate sitting on the other side of him, leaning in to say something.

I don't recognize his other teammate; while seated, he appears almost as tall as Nash, but his frame is lankier, and he has dark blond hair with movie-star white teeth. He's hot, objectively speaking, but Nash is downright mesmerizing. I can't seem to tear my eyes away from him.

A wolf-whistle yanks me back to reality and the brightly lit training room. My focus shifts to Christina, standing at the front of the classroom clad in black dress pants and a fitted gray LSU athletics polo. Behind her, Coach Ward leans against the wall, wearing similar LSU training gear. Soon, it'll be my uniform, too.

"Okay, team. I'm going to read off a list of athletes for each trainer." Christina raises her voice to be heard over the handful of players still chattering, holding up her black clipboard.

Coach Ward wields a reproachful look at the group, making a 'settle down' motion with his hands, and a hush immediately falls over everyone. He's a silver fox with the athletic body of someone half his age, broad shoulders and toned torso evident beneath his shirt. He's also incredibly intimidating in a quiet way—the kind of person who silently commands a room. Though rumor has it, on the rare occasion that he does ream out the players, his yells echo throughout the entire first floor of the building.

Christina continues, "Athletes, this will be your assistant student trainer for the semester. Today, they're going to run each of you through an individual assessment while I train the rest of the group. We'll go in order, so if your name is called first, please see your trainer as soon as this is finished. Everyone else can gather in the main gym."

As she begins to list off names, my heart rate—already double what it should be, according to my Apple Watch—skyrockets to an all-time high. Preston's group is first, and Nash isn't in it. I fiddle with the sleeve of my jacket while I wait, barely able to breathe. The odds are fifty-fifty now, which is far too close for comfort. But with any luck, Nash will be with Julianna instead of me.

"Violet"—Christina gestures to me with her clipboard and glances down at her list—"James Anderson, Ryder Smith, Brent Benson, Nash Richards, Connor Haas, and Spencer Davidson."

My chest tightens at the fourth name, vision starting to tunnel. I can't hear what Christina says next because I'm too focused on keeping the blueberry bagel I ate for breakfast from making an appearance on the training room floor.

Christina finishes reading out the rest of the names in Julianna's group, directing us to break into our respective trainer-athlete pairings while the remainder head to the gymnasium to warm up. Everyone proceeds to disperse around the room, moving purposefully to their next destination. Nash strolls through the gymnasium doors without looking back.

Once he's out of sight, I manage to regain some semblance of normal functionality, and my first intake runs smoothly. My athlete is polite and cooperative, well-versed in evaluations like the one I'm conducting. It helps that all the players were already assessed by the training and medical team; this is purely for my own experience, to replicate real-life practice.

Before I know it, I'm finishing my third assessment with Brent Benson, a junior defenseman who struggles with chronic Femoroacetabular Impingement in his hip. I can already tell I'm going to learn an immense amount over the course of the semester. Hands-on, immersive education provides a million times more learning opportunities than a lecture ever could.

This would be the perfect internship if not for the whole, 'working with the ex who pulverized my heart' factor.

Brent hops off the table, raking a hand through his unruly copper curls. "Want me to send the next guy in? Who is it?" He reaches over to grab his light gray LSU hockey sweatshirt off the chair next to him.

"Nash," I tell him, realizing only too late that being on a first-name basis with him makes us sound overly familiar. "Uh, Nash Richards."

He nods, pulling on his hoodie overhead. "I'll let him know."

"Thanks."

Brent's tall figure disappears into the gym, leaving me alone in my assessment area. Filaments of memories with Nash whirl through my brain, haunting and intrusive. Our first kiss, first time, first fight. He was my first everything. First heartbreak, too. I grit my teeth, shoving down the thoughts.

A split-second later, Nash crosses the threshold dividing the rooms. My pulse goes haywire, and I have the most ridiculous urge to hide behind the assessment table. Or leave. Leaving sounds like a pretty solid plan. Who needs to graduate? Degrees are overrated.

He dawdles over to my corner at an impossibly slow pace, stone-faced like he's heading to a goddamn funeral. I'm not happy, either, but I like to think I'm hiding it better than him.

When he comes to stand next to me, he looms, more than a full foot taller than me. Larger than life, especially this up close. I'd forgotten how gigantic he is—he's easily the biggest one on the team this year. And of course, they stuck him with me, the smallest athletic trainer. Probably as some kind of test. If only they knew what a test it was going to be.

With a deep breath and a prayer, I try to steady my voice. "Hi."

It's the first thing I've said to Nash in over two years.

"Hey." His voice is flat, expression to match. He seems wholly unimpressed with being stuck together; wholly unimpressed with me in general, like I have zero effect on him whatsoever.

Wish I could say the same about his effect on me.

When I fail to say anything further, he heaves a weary sigh, scanning the curtained area. "Where do we start?"

"Um..." Even though I just performed three intakes, I have no idea what I'm doing. The moment Nash started to head in my direction, everything I learned in school and clinical placements flew out the window. As far as my mind is concerned, it might as well be the first day of freshman year.

I steal a glance at Julianna, who's talking to her athlete while recording notes on the assessment form, and my brain sputters like a rusty engine kicking into gear. "Have a seat so I can ask you the preliminary questions."

Nash sinks onto the gray vinyl therapy table and places his elbows on his muscular thighs, watching me with a blank expression. It's impossible to tell what's going on in his head. Shutting people out is his superpower, and right now, he's harnessing that to its fullest.

The intricately inked designs along his right forearm catch my attention, dark swirling patterns encasing his corded muscles. Then my gaze slides lower, to his hands. They're twice the size of my own, his fingers still visibly rough and callused like before. A tiny shiver runs through me. Those hands have been on my body. Those fingers have been inside me. Other parts of his body have been inside me, too.

Focus, Violet.

I grab my clipboard and pen, perching on the black pleather stool across from him. My hands are trembling, and I clutch the clipboard tightly to hide it. It's painfully awkward as we run through the items on the athletic training intake form, verifying personal information like his full name and date of birth. While the intake questionnaire buys me some time before I have to touch Nash, it's unnerving in its own way because I already know a majority of the answers other than a few minor developments over the past two years.

Scanning the list, I move on to the next item. "Do you have any concerns, injuries, or other issues that are bothering you?" My pen hovers above the page, ready to record his response.

"No."

Liar. Every high-level competitive athlete has at least one chronic issue, and I am confident Nash has more than that.

"You sure about that?" I arch a brow, glancing up at him. Now that we're closer, faint blue circles line his eyes. He looks tired; weary in a way that sleep won't fix.

Nash meets my gaze evenly. "Positive."

Clearly, I'm not going to get anywhere with him stonewalling me, so I let it go. The physical assessment will reveal more than the intake interview, anyway.

"Any history of concussion?"

He nods. "Last year. December."

Worry ghosts through my mind, even though he's not mine to worry about anymore.

"On the ice?" This isn't even on the form; I just want to know.

"Yeah, when we were playing against the Vipers." His mouth tugs into a frown and he shifts his weight, like recalling the event is physically uncomfortable. "Hit gone wrong. Slammed into the boards at full speed."

My stomach lurches at the visual but I just nod, keeping my eyes fixed on the form while I take notes. "Loss of consciousness?"

"No. Mild dizziness. A little disoriented."

"How long did your symptoms persist?"

When I look up again, something flashes across his face. "About two weeks."

In other words, he was playing again after two weeks, but I'd bet anything his symptoms weren't gone. Dammit, Nash. He'll never admit it, so I bob my head in acknowledgment and continue to record his answers.

"Any lingering symptoms from the concussion?" I ask. "Vision issues, dizziness, headaches?"

"No." Now he's being honest with me again.

The rest of the intake questions follow in kind, with Nash telling me what he thinks I want to hear, alternating with the truth as it suits him. I'm pretty sure he's generously padding how much he sleeps and underestimating his alcohol intake by a wide margin, but I don't bother calling him out on it. Things are strained enough between us as it is.

We reach the end of the questionnaire, and I set down the clipboard, forcing a smile that feels woefully like a grimace. "Okay. Let's check you out."

Everything else around us fades, and my heart roars in my ears. In theory, the first step is standing up, but my butt is frozen to the seat of my stool.

This is the hardest part yet.

I swallow. "I'm going to have to…um, touch you."

"I know." Nash shrugs a broad shoulder, seemingly indifferent to the idea. "I'm used to being poked and prodded."

And I'm used to poking and prodding—just not poking and prodding *him*.

His steely gaze follows me as I approach him, strong jaw tense and brow lowered slightly. There's something heavy between us, and I'm not sure if it's tension or chemistry. Maybe it's both. My heart clenches, and a wave of sadness hits me from out of nowhere. How did we end up strangers? Sometimes I still don't know.

Then I remind myself where we are and what I'm supposed to be doing.

I come to a halt an arm's length away, still unable to bring myself to touch him. "How's your shoulder?"

"Great."

He's so full of shit. I know firsthand that his right shoulder has bothered him since freshman year. His chart indicates it caught up to him last year when he experienced an acromioclavicular joint injury and missed the second half of the season, which must have been devastating for him. It's not the type of issue that magically goes away, either, especially with repetitive use and lack of rest.

"Let me take a look." I take a step toward his left.

Nash inclines his head to the other side. "It's the right, Vi."

Like I could ever forget.

"I know. I want to check them both." With any luck, starting on his good side will help him let his guard down a little.

My fingers land on his deltoid, and something twists in my gut. His skin is warm and smooth beneath my hands, muscles fuller and more defined than the last time I touched him. He still wears the same cologne, too. Familiar undertones of citrus and spice evoke another wave of bittersweet memories, some of which I wish I could forget and others I still cherish, even though they hurt.

Nash keeps looking straight ahead, barely acknowledging me. The ache within me intensifies in response to his non-response, seeping into the cracks in my heart. Why does he have such a strong effect on me after all these years? What the hell is wrong with me?

Across the room, laughter erupts from one of the other stations. Julianna and Preston are smiling and making small talk with each of their respective players, the way we're taught to in order to build rapport with an athlete. The other guys appear to be making an effort to be friendly in return like my previous three assessment subjects did.

My current athlete is sullen and silent.

Christina strolls by, poking her head into my assessment area, and Nash stiffens slightly. She's been doing rounds through the room the entire time but naturally, she's shown up to check on me at the worst possible time.

"How are we doing over here?" She gives us a bright smile, eyes traveling back and forth between us.

"Great," I lie. "He's a model athlete."

"Perfect. Let me know if you need any help with your findings."

Christina disappears to check in with Preston while I try to assess Nash's range of motion in his right shoulder. He sucks in a sharp inhale and the joint locks up. I make another attempt, but he actively resists me.

"Would you chill out?" I hiss. Obviously, it isn't professional to snap at your athlete, but most athletes don't actively fight you, either. And most aren't your ex-boyfriend. I'm going to give myself a pass on this one. Not like he's going to file a complaint.

His gaze cuts over to me. "What?"

"You couldn't be more tense if you tried."

"I'm sore from dryland yesterday."

"You're practically fighting me." It's a bit of both, though. I can tell he has some pain points, but he's also resisting my attempts to do much of anything with his body. Given that he's a giant, force isn't really a viable option, not that it would make for an effective evaluation anyway.

"I need to check your external rotation." My fingers brace his elbow, making another attempt to assess his range of motion with little success. Frustration surges within me and I snap at him before I can stop myself. "Stop resisting."

"Maybe you're being rough," he says through gritted teeth.

"I'm half your size, and you're trying to say I'm beating on you?" Drawing in a deep breath, I hold it and count to five, channeling my patience. I'm sorely tempted to jab him in a pressure point, but I refrain. Barely. I lower my voice before speaking again. "You're sore because you have several injuries and you're compensating for them, but you already know that since they've clearly been around for a while."

Nash grunts but says nothing. He's always ignored his injuries and clearly, still does. His pain tolerance must be through the roof. I'm not sure I'd have caught the full extent of it if I couldn't read him so well. He might have been able to pull one over on Preston or Julianna.

"Look," I tell him. "We don't have to be BFFs, but the least you can do is cooperate with me. I still have to do my job."

"Fine." He lets out a heavy exhale, and the tension he's holding diminishes a fraction.

For the last few minutes, I complete the rest of his biomechanical assessment while we speak only as much as is absolutely necessary. As time passes, Nash gradually relaxes more, whereas I grow more and more apprehensive with each new finding. His right shoulder and left knee both have issues that warrant further investigation, and neither has been flagged on his file.

"How long has your left knee been giving you trouble?" I release his left foot, lifting my chin to peer up at him.

He doesn't miss a beat. "It doesn't."

Right.

"Are you playing this weekend?"

"Of course." Nash sounds borderline annoyed, like it's a stupid question. "Why?"

My eyes dart around the room for onlookers, but we're in the clear. Everyone else is occupied. "How did you pass your preseason screening?" I whisper.

Nash doesn't look at me. "Don't know what you're talking about."

"You're a mess." I don't know how he faked it with the rest of the training team. Maybe they caught him on a good day. Or maybe they're choosing to look the other way because the team needs him. While Coach Ward and Christina are both highly respected, and I'd like to think they're both above doing that, it happens more than it should in elite college sports.

"I'm fine, Vi."

Worry starts to swirl in my gut, working into a cyclone of panic. I have no idea how to fill out my assessment chart for him. If I'm honest, there's a good chance Nash won't be playing for a long time. I don't want to be the reason one of the best players on the team gets put on the injury list. Especially when our head trainer missed—or chose to miss—whatever is going on.

"You're lucky you got assigned to me," I murmur, reaching down and taking hold of his right ankle. Even his feet are enormous. His white Nikes must be a size thirteen, at least.

"Why's that?"

"Because anyone else would tell Christina and Coach Ward to bench you."

CHAPTER 4
JUST FRIENDS
NASH

THE UNIVERSE IS FUCKING with me. It's the only possible explanation.

Christina dismisses us, marking the longest ninety minutes of my entire life, and the team slowly filters out the doorway of the training room. All of the other guys are in great spirits, fist-bumping and laughing about how we're going to clobber the Panthers in tomorrow night's game. I hang back from the rest of the group, distancing myself from them so I don't have to engage.

As I cross the threshold into the hall, the metric ton of weight I've been carrying on my shoulders lifts partially. At least it's over for today. Too bad I'll have to go through this mindfuck several times a week for an entire goddamn semester.

Slowing to a stop, I search the hallway for Vaughn—the only person whose presence I could tolerate at the moment—but he's missing in action. His assessment was last; maybe he's still inside with his trainer. I have an hour until my next class, so I pull out my phone and shoot him a text letting him know I'm grabbing lunch in the athletes' lounge if he wants to meet and study for a while.

A split-second after I hit send, Violet appears from out of nowhere, and the load crashes back down on me like a ton of bricks. She comes to a halt in front of me, tucking a lock of wavy blonde hair behind her ear. Her hair is shorter than it used to be, hitting just above her shoulders, and while it looks good, somehow I find the change unsettling.

"Can I talk to you for a second?" she asks, twisting her hands.

"I guess." I follow her off to the side of the hallway, where we're partially shielded by the built-in trophy cases. Behind Violet, a massive mural of the LSU logo adorns the wall in black, white, and gray. A steady stream of students passes by, their animated chatter granting us some degree of privacy.

Shifting my duffel on my shoulder, I glance over at my teammates gathered down at the other end of the hall. Fortunately, they're too preoccupied to notice us. When my gaze falls back to Violet, it's like being speared with a hockey stick in the gut. Her face is familiar yet foreign. It's a face I've spent two years trying to forget, even though I know I never will.

"I have class in a few minutes," I lie, looking past her into the crowd. "What's up?"

Seeing her is even more difficult than I expected. It's not just awkward; it's torture. Same big blue eyes and cupid's bow lips, but the person beneath them is a stranger.

"This tension between us is too weird." She lets out a heavy sigh, and her expression is so hopeful that it almost stirs emotion within me. Almost, but being dead inside helps quell those feelings nicely. "We have to work together all semester. Can we call a truce? Be friends, maybe?"

Friends? That's cute.

"You and I both know we can't be friends."

Violet plants her fists on her hips, tilting her head defiantly. "Why not?"

"Why do you think?"

Behind Violet, Vaughn strolls out of the classroom, scanning the hallway. When his eyes land on us, they widen, and he throws me a questioning look. I give him an almost imperceptible shake of the head to let him know to keep walking.

Despite my attempt to be discreet, Violet notices our unspoken interaction. She surveys our surroundings warily, lowering her voice to a yell-whisper. "Are you seriously trying to play the victim? After everything you did?"

An errant surge of irritation comes rushing back to me. While I wasn't exactly a model boyfriend near the end, it doesn't change the fact that Violet jumped right into someone else's bed the moment we broke up. After seven months together, she moved on in the span of a weekend. Who knows, maybe it was even sooner. Given the timing, I'm not convinced there wasn't some overlap.

"Can't have hurt too bad considering how quickly you found someone else. How is Jay these days, anyway?"

Violet stiffens, indignation stretching across her pretty face. "Were you keeping tabs on me or something?"

Obviously. It's like she doesn't remember me at all.

"I know everything that happens on campus."

I hadn't even given Violet back all her stuff yet before one of my friends spotted her walking hand in hand with Jay McAllister, some idiot from the baseball team. She barely had time to delete me from her social media first. She and Jay didn't last longer than a couple of weeks, but I still want to punch him in the face whenever I see him on campus.

Her mouth sets in a line and she takes a step closer, followed by another, until we're almost toe to toe. She still smells the same, spicy cinnamon and sweet vanilla, which has always reminded me of a cinnamon roll with frosting. It is, unfortunately, every bit as appealing now as it was back then.

Our physical proximity triples the load bearing down on my shoulders, crushing my chest along with it. It takes conscious effort to keep my breaths slow and even as a strange combination of resentment and desire courses through my veins. Part of me still wants her, even though I'm pissed.

With our height difference, Violet has to crane her neck to look up at me. In the crowded, noisy hallway, our confrontation continues to go unnoticed.

Fury gleams behind her light blue eyes. "He asked me out, and I was single. Is that some sort of crime, now?"

"You were single for all of two seconds."

"Not that I have to explain myself to you, but that was a rebound. It didn't mean anything."

Maybe not to Violet, but it sure spoke volumes to me.

"I bet."

It's not like I didn't move on. Obviously, I did—because damned if I was going to let it look like I was moping around pining after her. But it took months before kissing someone else didn't turn my stomach.

"You have the balls to complain that I moved on too soon when you're the one who broke us in the first place?" she hisses.

My grip on the strap of my bag tightens. Does she think I don't fucking know that already? I'm well aware of the starring role I played in the failure of our relationship, but she played a part, too.

Her tone turns skate-edge sharp. "You ditched out on Easter dinner with my *family.*"

Guilt is something that rarely troubles me, but even I'm not immune to experiencing a hint of it when she brings that up. Instead of going with Violet to meet her parents and sister, like I was supposed to, I may have taken a boys' trip with a bunch of guys from the team at the last minute. Can't deny that I handled it badly, even if I had my reasons.

"Why the hell are you even here?" I deflect, because I can't really defend what I did. "You could have chosen from like, twenty other varsity teams to work with other than the team."

"Don't flatter yourself. It wasn't my call." Violet takes a giant step back and crosses her arms over her black long-sleeved LSU zip-up, leveling me with a glare colder than I've ever seen before. The temperature in the hall drops at least ten degrees. "I never would have chosen to inflict your presence upon myself, especially not for an entire semester."

"That makes two of us."

She huffs and shakes her head, tipping her chin to look up at the ceiling. Beneath the fluorescent lighting, her eyes shine, turning glassy. Guilt flickers in the back of my conscience again, but I tell myself it's misguided. I don't owe her anything, especially not anymore.

"This is what I mean about being friends, Violet. It'll never work."

"Fine." She draws in a breath, narrow shoulders rising, and her gaze snaps back to me. "Fuck you, too." Turning on her heel, she stalks away, sleek blonde hair bouncing with each step. She disappears into the sea of people, leaving me holding all the words I should have said instead.

CHAPTER 5
A CAREER-ENDING DECISION
NASH

MY AFTERNOON HAS BEEN a complete clusterfuck.

After getting felt up by my ex-girlfriend in the most awkward manner possible and forcing myself to eat a lunch I don't even want, I attend three lectures in a row—because my Thursday class schedule is a nightmare—and absorb precisely zero information from any of them.

When I hit the library to study for an hour before my late afternoon practice, I open my laptop to discover that the scarce notes I managed to take earlier this afternoon don't make any sense; they might as well be written in Latin. I'm going to have to hit up my classmate, Ben, to ask if I can borrow his. He'll probably find it more than a little bit odd since he was sitting next to me in class the entire time.

Since my engineering homework is a bust, I try to focus on my general elective instead: the Psychology of Human Sexuality. While it sounded like a good idea when I registered last spring, it's a decidedly different story now. Our first unit is on attraction, love, and communication, and for some reason, the subject matter keeps sending my mind right back to Violet. Maybe it isn't too late to switch to a different option, like Abnormal Psychology. It would be far more fitting for my current state of mind.

Things continue to go downhill when my phone buzzes in my coat pocket and I slide it out to find a message from the last person I want to speak to. Fucking hell.

> Doug: Saw your last game. Call me. We need to discuss.

> Me: Okay, I'll give you a shout tonight.

> Doug: Now, Nash. I know you aren't in class.

> Me: I'm studying in the library before I head to practice. I'll call you on my way home.

> Doug: See that you do, or you may find that your phone is unexpectedly disconnected.

I read and re-read his last message, jaw clenched tight enough to grind my molars into dust. Thanks to his six-figure income, I didn't qualify for student aid or government loans. I was denied private loans because I have insufficient personal credit history and lack a cosigner. And as a Div I athlete with a demanding STEM major, holding down a part-time job is literally impossible. Otherwise, I would tell him to shove his phone plan up his ass.

Tamping down on the urge to release a tirade of curse words in the library stacks, I begin to pack up my stuff before I lose my temper, shoving my textbooks into my bag and yanking the zipper shut so violently that the people at the neighboring table turn and stare. Maybe a decent meal at home after practice will help get my head straight. Fuck. Practice. I'm not in the mood to see the guys, and I'm *especially* not in the mood for the inevitable locker room talk about the "hot new trainers."

Crisp autumn fall air hits my face as I burst out of the library, cutting across the quad dotted with lounging students and towering trees bedecked in shades of orange and gold. I breathe in deeply, focusing on the scent of earth and fallen leaves, and try to calm my mind. It's impossible. I'm more keyed up than I am before a game.

Halfway to the parking lot, I round a corner and spot Violet coming out of the Arts building with the male trainer who's also interning with our team. I think his name is Preston, or maybe Parker. Something preppy like that anyway, which suits him to a T. He looks like the type who goes to brunch at some country club every weekend and whose parents may or may not have purchased his way into college. His full name is probably Preston Vanderbilt the Third or some shit.

They're deeply immersed in conversation, smiling and clutching identical cups from The Beanery. It's downright nauseating. Turning away before she sees me, I make a slight detour to avoid them, mind reeling. Then a disturbing realization plows me over like a Zamboni traveling at full speed. Holy shit. Are they dating? Am I going to have to watch that loser simp over her all semester?

Yup. The universe is *definitely* fucking with me.

Once I get to the locker room, I try to get my head back in the game and off Violet, with limited success. Lost in my own thoughts, I ignore the rest of the guys and skip the usual small talk, changing in record time so I can be one of the first out on the ice. We have a new drill to master this evening, and it's more complex than the other ones we've been working on so far this season. With everything else going on, I need to stay off Coach Ward's shit list.

I grab my freshly sharpened Bauer 2X Pros and shove them on, kicking my heel against the floor to get my foot all the way to the back. Grabbing hold of my laces at the third eyelet, I tighten them, continuing upward until I'm finished, and then I repeat the same process with my other skate. As I work, my brain churns on spin cycle, everything swirling faster and faster until I'm nearly dizzy. Violet, hockey practice, Doug, my contract with Chicago, my shoulder, classes, our upcoming games, my knee, Violet again.

"That Violet chick is hot, huh?" our team captain, Marcus, pipes up, bringing me back to Earth. My laces slip through my fingers as I'm tying them, ruining the bow. Tugging the ends free, I start over, wishing I could make a noose around his neck instead.

"Don't even think about it," I mutter, leveling him with a menacing glare. Marcus is your stereotypical fuckboy, probably one of the worst on the team, and the idea of him so much as looking in

Violet's direction makes my skin crawl. I don't care if he's our captain, it isn't happening.

"What? Why not?" Marcus gives me an easy smile, clearly under the impression that I'm joking.

I look down, re-tying my bow. "This information doesn't leave this locker room, but Violet is my ex."

"You hit that? Nice, Richards." Marcus holds up a fist to fist bump me, which I pointedly ignore, double knotting my laces. If my fist makes contact with any part of his body right now, it's sure as hell not going to be his hand.

"I did not 'hit that.' We dated for a long time. Which means Violet is off-fucking-limits." I finish tucking my laces into my black and white socks and glance up to confirm that he's gotten the message. When he sees the expression on my face, his lighthearted expression morphs into that of mild terror. Marcus is a decent center, but unlike me, he isn't a fighter.

Pulling my stick off the rack, I add, "And if that little tidbit about our history gets back to Coach or Christina, you'll be shitting out your teeth for a week." The last thing I need is Coach Ward watching my every move during training for signs of "inappropriate behavior."

"What's this about Violet?" Ryder, a second-year defenseman on the bench across from us, cranes his neck. He ducks closer, giving us a conspiratorial look. "She's a dime, huh?"

The din in the dressing room gradually dies down as the other guys stop talking, trying to listen in on the conversation without being obvious. Ryder has no volume control, so he makes it really easy for everyone.

From down on the other end of the bench, Connor slams down his protective gear. "Right? She can rehab me any day."

My grip on the Bauer Nexus Geo in my hands tightens until I think it might snap in two. Thing is, I know Connor is kidding, but it feels like a skate blade to the brain even as a joke.

"Yeah, I think I pulled my groin," Ryder adds. "Might need her to check it out."

Several of the guys laugh, while a few others murmur or nod in agreement.

I shoot them a warning look. "Shut the fuck up." Ryder is in Violet's training group, so I especially don't appreciate his comment.

He recoils, but Connor merely smirks because he doesn't think I would beat his ass. Usually, he'd be right but in this case, I absolutely would. It's going to be hard enough seeing Violet every day, and I don't need one of my teammates banging her on top of that. Or worse yet, one of my roommates.

Not to mention, none of these tools could handle Violet in the bedroom to begin with. They would have no idea what to do with someone like her. Beneath that deceptively innocent exterior, those big doe eyes and tight little body, Violet is a dirty talking goddess. She's also kinky. I'm talking, we-had-a-safe word, kind of kinky.

A sudden flashback assaults me out of nowhere, a memory of her nails digging into my back. Her voice in my ear, begging me not to stop. Begging for me to give it to her harder. Begging for permission to come.

The most ironic part is, Violet was a virgin when I met her. It's not lost on me that I corrupted her and sent her out into the world after we broke up. I can't think about the implications of that too closely, or I want to punch things. Starting with myself.

Goddammit.

"Listen, fuckers." All eyes in the room fall to me. "All any of you need to know is that Violet is one hundred percent out-of-bounds. If any of you even think about touching her, it'll be a career-ending move. Because I will end you. Immediately."

A good portion of the guys, especially the first- and second-year players, exchange alarmed looks. One eyes the exit like he's considering making a run for it. And a few others glance away like if they don't look directly at me, maybe the threat will vanish.

Ryder lets out a low whistle, holding up his black CCM-gloved hands. "Chill, Richards. I'm kidding."

"I'm not." Another wave of rage grips me, along with the

desperate need to escape. I storm across the room and yank open the door, heading out onto the ice. Someone lets out another low whistle as the door slams shut, followed by muffled voices asking what the hell is wrong with me.

I don't know the answer to that, either.

CHAPTER 6
DENIAL, PARTY OF ONE
VIOLET

IT'S FRIDAY NIGHT, I'm still ticked off about how things went down with Nash yesterday, and to add insult to injury, he's been living rent-free in my head ever since.

"We can't be friends."

Asshole.

Bass throbs in the background of Overtime as the music switches to a new R&B song by The Gruuv; it's an angsty number about an old lover, and it could not be more ill-timed. The same could be said for coming here tonight. In all of my stress, I forgot the Grizzlies had a game at seven, and the place is packed from wall-to-wall with people flying high on a post-game win. By the time I realized my error, Jules and I already walked through the doors and snagged a booth. Since we made plans to meet other people here, it was too late to do anything about it.

I tear another piece off the paper coaster, adding it to the pile of tiny cardboard shreds next to me. Despite the celebratory atmosphere, I'm firmly in moping mode. All I want to do is go back to my apartment, cocoon myself inside a cozy blanket, and watch Love Island while eating a pint of cookie dough ice cream. Maybe have a bonfire with all those law of attraction books while I'm at it.

Julianna returns from the bathroom and slides into our booth. "I know you're bummed, but at least we're together, right?" She picks up her strawberry margarita glass, offering me a sympathetic smile over the salted rim.

"Right. That definitely helps."

She beams. "Plus, my brother's friend interned with Christina two years ago and he landed a spot training an AHL team right after graduation. She's a freaking genius."

"Totally." I force a smile, trying to sound enthusiastic, but it comes out flat. Part of me feels ungrateful. Objectively, this opportunity is an amazing career steppingstone. It should help me after graduation…if I survive that long.

After yesterday, I've been having some serious second thoughts not asking for a reassignment. I'm my own worst enemy—in more ways than one. Because the first thing I did last night when I got home was something most people do far sooner, post-breakup.

The thing I said could only bring trouble.

The thing I swore I'd never do.

I Googled my ex.

And I went deep. First, I discovered that Nash either has zero social media presence or it's so locked-down he's a ghost. Then I fell down a rabbit hole of newspaper articles, Internet forum gossip, and wild speculation, trying to piece together the time I missed.

Shortly after we broke up, Nash was selected as a second-round draft pick by Chicago, which is a huge accomplishment in and of itself. He had an amazing sophomore year before experiencing an undisclosed injury last January, prompting rumors and conjecture regarding the nature of his issue and whether he had surgery. Based on his chart and his assessment, I already know it was his shoulder, and he didn't.

After missing half a season, he must be under an unimaginable amount of pressure to perform this year.

"Still," Julianna says. "The whole thing is kind of wild, huh?"

"Very unexpected," I reply truthfully, finishing the last of my second rum and Coke. As the alcohol starts to kick in, warmth spreads through my body and I begin to unravel, decompressing from the ball of stress I'd turned into. Maybe things will be okay.

But probably not.

"It'll be great having Preston with us too," Julianna adds.

Immediately, my unraveling stops. Will it? Preston and I have been friends for more than a year, but lately, we've had this different, flirty dynamic going on. Since he's in the same program, it's made for some awkward situations where neither of us knows how to act. We're not quite "just friends" anymore, but we're not quite more than that, either. We're stuck firmly in the friendship gray zone.

Technically, nothing has happened between us yet. We've been doing a bit of a dance, alternating between getting closer and drifting further apart. More specifically, he keeps trying to get closer, and I keep pulling back. He's broached the subject of "us" a few times now and I've blown it off, telling him I'm not ready for anything serious right now.

I don't know what my problem is. Preston is perfect, both on paper and in-person. He comes from a nice family and he's the kind of guy who's destined to get married and have a nice family of his own someday, replete with a big white wedding, white picket fence, a couple of kids, and the whole nine yards. My ten-year plans include the same things, so it's a logical match. Everything I want. Or should want, at least. So why don't I?

Claire claims I'm afraid of getting hurt again, and she's probably right. I've had a few boyfriends since Nash, but I haven't let anyone else into my heart. Because he didn't just break it—he decimated it.

When I don't respond, Julianna looks at me inquisitively. "What's going on with you and Preston, anyway? Is it going to be weird to be working together?"

"No, it's okay. I mean, I'm okay. I don't know about him. He seems okay. I'm sure we're okay." I wave her off, but my rambling and repetitive word use is a dead giveaway that things are not even a little bit okay.

"Are you sure?" Julianna tilts her head.

I swallow a mouthful of gravel. "Yup." Being stuck with Preston and Nash in the same room every day. Awesome. I haven't even dated that many guys. What are the odds of this happening?

Her coral-painted lips fold into a frown, but she says nothing.

She doesn't need to, it's more than obvious that I'm hiding something.

"Coach Ward is a silver fox, huh?" I offer, trying to change the subject. It's true; I've never been super into older men, but he's the exception. He'll make for nice eye candy while the rest of the world burns down at my feet.

"Right?" Julianna's hazel eyes widen. "Lucky Mrs. Ward."

A gust of cool air whooshes past as the double doors behind us burst open, and a mass of students push into the pub. Most are clad in black-and-white Grizzlies gear, coming from the home game that just wrapped up. I spot Claire in the crowd, and she gives us a wave, pointing at the bar to indicate that she's going to get a drink.

Behind her is a group of strangers, plus someone I recognize— Vaughn, Nash's best friend and a forward for the Grizzlies. When Vaughn turns, I catch a glimpse of who's standing behind him, and my heart comes to a screeching halt. If I were hooked up to an electrocardiogram, it would flatline.

Because standing less than twenty feet away is Nash.

He turns back to Vaughn, shaking his head and laughing. They're accompanied by the rest of the team and, of course, a generous handful of drop-dead gorgeous girls who are hanging all over them. Clearly, nothing's changed on that front.

"Oh my God." Ducking, I try to make myself less visible. I knew coming here on game night was a mistake; we should have left while we still had the chance. "Let me come sit beside you."

Stealing another glance in Nash's direction, I confirm he hasn't seen me yet. If I can make this fast, hopefully he won't. Julianna turns around and cranes her neck, trying to see what the issue is, but I'm already out of my seat, gesturing for her to stay down. Pulse galloping, I slide in beside her, safely hidden behind the tall back of the vinyl booth.

"What on earth is going on?" she asks.

"Nash just walked in."

Julianna grimaces. "You're hiding from him?"

It doesn't make sense to me, either, considering I'm about to spend an entire semester working with Nash and his team. But I'm not ready to face him again, especially not without the opportunity to prepare myself first via rehearsal and self-administered pep talks. Maybe some prescription sedatives, too.

"I'm not hiding from him. I just don't want him to see me." Quickly, I add, "Don't tell Claire I'm hiding from him. She'll tell me I should keep my chin held high and all that jazz, and I'm not in the mood."

Claire strolls up, trademark vodka cran in hand, and slips into the vacant spot where I was sitting. "Are we playing musical chairs, or what?"

"There was a draft," I lie, trying in vain to drain additional alcohol from my empty glass. Realization dawns on Julianna's face that I can't risk going up to the bar and being seen.

"I'm going to get us refills," she announces. "Be right back."

I slide out of the booth to let her out, shooting her an appreciative look. "Thank you."

"So? How was your first week?" Claire sets down her drink, leaning over the table expectantly.

"About as good as you'd expect, which is to say, awful."

"I bet." Sympathy flashes across her face. "It's not too late to ask for a different placement. If you explained the situation, I'm sure the department would understand. I mean, it's not your fault."

Over by the bar, Preston and his friend Silas walk up to join Julianna. They were both at the Grizzlies' game tonight, and neither knows about my history with Nash. If I have my way, that's how it'll stay. The fewer people gawking at this trainwreck of a semester, the better.

"I don't want Preston hearing about this, okay? We can recap later at home."

Claire's lips roll into a line like she wants to argue, and I'm grateful she doesn't. We discuss her capstone marketing presentation for Gatorade while the hockey team grabs a table in the opposite corner, placing Nash in my line of sight with his back turned away. We're clear across the room so fortunately, he doesn't seem to notice me.

But I can't not notice him.

And the longer I look at him, the more I realize I'm not prepared to face him all semester.

Preston, Silas, and Julianna turn away from the bar with a fresh round of drinks. As they pass by the groups of tables, four girls huddled near the entry openly ogle Preston. At six feet tall, with perfectly tousled sandy hair, and a dimple in one cheek, it's a common occurrence. Despite that, he's oblivious to the effect he has on them. It's not that he lacks confidence, it's that he's the Golden Retriever of men; hopelessly good-natured and too pure for his world.

Probably too pure for me, too, but that's another problem entirely.

Julianna passes me my drink, and I down half of it in two large gulps. She shoots me a worried look. Preston eases into the spot where she had been earlier, next to me. A wave of his cologne floats over to me, pleasant and clean smelling, but it doesn't make my stomach do a somersault like Nash's cologne.

I wish it did.

Preston bumps me playfully with his shoulder. "You must be pumped about this semester, huh? I know you love hockey."

"So pumped," I agree, but it comes out flatter than a deflated balloon.

Something flashes across his face, a mixture of confusion and disbelief. Clearly, I'm not selling it. Had I known what this semester had in store for me, I would have invested in acting classes over the summer.

Much as I try, I can't seem to feign cheer with the rest of the group, and by the time I finish my third drink, it's obvious that I'm miserable. Tipsy, but miserable. I keep catching myself staring at Nash, forcing myself to look away, trying to make conversation with everyone at our table, and finding my eyes drifting back in his direction. Rinse and repeat, like some toxic cycle.

Preston shifts to face me, his slate-blue eyes scanning my face. "How did your assessments go? We didn't get a chance to finish recapping earlier."

"They went pretty well. It's just been a long week. You know, didn't sleep well with all of the anticipation and now it's catching up to me." This seems like a perfect excuse to bail, so I add, "I think I'm going to call it a night, actually."

Claire is lost in conversation with Silas, who she's been rocking a crush on forever, but Julianna's gaze rockets over to me. "Do you want me to leave with you?"

That had been our plan—split a rideshare back to the apartment later. Still, I'm willing to suck it up and pay for it myself if it means escaping my elephant ex lurking in the corner of the room. It's not even eleven p.m., and Julianna seems to be having fun. I don't want to drag her down with me.

"I'll drive you," Preston offers, pointing to his half-empty pint of beer. "This is only my first."

"Thank you, but you don't have to," I tell him. "You guys only got here an hour ago."

He reaches for his jacket and waves me off. "It's no problem."

I bite the inside of my cheek, debating whether to argue. It's hard to justify saying no without sounding rude, and if I'm being honest, I'm not a huge fan of taking rideshares alone. It's always made me feel uneasy.

"Okay. Thanks."

There's also a teeny, tiny, petty part of me that likes the idea of Nash potentially seeing me walk out of here with another guy. I know it's awful. I know it's wrong. But it doesn't change the fact that I do. After the way he acted to me, it would be sweet in-your-face.

Of course, that's assuming Nash even cares, which is a big assumption to make. There are countless tales floating around campus about the girls he's hooked up with since we broke up. While I don't always believe the rumor mill, I've heard enough to know this is a "where there's a smoke, there's fire," type of situation.

Just one reason of many why I need to steer clear of him, so I don't get burned.

Again.

CHAPTER 7

MR. WRONG
VIOLET

THE DRIVE HOME is only a couple of minutes, filled with easy conversation and speculation about what our internship will hold. Preston and I compare notes on the impressions we've gotten regarding the athletes so far. When the topic turns to Nash, I offer a vague response and change the subject to Christina. It's a little clumsy, but Preston doesn't seem to notice.

But the closer we get to my place, the more my nerves ratchet up, because I'm not sure what kind of parting Preston expects. Is this merely a friend offering me a ride home, or is this something else? Something more?

What do I want it to be?

I don't know the answer to that.

By the time Preston pulls into the street parking in front of my house, I'm brimming with anxiety. He parks and gets out, opening my car door and closing it behind me. I start up the sidewalk and he wraps an arm around my shoulders, pulling me closer—and answering my unspoken question.

We reach my front door and the motion-activated LED flicks on, bathing us in a blue-white glow. At least Claire and Julianna aren't home, affording me some degree of privacy while I attempt to navigate this.

Keys in hand and heart galloping, I turn to face him. "Thank you for the ride."

"No problem." Preston flashes me a perfect grin, and then his smile fades, blond brows knitting together. "Don't get me wrong, I'm glad we're together this semester, but I don't want it to make things weird between us. Are you okay with all of this? You seemed a little off tonight, and I wasn't sure if that was why."

Little does Preston know, he's the least of my worries when it comes to the internship.

"I think it'll be fine. Don't you?"

The corner of his mouth tugs. "Oh, I'm good with it. Especially the part where I get to see you every day."

There are a hundred girls on campus who'd kill to be in my shoes. I should be flattered, but what I feel is closer to panic. I nod but say nothing, unsure of how to respond. A few more seconds pass, an awkward silence hanging between us in the cool night air.

"Thanks again." I step forward to give Preston a hug and he wraps his arms around me, giving me a squeeze. He smells good, objectively, like a mixture of laundry soap and expensive cologne, but nothing about it makes me want to bury my face in his neck and inhale his skin. Something's missing. Is that what they call pheromones?

We remain intertwined for a few moments longer than platonic friends normally would before slowly pulling apart. Our gazes meet and his eyes darken, sending my pulse racing again. I know the look he's giving me. It's the universal male, 'I'm about to kiss you' look.

Do I want him to kiss me?

I'm still not sure.

Suddenly, I realize what's holding me back: I'm broken. Utterly broken. I have a six-foot-something, undeniably gorgeous—not to mention, nice—guy standing at my door, and all I can think of is the jerk who's sitting with his friends and groupies back at Overtime. You know, the one who smashed my heart into itty, bitty pieces and ground those pieces to dust for good measure.

Resentment kicks up within me, revving like a high-powered motorcycle engine. Bad enough that I let Nash ruin my past forty-eight hours. Now I'm letting him ruin my dating life, too? No. Not going to happen. I'm moving on. I have moved on. Welcome to Moved On City, Population: Me.

Preston's hands slide around to my lower back, and a nervous smile tugs at my cheeks. My stomach backflips with anticipation as he leans in, bringing our lips together.

Then, nothing.

Much to my dismay, I feel nothing on an emotional or physical level in response to Preston's mouth pressed against mine. Don't get me wrong, there's nothing wrong with the kiss; his lips are soft and his breath smells like peppermint. But there's nothing right, either. No flutters in my stomach, no pull between my legs, no wanton rush of heat from head to toe. Nothing, except for a massive wave of disappointment.

Still clinging to the faint possibility that something will ignite a fire within me, I part my lips, kissing him back. His tongue moves against mine in a way that can only be described as skillful. It's not too rough or too soft, and there are no teeth or excessive amounts of saliva involved. It feels...nice, I guess. But aren't first kisses supposed to be more than nice?

His hands remain firmly within PG territory, with one around my waist and one bracing my upper back between my shoulder blades. It's the portrait of a Hallmark movie kiss—there's zero passion to be found.

As if reading my mind, his hand slides higher up my back, coming to rest on my neck. Now we're getting somewhere. If he could just sink his fingers into my hair and pull, taking control a little, I might be able to work with that. Push me up against the door behind me for good measure. But he doesn't. He cradles my head gently, and it's sweet while frustrating at the same time.

Because this isn't his fault. It's no one's fault, though it sure as hell feels like mine. Preston ticks all of the ideal boyfriend boxes; smart, ambitious, handsome, and considerate. I want to like him, and I'm trying to right now. Unfortunately for both of us, it doesn't appear to be working. I can't create chemistry out of thin air, no matter how much I wish I could.

My hands loop around his shoulders while he angles my face, deepening the kiss. I'm still searching for the spark and coming up hopelessly empty-handed. Foolishly, I had hoped that our friendship would somehow translate into physical compatibility. Maybe that's part of the problem. He's my friend, and it's hard to see him as anything else.

Is it possible for your brain to be attracted to someone while your body isn't? It feels like that's the explanation here. On an intellectual level, I know I should be into this. On a physiological level, I'm simply not.

Plus, even if I assume Preston is playing it safe because he's trying to take things slow with me, I can tell—I just *know*—that he doesn't have some secret, well-hidden kinky side like I was hoping he might.

Like I do.

While I sort of suspected this going in, I am more certain than ever that he'd be appalled if he knew what turned me on. Preston is not the kind of guy who's going to order me to get down on my knees, lavishing me with that perfect blend of sweet and sordid nothings. He's not going to push the envelope between pleasure and pain, degradation and praise. And he's definitely not going to get off on it if I fight him, even if we're role playing.

The unfortunate reality is, some of the boxes on *my* boyfriend checklist are a little out of the norm. No one's ever checked them off…except for Nash.

Preston slowly ends the kiss, and I plummet back to reality, horrified at the sudden realization of who I was thinking of instead.

He flashes me a flirty grin. "I'll text you this weekend."

"Sure," I whisper, ignoring the gnawing in the pit of my stomach. "Sounds good."

What the hell did I just do?

His hand lingers around my waist while I fumble with my keys and unlock the deadbolt, pushing the door open. With another peck on the lips, Preston releases me, waiting until I'm safely inside before he turns to leave.

Hands shaking, I lock the door behind me and toss my keys into the dish on the entry table with a clang. Leaving the lights off, I shuffle into the pitch-black living room as a kaleidoscope of emotions blossoms in my chest, sinking into the pit of my stomach. Guilt, anger, regret, longing, resentment, sadness, along with other things I can't even put into words.

Lowering onto the couch, I rest my head in my hands while hot tears prick at my eyes, threatening to overflow. My teeth sink into my lip, trying to bite back a sob.

I have never been more frustrated in my life.

More than that, I feel hopeless. Defective. Damaged beyond repair.

Since Nash and I have broken up, I've been batting zero for five. I've kissed five perfect-on-paper guys with precisely zero butterflies.

I want those goddamn butterflies—and only Mr. Wrong has ever given them to me.

CHAPTER 8
BAND-AIDS AND BULLET HOLES
NASH

THE WEEKEND PASSES in a blur of hockey and booze.

I rarely drink to excess anymore, but I made an exception after I saw Violet leave Overtime with that douche, Preston. Once my judgment was sufficiently impaired, I let Connor drag me to a massive house party that was packed with puck bunnies, none of whom even remotely held my interest because all I could think of was a tiny blonde athletic trainer who hates my guts.

As is to be expected when you're out partying with Haas, I didn't get home until sometime after four a.m. Friday night. Or Saturday morning, technically. By the time we rolled out of bed around noon, we both wanted to die, which we cured using the oldest remedy there is: drinking and doing it all over again.

Needless to say, now that it's Monday, I still feel like shit, and I remember why I stopped doing that.

But seriously, is Violet dating him? What the fuck?

Shaking off the thought, I cut across campus beneath the cloak of morning twilight, draining the last of my coffee while I try to figure out how to navigate things with Violet. Not only was I an asshole to her last time we spoke, but my shoulder has also been giving me more trouble than usual. While I've known my AC joint was fucked up again for a while—or maybe it never fully healed after last season—it's gotten significantly worse over the last few practices. I can't afford to miss any games, which means I need Violet's help. Thing is, I know I don't deserve it, and I'm not sure she's going to give it to me.

When I arrive at the hockey training facility, Violet is the only other person present, as I'd expected because she's always been obsessively early like me. It's a good opportunity to catch her alone and potentially smooth things over. Or for me to make them even worse, which is also a strong possibility.

Lingering in the doorway, I watch her for a moment while she kneels, pulling out various training accessories from the wooden cabinets lining the wall. Pylons, multi-colored exercise bands, and medicine balls in an assortment of weights. Her pink hooded LSU sweatshirt rides up slightly, revealing black athletic pants that show-case her perfect, perky ass. It's impossible not to stare. I can't believe I fucked things up with her. I am such an idiot.

I'm also being a creep.

Get it together, Richards.

I rap on the doorframe before entering so I don't startle her. "Hey."

Violet's pale blonde ponytail jerks as her head snaps up. Her blue eyes narrow at the sight of me, leveling a blistering scowl in my direction. "What do you want?"

Okay, I guess I deserve that.

Glancing around, I confirm that no one else is in the training area before I cross the room to join her. The apprehension on her face grows with every stride I take. I guess I deserve that, too, though somehow it hurts more than anything she could ever say.

If only I could have kept my fucking mouth shut instead of throwing the past in her face. But broken people break things, and I leave behind a path of destruction in my wake.

"I need a favor," I tell her. "A small one."

Her light eyebrows jump. "A favor? Ha. No."

Undeterred, I take a step closer, ducking to catch her eye. "I need you to tape my shoulder before practice. Quickly, before anyone else gets here."

Violet meets this request with a blank stare before turning away, saying nothing. She resumes preparing for dryland, yanking open a nearby drawer with a surprising amount of violence and sending the contents rattling noisily. Pretending I'm not here, she sifts through the items, setting aside another handful of colorful exercise bands.

I clear my throat. "Could you?"

She stiffens and slams the wooden drawer shut, dusting off her hands. Straightening to full height, she squares her shoulders, her delicate nostrils flaring. She's still comically tiny next to me, and despite the broader situation at hand, I fight a smile at the sight of someone so small trying so hard to seem intimidating.

"Could I?" she echoes. "Yup. Am I going to? Nope."

I can't decide whether she's frustrating or cute. It's kind of both. It's also troubling, because my defenses are already disintegrating around her.

"Come on, Vi." I lower my voice, giving her an imploring look that used to work well in a variety of scenarios. Still might work if she has any soft spot left for me. I suspect she does, even if it's well hidden. "My shoulder was killing me all weekend, and I can't afford a repeat of what happened last year. I need all the ice time I can get. Chicago's assistant general manager has me under a fucking microscope."

Her demeanor relaxes a fraction before she flinches like she caught herself. She grabs a blue balance disk off the nearby shelf, clutching it to her chest like a shield. "Why the hell should I help you? We're not friends. Remember?"

I suppress a grimace at my words being thrown back in my face. It's fully deserved, even though the reason I said that is the opposite of what she seems to think.

"Because I need you, and you know it."

Violet presses her lips together, glaring at me for a beat. I study her more closely, and my chest tightens. Because beneath the hostile front she's working so hard to put up, there's barely concealed sadness in her eyes.

I feel like I should apologize for the other day, but the words get caught in my throat, so instead, I add, "Please."

A few more seconds tick by. Her gaze darts from me to the rest of the room a few times, her expression flickering between irritation and something I want to call pity. Not normally an emotion I shoot for with women, but in this case, I'll take it.

Voices echo in the hallway but pass by without entering, a reminder that the other players are going to start arriving soon. Selfishly, I wish she'd move things along; the longer this goes on, the more likely it is that someone else will walk in. But her waffling is better than her saying no, so I opt to say nothing and wait her out instead.

"Why would I do anything for you when you clearly can't be bothered to put in the work behind the scenes at home?" Violet asks, still hugging the balance disk to her body.

"I've been icing my shoulder."

"Which is only one of several things you should be doing." She draws her lush bottom lip into her mouth, releasing it. "If you want my help, you're going to have to commit to sticking to your rehab exercises for the next month. All of them."

"Tried," I tell her honestly. "Didn't notice any difference. They're a waste of time."

"I'll change up your rehab protocol, then. You agree to stick to it for one month or no deal."

Christ. I'm not going to win this one, am I? I'd forgotten she can be almost as stubborn as I am.

"And I'll know if you're lying to me," Violet adds, throwing the balance disc down onto the ground with an ear-splitting smack. "I'll be able to tell if you're slacking off."

"If it means you'll help me, it's a deal."

Beneath the pink fabric of her hoodie, her narrow shoulders heave in a resigned sigh. "Fine. But for the record, I'm only doing this because I know you'll play without the tape if I don't help you, and that will make life more difficult for both of us in the long run."

Wordlessly, she strides past me to the supply closet, pointing me in the direction of a therapy table in the corner on her way by. I trail behind her, waiting in the partially curtained-off assessment area she indicated. A split-second later, she turns back to face me, holding a brand-new roll of neon pink kinesiology tape and a pair of fabric scissors that I'm borderline worried she might stab me with.

Wait. Pink tape? No. Hell no.

"I'm gonna need black," I call over. "Or blue. Red. Green. Maybe purple in a pinch. Anything but that." While beggars can't be choosers, I do have some degree of pride, and Barbie pink isn't going to fly.

"Seriously?" Violet gestures with the KT roll in exasperation. "It's *tape*, you overgrown man-child."

"Do you know how much shit I'll get if I show up in the dressing room with pink tape all over my shoulder?"

For a moment, it looks like she might lob the tape at my head, and I don't fully blame her. Then determination stretches across her face, and I know I've lost the battle. In fact, I'm pretty sure I handed her the winning ammunition.

"Guess that's a price you're going to have to pay." She slams the closet door shut and marches over to me, ripping open the clear plastic packaging with a worrisome ferocity. "Sit."

Given her reluctance to help me and the time crunch I'm facing, I know better than to argue any further. I obey her orders, sinking down and slipping my arm out of my white t-shirt to offer her my bare shoulder. When her gaze lands on my skin, a bubble of laughter escapes from her bare lips. It's melodic, a sound I missed more than I even realized.

She inclines her head, blue eyes twinkling with amusement as she studies my pitiful handiwork. "You tried to tape your shoulder yourself?"

"Tried," I admit, reaching over and yanking off my pathetic attempt, tossing the balled-up KT tape into the nearby wastebasket. "And failed."

Violet's cool fingertips land on my skin, prodding and assessing as she steadies my arm with her other hand, taking the joint through its range of motion. Our bodily contact stirs up all kinds of conflicting emotions within me and I close my eyes, trying to ignore the fact that she's the one touching me, but it doesn't work—my body still knows.

When I reopen my eyes, her full mouth is pulled into a frown. Her frown deepens as she continues her assessment, confirming my worst fears. It's more fucked up than I thought.

"Taping this is like putting a band-aid on a bullet hole," she murmurs.

"Better than no band-aid."

Her gaze lifts to mine, brimming with concern. "Barely."

Brow furrowed in concentration, Violet stretches the tape across my skin until it's perfectly taut, snipping off the section at the end. She works methodically, forming a crisscross of lines to support and stabilize the joint, explaining what she's doing and the rationale behind why she's doing it. It's not clear to me whether she does this for all her athletes or whether she's trying to help me in case I find myself in another solo-tape emergency situation down the road.

She's so close that I can smell her perfume, and my body instinctively starts to respond. It takes every shred of willpower I possess to resist the urge to lean in closer, pressing my nose to the crook of her neck like I want to. But I know I wouldn't be able to stop myself there, and it would quickly escalate into me doing something more, like biting that fleshy spot above her shoulder. You know, the one that always pushed her over the edge when she was close.

Though, I wonder how she'd react if I did.

To stop myself from doing something stupid, I clutch my phone in my free hand, keeping my gaze fixed on the blank wall ahead. A barrage of memories begins to play through my mind like a high-light reel of regrets.

Violet watching from the stands at every single home game, sitting with the other team girlfriends. Coming out after to find her wearing my jersey, looking fucking adorable. The way she knew not to push me when I was grouchy after a loss. The time I was so sick with the flu I missed three practices in a row. My roommate peaced out like I had the plague, but Violet wasn't afraid of catching it. She took care of me without a single complaint, staying with me for two days in my cramped dorm room while forcing me to drink liquids and take Advil at regular intervals. Then she got sick right after me, and I did the same thing for her.

Violet leans closer, reaching across my body to secure another piece of tape, and her breasts brush against my bare bicep. She lets out a tiny gasp, pulling away like she's been burnt. Averting her eyes, she stretches another line of tape across my skin. I opt to ignore the incidental contact for both of our sakes.

Being with her was great...and it was terrifying. The more Violet and I bonded, the more I freaked out inside. The closer we got, the more I started to pull back. Prioritizing her less and putting my friends first. Going out with them instead of staying in with her. Getting way too drunk, way too often. I never cheated, never crossed a line with anyone else or even wanted to, but toward the end, I was a shitty boyfriend.

It's my fault she rebounded right into the arms of another guy. Deep down, I know that.

"There. All done." Violet's voice is clipped, yanking me back to reality where she's regarding me with clinical detachment. It's the polar opposite of the way I see her—which on some level, is like she's still mine, as irrational as that may be.

I glance down. Her work is precise and tidy, a far cry from my crooked and wrinkled tape job, and the joint feels more stable already. As she mentioned, it's not a fix, but it'll help.

"Thanks," I tell her, hopping off the table. "I owe you."

She turns away, refusing to look at me. "That you do."

CHAPTER 9

HIGH POTENTIAL
NASH

MY SECOND WEEK of training with Violet went marginally better than it did during our first week. Instead of trying to pretend we're strangers, we've resigned ourselves to an uneasy level of familiarity. It's still awkward but less overtly hostile—like a reluctant, grudging détente. It helps that we haven't been alone much. It's a little easier to pretend the past never happened when we're not allowed to talk about it.

Her tape job has been helping with my AC joint situation significantly. If I could somehow talk her into re-taping it every three to four days, I'd be set, but the chances of that happening are slim. Who knows, maybe the stretching and rehab she said she'd give me will help. Now that I promised her that I'd do them, I have to keep my word.

"Richards, hold up a sec." Connor jogs to catch up with me as I pass by the Center for Management Studies on my way to my car. I swear he's got a sixth sense for when I want to be alone. It's quarter to five, I'm fucking spent, and all I want is to zone out in front of the TV while inhaling a fridge's worth of food.

"Banks is inside talking to Potter about our comms quiz," he adds, nodding to the modern, glass-walled building. Connor and Vaughn are both in the business faculty, majoring in finance and sports management, respectively, and they register in classes together when possible. "Should be right out."

Moments later, Vaughn pushes through the oversized glass double doors. We continue to the parking lot where he and I are both parked, dodging students in our path. A few of them turn and stare, mostly at Vaughn, who's been featured all over campus in our school's new athletics advertising campaign. Posters, billboards, you name it. He is officially even more LSU-famous than he already was. I was more than a little relieved to be spared that "honor."

"We're going to Gino's," Vaughn says. "You in?"

"Nah, I'm gonna pass." Normally, I'd never turn down pizza. At the moment, I am decidedly not in the mood.

"Why?" Connor gestures with his stainless travel mug which, knowing him, could contain anything from double-strength coffee to straight vodka, possibly both. "You have to eat. You're telling me you'd rather cook? Or order in cold takeout?"

"Been a long day." In truth, everything after training went smoothly enough, but it seemed twice as exhausting as normal. Fourth-year engineering courses like Applied Hydraulics and Advanced Structural Analysis are brutal enough without throwing an ex-girlfriend into the mix.

Connor narrows his eyes like he's scouring my face for a tell. "You've been weirder than usual lately. Is this about the Violet thing? You're not still hung up on her, are you?"

Unfortunately, discretion isn't something he's familiar with, and he's speaking loudly enough to be heard in Canada.

"Dude," Vaughn mutters. "*Volume.*"

My head whips around, scanning our surroundings for anyone we know. "Seriously, Haas. Maybe you should get a megaphone and tell the whole school. Make a fucking TikTok, while you're at it."

Connor lets out a low whistle. "Oh, I get it now. You need to get laid."

"I need lots of things."

"Nash!" A female voice in the distance cuts in, interrupting us before Connor can respond.

I look over my shoulder to find Candice barreling in our direction, her glossy pink lips breaking into a too-broad smile. Her high heeled boots click against the concrete as she draws closer and I reluctantly slow to a stop, nodding for the guys to go on without me. Acting like I didn't see her doesn't appear to be a viable option, especially when she just shouted my name at full volume, and we've already made eye contact.

"Speaking of laid…" Connor says under his breath.

Vaughn starts, "Do you want us to—"

"I'll catch up with you guys at home."

"Bzzt. Wrong. You're coming to Gino's. I'll save you a seat." Connor throws me an air pistol as he walks backward. Vaughn rolls his eyes, tossing me a wave before turning away to catch up with him.

Before I can argue, Candice launches herself at me, wrapping her arms around my neck and enveloping me in a cloying floral-scented hug. I half-heartedly return the gesture while she mashes her breasts against my chest. I think the goal is to tempt me, but I'm mostly annoyed by the unsolicited physical display of affection. We don't hug—unless we're naked.

She releases me, looping her slender arms around my waist instead. "I missed you."

Our extended bodily contact begins to give me claustrophobia, and I take a step back until her grip on me breaks, her hands falling to her sides. She looks slightly affronted, but I don't really care. This public thing she's pulling isn't us. At all.

"Been busy with preseason."

Candice makes a pouty face, fluffing her dark brown hair. "Too busy to text, apparently."

"Yeah. Really slammed." If I'm being honest, she hasn't been on my radar, but openly admitting that would be harsh even for me.

"What about tonight?" Taking a step closer, she draws a small circle on my chest with a pink fingernail, fluttering her long eyelashes. "Are you busy then?"

After the past couple of days, I have no shortage of pent-up frustration, both sexual and otherwise. In theory, hooking up with Candice later could be an easy enough solution. She is, objectively, a perfectly nice chick. Low drama, low maintenance. No issues, save for the fact that we seem to be on slightly different pages regarding the nature of our relationship. And while Candice isn't in the same league as Violet, she's still hot.

But the last time we were together over the summer, it was like Candice was putting on a big show in the bedroom for my benefit. Her moves were practically choreographed, her lines almost like they'd been rehearsed. It was the same old, "spank me, fuck me harder" shit that all women seem to be whipping out lately. Don't get me wrong, I'm a kinky motherfucker. But fake kink is even worse than vanilla sex, and you can *always* tell when it's fake.

What's the end game there? To get me to like them more? That's not what a no-strings hookup is about, and that's not going to happen. Fact is, you can't skirt the edges of decency with a stranger. Can't push someone's limits until you know them. And you can't be involved in a power exchange without ground rules. I'm not going to choke some chick I'm casually fucking, even if she asks me to—and a couple of them have, present company included. As a high-profile athlete, Doug has always drilled into my brain that I need to be mindful of potential optics, and there's too high a chance of something like that being misinterpreted or used against me later.

Guess that's what I get for sticking to casual hookups. There's no emotional connection and there is definitely no trust. Just two people using each other's bodies as an alternative to masturbation.

Of course, none of this used to bother me until Violet teleported back into my life. It's hard to forget the fact that our bedroom activities were anything but vanilla. It was Baskin Robbins and the thirty-one flavors of fucking. She's almost as deviant as I am. Almost.

"Nash?" she prompts.

I force my attention back to Candice standing in front of me and try to seriously consider her offer. My body fails to respond. Not even an inkling of interest down south. Great. Violet is cock-blocking me when she's not even within sight.

"Tonight's no good," I tell her. "Maybe another time."

As I depart, she calls out something like 'text me later,' and I pretend not to hear.

Right before I reach my SUV, my phone vibrates in my back pocket. I pull it out expecting to find Connor harassing me again, only to discover Doug's name flashing on the caller ID instead. My stomach pole-vaults into my throat, and I silence the ringer, letting the call go to voicemail. I'll have to call him back later, once I get some dinner into my system. While I can delay it, I know I can't avoid him forever—even if I wish I could.

Cool relief washes over me when the ringing stops, but it's short-lived. Two seconds later, my phone starts buzzing again. Hitting the push button start, I let my car idle while I stare at the blinking screen. I should have expected him to keep calling. He has my class and training schedules, and he knows I'm free. I mean, I could be in the shower, in bed with a chick, jerking off, or doing any number of other things that require my attention, but as far as he's concerned, if they aren't school and they aren't hockey, they aren't valid.

My phone continues to ring, and for a brief, shining moment, I have the strongest urge to find a cigarette. I don't even smoke—never have—but this is the kind of conversation that could drive a person to start. Alcohol would also work, but sadly, there are no bars in my immediate vicinity, either.

Bracing myself, I swipe to accept, clamping down on the overwhelming urge to address him by name. Antagonizing him will only make it worse, and it's bad enough as it is.

"Hi, Dad."

Doug Richards. Nationally renowned minor hockey coach, head of the prestigious minor hockey program at Copperhill Sports Academy, and world-class asshole. AKA, my father.

"How's your preseason going?" His voice is gruff, words slurring together slightly in a way that tells me he might have started to hit the bottle earlier than usual today. Maybe his girlfriend, Shannon, is away for work this week. As a flight attendant, she travels a lot, but I don't keep close tabs on their schedule.

It's unclear why my father bothers to ask me about my career when he already knows the answer. I'm more than aware of the fact that he keeps meticulous track of me. He watches my games on TV, checks the post-game replays, haunts the online NCAA gossip forums, and records my stats on a spreadsheet so religiously, it's like he belongs to The Church of Hockey Statistics. Hell, he knows my numbers better than I do. Always has.

I swallow the shard of glass in my throat. "Good so far."

Our first few games have gone well overall, both in terms of the team's performance and my individual defensive play. Not perfectly, but that's what the preseason is for—to iron out all the kinks, get the players used to working together again, and prepare for the games that actually matter in the standings.

He obviously disagrees, because his tone sours. "Then why are you down on the second line?"

"Coach Ward is still moving us around to find the best fit." I grit my teeth, working overtime to keep my voice level. It's a good thing we aren't on FaceTime because civility would be much harder to fake.

Lines change all the time. Next week, I could be on the first or the third. It's about the team as a whole. If you shove all the weakest players down to the bottom, you're handing your opponent a scoring opportunity whenever they set foot on the ice. At the same time, you don't want to stick your superstars with dead weight. Managing the roster is an art, not a science. It's not just about me, either, contrary to what my father is implying. As a seasoned hockey coach, he damn well knows that.

It doesn't matter. If I were on the starting line, he would find something else to criticize.

My father harrumphs. "After all the opportunities you've been given, I didn't raise you to be a mediocre, middle-of-the-pack player."

I have a full-ride scholarship to play on a D1 hockey team at one of the top schools in the entire country. Objectively not middle-of-the-pack nor mediocre, but he has a way of making me feel like less than either of those things.

"Doing my best," I tell him, careful not to sound argumentative. "Games against the Vipers and the Orcas were strong."

Instead of agreeing, he merely grunts because offering even a sliver of validation would be too much to ask. A dull, empty ache settles into my chest—a hunger for his approval. As much as I hate my dad sometimes, I still crave his praise. I hate myself for that, too. I know I'm never going to get it.

That knowledge doesn't stop that little voice in the back of my head, though. The one that says maybe, just maybe, if I can be better, it'll be good enough for him someday. If I work hard enough...

"Highly disappointing performance against the Wildcats," he cuts in.

Searing frustration surges through me, and I smack the steering wheel with the heel of my palm, praying he doesn't hear the impact over the other end of the line. Of course, he *would* single out the only loss we've had so far this year.

"Yeah, I guess it wasn't our best." We only lost by one goal, but who's counting? A loss is a loss, as far as he's concerned.

Something in my response must trigger him because he launches into a technical lecture about defensive zone coverage that I've heard a thousand times before. Like always, I tune out completely, interjecting with "right," and "makes sense" every so often to create the illusion that I'm listening. Really, there's no need to. I know every rant of his by heart.

The longer we talk, the hotter the interior of the car becomes, even with the air conditioning on full blast. While it's warm for September, the real issue is the person on the other end of the line. I strip off my hoodie and fiddle with the climate control while he rattles on, reiterating concepts so elementary, it's offensive. I learned this shit in the minors. Not to mention, you don't get drafted after your freshman year of college like I did if you don't under-stand the fundamentals of hockey.

Despite the contract awaiting me after graduation, Doug doesn't think I'll make it, and he makes that abundantly clear on a regular basis. He's been especially skeptical ever since I had the audacity to injure my AC joint last year. He enjoys nothing more than comparing me to the big names he's worked with, including one first-round draft pick who went pro at eighteen years old a few years back. No NCAA, no farm team, just a coveted golden ticket straight up to the league. It's beyond exceptional; a generational talent.

According to him, I should have been that generational talent—and he never lets me forget it.

I tune back into our conversation right as he's wrapping up. "I'm only hard on you because you have so much potential. It's time you started living up to it."

The line goes dead before I can respond.

CHAPTER 10

THREE OPTIONS
VIOLET

PERFECTIONISM IS A FUNNY THING. No matter how hard you try to reach it, it always manages to slip through your fingers at the last minute, stealthily evading your grasp. Could have, should have, would have. I try to tell myself that "good enough" is, well, good enough, but it's a tough sell when it goes against the way you're wired.

"Are you still working on that? Let me look it over for you," Preston offers, nodding at my laptop screen.

We're camped out in the training room working on an assignment creating an entire training session from scratch. Next week, we'll take turns leading the team through each session by ourselves. It was the three of us earlier, but Julianna had to duck out for a dentist appointment.

While it's been okay so far—almost like old times, before the tension between us developed—I'm still worried that might change. I want to avoid another potential kiss scenario. I'm already regretting the first one, and I don't know how to talk to Preston about it. The whole, 'it's not you, it's me' thing seems painfully cliché, even though in this case, it's one hundred percent true.

"Thanks," I tell him. "But before I let anyone else see this mess, I still need to iron out a few details." As in, all of them. I'm on draft number three and it still doesn't seem quite right. While there's science behind athletic programming, there's also a certain amount of art; a way that the pieces have to fit together holistically. For this assignment, I haven't yet found it. However, accepting Preston's help could be construed the wrong way and after what happened between us, I'm trying not to lead him on.

He resumes packing up his things, shoving his final textbook into his bag. "You sure? I can stay if you need help. Or company."

"I'm sure, but I appreciate the offer."

There's an awkward pause. For lack of knowing what to do, I stand and push the chair back, taking a step closer. We hug goodbye while I make a point not to offer him my face. Though, I'm not sure he'd try to kiss me in here, anyway. That's more Nash's style.

Two more drafts later, the printer on the cabinet beside me spits out my four-page document. I re-read it one more time, giving it a final once-over until I'm confident that I've caught all my typos, corrected any mistakes, and polished all the rough spots. Somehow, I can't shake the feeling that I need to compensate for the Nash situation by being a model athletic training intern. It makes absolutely no sense, because none of the faculty even know there *is* a Nash situation. With any luck, I'll keep it that way.

Satisfied, I turn and reach for the stapler, startling when I notice a hulking figure looming in the doorway. My hand flies to my chest in surprise and the papers slide through my fingers, falling to the floor. I lean down and gather the pages, fastening them with a staple before shoving the assignment into Christina's inbox on top of the desk.

"You scared me," I tell Nash, trying to ignore my galloping heart.

"Maybe because you're working alone in the middle of the night." He pushes off the doorframe and strolls over to me, his heavy footsteps echoing against the tile. He's wearing a black long-sleeved tee and gray joggers, with his hair neatly styled instead of hidden beneath the baseball cap he was sporting earlier. It's a far cry from the creepy intruder that I feared he might be, but scary in his own way because he looks so good that it nearly incinerates my self-control on the spot.

It's frustrating, too, because I'm still angry with him. Or at least, I'm trying to be.

Hating Nash would be so much easier if I didn't have the underlying urge to tear off his clothes all the time.

He shrugs off his black nylon book bag, leaning one hip against the desk. His cologne wafts over to me, and my stomach does a pirouette. I discreetly scoot my rolling chair back a few inches to put more space between us. He either doesn't notice or chooses to ignore it.

His brow furrows as he scans the room, searching for signs of anyone else, and when his forest green eyes land back on me, there's concern beneath them that I didn't expect. "What are you doing here so late, Vi?"

When I glance at the clock on the wall, I discover it's past ten p.m. I thought it was more like eight, maybe eight-thirty at the latest. There are no exterior windows in the training room—the glass partitions look out onto the gymnasium—so it's easy to lose track of time.

"Had to create a training plan for next week and submit it to Christina before midnight. I usually do my homework at school because I can focus better. At home, I get distracted and start to get off track." Why am I giving him so many unnecessary details? I catch myself and stop abruptly. "What are *you* doing here so late, lurking in doorways and scaring innocent co-eds?"

"I left my stuff in the locker room so I didn't have to drag it to the Schuyler Center. When I came back to get it, I saw the light and wondered what was up. No one's ever in here this late."

"Schuyler Center? Why were you all the way over there?" Nash is a civil engineering major, and the Schuyler Center is a social sciences building tucked away on the opposite end of campus from the engineering faculty.

"Met my group for our sociology project and promptly wasted the whole goddamn evening. No one could agree on a topic. We pissed away more than two hours arguing." He rolls his eyes, much like I imagine he did the entire time. In addition to lacking any shred of tact, Nash has very little patience.

"Ugh," I groan. "Group projects are the worst."

"Tell me about it. I can already tell I'm going to be the one rewriting this piece of shit paper before we turn it in." Nash smirks. "I guess that makes me the Violet of the group."

A gnawing feeling forms in my belly. It's a familiar sensation at this point, one that makes an appearance every time Nash demonstrates that he remembers something about me. In a strange way, it was easier to move on when I told myself he'd forgotten.

"In my defense, I only did that a couple of times."

His mouth quirks. "You mean, every single time."

Having a civil, back and forth conversation with him is strange and normal all at once. When we both let our guards down like right now, things flow a little too easily between us. Which is why I need to reinforce my emotional walls to keep Nash far, far away from my heart. Should be easy enough. All I need to do is focus on remembering how badly he broke it.

"Well." I clear my throat, reaching for the mouse to shut down the computer. It chimes, and the screen goes black. "I was just leaving."

Nash stands back up and slings his bag over one broad shoulder, but he doesn't move to leave. "Me, too. Where are you parked?"

"Um… I'm not. I'm taking the train home." I'm reluctant to admit this because the transit station is on the other side of campus, and it is shady as hell. In addition to being dank and decrepit, it borders a high-traffic main road that divides the scenic LSU campus and a less savory part of town. I frequently stumble across homeless people sleeping in the station stairwells, and more alarmingly, have witnessed more than one drug deal go down while waiting.

However, taking a rideshare everywhere isn't economically feasible, and I haven't gotten behind the wheel of a car since last winter. I don't have any intention of that changing, at least not any time soon. I might be forced to revisit that after I graduate, depending on where I land a job, but that's tomorrow's problem.

"The train?" A frown tugs at the corners of his mouth. "Why?"

"My car's in the shop." It's easier to tell people this than to explain the truth, especially to him.

A muscle in his jaw twitches. "Do you mean the same transit station where three people got mugged last week?" His deep voice is stern, the effect far hotter than it should be.

"I guess so?" I squeak. Hadn't heard about that, but it sounds pretty on-brand for West Campus transit station.

"I'll drive you home."

Alarm bells sound in my head. Going places with Nash. Alone. *Bad idea. Bad, bad idea.*

"Thanks, but that's not necessary." I reach down, retrieving my purse from the drawer I'd crammed it in earlier.

When my gaze lifts back to him, Nash's expression turns stormier than a Category 5 hurricane. "It's late, it's pitch-black outside, and you're pocket-sized. The campus Safewalk program exists for a reason. That's not even factoring your CSI transit situation."

While I hate to admit it, he does have a point; in addition to the mugging incidents in the transit station, there's been a rash of unsolved night-time sexual assaults on campus lately. But still, it's not like my ability to take care of myself magically disappeared when Nash plummeted back into my life like a fiery meteor of bossiness. I always keep my keys in my fist when I'm walking and have my phone at the ready. I'll be okay. I think.

He rakes a hand through his dark hair, mussing the perfectly styled tresses. "Why are you working late by yourself, anyway?"

"I wasn't by myself. Preston was here, too."

Nash nods, but his expression tightens at the mention of Preston's name. Then something else registers across his face: disapproval. "Wait, he *left* you to take the train home alone?"

"I'm not helpless."

"I knew I didn't like that guy," he mutters, half-under his breath but still loud enough for me to hear.

I open my mouth to defend Preston because he's still my friend if nothing else, and immediately think better of it.

"I'll be fine, Nash. See you tomorrow." Slipping into my black wool coat, I grab my tote off the table and brush past him with my chin held high, but it's hard to look dignified when my overloaded book bag puts me comically off balance. Between my anatomy text-book and the extra training materials I'm taking home to study, it must weigh fifty pounds.

In a few long strides, Nash beats me to the door and stands in front of the doorway, blocking it with his body like a gigantic human barricade. I come to a screeching halt, glowering up at him.

"Three options, Vi. Either I drive you home"— he holds up three fingers to illustrate, ticking them off one by one—"you get campus Safewalk to come escort you, or I walk you to the train and wait with you. Take your pick."

CHAPTER 11

TARGET PRACTICE OF THE HEART
VIOLET

I LIKE how Nash has framed these scenarios as my only choices. Typical.

Scowling at him, I shift my tote on my shoulder and try to ignore the fact that I'm more tilted than the Leaning Tower of Pisa under its weight. "Why do you think you can order me around?"

"If you don't choose, I will." Nash folds his muscular arms, biceps flexing as he leans against the charcoal gray doorframe. His oversized form fills a stunning amount of the doorway, eclipsing a good portion of the light streaming in from the hall.

The most paradoxical mixture of emotion swells within me. Irritation, mingled with something else that I can barely admit, even to myself. Excitement. While his protective act might be a little old-fashioned, it's proof he still cares, and the circle of people he cares about is minuscule.

When I don't respond, he adds, "Fine. Fourth option: I can follow you if you're going to be stubborn about it."

"Wouldn't that make you one of the creeps you're warning me about?"

"I'm a lot less scary than the ones running loose out there." He jerks his thumb behind him.

"Others would disagree." Most people would jump out of their skin if someone like Nash was following them at night. He casts a pretty terrifying shadow.

"Less scary when it comes to you, anyway." Another pause follows. He cocks a brow, voice dropping until it's nearly a growl. "Don't make me carry your ass to my car."

I wouldn't put it past him to do that.

Sighing, I motion for him to move out of my way. "Fine. Let's go to the train station."

Instead of clearing a path, Nash reaches for me, and my breath hitches. For a split second, I'm not sure what he's about to do. Wordlessly, he lifts my bag and slides it off my shoulder. His fingers brush against mine, sending a tingle of electricity shooting up my arm. It travels all the way to my chest and into my stomach, moving lower still.

When he slips it onto his good shoulder, an invisible fist tightens around my throat at the thoughtfulness of his gesture. Bittersweet—kind of like him.

Spending time with Nash is like putting my heart up for target practice.

Pulling the door to the training room shut behind me, I lock it and double-check the handle before we head down the deserted, half-lit hall. It's silent aside from our echoing footsteps and the faint hum of a vacuum running somewhere in another part of the building.

When we reach the main doors to the facility, Nash holds the door open for me before following me outside. Cool evening air greets me, laced with a subtle chill that tells you fall is well under-way. I go to make a left, but Nash grabs my arm and steers me in the opposite direction. "No. This way."

I come to a halt and plant my feet, resisting his pull. "What are you talking about? I catch the train nearly every day." Claire and Julianna let me hitch a ride with them whenever possible, but our schedules don't always align.

"Don't know what to tell you, but this way is faster." He releases me and gestures for me to get going. I don't even bother to argue because I'd have better luck arguing with a hockey stick. Even sticks bend, which is more than I can say for Nash.

Moments later, we pass behind the performing arts building, which is the halfway mark to the transit station. As luck would have it, his way actually *is* faster, and I'm sure he'll make a point to remind me of that. Often.

As we navigate the darkened campus beneath overhead street-lamps and the faint glow from lit-up buildings, the cordiality between us starts to fade. Threads of tension weave, pulling tighter and tighter until I feel like I'm suffocating. While Nash seems comfortable with our lack of conversation, it drives me a little crazier with each unspoken step, especially because I still don't know what he wants.

"I thought you said we couldn't be friends," I blurt, stepping off the curb to cross a utility road.

His gaze slides over to me. "We can't."

"Then why do you care what happens to me?"

We slow to a stop under a yellow-tinted streetlamp. It casts half of his face in shadows, making him even more difficult to read than usual.

"Same reason I can't be your friend."

I stare at him for a few heartbeats while the implications of what he said hang in the air. I don't know how to respond, so I resume walking.

In my peripheral vision, a glimmer of playfulness shines through his solemn exterior. "Besides, if something happens to you, who else is going to maim me on the training table? I suspect Preston and Julianna don't pack the same punch."

"I didn't *maim* you," I tell Nash. "It's not my fault you're battered and bruised. You should book a sports massage. It'll help with some of the tension you're holding in your neck and shoulders."

"Not a big fan. I'd rather have you rub me down."

I elbow him in the ribs, though his innuendo is a sign he's defrosting to me, however marginally. "Are you like this with all your trainers?"

He smirks, but it quickly fades. "No. In all seriousness, though —and I'm not trying to be a dick this time—why are you working with the team?" Unlike the last time he asked this, he sounds more curious than confrontational.

"Like I told you, it wasn't my choice. Placements were supposed to be determined according to a ranked-choice system. My top picks were the women's hockey team or one of the basketball teams. Unfortunately for me, you guys are such special snowflakes that you require the top students, and my choices were disregarded."

"You're one of the top students in your program?"

Despite his neutral tone, I bristle at the question. "Is that hard to believe?"

"Of course not, Vi. You've always been crazy smart."

Nash holds the train station door open for me and we enter the musty stairwell, greeted by the faint odor of stale urine and rotting food. The stench intensifies as we scale two flights of stain-covered concrete stairs. On the second-floor landing, a scruffy man is slouched against the wall beside the doorway snoring loudly, surrounded by several empty cans. He seems harmless, but Nash doesn't even need to say anything for me to know he disagrees. Strongly.

Without a word, he yanks open the door at the top, gesturing for me to go first. The slumbering man doesn't stir. As I squeeze past Nash, our bodies brush, and I try to ignore the sparks of desire that shoot through my body. It's just hormones. Biology. It doesn't mean anything.

I step beneath the dingy spotlights that cast down from the ceiling, illuminating the graffiti-covered walls. A piercing wolf-whistle echoes behind me. I glance in the direction of the sound to find three guys standing a few feet away, leaning against a bank of ticket machines while smoking what smells like a joint.

"Wanna party, hot stuff?" one of them calls out. They all cackle obnoxiously, like this is the wittiest line anyone has ever thought of. Someone else utters something that I can't quite discern, except to say that it's definitely lewd.

Nash's broad figure steps out of the shadows, and their laughter dies down, either because they know who he is or because he looks like he's about to commit three homicides. Possibly both. He slowly turns to look down at me, unblinking, with an expression that says, 'are you fucking kidding me?' I flash him a sheepish smile, and his right eye twitches almost imperceptibly, vein in his forehead throbbing, ready to explode.

It's like the universe is conspiring to make this situation look as sketchy as possible.

I have a feeling this is the first of many chaperoned walks.

We approach the platform, and Nash scans our surroundings while we wait. He's quiet; too quiet, like the calm before a storm. After another inspection of the premises, his jaw tightens, cords in his neck tensing.

"Nope," he says. "Let's go." He begins walking, taking my backpack with him.

"What?" I hustle to catch up with him, which is no easy feat given that my legs are half the length of his. "Go where?"

"To my car, obviously."

I want to blame the late hour or my fatigued state for why I don't argue with him, but I can't honestly say those are the only reasons.

CHAPTER 12

FUNHOUSE MIRROR

THE PROBLEM with being part of a team is that even when only a handful of you behave like idiots, *everybody* suffers.

After fifteen minutes of dynamic stretching and on-ice warm-ups, Coach Ward has gathered us at center ice to deliver his game plan for practice. He's standing in front of the group, waiting for everyone to give him their attention—and he's getting more and more pissed by the minute.

I shut up right away because I am well-versed in the consequences when you don't. Unfortunately, a number of other guys are rowdier than usual, and they continue to keep talking.

And talking.

Coach Ward folds his arms, leveling an icy glare into the crowd, and the din slowly dies down.

"…fucking stupid." Connor is the last one audible in the silent arena. His mouth clamps shut, and he snaps to attention like he got caught with his hand in the cookie jar.

"All right." Coach Ward clears his throat, shooting Connor a reproachful look. "In light of how long it took everyone to settle down, I think we need to work on our focus today. We can start with one-on-ones in the corner."

A collective groan sounds. Battle drills like one-on-ones are almost strictly about effort, which is why they suck. You can't coast in a battle drill. Work harder than the guy you're battling. Win the puck. That's it.

"Defense, your job is to protect and keep the puck. Offense, your goal is to get possession. We'll cycle through everyone. Show up, work hard. Let's go." He blows his whistle, dismissing us, and we disperse.

We toil through one-on-ones for what feels like hours while I mentally coach myself through each drill. Position before possession. Stabilize your body. Leverage your edges. Create a wall. Keep the puck. Repeat.

For the duration of the exercise, I grind my ass off, too occupied to notice what anyone else is doing. But there must be an issue with some of the other guys' performance or effort because Coach finishes us off with skating lines; all hard stops and starts with no puck, also known as a bag skate. And by finishes us off, I mean he nearly kills us.

"That was grueling." Vaughn coasts off to the side and pushes back his cage, taking a drink from his water bottle. He pours the rest of his water over his face, wiping his face with the hem of his black practice jersey. "Was that your bright idea, Parsons? Did you contribute to that nightmare of a practice plan?"

Drew leans on his stick and shrugs, which is as good as him pleading guilty. "You know what they say, the things that hurt are the ones you need most."

"You're a sadist," I tell him.

Though in truth, if any of us are, it's probably me. But only under the right circumstances.

My shoulder throbs, dull pain radiating into my upper back, a nagging reminder that something is wrong. Violet's tape job has been gone for a few days now since the adhesive wore off, and I'm sorely missing it. I wonder again if I could convince Vi to tape my shoulder on the regular. Maybe I'd pushing my luck, but if I keep up my end of the bargain performing my rehab and stretching, I think there's a decent chance she'll bite.

Signature dramatic flair in full force, Connor flops onto the half-wall, draping his upper body over the boards like a rag doll. "If the bag skating at the end was your idea, Parsons, you're officially evicted."

"I'm on the lease," Drew points out.

"I don't care," Connor mumbles, still face down. "I'll leave your shit on the lawn."

"Move it, Haas. You're blocking the gate." I jab him in the leg with the blade of my stick. He grunts in response but makes no effort to move. "Don't make me spear you."

In theory, I could get past without him moving. I could simply hop the boards, like we do all the time. But in reality, I'm way too fucking tired to do that. Connor eventually relents, and we shuffle into the dressing room to hit the showers.

As we get dressed, Coach Ward circulates through the locker room, giving individual feedback. I yank on my jeans and zip up the fly, half-listening to his comments while I speculate about what he'll say to me.

"Solid as always, Parsons."

Pretty fair assessment. Drew is nothing if not even.

"Haas, watch your temper in those battles."

I stifle a laugh because Connor is a hothead at the best of times.

"Good effort out there, Banks. Nice stick lifts."

He's right. Vaughn crushed it out on the ice today. Our matchup was intense. I used to be able to overpower him with my size advantage, but the fucker has some good moves this year.

Coach Ward turns to me. "Richards, come see me after you finish getting dressed."

Okay, then.

———

Leaning back in the guest chair across from Coach Ward's desk, I scan the walls filled with championship photos while I try to figure out why I've been summoned. I haven't done anything to warrant a reprimand. At least, not lately.

While a lot of athletes would be shitting pucks right now, I'm not overly concerned. Thing is, coaches fall into one of two categories: the authoritarian, which is self-explanatory, and the players' coach. Ironically, while Coach Ward had a reputation for being intimidating—or scary, depending on who you ask—in my opinion, he's a players' coach through and through. He's relatively democratic, he cares about his athletes, and he isn't solely focused on winning at our expense. That's why this current scenario doesn't spark too much fear within my soul. I grew up with the other kind of coach breathing down my neck, and I know what scary actually looks like.

"Richards." Coach Ward leans forward on his desk, steepling his fingers. "I wanted to touch base with you to see how things are going. How's the semester been treating you so far? Are your classes going well?"

"Not bad," I say, crossing an ankle over knee. "Pretty demanding, as I would imagine most fourth-year programs are."

"And how's your father doing?"

Coach knows my father from the hockey sphere, which is a smaller world than you'd expect. He often asks about him—mostly for the sake of being polite, I think, because I've always gotten the impression he doesn't particularly like my father. I don't fault him for that. The only people who do are the ones who can't see through bullshit.

"He's good, Coach."

"Glad to hear it." He pauses. "The reason I ask is that you've been a little uneven lately."

"I'm sorry, can you clarify?" I hedge, praying this isn't about my shoulder. "Is there something specific you want me to work on?"

"Maybe uneven is the wrong word." His mouth pulls into a frown, his expression hinting at concern. "You're performing well. Phenomenal effort in those battle drills earlier, actually. But you seem incredibly distracted off the ice. I noticed it in dryland last week, and from what I can tell, it's been an ongoing thing. Is everything okay in your personal life? Anything you want to talk about?"

Oh, so this is about *Violet*. He just doesn't know that.

"All good." I force myself to meet his eyes. "Same as usual."

"Have you seen Dr. Schultz lately?"

"No, sir. Haven't had time to make an appointment since classes started back up."

He raises his eyebrows. "Maybe it's time to think about that."

———

Dr. Schultz is the Grizzlies' team sports psychologist, but she makes us call her Marie. She's a plump, middle-aged woman with long graying hair, a soft-spoken voice, and an even softer temperament. Even though her job title contains the word "sports," hockey-related topics only consume about half of our fifty-minute sessions at the most.

At Coach Ward's instruction, this is my first appointment back this school year. Long overdue, thanks to my hectic schedule. And, well, my avoidance of therapy.

I sink into the overstuffed navy-blue couch in Marie's office, clutching an extra-large coffee to power me through until I need to drive Violet home later. We've fallen into a routine of sorts on days when we both happen to be on campus after-hours. I meet her in the training room, we walk to my car, and I drive her home. As an added benefit, I'm able to better focus on my schoolwork when I'm on campus waiting for her. There are too many distractions at home, like Connor constantly trying to rope me into getting wasted on a weeknight.

Because of this arrangement, I end up staying late more often than I otherwise would—as in, every time Violet does, except when I have a game or practice. But she doesn't need to know that. It's a small price to pay for the peace of mind it grants me. Being with her is the highlight of my day. Twenty fleeting minutes where we get to be alone without the pressure and prying eyes of everyone else.

Marie rifles through a stack of yellow-lined papers, checking her session notes, and pulls out her blue pen, ready to jot down more on a fresh legal pad. "Last time we spoke, you said your mother's birthday was near the end of August, correct?"

"August twenty-third." I swallow, trying to squash the sour feeling brewing in my gut.

"Did you do anything to commemorate it?"

Guilt uppercuts me in the ribs, followed by a heavy, lingering sorrow that fills my entire body. "No."

She nods, marking something down. "Have you been to see her lately?"

"You mean, to her grave?" I haven't been there in months, and I feel like a shitty son for it, but the ugly truth is, it never gets easier. It never hurts less. And sometimes it's easier to stop picking at the scab, even if that makes me a selfish asshole.

Marie peers at me over her wire-rimmed glasses with what I've deemed "her therapist look," an inquisitive but encouraging expression meant to rope you into talking. "You used to refer to it as going to see her. What's changed for you?"

"Why does everything have to mean something?" Fucking therapy.

"It doesn't have to," she says neutrally. "Does it mean anything? Maybe it doesn't."

I don't know the answer to that, which is often the case when I'm perched on this goddamn velvet couch.

"I'm not sure." Taking a sip of coffee, I look out her office window at the quad below, watching students mill about the leaf-covered grass.

While hockey is the primary source of my stress, it's also my outlet for it. I cope with the pressure by beating the shit out of myself on the ice and in the gym six, if not seven, days a week, until I'm too tired to think about anything else. Then I collapse into bed and do it all over again the next day.

When that was no longer an option because of my shoulder injury last year, it was like a massive part of my life had been ripped away suddenly. I was lost. After a few weeks of stumbling from class to class like a zombie, with the grades to show for it, Coach Ward said he was concerned that I might be depressed and recommended I see the team's sports psychologist. And by "recommended," I mean that he said I had to get some help, or he was kicking me off the team.

I fought this suggestion because I wasn't sad like I assumed a depressed person would be—I was numb. Plus, I was adamantly opposed to the idea of therapy. The thought of sitting around talking about my feelings sounded about as pleasant as slitting my throat with a skate. Vaughn talked me into giving it a fair shot, and I finally relented. Once I did, vowing it would be a one-time thing, I realized it wasn't as bad as I'd imagined. Sometimes it's even kind of nice. It's validating.

That's not to say it's easy. It sure as fuck isn't. Some days, we talk about shit I would rather pretend never happened. Some days, it's like holding up a funhouse mirror and seeing my ugly, distorted reflection with all its flaws. There are a lot of them.

"Let's shift gears for a minute," Marie says. "How's hockey going?"

"Hockey is fine. Training, not so much." See? Her therapist look worked on me. I almost spilled about Violet without even meaning to.

She pauses, glancing up from her notes. "Can you elaborate on that?"

"Do I have to?"

"This is your time. You never have to talk about anything you don't want to."

Somehow, this tactic of hers always makes me feel guilty. I don't think that's the intent; I'm just not used to being given many choices outside of these four walls.

"Can we circle back to hockey?" I ask, shifting my weight on the plush couch. It's a little too comfortable, making it tempting to lay back for a nap. Fuck, I need to start going to bed earlier. "That's why Coach sent me here. Said he thinks my focus is off."

"Absolutely. We can work on some coping strategies. Why do you think your focus is off? Is something bothering you?"

Another sip of coffee masks my reaction. Dammit fuck. I'm fighting tooth and nail not to open the Pandora's Box that is Violet in this session. I've managed to skate around that topic with Marie for the better part of a year without getting into it, and I'm not eager to change that now.

"Stress in general. Can we work on some ways to compartmentalize it?"

"It's a little easier if I have some more background first." Marie's pushback is firm, but gentle. "How are things with your father? Is he a part of this stress?"

Despite Marie's coaching and undying patience, I have yet to set boundaries with my father like she's repeatedly suggested.

That means this is a question that's easy to answer honestly.

"He's always a part of the stress."

CHAPTER 13
ENDANGERED SPECIES
VIOLET

"TIME OUT." Claire slows to a stop on the path and bends at the waist, trying to catch her breath. "I have a cramp. The mother of all cramps, actually."

Gravel crunches beneath my feet as I come to a halt beside her, panting. Late morning sun filters through the trees, shining onto the gold and crimson leaves scattered on the ground. Fall is my favorite running weather; plenty of sunshine without it being not too hot or cold, not to mention gorgeous scenery.

"Press two fingers into the area and breathe against it," I tell her, unzipping my purple running jacket and tying it around my waist. "We can walk it out."

Claire does as I say, blowing out a heavy breath. We're three-quarters of the way into our 10K training plan, with the goal of running a race before winter hits and ten feet of snow on the ground make that nearly impossible. After that, we're going to try a half-marathon, but at over twice the distance, I expect it'll take us a lot longer to train for.

While Claire has full marathon aspirations someday, I'm not sure I'll ever work up to that. It seems pretty intense. Never say never, though. I like to keep challenging myself. Not only does it give me something to work toward, which is a great distraction from school, setting performance-related targets has helped me foster a healthier relationship with my body. As cheesy as it may sound, it's easier to ignore the bit of flab or cellulite when you know you can crush Dancer's Pose.

Rather than focusing on the scale, or what size jeans I'm fitting into any particular week, it's been so much better for me mentally to track things like my running split time or whether I can do a handstand in yoga. Okay, jury's out on whether the last one will ever happen. But I'm going to keep trying, even if I faceplant in the process. Again.

Claire sucks in a breath. "So, you don't think it's going to go anywhere with you and Preston, huh?"

Guilt, ever-present lately, seeps into the corners of my mind at her question.

"I wish it could, but I'm not feeling it. And I know you're going to say it's because I'm scared of getting hurt again, but I honestly don't think that's it. I tried, Claire. I even let him kiss me. There's nothing there. Crickets. Radio silence. Nil."

"Shame." She exhales again, digging her fingers into her abdomen over the top of her pristine white training jacket. Only Claire could rock white workout gear and keep it spotless. She straightens to standing, readjusting her black Lululemon headband. "He's such a nice guy. You'd make gorgeous babies someday."

We resume walking along the pathway as a few bicyclists fly by, throwing off a pleasant breeze as they pass.

"Trust me, I wish it weren't so. It'd make my life so much easier if I could convince myself to be into him." I wipe my forehead with the back of my hand, inwardly cursing my choice of attire; it's hotter than I expected today, and my full-length black leggings are a magnet for the sun's rays. "What about you? What's happening with Silas?"

Her smile is grim. "Think we have the opposite issue there. I'm the one he's not into."

I can't see how. Claire is the total package; not only is she gorgeous and funny, she's also pre-med and destined to be the best pediatrician in the tri-state area someday. Then again, with some guys, that is the problem—they're intimidated by her intelligence and ambition. Or worse yet, they try to compete with her and mansplain everything. She's been single for a while and bummed over it, especially after a string of especially bad dates, but I keep reminding her that those are the ones she wouldn't have wanted anyway.

"I feel like guys are utterly oblivious sometimes. Are you sure Silas even knows you like him?"

"I am not sure how I can make it any clearer to him, short of showing him my boobs."

"Guys *always* like that."

She laughs and swats me playfully, jogging on the spot. "Okay, let's go. Two more miles."

Twenty minutes and twenty-two seconds later, we reach our distance goal and walk the remaining couple of yards to a set of wooden benches at the entrance to the park. From a training perspective, it's ideal to stretch immediately after, plus it helps the sweat dry, which saves Claire's leather seats. She's a little particular about some things, including her car, the tidiness of our apartment, and how the fridge is organized.

"About Preston," she begins, placing her heel on the bench and leaning forward to stretch out her hamstrings. "Are you not into him because of Nash?"

"That's not it." My response is a little too quick and a lot too insistent. Even I know I'm full of shit, and Claire can always see right through me. "I mean, maybe it's part of it, but not all. I think being around Nash made me realize that Preston and I don't have the chemistry I need. But I don't think we would've worked out either way. Does that make sense?"

"Are you sure you're capable of seeing things objectively with him in the picture?"

"No," I admit. "I'm not." Ever since he came back into my life, I've been viewing things through Nash-colored glasses. I feel him everywhere; his influence is heady like a drug, intoxicating and impossible to ignore.

"How is it seeing Nash all the time, anyway?" Claire gives me a sympathetic smile, and I greatly appreciate that she's sparing me an 'I told you so' speech that I arguably deserve.

I steadfastly avoid her gaze, kneeling down to re-tie my pale pink shoelace, noticing I've nearly worn a hole in the toe box of my gray Asics. Maybe I need to size up before our race. "Oh, you know. We're both being professional."

This isn't untrue. Considering who I'm dealing with, Nash has been shockingly professional. So far, at least. I can't rule out that changing in the future because, well, it's Nash.

"It's awful, isn't it?" Claire reads between the lines.

"So awful." Pushing to stand, I drag a hand down my face, my fingers trailing through remnants of sweat. "It's awkward. And he's gotten better looking. How is that even fair?"

"You're not telling me you're still attracted to him, are you? After everything he did?" Her understanding gives way to open dismay.

"I mean…" Has she seen the guy?

Contrary to what I'd hoped going in, our chemistry is as present as ever—and I'm pretty sure I'm not the only one who's noticed. The way I feel around him, especially when we're close, is indescribable. I've never replicated that with anyone else, and with the way things are going, I'm deeply worried I never will.

But that's only the physical part of things. Rationally, I know there's so much more to it than that; a laundry list of things required to make a relationship work, none of which we have. Nash might tick the dirty boyfriend boxes, but the practical ones are all blank.

Which is why him driving me home—which he's now done several times—is more than a little hazardous. Being alone together presents the opportunity for all kinds of mistakes to happen. Sexy mistakes. Dirty ones, too.

Maybe I should invest in a chastity belt. Heck, better make it two. Is there something stronger than a chastity belt? Chastity pants? Chastity jumpsuit, maybe?

Claire sighs, pulling her heel to her glute. "Violet."

"I'm not going to act on it," I tell her.

I don't think.

————

Nothing feels better than a long, hot shower after a sweaty run. Okay, a few things do, but most of them are X-rated and not attainable without the assistance of a highly skilled partner.

I fasten the tie on my white terry cloth robe, bustling into the bathroom where Julianna is perched on the counter, forehead furrowed in concentration as she paints her pinkie toe metallic fuchsia.

She looks at me through the mirror. "I wish you could come out tonight."

"Me too," I lie, combing out my wet hair. It's so much faster to dry since I chopped off nearly four inches. Throw in the refurbished Dyson blow dryer I splurged on, and I can be ready in mere minutes. Best investment ever.

"You could meet up with us after, maybe? Ninety9 is supposed to be amazing."

Julianna and Claire are hitting a new club that opened last month. Claire got on the VIP list thanks to a girl in one of her classes who knows the owners, and they are both convinced this is an optimal way to meet guys. While dancing can be fun, I'm more than a little skeptical of their plan.

"Not sure if I'm staying over or not. I might sleep at my sister's to give her a hand with the kids, let her sleep in tomorrow, that kind of thing." I flip my head over, applying mousse to the roots, and work it in with my palms. One other reason my hair dries so quickly is that I have so little of it; it's thin and baby fine. In another life where money isn't a thing, I fantasize about getting extensions for volume.

"Boo." Julianna pouts. "We can try for next weekend, if it's any fun."

"Totally." And I'm not lying. I'd be open to it another night. But tonight is my parents' thirtieth wedding anniversary and they're celebrating with a big catered family soirée at their place.

In truth, I don't mind missing out on the club. I'm not sure what it says about me, but most of the time, I'd rather hang out with my family on a weekend than get wasted at a party like most college students.

Don't get me wrong, I love my friends, and going out can be fun sometimes. But it's one of those, a little goes a long way type of things. Many of the happiest occasions for me are when I'm hanging out with my sister, Grace, her three kids, and my parents. My brother-in-law Michael, too, but he's been deployed more often than he's home lately.

I say I'm an old soul, but Grace teases me by saying I was born to be old and married. While she got pregnant and married—in that order—young, at twenty-two, I am the one who always played wedding with dolls growing up. Maybe there is a part of me that's still a runaway hopeless romantic, as impractical as it may be in today's society.

One warp speed blow-dry later, I find a text from my sister, letting me know she's leaving to come pick me up. I'm already waiting outside when a beige minivan pulls up to the curb and its automatic passenger door slides open, revealing a matching beige interior.

"Mom-mobile, at your service," my sister announces.

My two-year-old nephew, Lincoln, is strapped into his car seat, clutching a Thomas the Tank Engine board book. Four-year-old Willow is sitting primly in her booster seat, poring over Giraffes Can't Dance. And Abigail, my brand-new baby niece, is fast asleep in her rear-facing bucket seat.

"Auntie!" Lincoln and Willow squeal in unison.

"Hi, cuties." I climb into the middle row, kissing Lincoln and Willow before fastening my seatbelt. I'd give Abigail a smooch, but Grace will kill me if I wake her and ruin her car nap. She specifically arranged her daily schedule to accommodate for the fact that Abigail would fall asleep on the drive to and from picking me up. Abigail is one of those unicorn babies who sleeps through the night at a young age, and my sister is terrified of jinxing it by deviating from their routine in any way.

"Thanks, Gracie," I add, waggling my fingers at her in the mirror.

"No problem." She signals and shoulder checks, pulling away from the curb. "It's nice to have a reason to get out of the house sometimes. I mean, one that isn't a pediatrician's appointment or to a sale on jumbo-packs of diapers."

"Yeah, I'm sure you really love playing taxi." Not to mention, Willow always insists that I sit in the back with her, so it literally is like Grace is taxi-ing us around.

"Violet, my idea of 'me time' is getting to hit Target alone. Let me have this."

I slip on my tortoiseshell sunglasses, stashing my purse between the captain's chairs. "'Kay. At least let me pay for Starbucks."

"Starbucks?" Willow claps her hands so quickly, they'd give the wings of a hummingbird a run for their money. "Can I get a pink drink?"

"I want a cake pop!" Lincoln shouts, kicking the seat in front of him.

"Inside voice, honey, your baby sister is napping," Grace says gently. I consider myself a fairly patient person, but her patience still amazes me. Her blue eyes meet mine in the rear-view mirror, but there's a smile behind them. "Now look at what you've done, Auntie."

I lower my voice, leaning closer to them. "One treat each, okay? As long as Mommy says it's okay."

"If you hop them up on sugar, you have to play with them," my sister singsongs.

"Deal."

When we get back to Grace's, I send her upstairs with her coffee for some quiet time. Or try to, because my sister is the epitome of someone who has trouble accepting things from other people, including help.

"You don't have to." Grace tucks a lock of curly dark blonde hair behind her ear, stealing a glance at the upstairs landing where her bedroom is. A hint of longing gleams in her eyes, betraying her protests. We both know she wants nothing more than to escape for a couple of hours. With Michael gone as much as he is, she rarely ever gets a break.

"Yes, I do. Now, shoo." I balance my vanilla latte and pumpkin bread in one hand, taking her by the elbow with the other and leading her to the stairway. "Go upstairs. Nap, take a bath, read a trashy magazine, watch Bridgerton. Do whatever you want. I've got the kids for a few hours."

"Okay. But I'm still establishing my milk supply and we're not doing bottles yet, so come get me if Abigail starts to fuss and I'll nurse her."

"I will. I promise."

I lead the kids into the kitchen to start prepping lunch, placing Abigail in her swing. By the time we're due to leave for our parents' house several hours later, everyone has napped but me. Lincoln and Willow have somehow consumed two entire boxes of Annie's Bunny Macaroni and Cheese between the two of them. Abigail spits up on two clean outfits, then blows through a diaper with a third. Grace has the chance to blow dry her hair for the first time in two weeks. And I'm exhausted, but happy.

———

It's practically a family reunion between all of the aunts and uncles, cousins and their children swarming my parents' sprawling two-story house. My mother ushers us inside, alternating between thanking me and scolding me for buying them a present, even though it's only a modestly priced bottle of Merlot. Difficulty with accepting things runs in the maternal side of our family, clearly.

A glass of champagne is thrust into my hand and then I'm inundated with a good half-hour of questions about my dating life and degree, heavy emphasis on the former.

"Violet." Aunt Ruth wraps me in a warm embrace. "How are you, darling? Do you have a boyfriend yet?"

You'd think I was a spinster, if that were even still a thing. I politely dodge and weave questions like this until dinner, during which I proceed to stuff my face with shrimp bisque, Boston salad, garlic mashed potatoes, and red pepper mousse-stuffed chicken. If I'm going to die alone like everyone seems to think, I might as well die well-fed.

Dinner wraps up with flourless chocolate cake that's good enough to marry. It might actually be better than sex. Wait. That's not entirely accurate. It's better than sex with anyone other than Nash. Nash blows this cake straight out of the water.

Oh, God. Claire's right. I am in danger.

Over in the living room, my father spins my mother around while a cheesy rock ballad pours out of the built-in speakers. They're laughing like drunken teenagers, traces of burgundy lingering on their lips from a few too many glasses of wine.

Whenever I start to become too cynical about love—which is fairly often, because I'm a college student in today's Tinder-riddled society—I look at my parents, and I know that it can happen for some people.

Of course, that's not to say it'll ever happen for me. Maybe it won't. But seeing them so in love after thirty years of marriage gives me some semblance of hope. It's out there, and it is possible.

"Thirty years," I murmur. "And they're still sickeningly in love."

Grace nods, a smile playing on her lips as she watches them. "They really are."

From beneath her black-striped nursing cover-up, Abigail's chubby little hand pops out and finds Grace's hair, yanking a curl, and I stifle a laugh.

"I don't think that kind of love exists nowadays." When I turn to face my sister, she raises her eyebrows, probably because she's been happily married to my brother-in-law Michael for four-and-a-half years.

"I mean, for people my age." Then I realize I just implied that my twenty-six-year-old sister is old.

Fortunately, Grace isn't one to take offense easily. Her cornflower blue eyes crinkle at the corners and she shrugs off my comments, reaching over to embrace me in a brief, a one-armed hug. "Don't be silly, Violet. It absolutely does."

Does it really, though? Grace met her husband back when they were in high school. She's been happily paired up for more than a decade, before dating apps doused the dating landscape in kerosene and lit a match. These days, love seems like a losing bet.

"You're only twenty-one," Grace adds. "There's no rush. Look at Kayla. She's perfectly happy."

Our cousin and I are different breeds, though. Our twenty-nine-year-old cousin Kayla enjoys living alone in her modern loft downtown, pulls eighty-hour work weeks at her high-pressure job, and takes vacations only when her job forces her to use her paid time off. She doesn't want to get married. Not now, not ever.

I do. Someday.

It's not like it's my only goal in life. But it's one of them.

Sometimes it feels taboo to admit that I want to get married. That's not to say I think there's anything wrong with Kayla and her priorities. I don't, at all. But there are times when I feel like I'm being simultaneously pressured to partner-up and judged for wanting to do so.

"Did you have butterflies?" I ask Grace.

She looks at me questioningly. "I'm sorry?"

I'm not making sense. I've only had a single glass of champagne, which means I must be drunk on chocolate cake.

"When you first met Michael, I mean." I trace the droplets of condensation coating the outside of my ice water glass with my finger absentmindedly, playing connect the dots. "Did you have butterflies around him?"

A wistful look appears across her face. "Absolutely."

I pause with my finger on the glass. "Do you still?"

Maybe butterflies aren't worth chasing if they fade over time.

"Sometimes. I mean, it's not all roses and champagne with three young kids. But when he kisses me…" She bites her bottom lip, her cheeks pulling into a smile, and I could swear, she literally glows. "Yes, I still feel them."

Selfishly, I think part of me was hoping she'd say no. Then I could tell myself that you don't need that euphoric rush; that all-consuming desire; that inexplicable thing I can't seem to find. At least, not with anyone new.

"Why?" Grace inclines her head, studying me.

"Just curious."

In my world, butterflies are on the endangered species list. Experienced with precisely one person, never to be found again.

CHAPTER 14
HOCKEY CODE
NASH

I'M LATER than I should be when I arrive at LSU's Apex Arena. Which is to say, I'm still on time, just not absurdly ahead of schedule like usual. Not only are we facing MSU again tonight, complete with that asshole Eriksen, but it's also the first time the athletic training interns will be on the bench during our game. In other words, Violet will be watching me play, and I'm more nervous about that than I'd like. I'm pretty sure she hasn't been to a single game since we broke up. I never saw her in the crowd or around the arena. Though selfishly, I always hoped I would.

As I push through the glass doors, I spot Candice standing with her friends by the concession area and I swerve back into the sea of people, taking an alternate route to the locker room. I have enough shit to deal with. Not adding that to my list.

My teammates mill about in various states of undress, talking game plans while upbeat music booms from a portable speaker. Drew swoops over as soon as he spots me walk in. As to be expected, he's flipped into his pre-game micromanaging alternate captain mode. Meanwhile, our captain, Marcus, is chilling with his buddies on the other side of the locker room without a care in the world.

"You good?" Drew has the energy of someone who's been mainlining caffeine. "Watch out for their defense tonight. I heard their Coach put a bounty on your head after what you did to Eriksen last game. Sonderquist is gunning for you."

Sonderquist is MSU's answer to, well, me. He's their stay-at-home defenseman; their enforcer. And if he's gunning for me instead of Vaughn, our top scoring forward, all the better. One of us was built to take the knocks—and deliver them—and one of us was built to win games.

"I'm good." I unbutton my dress shirt and slip out of my navy suit pants, hanging them both in my locker. If you ask me, the suit requirement before and after games is ridiculous.

Drew gives me a dubious look. "Remember to keep your head up."

"I always do, man. Besides, I'm not indispensable like Banks." I point at Vaughn, who's minding his own business while he gets dressed off to the side. He's not much for pre-game chitchat; says it messes with his focus.

Drew's eyes widen because I've given him something else to fret about, which wasn't my intention. I just wanted to get him off my back. For the life of me, I'll never understand worrying as much as he does. It doesn't change the outcome; it's an utter waste of energy.

With that said, it's not that Vaughn can't take care of himself. It's that it isn't his role. His job is to get the puck to the net, get it past the goalie, and do it all over again. My job is twofold: make sure no one takes him out with a dirty hit, and retaliate if anyone tries.

"Saw Candice hanging around outside," Connor remarks. I turn, finding that he's already tugging on his shoulder pads. Yikes. I'm later than I thought if Connor is already half-dressed. He's never on time.

"Yeah, I saw her too." Then I promptly headed in the other direction.

"Maybe she could help you get your mind off—you know."

"Maybe." I slip into my moisture-wicking base layers, avoiding eye contact with him. Connor doesn't understand what it's like to be so hung up on someone, you can't even fathom the idea of sleeping with someone else. And it's not a debate I care to get into here, of all places.

"Sex is like pizza," he says, catching my attention again. "Even when it's bad, it's still pretty good."

Up until a few weeks ago, I would have agreed with him.

Now I'm being forced to come to terms with what I'm missing.

Having Violet on the bench is a test of my focus, to say the least. While the trainers' job is to hang back unless they're needed, her presence is still a distraction, especially when I know she's likely watching me extra closely because of my shoulder. It takes a solid couple of minutes into the first period before I find my groove and manage to concentrate on the game instead of wondering what Violet's thinking about how I'm playing.

Like always when we face MSU, the game is a bloodbath. By halfway through the second period, the score is already tied three to three, with another goal against us that was called back for goalie interference. It's been highly physical, and there are penalties flying left and right, a handful of which I've drawn and three that I've taken. If you ask me, two of my penalties were bullshit, but it is what it is.

After an icing call, we end up taking a faceoff in the MSU zone that puts me face-to-face with my least favorite person. I've taken a few hits out on him already tonight, and he's decidedly pissed. Not to mention, limping slightly.

Eriksen juts his chin at our bench where Violet, Preston, and Julianna are standing with Coach Ward. "Who's the hot blonde on your bench, Richards?"

Rage flickers inside me me and I grit my teeth, shoving it down. Despite that, something about my reaction must give me away, because triumph registers across Eriksen's face. No big surprise there; Violet is my kryptonite. I do not, however, need this dickbag knowing that.

"You know her, don't you? Course you do. She's a nice piece of ass." He smirks, nodding at her. "Bet she'd be a great lay."

Anger sparks again, igniting into a flame, and I fight the urge to snap my stick over his bloated head. *Cool it, Richards.* Second period is too early to get tossed from the game, but if I'm stuck talking to him much longer, it's going to become a real possibility. Unfortunately, the officials are still off to the side talking to Coach Ward. What the hell is the hold up?

"She's one of our trainers," I tell Eriksen. "Save your weak-ass trash talk for the team."

He laughs, but it's sardonic. "Oh, *now* you care about hockey code? After what you did with my girl? That's fucking convenient."

To be clear, sleeping with Penelope was a perfectly consensual one-night deal. I had fun, she had fun, everybody came out ahead. Multiple times, in her case. And based on what Penelope said, it was desperately needed on her part after whatever the fuck Eriksen was—or wasn't—doing to her.

"Your chick hit on me first, man. If you were still together when it happened, take that shit up with her." I skate back a few inches, repositioning for when the puck drops. Hopefully, that will happen this decade.

Eriksen snorts. "Don't act like you didn't know who she was."

For fuck's sake. I can't even keep track of who the guys on my *own* team have slept with. But there's no point in arguing with crazy.

"Don't worry, Eriksen. I'm sure you'll break that dry streak sometime before the end of the season."

He falls quiet for a moment. Once he puts two and two together —which takes a while, because he's not that bright—his face reddens until it matches his crimson jersey.

"Fuck you, Richards." He spins ninety degrees to face me, his teeth bared in a snarl. I think he's shooting for Doberman, but the effect is more yippy small dog. "We can settle this after if you want."

A bout of laughter escapes the back of my throat; his challenge is that absurd. I have no idea why he's putting this on the table.

There's no way it would end well for him, and he should already know that after our last run-in. That said, I have better things to do than beat the shit out of Eriksen after the game.

"Thanks, but I'll pass. Might give Penelope a call and see if she's busy, though." Of course, I have no interest in following through on this threat. Pretty sure I deleted her number not long after I got it. I'm just fucking with Eriksen because I can, especially because he started this by trying to drag Violet into it.

At hearing this, Eriksen tosses his stick and lunges for me. I immediately skate backward and out of swinging range, because any fighting can get you tossed from a game—or worse—in college hockey. Sometimes I get away with pushing my luck, but I don't want to roll the dice with Violet watching.

The officials rush over and restrain Eriksen while he continues to yell at me, trying to get free from their grip. He gets sent off for a five-minute major, and the play restarts without him.

Violet is watching me closely when I skate back to the bench after my shift, questions written across her face. I can tell she's dying to ask what that was about. I'm sure I'll have to explain to her at some point in the future, but it'll require cooking up a sanitized version of events that do not include Penelope. Somehow.

Connor cackles, fist-bumping me as I hop back onto the bench. "That Eriksen shit was beautiful, bro."

"Doesn't take much with that one," I say, catching Eriksen's eye from where he's still seated in the sin bin. I throw him a wave and smug-ass smile, and he mouths, "fuck you" in return.

Every year, our team holds an unsanctioned end-of-year party and hands out unofficial awards called The Cellies. Some of the honors include "Best Lettuce" (hockey hair); "Best Off-Ice Game" (as in, with chicks); "Best Actor" (most dramatic dive after taking a hit); and "Best Celly" (most ridiculous post-goal celebration).

Last year, Connor and I tied for "Best Trash Talk." Connor is a heckler—his chirps are entertaining, sometimes to the point where the victim will even laugh because he's undeniably funny. I am not as concerned with entertainment and will go straight for the jugular, using whatever will piss off the other guy the most. The more you can rattle them, the less effective they'll be on the ice. Case in point, Eriksen.

Lines change, and Connor gets back on as Vaughn hops onto the bench. He reaches for his water bottle, squeezing it into his open mouth, and glances around, leaning in closer so Violet and the other trainers don't overhear. "Is that Doug I spotted over on the east side? A few rows from the front?"

"What?" My stomach lurches, gaze darting to the stands on the opposite side of the rink, but I can't make out any faces in the crowd from where I'm seated. While showing up unannounced is pretty on-brand for him, it's a little early in the season for one of his surprise visits.

"Thought I saw him, but I wasn't sure since you didn't mention he was coming."

Vaughn is painfully aware that I'm on edge when I know my father will be here and that my performance often suffers accordingly. Usually, I give him the heads-up so he can help keep my head in the game and stop me from getting too rattled by Doug's presence.

From the other side of me, Drew overhears. "Doug's here?"

"I don't know," I mutter. "Maybe."

Not that it should matter—Doug records my games on TV when he's not in attendance. He's always watching one way or another. It's like a ball and chain around my neck, weighing me down, slowly choking me. Still, having him here in person is a million times worse.

"Shit," he says. "Sorry, man. That's rough."

Another line change occurs, and I hop on for my next shift, making a point to skate even harder than usual. With every single stride, I dig into the ice like my life depends on it. On some level, I know I'm going to hit the wall before the game is over if I maintain this pace, but I can't seem to stop myself. I was a little off kilter to begin with because of Violet, and now I'm spinning out of control.

Connor winds up and makes a clean pass to Vaughn, who barrels for MSU's net while I skate backward, remaining in position to protect our zone in the event of a turnover. When the play brings

me over to the seating section Vaughn mentioned, I divide my attention briefly, searching the stands in my peripheral vision while
staying on top of the puck.

At first, all I see are the usual college students and local families. Then I spot Doug sitting down at the far end of the third row.

Fuck me.

From that moment on, I feel his eyes following me everywhere
on the ice. Judging every missed pass, every minor miscalculation,
every single misstep, no matter how small.

His voice echoes through my head, telling me what I did wrong
and what I should have done instead. It's a steady stream of
commentary inside my brain even when he isn't around, but it's
always louder when he is. Sometimes I want to take off my helmet
and bang my head against the boards to make it stop. But I've
already had one concussion in my career; better not make it two.

My game goes straight downhill from there. As in, off a fucking
cliff.

When I slam an opposing center into the boards, all I can think
is that I should have hit him sooner, hit him harder. Connor misses
my pass because he wasn't looking, and I blame myself instead of
him because I should have waited until he was ready or passed to
Drew instead. Our goalie, Joey, lets in a weak goal, but it's my fault
because I let the other team fire off a shot in our zone.

I can trace every single thing that goes wrong on the ice directly
back to something I did incorrectly or failed to do.

After my shift ends, I hop back onto the bench next to Vaughn.
My jersey is soaked with sweat, breath heavy, and I'm parched like
I've been without water for hours. Leaning in for my water bottle, I
chug half of it in a few greedy gulps.

"Yeah," I confirm, voice low. "He's here."

Vaughn glances over to where Doug is seated, then back to me.
"Didn't tell you he was coming, huh?"

If it seems weird to outsiders, that's because it is. What kind of
parent shows up randomly to their kid's game? I mean, barring
something like a fun surprise visit—which this absolutely is not.

Craning my neck, I make sure the trainers are still out of

earshot. They're down on the other end of the bench with Christina, checking out a freshman who took a puck to the ankle. "You know how it is. Sometimes he just appears."

Vaughn huffs, shaking his head. "Fucking fathers."

He can identify with daddy issues all too well, although his are the opposite in nature. Whereas my father is overbearing and controlling, his is a total fucking deadbeat. In and out of his life, comes and goes whenever he wants. If you ask me, they're both useless assholes.

"Fucking fathers indeed."

Coach Ward stalks over, studying me with a frown. Violet notices but quickly turns away and pretends to busy herself talking to Preston. I keep looking ahead, hoping Coach will move along to someone else.

After a beat, he leans down to talk to me so the other players don't hear. Vaughn shifts over, giving us some space, which is considerate given that most other guys would try to secretly listen in.

"Richards." Coach is more concerned than angry. "What's going on? You're squeezing the stick too hard."

Am I trying too hard? Most definitely. I'm at a twelve out of ten, maybe a thirteen, and I don't know how to dial it back. Couldn't if I tried.

The most frustrating part of this phenomenon is that it's utterly counter-productive; you get yanked out of the zone and plunked into your head, where you proceed to play like shit.

"I don't know, Coach. Just in my head tonight for some reason."

Understanding crosses his face, and I wonder if he knows Doug is here. "I understand, son. Try to use some of those strategies we discussed in chalk talk last week. Remember, the mental game is as important as the physical. Maybe more."

Our off-ice player development time, nicknamed chalk talk, touches on nutrition, mental health, school-life balance, and all that fluffy shit. Coach Ward is a big fan of stress management, and his lessons include crunchy-granola things like deep breathing, visual-ization, mediation. Maybe I haven't given it a fair chance, but none of it ever really jives with me. Deep breathing leaves me more agitated than when I started. I can never "see" visualizations the way you're supposed to. And meditation? Good luck with that. Not with the way I'm wired.

"I'll try," I tell him.

By the time the final buzzer sounds, we're down by two goals for a score of six to four. While I can't say it all falls on my shoulders, I sure as hell didn't help. I've made a litany of mistakes that I know of on the ice tonight, and I'm sure Doug has found a hundred more. I'll hear all about them soon enough. Funny part is, he'll be angrier than Coach Ward over the loss.

The mood in the locker room while we get changed is gloomy, with little chatter. None of us like losing to MSU. And losing to Eriksen specifically rubs a heaping handful of salt in the wound for me.

"You coming to Overtime?" Connor asks, toweling off his face, followed by his hair. He's fully naked and fully unfazed. While none of us are shy—when you shower together, you move past any sense of modesty pretty damn quick—some of us embrace the group nudity aspect more than others. For instance, most of us make a point to put on boxer briefs before we stand around shooting the shit.

Connor is also a little too comfortable being naked at home, much to Savannah's chagrin.

"I'll come, but I'm gonna drive tonight." I slip on my dress shirt, running a hand through my damp hair. Overdue for a haircut, but no idea where I'd even begin to pencil that into my schedule.

He makes a face. "You suck."

"Trying to cut back on drinking." Doug's presence is another reminder why. If there's any familial predisposition to alcoholism in my genes, I want to tread carefully. I still drink, but I make a conscious attempt to moderate it more than most other college students. Specifically, when it comes to binge drinking; aside from that one-off with Connor recently, I rarely ever get drunk.

"Plus," I add, buttoning my cuffs, "I have to go handle Doug."

Connor grimaces, because even he has some sense of empathy. "Sorry, man. Let me know if you change your mind on drinking after dealing with that."

"Will do."

Getting dressed doesn't take nearly as long as I wish it did. Time seems to speed up, propelling me to face what I dread most. My nerves skyrocket as I push open the dressing room door, exiting into the fluorescent-lit corridor, but there's no trace of Doug in the hallway. He's nowhere to be seen in the arena lobby, either.

I don't even need to check the parking lot to know he's already gone.

———

A normal person would probably be upset if their parent bailed immediately after their game. As far as I'm concerned, it's Christmas in October.

Vaughn walks out of the dressing room a minute after I do, immediately spotting me. We stand off to the side in the concourse, rehashing the game for a few minutes before deciding to shelve it for the night. Sometimes I have to force myself to take a break. Vaughn is much the same—a workaholic who doesn't know his limits. Or a hockeyaholic, I guess.

"What do you figure, want to hit Overtime?" I ask him. "You can ride with me."

He doesn't respond. Vaughn's one of those guys who's always present, in a very Zen sort of way. Unlike a lot of other people, he doesn't ignore you for his cellphone or look over your shoulder at a party, searching for someone better to talk to.

Only one thing could possibly distract him this much.

I follow his line of sight, and my suspicions are confirmed when I spot a pretty brunette with nearly waist-length hair, torn jeans, and black Chucks. She's standing with a smoke-show blonde in a pair of heeled boots that make her tower over the crowd. Vaughn's attention is firmly fixed on the brunette—otherwise known as the forbidden fruit.

"Banks." I shove him a little harder than I mean to, sending him slightly off balance.

His attention snaps back to me. "Sorry, what?"

"Are you done staring at Coach Ward's daughter yet?" I feel for the guy. It's rare that anyone captures Vaughn's interest, and the one girl who finally did is completely off-limits. Unfortunately for him, the number one-unwritten rule of hockey is that you never, *ever* go after the coach's daughter.

Not to mention, I'm pretty sure Luna doesn't even know Vaughn is alive. She might be aware of him due to his position on the team —nearly everyone on campus is—but he doesn't seem to be on her radar beyond that.

"Wasn't staring," Vaughn mumbles. "Just noticed her, that's all."

I fight a knowing smile. "Right." If he were anyone else, I'd rib him harder. But Vaughn is a rare breed. Unlike the vast majority of humans on this planet, he's not an asshole, so he gets a pass.

He clears his throat, casting one final longing look in Luna's direction. "Home is fine. Let's go."

"I said Overtime, you dick. Not home. You weren't even listening."

"Overtime works, too."

We catch up to the rest of the group, huddled by the front entrance. Candice, fortunately, has not yet appeared. Maybe she already took off after the game, or maybe she was here watching one of the other players. I mean, doubtful, but it would make things easier for me if it were true.

Savannah's face brightens when she sees us and she scurries up, copper hair flying, giving Vaughn a big hug. "Great game, you two."

Releasing him, she embraces me, and I lean down, hugging her back. She's a lot shorter than me so I have to stoop awkwardly, but I don't mind. Unlike Candice's hug, Savannah's doesn't come with an ulterior motive.

"Thanks, Savi. Are you coming to Overtime?"

"Wish I could, but I picked up an extra shift at work. Just gonna say bye to Drew and head out."

In a twist of poor timing, Violet, Julianna, and Preston appear nearby at the same time Savannah and I pull apart. Judging by Violet's expression, she caught our hug and doesn't know what to make of it. I'm not sure if making her jealous would help or hurt my case—whatever that is.

Hell, I still don't know what's going on with Violet and Preston. He could be her boyfriend, and I could be obsessing over her for nothing. Then again, I do know the feelings between us are definitely *not* nothing—regardless of whatever Preston's temporary role may be. He won't stick around long-term. Of that much, I'm certain.

Drew walks out of the dressing room and says a quick goodbye to Savannah before joining me and Vaughn. Ever the social fucking butterfly, he waves over the three interns, engaging them in conversation about the game and how they enjoyed being on the bench for the first time. The only thing that could make this worse is if Candice resurfaced. Fuck. Better get out of here before she does.

"Vaughn and I will meet you at Overtime," I tell Drew, giving Vaughn a nudge with my elbow. Setting off for the doors, I call over my shoulder. "Sound good?"

Drew looks at Violet, Julianna, and Preston. "You guys want to join? Come on, it'll be fun. Team bonding and all that."

My fist clenches around my keys. I had forgotten that Drew considers rudeness to be a mortal sin. He'd rather die than be seen as excluding someone. But now I might kill him myself.

Violet looks like a deer in headlights. Julianna bites her bottom lip like she's weighing the offer. But Preston is fully on board, and one is all it takes. Soon enough, we've all made plans to meet for drinks, and I'm sorely regretting my decision to be designated driver.

Mental note to smother Drew in his sleep later.

CHAPTER 15
RESCUE ME
VIOLET

WHY DID I let myself get talked into coming to Overtime with the team? It's about as awkward as can be expected. No, it's worse. I'd rather endure a gynecological exam. With an audience.

The only upside, however marginal, is that things between me and Preston have been surprisingly harmonious since our disastrous kiss. Maybe he's picked up on the heavy hints that I've been dropping. Or at least, I hope he has, because I want to avoid one of those awkward talks where you try to let someone down gently. I've never been good at them.

"The team is fun to watch this year," Preston says. "There's a lot of good talent. Especially Banks. He has some of the best hands in the entire division."

I glance down to the other end of the table, where Vaughn is laughing with the team. He's one of the only guys who doesn't have a girl hanging off him. Obviously by choice, because he's got the tall, dark, and tattooed thing down pat. There are a lot of rumors about him and why he's rarely seen with anyone, but I don't know the backstory. Nash never really commented on it.

"His goal in the third was amazing," I agree, turning my attention back to Preston.

"Our defense has come a long way, too." He leans forward,

gesturing with his beer. "Richards is crushing it this year. He must be doing better after that AC joint injury last season, huh?"

My mouth goes dry. "Seems that way, yeah."

It's not a total lie. To most people, it *does* seem that way. Nash has developed significantly as a player since I last saw him play over two years ago. Physically, he's filled out as well, which I'm sure makes for a scary sight barreling for you at full tilt on the ice. Probably why guys tend to dump the puck and run when they see him coming. His body checks must feel like getting hit by a freight train.

Julianna sinks down next to us, and Preston leaves to use the bathroom. Once he disappears, Jules reaches across the table and pats my hand, giving me an apologetic look. "Thanks for coming. I know this is weird for you."

More specifically, I had a mild freakout once we got to Julianna's car, and she talked me into coming once I calmed down enough to listen. She said it would be a good way to get to know the team, but I already know more than I want to about number twenty-seven.

While Jules may not admit it, I know it's a ploy for her to get closer to Marcus, the team captain. It's probably fair game for them to hook up since he's in Preston's training group and not Julianna's, but I get a bit of a sleazy vibe from him.

"It's okay," I tell her, lowering my voice so no one around us can hear. Logically, if I have to see Nash all semester, I might as well get used to it. Call it exposure therapy. "But you have to drive me home like we agreed. I can't be alone with Preston again. We still haven't talked about that kiss."

"Deal. You're coming home with me no matter what. We don't have to stay very long, either. Let's have one drink and go."

I relax into my chair. "Thank you."

To be fair, the rest of the team has been incredibly welcoming. Some in a friendly way, others in a flirty way that makes me think they have a death wish because Nash has leveled several murderous glares in their direction. Other than that, he's pretended like I'm not even here. I'm trying to do the same, but that's easier said than done.

On the side of the table where Nash is seated, the waitress appears with a tray of shots. While it's a weeknight, this isn't overly surprising. A lot of athletes party hard all week long, though I have no idea how they manage to keep up with their training. My attention slides over to them. I'm eavesdropping a little, but I can't help it.

"Tequila." Connor slides a shot glass over to Nash, who pushes it back and gives him a withering look.

"We're supposed to celebrate after we *win* games."

Connor retorts, "The alcohol is a consolation prize."

"Gonna need a whole lot of consoling after Coach Ward bag skates us for an hour tomorrow morning," Drew points out.

"No shit," Nash says. "Plus, I'm driving tonight, remember?"

This piques my interest. Maybe Nash doesn't drink and party as much anymore as I thought. He definitely did more than his fair share freshman year. Some people outgrow it in college, while others don't. Case in point, Connor.

"Ugh." Connor throws his head back. "You're all boring."

"Are you looking forward to the away game next month?" Julianna asks me, bringing my focus back to her.

"Super excited," I lie. Traveling with the team is a huge honor. But being stuck on a bus with Nash for three hours each way, and then at the same hotel for two nights, is more than a little problematic. Sleeping a few doors down the hall from my ex, sharing meals with him and the team, all while trying to pretend there was never an "us" in the first place.

Jules takes a sip of her rum and Coke, placing the glass back down on the table. "If you think about it, it's kind of like traveling for work. Our first work trip, which is exciting…"

I'm half-listening to her when some girl strolls up to Nash, eyeing him like he's the only guy in the whole place. Perfectly styled, dark glossy hair falls in front of her face as she places a hand on his arm and leans in closer, saying something in his ear. They're clearly well-acquainted, probably intimately acquainted if I had to guess, and seeing them together is like sandpaper against my heart.

He shakes his head in response to something she says and then his gaze lifts, scanning the crowded bar. Our eyes lock, and a jolt of electricity runs through my body. *Shit.* I've been caught. I immediately avert my eyes and pretend to focus on Julianna.

"You know what? I'm going to grab a refill after all," I tell her, pushing my chair away from the table as I stand. I'm certain I can still feel Nash's gaze weighing down on me, but I don't dare glance over to check.

Steadfastly avoiding even the slightest glimpse in Nash's direction, I weave around the other tables and approach the bar, ordering a second rum and Coke. Something about my face must reveal that I'm having a hellacious night, because the female bartender gives me a pitying look and tells me it's on the house. She turns away to mix my highball, and I stuff a handful of bills into the glass mason tip jar on the counter while I wait.

Is Nash still talking to that girl? I sneak a peek and confirm that, much to my dismay, he is. I hate that it bothers me. It's beyond none of my business. Obviously, he's been with other girls since we broke up. I've been with other guys, too. Still, knowing that and seeing it are two different things. I've let myself live in a cloak of complete obliviousness for the past two years. It was comfortable; warm and fuzzy, trimmed with denial. And thanks to that, the irrational part of my brain still thinks he's a little bit mine.

Though I have to say, from the looks of it, he's not really flirting back.

"Basketball is the superior sport, you know." A deep voice interrupts my thought spiral and I jump slightly, turning to find a tall, lanky guy peering down at me.

His chestnut curls tumble over his forehead and his grin is flirty, the dimples in his cheeks peeking through. The skin on the back of my neck tingles, and I steal a glance to my right, unsurprised to find this interaction has drawn Nash's attention. The brunette is still talking to him, gesturing animatedly, but his gaze is fixed on me with laser-like precision. I doubt he hears a word she's saying, and I'm filled with a warped sense of satisfaction at the knowledge.

"Are you here with the Grizzlies?" the guy asks, bringing my focus back to him.

I utter a nervous laugh. "Sort of. I'm doing my athletic training internship with the team."

"Nice," he says. "I'm Devin. Point guard for the basketball team."

"Violet. Uh, trainer for the Grizzlies. Like I said." Smooth, Violet. I'm not especially interested in Devin, but even if I was, it would be impossible to flirt when there's a furious giant shooting daggers at us with his eyes from afar. Which is Nash's intention, I'm sure.

Devin continues, "Why don't you come join our table for a—"

Before he can finish his sentence, Nash stalks up to the bar in a blur of menace and comes to stand beside me. Right beside me, so close that I can feel the heat rolling off him in waves. The clean, masculine scent of his cologne invades my airspace, and my stomach does a pirouette. Nash levels a poisonous glare in Devin's direction but says nothing.

Devin shoots him a bored look. "Need something, Richards?"

"Fuck off, Henderson." Nash slides an arm around my waist, sending a rush through my body that I want to call irritation but might be something else.

What a hypocrite. He had a girl all over him not even two seconds ago. Did I swoop in and act all territorial? No. I watched it from afar while pretending not to, like a normal person.

"It's not your place—" I start to say.

"Now." Nash juts his chin, his attention still fixed on Devin. "Unless you'd like to watch the rest of your season from a hospital bed."

Devin rolls his eyes, but it's clear he doesn't want to get into it with Nash. Most sane people wouldn't.

There's a pause as they engage in a silent, testosterone-fueled pissing match. Nash's jaw ticks, his steely glare intensifying. Devin eyes him for another beat as if considering, but I suspect he's fully aware that an altercation would not work out in his favor. Hockey is physical in a way that basketball is not. While Devin has a slight height advantage, Nash is twice as built and has years of experience fighting on- and off- the ice.

I nearly interject again, but something in my gut tells me there's more going on than I'm privy to at the moment. Nash's reaction is extreme, even for him.

Finally, Devin glances down at me with a cocky smile. "Come grab me later if you want."

"Not going to happen," Nash practically snarls.

Once Devin turns to leave, I swat Nash's hand away. An unwelcome chill spreads across my torso where his arm was. I've never been so annoyed with someone while also wanting to strip off all of their clothes. I'm a lost cause.

"You're an asshole."

"Never said I wasn't."

The bartender sets my drink on the black laminate counter, sliding it over to us, and Nash leans over the bar to order a beer. When he turns back to face me, instead of looking annoyed like I expect, his green eyes gleam with amusement. He's actually enjoying this. I should have known.

"You can't act like that every time a guy talks to me."

"Don't worry, I already told the team you're off-limits. Word will travel around campus from there, and that issue will take care of itself. No one who values their life will get within ten feet of you." He takes a sip of his beer, his lips forming a smirk against the mouth of the amber-colored bottle. It simultaneously makes me want to slap him and wish I were that beer.

Like I said, lost cause.

"Off limits? Why?" Bringing my drink to my mouth, I huff a sardonic laugh around the black plastic straw.

He tilts his head and gives me a look that says he can't tell whether I'm messing with him or I'm legitimately dense. "You know why."

"Trust me, I have zero interest in dating any of your teammates. But like I was saying, it isn't your place to scare guys off. We're ancient history."

"Hardly." Taking another step, he comes to stand directly above me, the warmth of his skin heating mine. "We were too many things to ever be ancient history."

My focus settles on his lips, and desire throbs between my legs at the memories of them all over my body. Dammit, no. I shouldn't be thinking like this, especially not under the influence of alcohol.

"Many of those things were bad," I manage.

"Many of them were good."

The good times *were* good. Delicious. Amazing. Sweet, even. But the bad times were brutal.

I pause because the only comeback I can formulate is too painful to verbalize out loud. Satisfaction flickers across Nash's face like he just won our argument. Maybe he did.

Nash rests his elbow on the bar, pointing behind me with the neck of his beer. "Circling back to our basketball player friend, do you know who that guy is?"

I follow his direction to the far corner where Devin is standing with a group of guys next to one of the pool tables. Based on the fact that they're all a head taller than every other patron, I assume they must be the rest of the basketball team. Basketball isn't as big of a deal on campus as hockey, so they don't get nearly as much airtime. I'm not familiar with most of the athletes.

Like Nash's team, they're accompanied by a handful of beautiful girls fawning all over them. Several of the guys even have multiple girls competing for their attention at once like some miniature, impromptu version of The Bachelor.

One thing I don't miss about dating an athlete? Groupies.

"He said he plays point guard. Beyond that, not a clue."

"Devin is a fucking creep."

I scoff, taking another ill-advised sip of alcohol. "There is some serious irony behind the idea of you protecting me. Not to mention, it's none of your business."

"It is absolutely my business." His voice deepens, turning gruff. "If Devin roofies your drink—which he's known for doing—I'm the one who will be taking care of you later because you're sure as fuck not leaving with him."

Roofies? A wave of nausea hits me, and I nearly choke mid-sip.

"Oh," I croak. I can't believe I didn't know this. I listed the men's basketball team as my second internship choice.

"I know several girls who've woken up in Henderson's bed with no idea what happened the night before. Enough that it isn't a coincidence." Nash pauses, raising his dark eyebrows. "You know, for someone in the athletic training program, you are shockingly out of touch with the athletics world."

For some reason, his comment stings. I guess I'm no longer accustomed to his searing lack of tact.

"Why, because I don't stay up to date on all the varsity gossip? Did it ever occur to you that might be intentional? I've been trying to avoid all the stories about you sleeping with half of the girls in our school."

The statement is a little too raw, and immediately, I want to take it back. Not because it's potentially hurtful, but because it shows how much I still care. Pretending Nash never existed was the only coping mechanism I had. I'm not indifferent to him, much as I wish I was.

A rare glimmer of hurt crosses his face, but he recovers quickly, and his tone hardens. "Well, some of that gossip might contain useful information. Like who the date rapists are around campus."

"How did I ever survive without you?" I take a sip of my drink, giving him a faux earnest look. I'd like to say I'm being difficult to keep up my walls, but the ugly truth of it is, part of me enjoys riling him up. I'm pretty sure, deep down, part of him enjoys it, too. Especially one part in particular.

Nash's jaw tenses, his irritation visibly ramping up another notch. I bat my eyelashes at him, and he narrows his eyes, slowly shaking his head—but I don't miss the tiniest hint of a smile playing on his lips. The rational part of me knows that it's wrong, but he's extra hot when he's angry. Possibly because it reminds me of the make-up sex that always followed our arguments.

God, we used to have incredible make-up sex. Clothes flying, frenzied kisses, and hands everywhere, tearing off clothes. If we were still together, this is the part where he'd drag me into the bathroom and fuck some sense into me.

Not that I want that to happen. But I'd be lying if I said I wasn't going to think about it later, alone in my bed.

"Between this and that murder trap of a transit station," he says slowly, "I'm not sure how you survived, either."

I set my glass on the bar, tucking an errant strand of hair behind my ear. "Now you're just being dramatic."

"Call it what you want." Grabbing our drinks in one hand, he places his other hand on my lower back, steering me back over to our table. "And don't expect it to change."

CHAPTER 16

IT'S A BOY

ONCE IN A WHILE, storing my things in the athletics center pays off.

Today is one of those days.

After stopping by my locker to swap out some textbooks, I spot Violet standing in the functional training area looking like a fucking feast. Skin-tight black compression leggings highlight every curve of her lower half, her loose-fitting grey tank top revealing a sliver of a hot pink sports bra beneath. Her hair is pulled into a ponytail on top of her head, her face is flushed pink from her workout, and she looks more fuckable than ever.

She finishes her quad stretch and sits down on the mat, moving into a set of supine stretches. I'm running late to meet Drew, which means I should keep moving and walk straight out the door, but my body has other ideas and before I know it, I'm standing at the edge of the mat in front of her.

Violet looks up at me and removes one wireless earbud, hitting pause on her phone. "What do you want, Nash?" Her pouty lips quirk, betraying her attempt to sound annoyed.

"Can't I say hi to my trainer?" I flop down beside her, covertly sneaking a peek down her sports bra. Goddamn, I missed her tits. They're even better than I remembered.

I would do bad things just for the chance to see Violet naked again. And then I would do bad things to her.

"I feel like there's an ulterior motive at play here." She releases her calf and switches sides, extending her left leg along the floor while pulling her right leg up. All that does is make me think about how flexible she was in bed—and outside of it. Like in the backseat of my car.

"I could help you stretch."

"There's no way you'd keep that G-rated."

Fair enough. In my defense, we'd both have more fun if my shoulders were holding up her legs. Naked.

"But if you want to make yourself useful, you could grab me a black foam roller from over there." Violet nods to the far right corner, where a wire basket holds an assortment of foam rollers and other accessories.

If this was anyone else, I would tell them to fuck off and get it themselves. But I'm trying to find a reason to stick around, so I walk over and grab one, passing it to her. I know from experience the black rollers are the firmest, verging on painful, but Violet likes a little pain. She likes it rough, too.

I almost wish I didn't know those things. Maybe life would be easier if I didn't.

"Thanks." Violet leans onto one elbow and pulls herself upright, readjusting to roll out her glutes. Is it weird to be jealous of a foam roller? Because I think I am.

She peers over her shoulder at me, and her bare lips tug into a smile that's half-shy, half-exasperated. "Are you going to watch me foam roll, or what?"

I mean, yeah. Is that an option?

"You're cute when you're all sweaty." I shrug, enjoying the way her flush deepens in response to my words, rosy hue traveling all the way down to her chest.

"Pretty sure I'm a total mess right now, but whatever works for ya."

Oh, it's working for me. I like clean Violet, sweaty Violet, dirty Violet. I'm especially into the last one down on her hands and knees, begging for me to give it to her harder with her hair wrapped around my fist.

I am so fucked.

Pushing to stand, I put some distance between us before I do something stupid in the middle of the fitness floor. Plus, if I let myself continue with this line of thinking, these joggers I'm wearing won't hide a thing.

"Have you been doing your stretches and rehab like you promised?"

"I have been, actually." Call it repentance. The one and only time I broke my word to Violet, it broke us in the process, and that was the biggest mistake of my life. "It's been helping." I almost hate to admit this because doing a million reps with a stretchy exercise band *seems* like it should be useless. You can't even feel anything while you're doing it. But it isn't a surprise that Violet is good at her job. She's been working on my shoulder a lot lately, and she knows where the issues originate. Some kind of strength imbalance, she said, but I didn't understand when she explained it.

Relief stretches across her pretty face. "Good. I'm glad."

My phone vibrates in my pocket. I'm sure it's Drew, wanting to know where the hell I am. Frankly, until just now, I'd been so wrapped up in Violet that I'd forgotten he existed.

"I'm running late," I tell her. "What time should I meet you later?"

She freezes, her hands splayed on the floor for balance. "I feel bad. You don't have to—"

"What time?"

Violet scrunches up her mouth before finally replying. "Seven?"

"See you then." Before turning away, I throw her a wink that earns me an adorable fucking grin. As I push through the doors into the hall, the grin on my face is even bigger.

———

Seven o'clock takes forever to arrive. By the time it does, I've hit Gino's off campus with some of the guys for dinner, completed all of my homework, wasted time on my phone, and read ahead in two of my classes. It's not that I mind waiting, it's that I'm impatient as fuck to see Violet. I don't know what I'm doing when it comes to her. All I know is that I can't stay away. Every time I try, I feel like a junkie going through withdrawals.

At six-fifty-one, my limited patience runs out. Packing up my books, I head out of the athletes' lounge where I'd been studying, down the hall to the training room. Violet is immersed in something at the corner desk with her head down.

I rap on the door, so I don't startle her. "Ready to go?"

She peeks over the computer screen and gives me a wry smile. "Just about. But you do realize that people take public transit every day and survive, right?"

"Maybe they're being reckless."

"Taking the train is reckless, now?"

I stroll over to where she's seated. "When you're the size of Tinker Bell?" Stepping around the desk, I come to a halt less than an arm's length away, peering down at her. "Yes."

Violet rolls her eyes. "I should have known not to underestimate your stubbornness. It is truly unparalleled."

"Thank you."

"That wasn't a compliment." She returns her attention to the computer screen, but the corners of her mouth quirk.

"It is to me."

I'm still intensely curious why she refuses to drive. I don't mind driving her home—fine, I like it—but I hate that she takes the train at night when I'm not around. Especially when she has a perfectly good vehicle parked outside her house. She can't seem to explain why she's having so much trouble with a brand-new Honda CRV—and despite her claims of engine troubles, it's there every time I drop her off, not at the shop. Something doesn't add up; I just don't know what.

Once Violet gathers up her belongings, I take her bag and we weave through campus along our usual route, having fallen into a routine that's grown predictable. There's a comfort that's developed between the two of us when we're alone; an ease that we don't get to enjoy when we're around everyone else during the day. It's much more difficult when team management, the other players, and even the other interns are constantly looking on nearby.

"How was your day?" I ask, holding the stairwell door for her.

She sneaks a wary glance at me. "Pretty good, why?"

"Can't I ask?"

"I guess," she says. "How was your day?"

Aside from seeing her in the training room earlier, it was shit. I slept like trash last night, woke up late this morning, slogged through classes all day, and then Doug called again and reamed me out for twenty minutes over my positioning in my last game.

It's easy to forget all of those things now that I'm looking at her, though.

"Better now," I tell Violet. Blush tints her cheeks, a small smile on her lips, but she doesn't reply.

We stroll down the row of parked cars, arriving at my SUV in the middle. I reach over to open the passenger side door for her, and she grabs my arm, shushing me.

"Wait." Her blonde eyebrows pull together, voice dropping to a hush. "Listen."

In the distance, a faint crying sound echoes through the shadowy parking garage. I can't place what it is, except to say it's not human. My best guess is some kind of scared or injured animal. Not a cat, I don't think. Possibly a dog.

Following the general direction of the whimpers, we scour the rows and check underneath vehicles until we spot a small puppy hunched in the far corner, next to a white sedan. As we draw closer, it becomes clear that it's a puppy. His fur is a mixture of black and tan, with a black muzzle and oversized, pointy ears. He reminds me of a police dog. A German Shepherd or something like that.

"Aww!" Violet gasps, making a beeline for the puppy. She squats down a few feet away from the puppy, gently patting her thigh. "Come here, buddy."

"Careful," I warn her. Her bleeding heart knows no bounds. I like that about her, but right now, I'm lowkey worried she's going to contract fleas. Or rabies.

Obviously, I'm not much of an animal person.

She glances over her shoulder at me, giving me a reproachful look. "Come on, Nash. He's a baby. He's not going to bite."

After a few more encouraging words and gestures, the puppy slinks over to Violet with his tail between his legs, head held low. I can't quite discern whether he's being meek because he's scared, or if he's lethargic because he's malnourished. While he's clearly still a puppy, he's not just small due to his age, he's scrawny. His limbs look too thin compared to his big paws, and I can practically count his ribs.

"Or he could be a she, I guess…" Violet holds out her hand and the dog sniffs it tentatively, slowly wagging his tail while she examines his neck. "No collar." She hums, studying him thoughtfully, and her mouth tugs into a frown. "He doesn't look well taken care of, either. Look how skinny he is."

"It's possible he's been missing for a while. Maybe he escaped from a house nearby. He could have owners looking for him." At least, let's hope he does. It'll make wrapping this up that much faster.

"Oh, I know." Her expression perks up. "We should take him to a vet. They can scan him to see if he's microchipped."

"Take him?" I echo. "Like in my vehicle?"

Doug handed down my three-year-old SUV when he bought a new one last year. It's still in pristine condition, and I'm a little particular about maintenance and upkeep. I've never had any kind of animal in it before unless Connor counts, and I'm not especially keen to change that.

Violet cocks her head in confusion. "How else are we going to get him there?"

"I don't know, I thought we could call the SPCA to come and get him or something." Violet volunteered there all throughout high school, which means she might be on board with this option. Like I said, she's a total softy for animals.

"They're a charity, Nash. They don't offer Ubers for dogs. County Animal Control Services will pick up strays, but they always take forever because they're hopelessly short-staffed." Her expression darkens, turning troubled. "Plus, we can't let this widdle guy go to the big bad pound."

"Definitely not," I agree, pretending like that wasn't my plan all along.

Carefully, she reaches over and picks up the puppy, gauging his reaction as she does. He's more than pleased with the development and lifts his head, trying to lick her face. As she hauls him into her arms and pushes to standing, his sex becomes obvious.

"It's a boy," I confirm.

"Huh?" She glances over at me, then down at the dog in her arms, and laughs once it clicks. "Okay, then."

We walk back to my car with the puppy while he leans his chin on Violet's shoulder, his dark eyes happily taking in the new view. Up close, it's even more obvious that he's desperately in need of a hearty meal and a long bath. It's clearly been a while since he's had the former and judging by his matted coat and the way he smells, I'm not sure he's ever had the latter.

"What if he doesn't have an owner?" I ask, voicing the obvious concern that neither of us wants to address.

"Let's hope he's got a good home that's looking for him and we can reunite them."

Typical Violet for you—always looking on the bright side. In other words, the unrealistic side. Now that I've had a better chance to look at him, I have a strong hunch this dog is homeless.

Violet hands me the wriggly puppy before climbing into the passenger seat. He whines, squirming in my grip, probably because I have no idea how to hold a puppy and neither of us is remotely comfortable with my attempt. Once she buckles her seatbelt, I lean down and pass him back to her, praying he doesn't pee on the leather seats. Or worse.

As I wind through the parking garage, the puppy begins to calm down. He occupies himself by pushing his nose against the passenger window, leaving behind a wet streak of puppy snot that I'll have to Windex away later. But if that's the only cleanup required after this car ride, I'll call it a win.

"He's shivering. Poor baby." She reaches for the climate

controls, switching the fan to full blast, and cranks the temperature up to ninety degrees—despite the fact that it's a solid eighty degrees outside. Immediately, beads of sweat start to form on the back of my neck and along my brow, but I say nothing. There's a pecking order inside this vehicle, and stray puppies trump asshole ex-boyfriends.

Arching her neck, she peers into the back seat. "Do you have a blanket in here?"

"You are greatly overestimating my level of preparedness for this situation."

"A sweater? Jacket? Anything?"

"I might have an old hoodie somewhere." Easing the car to a stop at the parking garage exit, I check my rear-view mirror to confirm that no one is waiting behind me before shifting the ignition into park. Then I reach behind me and feel around on the floor, grabbing a worn cotton sweatshirt and handing it to her.

She holds up the heathered gray fabric and her pale blue eyes widen as she takes in the faded LSU Grizzlies logo with the year beneath it. "Your freshman year hoodie? I loved this thing."

I remember. Violet used to wear it all the time, even though it was more like a dress on her. She claimed it was her version of a Snuggie, and she wasn't wrong. It's the reason I hardly ever wear it now; just seeing it conjures up memories of her prancing around in it, looking borderline ridiculous and incredibly cute at the same time. Ever since we broke up, it's been relegated to laying around my backseat in case of emergency.

Or in case of stray dog, I guess.

Violet drapes the sweatshirt over her thighs, creating a makeshift bed, and the puppy makes a few small circles before settling in, curling up in her lap. Still petting him with one hand, she fiddles with the radio, flipping from station to station. Some cheesy song pours out of the speakers, its lyrics bemoaning a cheating boyfriend in the same homeroom who apparently hooked up with the singer's "bestie." It's terrible, which means it's right up Violet's alley. Her taste in music has always been questionable.

A few blocks later, I realize I'm driving slower than usual because I don't want to jostle the interloper sitting in her lap. How did I end up with a dog in my passenger seat and Top 40 music on the radio? Only Violet could land me in this scenario.

"What breed do you think he is?" Violet coos, scratching the puppy beneath his chin. He leans into her hand appreciatively, looking like he's found doggie heaven.

"I don't know, some kind of mutt."

Her jaw drops and she clamps her hands over the puppy's ears, ducking down to whisper to him. "Don't listen to him. You're *adorable*."

"It's not an insult. With those tan and black markings and the shape of his ears and nose, my guess is he's at least part German Shepherd. But I doubt anyone would abandon a purebred, so there are probably some other breeds mixed in there, too."

A few minutes later, I pull into the parking lot of an after-hours emergency vet clinic that Violet called. Since the puppy is a stray, they said they'd check him out free of charge, which is a relief. I don't want to have to explain an enormous veterinary clinic charge on my credit card bill to Doug. It wouldn't go over well.

A tall, burly man with dark, tawny skin and a warm presence enters the room, extending his hand to each of us. "I'm Doctor Singh. I see we have a new friend, here."

After we give him a quick rundown, Dr. Singh does a cursory physical exam and declares him to be underweight but otherwise in good health, and approximately six weeks old. He holds a white, futuristic device to the puppy's neck, which I presume is the microchip scanner. It beeps, and his expression clouds over before quickly neutralizing again. Violet looks hopeful, but I already know what's coming before he says it.

"I'm afraid he doesn't have a microchip. Without a chip or a collar, there's no way to locate an owner."

In other words, this is the politically correct way of saying he's a street dog.

The way Violet's face falls is a sucker punch straight to the gut. She doesn't just look disappointed; she's devastated. Her chin trembles, and I can see her fighting to steady her breath.

Fuck me.

"The local shelter does intakes until nine p.m.," the vet tells us, opening a glass jar on the counter and scooping up a handful of treats. He tosses them to the eagerly waiting puppy, praising him for being a good dog. "If you hurry, you should make it."

Violet worries her bottom lip, eyes flickering between us and the puppy. He wags his tail, snorting while he sniffs around on the floor searching for more treats, blissfully oblivious to his fate hanging in the balance.

"Are they—" Her voice climbs, cracking. "Are they going to put him down if no one adopts him?" She scoops him up in her arms, clutching him to her chest. The puppy wriggles, whining to be set down so he can continue exploring the office, but Violet doesn't let him go.

"I can't say for certain, but the shelter tends to be quite full at this time of year." He avoids her eyes and turns, heading for the door. "We have free samples of dog food and treats in the back. I'll give you a minute while I get some for you."

I hope Dr. Singh doesn't gamble, because he has a horrible poker face. They are absolutely going to put him down if we take him to the shelter.

Violet spins to face me, stricken. "We can't let him get put down, Nash. Can you keep him for a while? Foster him until we find him a good home? I promise, I'll help find the right family to adopt him."

"I can't bring home a pet. The guys would kill me. Besides, I don't even like animals."

"But you like this one, right? Look at that widdle face." She stands on her tiptoes, holding him up so we're almost eye to eye. They both make puppy dog eyes at me, and the puppy whimpers for good measure.

It is disturbingly effective.

I groan. "Why can't you keep him?"

She sets the puppy on the floor, studying him longingly for a moment before replying. "I would if I could, but Claire's deathly allergic. A dog licked her hand while we were out for a walk last year, and she swelled up like a hot air balloon. My sister has her hands full parenting three kids while her husband is deployed, so she's out. And my parents have a grouchy old tabby, Herman, who would claw this puppy's eyes out in no time flat."

Her chest heaves, shallow breaths moving in and out rapidly like she's on the verge of hyperventilation. "But maybe I can see if they'd keep them in separate rooms..."

A dull ache settles into my ribs, ironclad resolve starting to crumble. When she stifles a tiny sob, something inside me breaks. She's cried too many times over me as it is.

I can't believe this is happening. I can't believe I'm about to do this. And I wouldn't, for anyone else.

"I can keep him for now."

Her blue eyes light up, slightly red and glassy with tears. "You can?"

"Temporarily," I stress. "Only until we find him a good home."

She throws her arms around me, squeezing me with an impressive amount of strength for someone her size. I hug her back, trying not to seem like a creep while I inhale her cinnamon-vanilla scent. I don't want it to end. And it does, all too soon.

Releasing me, Violet bounces up and down on the spot. "Thank you, thank you, thank you. I'll help you find a home for him. I know your schedule is hectic."

On the plus side, this gives me another excuse to talk to her.

———

It's dark by the time we head back to my vehicle, brand-new foster puppy in tow. He peed on the floor at the vet before we left, so at least we should be clear in that respect.

Halfway to Target for dog supplies, Violet asks, "What should we name him?"

"Name him?" I steal a glance at her, signaling to turn left onto the secondary road. "Why? This is temporary, remember?" I have a feeling I'm going to need to keep reminding her of that minor little detail. Knowing Violet, she's already attached.

"Yeah, but we can't call him 'the dog' or 'the puppy.' Dogs have feelings, too. He deserves a proper name." She tilts her head, studying him in her lap. "Let's name him something hockey related."

To her credit, she knows how to win me over.

We start throwing out random hockey slang, trying to find a term that fits. Violet immediately rules out all of the penalties, because she doesn't want the puppy to be named after what she deems are "on-ice crimes." She claims it might give him a complex. I think she's giving the dog entirely too much credit.

"Mitts?" I suggest, offering up a common nickname for hockey gloves.

"That's cute! Or Deke?"

Not going to lie, I'm more than a little impressed by the depth and volume of Violet's hockey knowledge. I always knew she was a hockey fan, but I'd forgotten to what extent. It's refreshing after constantly being surrounded by so many puck bunnies and posers. A lot of girls pretend to like the game to impress me, and it's painfully transparent. That's not to say I expect everyone to like hockey or to even care about it, but if you don't know hooking from tripping, or icing from an offside, do us both a favor and don't try to fake it.

"Deke's good," I say. "Or Biscuit?"

"Biscuit?" Confusion appears on her face.

"A hockey puck. But also, because he's tan-colored, kind of like a real biscuit."

Her mouth tugs at my inadvertent admission that I've given this more thought than either of us would expect. "I like it."

"Biscuit it is."

CHAPTER 17

THE REAL REASON
VIOLET

"YOU BOUGHT *FOUR* CHEW TOYS?" I sift through the Target bags, examining their contents. For obvious reasons, Nash did the shopping while I waited with Biscuit in the vehicle.

"I don't want him chewing my shit," Nash grumbles, pulling into a suburban neighborhood not far from campus. "The internet said it would help."

In addition to the toys, he purchased a black collar and matching leash, puppy chow, a brush, dog shampoo, food and water bowls, and a soft, fuzzy gray dog bed. It's endearing, if a little confusing. For someone who isn't into animals, he sure wants to make sure this one is well taken care of.

"All black, white, and gray, huh?" I ask. "Trying to make sure Biscuit matches the Grizzlies' team colors?"

Nash grunts but says nothing. Probably because I'm right.

A few minutes later, he eases into the driveway of a cute two-story house clad with slate blue siding and white trim, opening the attached garage with his remote. The house appears well maintained, the yard tidy. I'm not sure what I was expecting, but it wasn't this.

I peer through the window. "Nice place. Who takes care of the yard?"

"We take turns." He eases his SUV inside, squeezing in next to a black BMW X5 and killing the ignition. The garage isn't quite as pristine as the rest of the exterior, thanks to an abundance of hockey equipment all over the place. "Except Connor. He outsources his."

From what little I know of Connor, this does not surprise me. He's in my training group, so we're acquainted—though I've struggled to get a read on his personality beyond "fucking" and "getting fucked up." His words, not mine.

I open the passenger side door, expecting Biscuit to leap into the front seat, but he doesn't. When I turn around, I find him sprawled across the backseat, furry belly up, lights out on his new dog bed. Snoring.

Being a puppy must be tiring.

"Nash, look," I whisper, poking his bicep. Shit. Shouldn't have done that, it's all firm and muscle-y, and now my mind is going places it shouldn't. I have to touch him enough during training as it is; I really need to refrain from touching him when we're alone.

He glances over his shoulder, and his expression softens when he sees the sleeping dog. Even though Nash will never admit it, I think he could end up liking Biscuit if he gave him a chance. Debatable whether he is even open-minded enough to give him said chance, however.

"Think you can get him inside without waking him?" I ask.

Nash looks at me like I've lost my mind. "Doubtful. But I can try."

I grab the supplies and slip out of the vehicle, careful not to slam the door while Nash goes around to the passenger side to attempt sleeping puppy extraction. Even though he told me to let myself into his house, it still feels wrong. It feels weird being here in general, if I'm being honest. Nash lived in the dorms when we dated, and seeing his natural habitat seems oddly intimate. Like another part of him I've never gotten to know.

As with the exterior of the house, the interior is warm and cozy, and significantly cleaner than one would expect. The hardwood floors shine, the drywall shockingly intact. Other than the pile of enormous-sized athletic shoes by the door and the heap of hockey sticks in the garage, you wouldn't know four athletes lived here.

Vaughn is in the living room with his legs stretched out, typing furiously on a laptop. Surprise stretches across his face when he sees me bearing an armload of Target bags, but it's quickly replaced by a warm smile. "Hey, Violet."

"Hey." I slip off my boots on the entry mat, nudging them aside. I'm not entirely confident they escaped the pee incident at the vet unscathed—in fact, I'm pretty sure they didn't—and I don't want to track anything throughout the house. Actually, I'm surprised Nash even let me wear my boots in the car after that happened, but I opted not to question it.

Vaughn's surprise returns when Nash appears a split-second later, holding a tired looking, but awake, puppy in his arms. Nash sets Biscuit down, brushing the loose fur off his hands, and Biscuit takes off like a shot to explore the house, newly reinvigorated by the change in surroundings.

"Is this your puppy, Violet?" Vaughn breaks into a grin as he sets his laptop aside, watching Biscuit sniff underneath the couch. Biscuit pulls out a stray t-shirt, chewing it, and Vaughn bends down, gently taking it out of his jaws.

"Uh, no," I say. "Not exactly." Nash didn't seem overly concerned with how his roommates would react to the dog development, but I still don't want to be the one to break the news.

"We found him in the parking garage at school," Nash explains, slipping off his olive green Carhartt jacket and hanging it on the hook. "He's a stray. Violet can't have animals at her place, so I'm keeping him until we find him a home. You know, fostering him temporarily. Mostly because Violet sucked me into it."

I roll my eyes, fighting the rush of heat creeping into my cheeks. Truth is, I know he did this for me, and I think it's incredibly sweet. I'm just not sure what to make of it.

"We named him Biscuit," I add.

"Nice." Vaughn kneels, extending his palm for Biscuit to sniff and scratching behind his ears. "Hey, Biscuit. You can stay with us for a while, huh?"

Biscuit barks in response, his tail wagging like a windshield wiper on full speed. I toss Vaughn a bone-shaped chew toy and he plays fetch with Biscuit for a minute while I sift through the shopping bags, passing items to Nash to put away in the nearby closet.

Connor wanders into the living room, shirtless, lazily raking a hand through his wavy blond hair. "Did one of you dicks just bark?" His gaze falls to Biscuit, and he comes to a screeching halt in the doorway. "Why the fuck is there a dog in our living room?"

"I'm keeping him temporarily until we can find him a home," Nash says wearily, yanking the tag off the collar and fastening it around Biscuit's neck to make sure it fits. Biscuit looks down at it and begins to run in circles, trying unsuccessfully to chew it.

"You didn't think to ask us first?" Connor asks, tipping back his bottle while he eyes Biscuit with mistrust. Apparently, Nash isn't the only non-animal person in the house.

Nash's tone sharpens. "Why, do you plan on helping take care of him?"

"Hell no."

"Then don't worry about it. I'll deal with Biscuit, and he'll be gone before you know it."

Even though I know this can't be permanent, the reminder within the second half of his statement makes me irrationally sad. Realistically, I know all we can do is try to find him the best home possible. Preferably one that will allow me visitation rights, because I'm already attached.

Before Connor can respond, Drew walks through the front door, accompanied by the girl I saw hugging Nash after the Grizzlies game. Drew is a junior defenseman in Preston's training group, cute in a clean-cut sort of way. And she's gorgeous, with striking copper-red hair—the kind of color you bring to your stylist and beg for, but they can't replicate because it's natural. As a dishwater blonde who has to highlight the heck out of my hair to mitigate its default blah, paper-bag color, I'm envious.

"Violet, this is Savannah," Nash says, gesturing to her. "Sav, this is Vi."

Immediately, I recognize the name because he's mentioned her in passing several times. She's Drew's best friend, which means that hug I witnessed was likely innocent. Not that I'd been wondering about that or anything.

Savannah gives me a warm smile, her brown eyes crinkling at the corners. "It's so nice to meet you."

"Nice to meet you, too," I tell her.

"Oh my God. You guys got a puppy!" Savannah squeals, running over to Vaughn and Biscuit. She picks up a rainbow-colored chew toy, engaging in a game of tug of war with Biscuit, who digs in his heels and slides across the hardwood.

Drew shoots Nash a questioning look. "We got a dog?"

Nash sighs. "I'll explain later."

———

Our first time giving a doggie bath is eventful, to say the least. Biscuit alternates between drinking from the running faucet and shaking the water off his fur, drenching us and the rest of the small bathroom in the process. After the third round of us both getting soaked, Nash leaves to get an extra shirt of his so I can change into it while he throws mine in the dryer.

He returns a moment later wearing a clean pair of navy joggers and a white Grizzlies t-shirt that hangs off his broad frame so perfectly it should be illegal.

"You can change in my room," he says, handing me a folded gray t-shirt. "It's the one on the left. I'll watch this furry little maniac, but I'm not even attempting to shampoo him until you get back."

I would object to the "furry little maniac" label if not for the fact that it's accurate. Biscuit is incredibly sweet—not to mention, clearly eager for human companionship based on the way he's basking in all this newfound attention—but maniac is an apt descriptor. Obedience school is in his future, potentially multiple times.

"Thanks." I slip out of the bathroom, leaving Nash alone with Biscuit, and head down the hall to his bedroom. When I push open the door and flip on the light switch, my heart does a somersault.

Faint traces of his familiar cologne permeate the air, but beyond that, his room is wholly unfamiliar. While that's to be expected, it saddens me.

A laptop sits on his glass desk next to a framed picture of him with Connor, Drew, Vaughn, and Savannah on what appears to be New Year's Eve. Other than the photo and a handful of hockey trophies, the room is spotless and largely devoid of other personal items, which isn't a huge surprise since he isn't exactly the sentimental type. And as I'd expected, his queen-sized bed is neatly made, covered with black sheets and a matching comforter.

For a split-second, I entertain the most absurd, torturesome curiosity about how many other girls have been in that bed, and I immediately delete the thought.

Drawing in a breath, I shut the door and wriggle out of my pink waffle-weave crewneck, its damp cotton clinging to my skin. When I slip Nash's clean, well-worn T-shirt over my head, it swallows me whole thanks to our foot-plus height difference. There's tug of nostalgia in my gut at wearing his clothes again after so long, and another tug in my gut for all the things we missed in between.

I return to the bathroom and carefully step over a puddle of water on the tiled bathroom floor, gesturing to myself. "This is a dress."

Nash glances over his shoulder at me, his mouth tipping up at one corner. "I dunno, I think you look cute."

It's impossible to hide my giddy smile, and my heart does another somersault because clearly, it's taking up gymnastics as a new hobby. Such a small statement shouldn't have the impact it does. It wouldn't, coming from anyone else.

We finally reach step two of the bath process: applying soap. Nash passes me the bottle, still a little wary of the furry fiend housed in the bathtub. Leaning forward, I scrub rosemary-mint dog shampoo into Biscuit's fur while he cranes his neck, trying to eat the bubbles.

"Didn't we feed you before this? You must be growing." I laugh, blocking his efforts with my elbow and catching a sloppy lick on my forearm as more water splashes onto my jeans.

"I thought you said your vehicle was in the shop a few weeks ago," Nash says, kneeling beside me. "Every time I drop you off, it's still there. What gives, Vi? Is it still not fixed?"

The abruptness of his question blindsides me, and I don't have an answer at the ready. I try to think back on what I told him. Did I say it was in the shop? What a sloppy, stupid lie. Dammit, Violet.

I clear my throat, trying to keep my voice even. "What I meant was, it isn't running properly. I haven't taken it in to be fixed yet. I haven't had, um, time."

"Highly unusual to experience issues with a brand-new Honda like that. Usually, they're pretty reliable."

"Must be bad luck."

We're in close quarters, static electricity humming between our skin. In addition to the heat of his body, I can feel his eyes on me, watching my reaction while I keep my attention fixed on the puppy. Nash is difficult to lie to at the best of times, and I'm unprepared. When I catch his face in my peripheral vision, I know I'm busted.

His dark green eyes narrow, flashing with suspicion. "Uh-huh."

There's a weighty pause, and I look up at him. My pulse pitter-patters faster with every passing second. His gaze holds mine, unwavering, until I feel like he can see into my brain. I've lost my mind. I think I lost it the first day I had to assess Nash—probably the moment I touched him.

"What's actually going on with your car? Or with you, more specifically?" He's sporting his patented, 'don't waste my time,' look.

"Nothing." Looking away, I grab the plastic cup we brought upstairs and fill it with warm water beneath the tub faucet, trying to rinse off Biscuit. Unfortunately, he thinks this is a game, and he scoots over to Nash's side of the tub, just beyond my reach. His tongue lolls out of his mouth, tail wagging as he waits for my next move.

"Why don't you drive anymore?" Nash presses. "You've had your license since you were sixteen."

Panic rises in my throat. "I don't... like to?"

His heavy sigh echoes off the bathtub tiles. "Level with me, Vi. I did you a solid by keeping the dog. You owe me one."

"You're pulling out the Biscuit card so soon? I thought you'd hold onto that one for a while and save it for something good." I'm trying to be playful but his mouth sets in a stern line, unwilling to bite.

"I want to know. It's been eating at me."

I dodge his gaze again, focusing on rinsing the last suds from Biscuit's fur. Biscuit drinks nearly as much clean water as gets on his body, but the soap is gone so I call it a success and pull the plug on the drain. The water gurgles and Biscuit dances in a circle, his nails clicking as he watches the mini whirlpool.

"I just..." I trail off, scrunching up my mouth. Nausea creeps up on me. "Remember that multi-car pile-up on the freeway last January?"

"What about it?" Nash's brow creases, concern across his face ramping up.

An onslaught of memories I'd rather forget assault me, and I drew in a breath, trying to quell them. Pushing them to the back of my mind, like I always do, rather than re-live it.

"I was involved in that. Smack in the middle. I got hit by two different cars coming at me from opposite directions, and my car got pushed into the one in front of me. It was a total write-off."

"Holy shit. Were you okay?"

While he's fairly calm, I get the sense Nash is losing it on the inside. Usually, he's a pro at hiding his emotions, but right now the cracks are showing. The telltale vein in his forehead is a dead giveaway.

"A few bumps and bruises, but I wasn't seriously injured. The person in the car next to me was critically injured, though. They had to cut her from her vehicle. Anyway, long story short, I was too scared to drive after it happened and then it just sort of—" my voice cracks, and I swallow. "Snowballed from there."

"Vi. I'm sorry." His hand lands on my upper arm, his voice gentle. It hurts in a million different ways. Because I don't like talking about this, because I miss him, because it makes me think of all the would-have, could-haves I've been working so hard to ignore.

"It's stupid, right? I'm not even the one who got hurt." I think about that all the time; it's selfish of me to be scared like this when other people ended up far worse off than I did. Even though no one died, several were critically hurt. All the same, I can't shake the feeling of terror I get when I even think about getting behind the wheel of a car.

It's also more than a little embarrassing that, as a grown adult, I am too scared to drive.

"It's not stupid." Nash's heavy arm wraps around my shoulders, hugging me. Hot tears rise behind my eyes, and I blink them away. We linger that way for a few moments, neither of us saying anything. The closeness is both comforting and upsetting all at once, because it feels so good, I don't want him to let me go.

"I know I'll have to get past it eventually, it's just easier to put it off until later."

In the empty tub, Biscuit whines expectantly, leaning forward on his paws in an attempt to escape. Nash squeezes me again before he grabs a towel from beneath the sink, drying off the dog and lifting him out of the tub. The instant Biscuit's feet hit the floor, he zooms out of the bathroom and gallops down the stairs. Distantly, Vaughn laughs and says something I can't make out.

I sniffle, wiping away an errant tear from the corner of my eye. "I should get home. It's late, and I have an early lecture tomorrow."

———

Once I change back into my dry shirt, Nash leaves Biscuit in the care of Drew and Vaughn while Connor side-eyes him from the other couch. Our drive home is quiet, mostly because I'm exhausted and nearly falling asleep in the passenger seat. Nash slips off his jacket, passing it to me to use as a makeshift pillow, and I doze off briefly before I feel the car slow to a stop, waking me.

It's a strange reversal of the scenario with Preston. Whereas I didn't know what I wanted to happen with him, I know exactly what

I wish would happen with Nash, even though I also know it's a bad idea. Maybe I'm a little unstable from the long day. I've been up since six to run with Claire before class, and I was expecting to arrive home several hours ago. Instead, Nash and I rescued a puppy, hugged twice, I saw his house and his bedroom, and I topped it all off with spilling a personal secret to him that hardly anyone knows. Draining would be an understatement.

Leaving his car running, he wordlessly walks me to my front door. We come to a stop, bathed in moonlight and chill fall air. Someone must have left our motion-activated porch light switched off, because it doesn't trigger.

"Thank you," I say, shifting my bag on my shoulder. "I know you're not a huge animal guy, but it means a lot to me that you agreed to help him." Though for someone who doesn't like dogs, he seems like a natural. Biscuit was following him around before we left like his newfound best friend.

"As long as you help me with the adoption process like you promised."

A wave of grief hits me. I'm not sure if it's over Biscuit, or us. "I will."

Something unspoken hangs in the air. Maybe it's the closure we never got.

Nash ducks his head, catching my eye. "You still know my number, right?"

"I do," I admit, breaking eye contact. Know it? I can still dial it blindfolded, backward, and upside down. And I've had to talk myself out of doing just that countless times.

"Text me, then, 'cause I can't text you."

"Why not?" I look up at him in confusion.

His jaw tightens, but it's hurt I detect and not anger. "You changed yours."

"Oh. Yeah, guess I did." Changing my number was one of several tactics I employed to help ease the post-breakup transition. Rebounding with Jay McAllister was another. So was dyeing my hair brown. Briefly flirting with the idea of transferring schools.

Consuming a billion self-help books. And taking up knitting for all of two weeks.

Most of them didn't work. Okay, none of them did.

"Why did you do that? So I couldn't call you?" A rare flicker of vulnerability appears on his face. Every once in a while, I see pieces of him like this that I suspect no one else ever does.

"No." I huff, scrambling to fight another tide of tears creeping in. With my emotional batteries drained, the truth tumbles out before I can stop it. "I changed it a few months after we broke up so I could tell myself that's why you weren't calling me. You know, instead of the real reason."

"What do you think the real reason was?" Nash's voice is uncharacteristically soft.

"That you didn't want to."

"No, Vi. I didn't think you wanted me to."

I did. So badly it still hurts.

"But you must have tried at some point, if you know I changed my number."

"Yeah, I tried to call you last year." He looks a little sheepish. "I was drunk after Vaughn's twenty-first birthday party."

"What were you going to say?" My heart squeezes in my chest, simultaneously swelling with hope and contracting with fear.

One corner of his mouth lifts. "I have no idea."

Suddenly, the porch light next to us flicks on. A sign that either Julianna or Claire is up, possibly both. Nash's eyes stay glued to me, and my breath stills. I take a small, micro-step forward, and he does the same. There's a moment's hesitation before we close the rest of the distance, and his strong arms wrap around my body. We fit perfectly—like a missing puzzle piece snapping into place. The urge to cry amplifies a thousandfold but I stuff it down, vowing to save it for once I'm inside.

He squeezes me tighter, and my sadness dissipates, replaced by a sense of deep relief. It feels like I've been holding my breath the entire time we've been apart and now I can finally let it go. I rest my cheek against the worn cotton of his hoodie and let my eyes drift shut, listening to his slow and steady heartbeat, savoring every second of being in his arms. It's been so long since I was held like this, warm and secure, fully comfortable. Obviously, I've been hugged, but it hasn't been the same. There's an intimacy with him I've never had with anyone else.

I glance up at him, trying to gauge whether he's feeling the same things that I am, but his expression is difficult to read. My pulse kicks up as he leans closer, his stubble scraping my skin. His nose brushes mine, and time stops, our lips hovering less than an inch apart. My brain and body are at complete odds, waging a civil war inside my head. My body thinks we're home, while my brain says to run. My heart, which should be the tiebreaker, has recused itself from the vote due to a lack of impartiality.

I want more than anything for him to kiss me, and it terrifies the hell out of me.

"I should go," I whisper, turning away.

Nash slowly lets me go, but one hand lingers on my waist while I fumble for my keys, unlocking the front door with shaky hands. Tugging it open, I force myself to take a step away from him that I don't want to take, and shift to face him.

"Thanks again."

He gives me a half-smile that's as sad as the way I feel. "Of course. Night, Vi."

CHAPTER 18

TIMING IS EVERYTHING
NASH

I AM NOT A SUPERSTITIOUS PERSON. Unlike most other athletes, I don't carry around good luck charms or adhere to specific pre-game rituals under some misguided belief that it will influence the final score when the buzzer sounds. I don't believe in signs, the supernatural, or serendipity.

But the fact that Violet's car accident happened a mere day after I got sidelined last January is fucking with my head.

Vaughn pokes my shin with the toe of his stick. "You okay?"

Other than the two of us out on the ice, the arena is empty. I agreed to stay behind after practice to help Vaughn work on his puck battles, but I'm not sure what good it's done when my mind has been elsewhere the entire time. He's beat me every single round, and I don't think he's had to work very hard to do it.

"I don't know," I admit, idly stickhandling the loose puck. "Do you ever feel like there's a significance to the timing of certain things?"

"Yeah," he says. "I do."

His answer doesn't come as a huge surprise. Vaughn is a lot more spiritually-minded than I am. While he isn't religious, he believes in a higher power, a greater good, and that there's more to life than what we experience on the physical level.

As far as I'm concerned, life is random. An accidental

byproduct of circumstance. No purpose, no plan, no meaning. A little nihilistic, maybe, but it's the only way I've been able to reconcile the world and my experiences within it thus far.

"Is this about Violet getting assigned to the team?" Vaughn skates backward a few strides, motioning for me to pass.

"Yes and no." Winding up, I level a shot in his direction, and the smack of the stick connecting with the puck echoes through the air. "Remember that big pileup on the freeway last winter? She was involved in that the day after I blew my AC."

He catches my pass, looking up at me with concern across his face. "That's awful. Was she okay?"

Even though I'd trust Vaughn with my life, I can't break Violet's trust and share the details.

"Mostly. Physically, anyway. Seems like weird timing, doesn't it?"

Unfortunately, I remember that day all too well. I was icing my shoulder on the couch, fuming over landing on the injured list in the midst of a hot streak when a breaking news report interrupted the football game I'd been watching. Once a serious car accident with multiple injuries came on screen, I watched with mild interest for half a minute and went to go take a shower. The cable programming had switched back to the third quarter by the time I got out, and I promptly forgot about the entire thing.

Until now.

Little did I know, when the news helicopter's video panned across the scene of the accident, *Violet* was in one of those cars. What if she'd been hurt? Would I have even known?

"Hmm." Vaughn looks down, leisurely dragging the puck back and forth.

"What does 'hmm' mean?"

He cocks a dark brow beneath his cage, a ghost of a smirk on his face. "Unless you're ready to own up to your feelings for her, you probably don't want to hear it."

"For fuck's sake, Banks. Are you going to make me say it?"

"Oh, *I've* known for a while. It's obvious from the way you look at her. But I wasn't sure if you were still in denial." Vaughn flips up the puck with the blade of his stick, catching it in his black glove. Inclining his head to the bench, he skates over to the side, motioning for me to follow. In other words, I've wasted enough of his time zoning out on the ice tonight. Fair enough.

"I'm well past the denial stage," I mutter, catching up with him in a few strides, stepping off the ice behind him. "Now tell me what 'hmm' means."

"I don't know if the close timing of the two events necessarily means anything other than shitty luck, but your reaction to this says it all. It bothers you because you wish you could've been there for her, and you wish she could have been there for you." He leans a padded shoulder against the dressing room door, shoving it open. The motion-activated lights flicker on, illuminating the changing area as I follow him inside. "Though if you ask me, I think you're more bothered about not being there for her than the other way around."

Bothered? I'm fucking broken up about it. True, I couldn't have prevented the car accident, or necessarily even mitigated how traumatizing the event was for her. Still, I like to think I could have done something—anything—to make it a little better after it happened.

Vaughn yanks off his white practice helmet, running a hand through his damp hair. "For what it's worth, Violet looks at you the same way."

Does she?

I untie my skates, letting his words sink in. On some level, I know Violet cares about me. But what I don't know is whether we're on the same wavelength or if I've been permanently relegated to the friendzone after fucking up my first chance. I'll always want more than that with her.

After we shed our sweaty gear, we hang it in our stalls to air it out and hit the showers in silence. Now, more than ever, I'm thankful for Vaughn's intuitive ability to sense—and respect—when someone doesn't want to make conversation.

Climbing under the spray, I turn the temperature dial higher until it's nearly scalding, closing my eyes as the stream of hot water pours down on my bare skin. No matter what I do, my mind keeps going back to the accident. To the stomach-turning knowledge that Violet was trapped alone, frightened out of her mind when I didn't have the slightest fucking clue. More than anything, I don't want that to happen again. Vaughn is right. I want to be able to be there for her.

This revelation leaves me more confused than ever. The absolute last thing I should be doing is complicating my senior year with a serious relationship. And there is no casual when it comes to me and Violet.

If she's even willing to forgive me in the first place.

———

Other than a very excited dog, the house is empty when I get back from practice. Drew came home to feed and let Biscuit out earlier before going over to Savannah's place, Vaughn had to babysit his little sister, and Connor is out doing… whatever it is that he does.

Halfway through the New York vs. Boston game, Connor comes inside through the garage and proceeds to storm around like an elephant, making a racket as he tends to. A few minutes later, he appears in a head-to-toe black Grizzlies sweatsuit with the hood up, looking like he's about to go rob a bank or something. I don't even bother asking, because with him, I generally don't want to know.

Connor flops onto the couch next to me, untwisting the cap on a bottle of blue Gatorade. "How's the puppy home search?"

"Not good. Violet's standards are sky high."

The good news is, the response to my ad has been surprisingly enthusiastic. In the past couple of days, I've been inundated with multiple would-be adoptive homes for Biscuit. I've forwarded Violet every single message of interest I've received so far, and she's promptly shut them all down. In her defense, some of her objections have been legitimate, like the couple who had five children and said they wanted a "low maintenance pet". Biscuit is many things; low maintenance is *not* one of them.

But some of the other potential owners seemed perfectly suitable, and Violet still immediately vetoed them. I'm not sure anyone is going to be good enough to adopt him, in her eyes. Even worse, I sort of empathize with her point of view. While initially I was eager to pawn him off on the first willing owner, the thought of handing off Biscuit to just anybody doesn't sit right with me. I can't believe I'm even saying that—he's a dog, for crying out loud. Yet somehow, I feel oddly protective of him, even if he is a total pain in the ass.

"Keep searching, fucker, because Biscuit chewed up my new shoes this morning." Connor reaches over and grabs something from behind the couch, holding up the remains to illustrate. The white leather uppers are in tatters, matching rubber soles mangled beyond recognition. They look like they've been put through a paper shredder. "These are Golden Goose. Or they *were*."

I snort. "Good. They were ugly."

He sets the mangled corpse of his sneakers on the coffee table across from the couch. "First of all, you don't know shit about fashion. Second, you're going to pay to replace them."

Pay for his overpriced footwear? Not gonna happen. Plus, there is some degree of irony in Connor—who doesn't give a shit about picking up after himself or helping out around the house—having something he values ruined.

"Consider us even for the time you got drunk and crashed in my bed with that chick from Alpha Phi." I wasn't pleased to come home after a late-night hookup a few months ago to find that the guys had thrown an impromptu party—and Connor was sprawled across my bed ass-up, buck naked. The only thing worse would have been finding him *face* up.

He barely even stirred when I tried to wake him. I was about to drag him out by his ankles until I realized there was a chick asleep underneath the covers beside him. I might be an asshole, but even I'm not that much of an asshole.

In the end, I crashed on the couch and had a knot in my neck for a week to show for it.

"Someone else was in my room. What was I supposed to do?"

"I don't know, go bang Rosalie in your car? Rent a hotel room by the hour? Not contaminate my bed, that's for sure."

Connor tips his head back and laughs, propping his sneaker-clad feet on the ottoman. "Ah, that was quite the evening. Worth it."

"I had to get new sheets, you dick."

"You know you could have washed them, right?"

"Maybe with kerosene."

"You're so dramatic." He rolls his eyes, tipping back his blue Gatorade. "Speaking of hookups, what's going on with you and Violet, anyway?"

Good fucking question. I'm still processing my talk with Vaughn. And Violet caught a ride home with her roommate earlier, so I didn't have the chance to see her after training this morning.

"Nothing."

"Nothing?" His brows lift. "You're going to pretend like you're not trying to get back together with her? Why else would you let her talk you into saving some mutt?"

"He's a mixed breed," I mutter.

As if on cue, Biscuit trots up to the couch and leaps into my lap, nearly crushing my balls. He places his front paws on my chest, leaning forward. Big black eyes peer into mine, cold, wet snout pressing against my nose. Holy hell, his puppy breath is atrocious. I need to start brushing his teeth like the vet said.

Dodging his licks, I move him down onto my lap, scratching his ear to distract him from trying to kiss me. Because breath aside, he was licking his crotch less than a minute ago.

Connor watches the production like I'm some alien life form. Maybe I am. How did I end up with a puppy? Oh, that's right, I'm whipped over Violet.

He blinks, shaking his head as if to clear it. "Stop changing the subject."

"I don't know, okay?" I snap. Biscuit whines, his ears drooping in response to the edge in my voice, and I absently pat the top of his head to comfort him. "It's complicated."

"What's the deal with her and Preston?"

A surge of irritation courses through me. Potentially unjustified since I don't know what—if anything—is happening between them. It may or may not even be a thing. However, what I do know is that Preston absolutely *wants* it to be a thing, and that's bad enough.

"I'm not sure." Glancing down to avoid Connor's prying gaze, I resume scratching Biscuit behind the ears, and his left leg starts thumping in appreciation.

"He's into her."

Thanks, tips. Anyone with a set of eyes could see that.

My jaw sets on edge. "I know."

CHAPTER 19

I KNOW LOTS OF THINGS
VIOLET

THE GOOD PART of this internship situation is, I see Nash all the time.

The bad part is, I see Nash all the time. Even when I'm trying to do things like focus on homework and training plans. His presence is beyond distracting, both when he is and isn't physically present.

In the middle of prepping for next week's training, I glance up from my clipboard to find Nash exiting the locker room area. He hoists his book bag onto his shoulder, trying and failing to hide a wince as he does. No surprise there; his shoulder has been bothering him all week. He can try to compensate, but movement patterns don't lie.

"Is it your shoulder again?" I call over. "Let me see." Christina has left for the day, and no one else is around, which makes it a good time to check out what's going on with him.

He avoids my eyes and throws me a dismissive wave, heading for the door. "It's all good, Vi. I'll see you at the game tonight."

"Obviously, it's not." Stupid, stubborn man. I'm not sure whether I'm more irritated or concerned. He has a unique knack for evoking both emotions in me.

When it becomes clear he's going to blow me off, I throw down my pen and march over to the door, blocking the exit. Straight out of his own playbook, like he did the day he walked me to the transit station.

Nash comes to a halt, which is fortunate because he could plow me over without even feeling it. He cocks a dark eyebrow as he peers down at me, a combination of amusement and annoyance across his handsome face. We remain planted in the doorway, locked in an unspoken stalemate. He could pick me up and move me out of the way in zero-point-two seconds if he wanted. But for some reason, he doesn't.

Clutching his elbow, I steer him through the room, over to the therapy table. Or he lets me steer him, rather, because there is no way I could drag this enormous human being anywhere against his will. He takes one step for every two I do.

Once we reach the table, I give him a shove that sends me more off-balance than it does him. "Sit down."

He complies, easing down onto the upholstered surface with a smirk. "I like when you play rough."

Even with him seated, the height difference between us is an impediment. The last athlete on this table must have been far shorter than him because the table is raised higher than normal. Or maybe Preston was using this area with someone; he's pretty tall. I grab the remote, lowering the table a few inches so I can see properly.

"Show me." I cross my arms, nodding at Nash's shoulder.

He reaches over and rolls up the sleeve of his black t-shirt, exposing his muscular upper arm. In this case, it doesn't provide enough access for me to observe what's really going on. I think he knows that, too.

I sigh. "I need to see all of your shoulder. Just take off your shirt, Nash. Nothing I haven't seen before."

With a shrug, he grabs the back of his shirt and yanks it off, wincing slightly. Miles of sculpted muscle beneath smooth, taut skin greet me. His hair is still slightly damp from a post-practice shower, recently applied cologne floating over to me and wearing away at my self-restraint. Freshly showered Nash is my favorite kind.

Stay professional, Violet.

Trying to stay on task, I run him through a few basic tests, most of which he fails to varying degrees. Then I manipulate his shoulder to confirm my suspicions. He tenses almost instantly.

"Does that hurt?"

He inhales sharply, talking through gritted teeth. "What do you think?"

My ubiquitous worry about him climbs up a notch. Nash has a high pain threshold. If he is showing that he's in pain, it's an eight out of ten at least.

"Your AC joint is getting worse, you know."

"It'll be fine."

"Fine like it was last year?" The words slip from my mouth before I can stop them. I don't want to fight about it. This isn't a matter of me needing to be right. I want him to listen before he ends up sidelined again. Because for some reason, I still care about Nash and I know how important his hockey career is to him.

On brand as ever, he ignores my question and lobs a curveball at me instead. "You dating Preston?"

I not-so-accidentally let my thumb slip onto a pressure point in response to that question.

"Ouch," he hisses, leaning away. "How are you so tiny, yet so violent?"

"Pressure points," I murmur, making a point not to glance up at him as I extend his elbow.

"Are you avoiding my question?"

I arch an eyebrow, meeting his eyes before returning my attention to his rotator cuff. "Not that it's any of your business, but no. I'm not. Why, are you dating that brunette who was all over you at the pub after the game?" Fair's fair, I guess.

"No. You're the only girlfriend I've ever had."

"Is that supposed to make me feel special?" My throat tightens, and I swallow it down.

"I don't know, does it?"

Curse my stupid, hopeful heart. I know it shouldn't, but it does. This is top tier 'pick me girl' mentality. Nash stood me up on Easter to go take a road trip with his boys—I'm not special.

I look away because it's hard to lie to his face. "It doesn't."

Clearing my throat, I refocus on the task at hand and we both fall silent.

"How's Biscuit doing?" I ask, trying to distract from the topic of Preston as well as the assessment itself.

"Great." Nash's smile is rueful. "Since I've brought him home, he's only destroyed three shoes, one iPhone cord, and chewed half a Finance textbook. You should come visit him."

"I will. Thursday, maybe? We could take him to that dog park you mentioned." Frowning, I check his limited range of motion again. "You need to take some time off."

"Can't." He reaches over, grabbing his shirt from the end of the table. His abdominal muscles ripple as he pulls it back on, vanishing beneath the wall of black cotton. "Game tonight. But if you could tape my shoulder before then, that would do me a solid."

A fresh onslaught of irritation sparks within me at his glib response. "You can't keep playing like this."

"This is Hockey 101, Vi. If you take a hit, shake it off and get back out there. If something gives you trouble, work harder until you master it. If something hurts, push through the aches and pains until they disappear."

"And if you keep it up, you're going to need surgery," I counter. Where on earth did he get this ridiculous idea from that he should push through injuries instead of resting? Coach Ward would never subscribe to that kind of philosophy. "Then you'll be out way longer than a few games."

"I'll deal with that if and when it happens." Nash slides off the table, coming to loom over me again. Another wave of his cologne envelops me, adding attraction to the confusing jungle of emotions I'm trying to navigate.

Balling my hands into fists, I prop them on my waist and glare up at him. "You're so hard-headed, you barely need a helmet."

His broad shoulder lifts in a shrug, but he says nothing. In addition to his hockey prowess, he's a gold-medalist in stonewalling.

"I should tell Christina and Coach Ward." I shake my head, turning away to gather up my purse and school books. My next class isn't for an hour, but I'm too annoyed to stand still doing nothing.

"Maybe," he says. "But you won't."

"How do you know?" I yank the zipper on my book bag shut with more force than necessary, resisting the urge to pick it up and smack him with it.

"Because I know you."

It's the truth in this that bothers me most of all.

My grip on the book bag strap tightens. "Don't flatter yourself. You used to know me, but not anymore."

In my peripheral vision, Nash steps closer, and his voice drops. "Oh, I know lots of things."

I lift my chin to look up at him again and this time, he's the one backing me into the therapy table. One step; two steps; three. My hamstrings hit the edge, and I come to a stop, heart rate skyrocketing.

I'm cornered.

Wordlessly, he takes the bag from my hands, setting it aside. Grabbing the backs of my thighs, he scoops me up and sets me on the table. Fortunately, he's more gentle than I was with him.

Nash's lips tug as he peers down at me. "This table is really low."

"I'm really short. Or you're really tall, depending how you look at it." This quote from the night we met slips out before I can stop myself. Though, he probably doesn't even remember.

"Bit of both, really." His mouth pulls into a heart-stopping grin.

A dull ache forms in my chest, because he does.

He leans down and plants his hands on either side of my body, stapling me to the spot. It's so quiet in the room, the only sound is our soft inhales and exhales. For the second time lately, we're close enough to kiss, close enough that I can smell the cool mint gum on his breath. All I can think about is his lips pressed up against mine, tasting that mint on my tongue.

"What are you—" I falter. Sentences are a challenge right now. "Someone could come in."

Nash, of course, is unfazed by this possibility. Rules have never concerned him all that much.

He tucks my hair behind my ear, tilting my face up to his with his finger. His movements are slow and deliberate, like a predator sizing up his prey before coming in for the kill. Heat unfurls in my center, my body instinctively responding to him like it always has.

I'm in trouble.

His gaze pins me to the spot, and I start to get lost in the endless depths of his eyes, drinking in the subtle details that can only be seen within intimate range. Up close, the rich green is a prism of colors. Gold burst like rays of sun around his pupil, darker ring of emerald framing his iris, with hints of moss and olive. They're unlike any color I've ever seen, like the depths of a forest kissed with honeyed beams of sunshine.

There's no lack of pheromones here; an inconvenient fact that's slightly easier to ignore when everyone else is around. Now that there are no witnesses, I have a nearly overwhelming urge to wrap my arms around him and bury my face against his skin, inhaling his divine, familiar scent until my lungs explode. I know the sound he would make, too. Low and throaty, on the verge of a growl.

My hands stay glued to my lap.

A maelstrom of feelings surges through me, lust and fear rising with every passing moment until they threaten to overflow, and I break eye contact. He steadies my chin between his thumb and index finger, turning my face back to look at him. When our eyes collide again, it rocks me. Time hasn't diminished his effect on me; if anything, it's strengthened it. The tiny, almost imperceptible smirk that forms on his lips tells me he's fully aware.

Nash watches me intently, tracing my bottom lip with the calloused pad of his thumb. "Like I was saying, I know lots of things." He drags his thumb lower, caressing the delicate skin behind my left ear. "For example, I know if I kiss this spot right here, you'll arch your neck and let out the sexiest fucking whimper I've ever heard."

I don't know about sexy, but it's taking all my strength not to whimper right now.

He inclines his head, dragging a rough palm down the column of my neck. My heartbeat flutters in a way that cannot be physically healthy for a twenty-one-year-old. I'm going to need a pacemaker by the time this internship is over.

"If I bite here, you'll moan." He squeezes the flesh where my neck meets my shoulder. There's a throb between my legs in response, confirming his theory. I have a couple of sweet spots, and that's one of them. But he knows them all.

"And if I move lower..." His fingertips ghost along my collarbone, his touch feather-light. I draw in a breath as his hand splays, slowly drifting down the swell of my breasts. My breath hitches, and goosebumps wash over my skin. I watch him, mesmerized, slipping deeper under his spell with every passing second. He continues until he's nearly at the neckline of my tank top, and my nipples tighten in anticipation of his touch.

Before he reaches his intended target, the door to the training room flies open and we both startle, pulling apart. Adrenaline shoots through my veins, a mixture of fear and disappointment echoing through my body.

Nash straightens, taking a giant step back, and I scoot off the treatment table just as James Anderson, a ginger-haired freshman on the team, barges in.

"Sorry, forgot my headphones in the training area." James throws us an apologetic glance, but it seems like he thinks he was interrupting something a lot more innocent than it is. He disappears into the next room, leaving the two of us alone in the aftermath of a massive slip in judgement.

"No worries," I call out weakly, even though he's already gone. "Just wrapping up."

Turning back to Nash, I pat him on the arm in a way that's meant to be friendly but is more awkward than anything. "Well, your shoulder looks fine for now." My voice is excessively loud, trying to legitimize his presence in case James can overhear. "Make sure to ice it when you get home and do those stretches I showed you."

James reappears with a pair of white earbuds in one hand and stands in the far doorway. He rakes a hand through his copper curls, eying us uncertainly. "I had a quick question for Violet if that's okay. I wanted to make sure I was doing that exercise you showed me correctly because I'm not feeling it in my adductor."

"Sure," I say. "No problem."

Nash clears his throat and gives me a meaningful look. "I should get going." He grabs his book bag, slipping it onto his good shoulder, and turns to leave.

"I mean it," I tell him under my breath. "Ice. Stretch. Rehab exercises. Try to rest as much as possible."

"Will do," he says over his shoulder, but we both know he won't.

CHAPTER 20

YOU'RE MINE
VIOLET

IT'S A DOUBLE-HEADER: the team is fresh off the win and it's Marcus's birthday. Which is how I ended up here, at the house Marcus shares with his roommates—and across the room from Nash, who's acting like nothing even happened between us earlier.

I mean, I'm not sure how else he could act. What is he supposed to do, tell everyone he felt me up in the training room this morning? But he's acting so normal, so unaffected, that it's making me *more* rattled. He's got the upper hand, and I hate it.

First, I had to watch him crush it out on the ice tonight—which, by the way, is such a turn-on that it could be considered foreplay. Now, I'm stuck looking at his stupid, handsome face and his stupid, tattooed arm, clutching that stupid bottle of beer with his stupid massive hand, trying to appear impervious to his appeal when I am anything but.

At this rate, I won't be able to function around him soon.

Julianna nudges me. "Want another drink?" She's perched on Marcus's lap to my left, a development she seems thrilled with but that somehow leaves me uneasy. I can't pinpoint why, when he's never been anything but perfectly pleasant to me.

I glance down at my empty mango White Claw. "Thanks, but I think I'm okay."

New, self-imposed rule: one-drink limit in Nash's presence.

Nash stands up and goes into the kitchen, presumably to get another beer. Everyone else is in the middle of some massive drinking game, the rules to which I don't understand. Either way, they're occupied enough that they won't notice my brief absence or if they do, they won't think much of it.

"I'm going to use the bathroom. I'll be right back," I tell Jules.

She nods, turning back to Marcus as he continues a story about their win in the championship semifinals last season. In this account, he's the hero, but it doesn't quite align with the version of events Nash relayed to me when he drove me home the other day. My radar pings again, and I make a note to speak to Julianna once I figure out a way to approach the topic.

Stepping over people scattered haphazardly around the living room, I squeeze through the crowd, slipping into the kitchen at the same moment Nash turns away from the fridge with a fresh beer in his hand.

He isn't even a little surprised to see me standing here. If anything, he looks like he expected it. It's like he's playing four-dimensional chess, and I'm a pawn.

Laughter erupts in the living room, but the kitchen is silent as I step closer to him. "We need to talk."

Nash's brows lift, thinly veiled amusement on his face. "About what?"

"You know what."

"Okay." He cracks his beer, tossing the bottle cap aside with a clink. "Shoot."

Shooting him sounds like a great idea, actually.

I go to speak, but immediately realize this room is entirely too open, too exposed to the party and potential eavesdroppers. Surveying the open main floor for alternatives, I come up frustratingly empty-handed.

"Let's just—go upstairs for a minute," I tell him, growing flustered in the face of his calm exterior.

With a shrug, he sets down his beer and follows me. The fact that he seems to think he needs both of his hands free for this discussion is worrisome. If anything, I should have made sure both his hands were occupied with something else.

I'm not sure I've thought this through. Okay, I definitely haven't. But too late, now.

Fortunately, the stairwell is sheltered from the living room such that no one can see us ascend. We reach the top of the stairs and I yank open the door to the first bedroom on the left, shoving Nash into the empty room. Or more precisely, I try to shove him, and he saunters into the bedroom purely of his own accord because my efforts don't move him an inch. At least he's in a cooperative mood, but I can't count on that lasting long once he hears what I have to say.

Music and party chatter fades as I close the door behind me, sealing us in. My trembling fingers search the wall beside the door, landing on the light switch, but when I flip it, nothing happens. I try again. Still nothing.

Great. We're in the dark—alone. Solid plan, Violet.

"What was that about this morning?" I yell-whisper.

A deep laugh rumbles in front of me. "What about it? Are we picking up where we left off?"

God help me, part of me wants to. The insane part.

Because the truth is, I didn't mind it one bit. My objections didn't kick in until later once I sobered up from Nash's influence. Then, the gravity of the situation hit me. If Christina or Coach Ward had walked in, it could have been catastrophic. Mostly for me.

Word has it, Coach Ward also warned the team to remain professional with the trainers. But unlike me, Nash wouldn't be breaking any official rules. Plus, as their top stay-at-home defenseman, the team needs Nash too badly to bench him. If we were to get caught together, they'd probably kick me out of my internship and let him keep right on playing. Double standards for the athletes are par for the course.

My eyes adjust to the dark, and his hulking silhouette comes into view a few feet away. Electricity thrums between us, like two halves of a circuit waiting to be connected, making my plan to speak to him privately seem more ill-advised than ever.

I take half a step back, hitting what feels like a dresser behind me. "You can't just try to seduce me in the middle of the training room."

"Fine. I'll seduce you here instead." Nash draws closer, and my breath snags as his hands slide around my waist, claiming the sliver of bare skin beneath the hem of my cropped shirt. Every nerve ending in my body lights up like a Christmas tree, my brain short-circuiting from the sudden galvanized surge.

Second thoughts murmur in the back of my mind, voices of reason reminding me he's the only one who ever broke my heart. It would be foolish to let him have it again, and that's almost a certainty if we head down this path. There's no half-hearted or half-assed when it comes to us. It's in or out, all or nothing.

"Do you always have to be inappropriate?" I'm trying to sound assertive, but my breathy protest is unconvincing even to my own ears.

"You're the one who yanked me into a dark room alone, Vi."

"Oh my God. You're so…" My train of thought derails as Nash lifts me off the ground, setting me on the dresser. Broad palms rest on the top of my thighs, heat radiating through the denim of my jeans and winding all the way up to my core, dissolving what little willpower I have left. With every second his hands linger on my body, those voices of reason get a little quieter.

A rough finger caresses my cheekbone, trailing down to my jaw. "Charming? Irresistible?"

I can't see his face in the dark, but I can hear the smirk in his voice.

"The word I was looking for is infuri—"

Before I can finish, he grabs my face and his mouth crashes down on mine. A rush runs through my entire body, and I resist for a split-second out of surprise before my instincts kick in, lips parting. He seizes the access that I grant him, pushing into my mouth with a low groan that vibrates down my throat. When his tongue slides against mine, a stadium's worth of butterflies in every color, shape, and size imaginable explode in my stomach. The flutters travel all the way to the tips of my fingers and toes.

Oh, I missed this.

Slanting his mouth, Nash deepens the kiss, faint traces of beer mingling with his unique taste. It's an intoxicating blend that leaves me lightheaded and longing for more, completely under his spell within a matter of seconds. His arm wraps around my waist, firm planes of muscle crushing me to him. My fingertips tug at the soft hair at his nape, earning me a deep, gravelly sound of appreciation and an even tighter embrace. His tongue plunders my mouth, ravishing me, and the voltage between us surges until it sizzles.

I've spent years fantasizing about being kissed like this again. It's claiming and demanding, bossy and insistent. It says *you're mine*, even though I know that isn't true.

Almost as if he can hear my thoughts, his fingers twine in the roots of my hair, yanking with zero hesitancy, and his teeth sink into my lower lip. A needy whimper escapes the back of my throat at the divine blend of pleasure and pain, a long unmet need finally being fulfilled. Everything lights up with white-hot passion, and my fingernails dig into his skin to urge him on.

He growls and releases his bite, slipping beneath my shirt and squeezing my breasts over my thin, lacy bra. His caresses are warm and rough, familiar yet thrilling, and I never want it to end. My head tips back with a shaky exhale as my nipples harden, skin heating beneath his hands. I'm gone, so far gone. He's an addiction I've fallen straight back into, hooked on the way he touches me and already aching for another fix.

"Why do you always smell so fucking good?" His words are a heated, husky whisper against my throat. My inhale catches in my lungs as his tongue drags along the column of my neck, his teeth sinking into that sweet spot that makes me whimper.

His hands slide beneath my thighs, hauling me to the very edge of the dresser so abruptly that I tip forward into him. He catches me, his strong, thick fingers digging into my ass with a bruising hold, and I gasp as his hard length presses that perfect, sensitive spot between my legs. It's decadent; a slow grind; an agonizing rhythm meant to take me to the brink and keep me there.

Faintly, I remember that we shouldn't be doing this. We especially shouldn't be doing this while the rest of the team is down-stairs. Someone could walk in at any minute. But if anything, knowing how wrong it is only makes me want it more. After all, the risk has always been part of his appeal.

"You're wet for me right now, aren't you Vi? I bet you're fucking soaked." His voice is thick with desire and full of filthy memories.

I don't need to speak up to confirm his theory; we both know it's true. It's like diving into a river after a dry spell.

His next thrust makes my mouth fall open, my thighs clenching with pleasure.

"Oh, God." I bury my face in the crook of his neck, clinging to him as I tilt my pelvis to meet his, chasing that incendiary high. Am I really about to get off from simply dry humping? I can't decide whether it's hot, because I have a six-foot-four hockey god grinding between my legs, or sad because I've been so orgasm-deprived that this is all it takes. Maybe a bit of both.

"Damn, I missed your sounds. It's been way too long since I've seen you come."

Sheer, unadulterated need throbs between my legs like a steady, beating drum growing louder and more insistent by the second. My eyes squeeze shut as my back arches against him, seeking friction and desperate for release. His movements slow to a torturously languorous pace, infusing my body with bliss, holding me right on the edge without letting me tip over.

Flames spread across my skin, and my breathing turns ragged, my underwear drenched with arousal. With another divine rock of his hips, I gasp and dig my heels into his backside, trying to pull him closer. His hands bracket my waist, holding me in place and hindering my efforts.

"Nash." A whimper slips through my lips. I'm fevered, frantic with need. "Please."

A low hum rumbles in his chest. "Good girl."

With a grip on my body that teeters on punishing, he yanks me against him again, capturing my cries with his mouth while I fall apart beneath his hands. It's an explosive euphoria; mind-melting pleasure. I hear colors, feel sounds, so weightless I'm not sure I'll ever come down.

When I finally float back to reality, I'm boneless and breathless in his arms. Nash cups my face, and his lips find mine again, but this time it's a soft kiss, tender and savoring. His hand wraps around my neck, my heartbeat pulsing beneath his fingertips.

He pulls back, his nose grazing mine. "Vi—"

Behind us, the door creaks and swings open, obliterating my post-orgasm high. Light pours into the room from the hallway like a spotlight trained on the two of us. Our connection shatters, and my hand flies to my mouth, fingertips landing on kiss-swollen lips where the taste of him still lingers.

Nash's hold on my waist tightens, and he pivots so he's partially blocking me from view. Behind him, Shea O'Connell appears in the doorway and drunkenly stumbles in like a baby fawn learning to walk.

A few steps into the room, Shea freezes, surveying the two of us with utter befuddlement across his face. "Shit. This isn't the bathroom."

He tips his head back, laughing hysterically at this revelation for a good couple of seconds. Then his gaze falls back to us, and his laughter dies abruptly when he finally registers what he sees: me, perched on a dresser with Nash standing between my legs, and Nash leveling him with a murderous glare. He looks like he's two seconds away from throttling Shea.

Shea's glassy eyes widen. "Uh…Sorry, Richards. Didn't mean to interrupt." He reaches behind him for the brass door handle, gripping the knob tightly like it might somehow keep him safe from Nash's wrath.

"You didn't interrupt, because you were never here," Nash tells him, a lethal calmness to his tone.

Shea is drunk, but not too drunk to not catch on, and he quickly shuffles backwards out the room. "Right, of course not. Catch you later."

He shuts the door behind him with a quiet click, enclosing us in darkness again. Nash reaches behind me and switches on a small table lamp, putting us face-to-face in the aftermath of what just transpired. We're both breathing heavily, but I'm panting more than after a full 10K.

"Fucking freshmen," he mutters, rolling his eyes. "*Again.*"

"Seems to be a common theme," I murmur.

His expression softens. "Are you okay, Petal?" He ducks his head to catch my eye, and his hands wrap around my waist, thumbs slowly stroking back and forth.

My chest pulls tight at the familiar nickname. "Yeah, I'm fine."

It's a lie; I'm reeling, nearly dizzy from his influence. And beneath that, I feel vulnerable. Painfully vulnerable in a way only Nash can evoke, and I hate it.

Because there's an ease in the way he touches me. A determination. Or maybe straight-up domination. Every other guy I've been with has been timid, engaging in an apprehensive game of trial-and-error while they tried to figure out what worked. Tried, because none of them ever did. Nash handles my body like an expert. Holding, squeezing, owning.

Maybe it's not a fair comparison. He's had a lot of practice. Besides, sex was never the issue. Everything else was.

His gaze pins me, watchful. "You kissed me back."

Like there was ever any question whether I would.

"I..." Grasping for a response, I come up empty-handed. "I should get going. Claire and I are supposed to go for a run tomorrow morning."

Nash nods, but he doesn't take his hands off me. His lips brush against mine softly, our tongues meeting. The butterflies start an all-out riot in my belly all over again, clamoring for more. He pulls away and rests his forehead against mine, squeezing his eyes shut for the briefest moment in a way that almost looks pained. "I missed you, Vi."

My throat clenches. "I missed you, too."

With a sigh, he picks me up and sets me back down on my feet, his hold on me lingering until the last possible second before we step out into the empty hall. He squeezes me in a silent goodbye, and I let him go downstairs first while I lean against the wall, trying to catch my breath.

Once Shea vacates the bathroom, I dart inside, locking the door behind me. In the yellowish vanity lighting, my makeup is smudged, composure demolished. Mascara flakes line my eyes, concealer rubbed off, cheeks flushed and lips reddened from kissing. Turning on the tap, I clean up as much as I can with soap and water, but it still looks like I've been crying, at best—or having sex, which I nearly was.

It takes several rounds of box breathing before I'm level-headed enough to face everyone again. The minute Jules lays eyes on me, she kindly offers to bail without asking a single question. I explain some of what happened to her on the ride home, but not everything.

Later that night, sleep evades me. I lay in bed, tossing and turning for hours.

One question echoes through my mind.

How can he be Mr. Wrong when he's the only one who's ever made me feel this way?

CHAPTER 21

RISK-BENEFIT ANALYSIS
NASH

KISSING VIOLET WAS either the stupidest or smartest thing I've ever done.

Problem is, I'm not sure which.

It's all I've been able to think about ever since.

Late afternoon sunlight pours into Marie's office through the floor-to-ceiling windows, the sun rapidly descending in the sky; it's four-thirty p.m., and I have an evening practice after this. Not ideal timing for a therapy session, in my opinion, but Marie was so booked up that I didn't have much choice. And the appointment was badly needed because I was losing my shit.

"You haven't talked about Violet very much." Marie's tone is gentle, her words carefully measured because she knows pushing me is the best way to guarantee I'll clam right up. "Is there a reason?"

That's because it hurts to even think about, let alone recount how I single-handedly decimated a good thing. I took a wrecking ball to our relationship, smashed it to pieces, and walked away.

I neutralize my expression while my grip on the arm of the couch tightens, navy velvet bunching beneath my fingers. Marie's attention drops to my hand, evidently noticing the gesture, but she says nothing. Drawing in a breath, I release my grasp. "I don't like to talk about it. Or think about it."

She gives me a small, sympathetic smile. "It's hard for you."

"It is." The two simple words are difficult to force out. Suddenly, throwing myself out that window seems like a more appealing alternative than discussing this.

"You must care about her a lot."

A knot forms in my chest, winding around my throat. "Yeah."

What kills me is, I've never told Violet that directly. When she said she loved me, I couldn't bring myself to say it back—which goes to show how dysfunctional I am. I'd like to fall back on the whole, "actions speak louder than words" concept to defend myself, but I'm not so sure I'm great at showing how I feel, either.

"You've mentioned that you dated," Marie says. "What exactly happened?"

With significant coaxing, I recount the high-level version of my history with Violet, both past and present. From the sweet start to the bitter end and everything in between. I'm sure Marie sees all kinds of things clicking into place, because it basically confirms what she and I both already know.

According to a previous session we had this spring, she believes I have "attachment issues." What she didn't say, and what I later found out via Google, is that's shrink speak for "emotionally fucked up." Supposedly, my issues stem from growing up with a temperamental, impossible-to-please father. That checks out; I don't think anyone could grow up under his roof and emerge in one piece mentally or physically.

It's not an excuse, but it's a major contributing factor as to why I screwed things up so spectacularly with Violet the first time around. Emotional intimacy is scary as hell for me, largely because I haven't experienced much of it. From what I remember of my mother, she was kind and loving, but she's been gone since I was four. From ages four to eighteen, I was on my own emotionally. Doug was worse than neglectful; he was a toxic presence in my life.

Since I came to college, I've been navigating adulthood on my own. Trying to undo all that damage from my father. Or trying to live with it, at least.

My friends are the only true family I have. Even then, male

friendships are different than a romantic relationship. We mostly bond over shared interests and doing shit together. Being with Violet represents something much deeper; something much more significant. It requires openness and reciprocity, trust and understanding, none of which I'm particularly skilled at. And the stakes are exponentially higher.

When I finish explaining, Marie pauses. "What do you think will happen if you let Violet in?"

"I don't know. I just…every time I start to, I panic. My brain slams on the brakes. I want to leap out of the car and run. Figuratively, I mean."

She hums thoughtfully. "What are you afraid of?"

Everything.

"Getting hurt."

It's not a logical fear. I know this on a cognitive level, but it doesn't change the dread that creeps in when I think about getting closer to her again. I have no real reason to suspect Violet is going to hurt me. That was a one-way street in our relationship, which she definitely didn't deserve.

"But this time around," I add, "It's different. Because I think my fear of losing her again might outweigh that."

"You're saying you might be willing to take the risk?"

I shift in my seat, my agitation from this conversation driving me to physical discomfort. Beads of sweat form along the back of my neck, T-shirt sticking to my skin. Is it hot in here? It feels that way all of a sudden. Violet makes me feel things, and my life is exponentially easier to navigate when I don't.

"I'm not sure I have a choice. I'll never forgive myself if I let her get away again." Long-repressed regret trickles into my brain, seeping through the cracks of my consciousness. "But that doesn't make it any less scary. I'm convinced I'm going to fuck it up again."

"In what way?" she asks gently. "Everyone makes mistakes, and no relationship is perfect."

"Fuck it up like, not be enough for her or what she needs."

I've never been enough for Doug. What if I disappoint Violet, too?

Marie makes another flurry of notes on her notepad and pushes her wire-rimmed glasses up the bridge of her nose, glancing up at me. "This is noteworthy progress, Nash. We went from a general fear to one that's quite specific. You said you were scared of getting hurt, but it sounds more like you're scared of hurting Violet. Does that resonate with you at all?"

It resonates a little too much.

"Kind of," I admit. "I don't want to be Doug version two-point-zero."

The words hang in the air, and Marie's expression softens. "You're not your father, Nash."

I wish I could believe that.

Sometimes I catch myself reacting to things the same way I know he would. Sometimes I look in the mirror and see his face, and it makes me want to take the mirror off the wall and smash it. Sometimes I wonder how, or even if, I can break out of the mold he's tried to force me into.

One of my biggest fears is that I might not be able to.

"What do you think will happen if you don't let Violet in? If you continue this pattern of behavior from before where you push her away when you get too close?"

"I'll lose her again." Justifiably so.

She raises her eyebrows at my admission. "Would that hurt?"

So much I can't even let myself imagine it.

"Yes."

———

Nothing like following your therapy session with a call from the person who sent you there in the first place. For fuck's sake. His timing is nothing short of impeccable.

"Hi, Dad." I pull into the arena parking lot and shift into park, letting my car idle. There are fifteen minutes until I need to start getting dressed, but I don't bother mentioning this time constraint; I'm sure he's already aware. His controlling tendencies have gotten progressively worse throughout the course of my college career. I'm surprised he hasn't placed a tracking device on my vehicle. Hell, maybe he has.

"I was watching your last game," he says. "Your gap control could use some work."

Is that so? Just last week, Coach Ward remarked that I have some of the best gap control in the entire conference.

"Noted." Leaning back in the leather seat, I pinch the bridge of my nose, squeezing my eyes shut. I sense a headache coming on. I don't get them very often; Doug is my only trigger.

"More turnovers than I'd like to see, as well. Is Coach Ward even addressing these things with you?" I can picture the scorn across his face like he's standing right in front of me, his gray-flecked brows lowered, upper lip lifted in a sneer. "I have some real concerns about the coaching team at your school."

Shifting in the driver's seat, I groan inwardly. Coach Ward and I have had our fair share of differences over the past few years, but his credentials speak for themselves. He played for fifteen years in the league before retiring due to injury and he has three cups to his name. A couple of LSU championships behind him as Head Coach, too. Pretty sure the guy knows what he's doing, but I know better than to argue that point.

"Don't worry," I tell Doug, trying not to sound as weary as I feel. "Coach Ward has it handled."

He scoffs. "Does he? You're looking a little soft on the puck lately, too. Make sure to work on those stick checks in practice this week."

My grip on the steering wheel tightens, a flicker of anger igniting in my chest. While all players have their weak spots, being soft on the puck has never been one of mine. Sometimes, I'm not sure whether Doug is intentionally trying to gaslight me or if believes the shit he says.

"I'll remember to do that." Hell, I couldn't forget his criticism if I tried.

He offers me a crumb by acknowledging that my positioning has been "satisfactory," and promptly launches into an interrogation about our practice drills. I take a sip of water, trying to swallow the frustration brewing within me, but it's futile.

After my mom died, it was just the two of us. I wanted to please him so badly. And when I started playing hockey, it seemed like it worked. I remember how proud he was of me when I learned how to skate. Even during the introductory years of minor hockey, he was encouraging, if a little intense. At least back then, there was some praise sprinkled in with the criticism; some approval to help keep me going.

I don't know when it changed—if there was a specific tipping point or if it was merely a slow, inevitable decline. The higher my tier, the worse it got, until I started playing elite-level hockey and his expectations became downright unattainable. Like I should have somehow been able to control whether our goalie let past ten goals in a game. I might play defense, but I'm not a fucking magician.

Slowly but surely, he grew more and more critical. Nothing was ever good enough. Eventually, I started to dread getting home after losses because I knew what was coming. I guess attending the school where he worked made it easier for teachers to overlook the bruises.

Our call wraps up with another detailed list of my shortcomings followed by a brusque parting. Switching off the ignition, I sit in silence and stare out into the half-full parking lot, attempting to shake off his barbed words. In less than five minutes, I need to walk into practice and forget the metric ton of radioactive negativity he just poured over my head. Nothing lessens the string of his sharp tongue other than time and distractions, neither of which I have at my disposal.

Turns out, being talented was actually the worst case scenario. If I had sucked, he would have eventually lost hope and moved on. Maybe he would have badgered me about my grades or something else, but nothing triggers the same level of obsession in him like hockey. Probably because he never played a single minute as a pro. Never got drafted to the league, either, which means I've already accomplished more as an athlete than he ever did. But that's his dirty little secret, and one he goes out of his way to hide from anyone else.

On some level, I know my father is living vicariously through me. And in a fucked-up way, I can almost empathize with that. But what I still don't understand is why he can't celebrate my successes instead of constantly tearing me down. No matter how high I climb, no matter what I achieve, he always expects more. Success is a moving target in his eyes.

One I'll never hit.

CHAPTER 22

HEART VS. VAGINA
VIOLET

I CAN'T GET that kiss out of my head.

Unfortunately, this means I'm obsessing over it while I'm sitting in the middle of the library across from Julianna, attempting to study. Normally, Strength & Conditioning Program Design is one of my favorite classes. Right now, it seems drier than cardboard. After less than half a page, the words begin to jumble together, sliding into a meaningless blur.

If kissing Nash was better than ever, what would everything else be like?

The question sends me straight down a rabbit hole of memories, right back to our first time. I was a virgin; he wasn't. It was good—great, if we're comparing it with all the other first-time stories I've heard from my friends. I even had an orgasm, which is apparently more than most women get their first time. And the sex after that? Better and better. Needless to say, it created some unrealistic expectations on my part.

Losing my virginity to Nash was like having a Ferrari for my first vehicle—and moving on to other guys was the equivalent of downgrading to a used, rusty Honda Civic. Sure, the Civic is a fine, reliable car. There's nothing *wrong* with it. It might get you where you need to go…eventually. But it's no Ferrari. The Ferrari might be a little impractical, but the performance can't be beat.

For all of Nash's numerous shortcomings in the boyfriend department, he was a giver in the bedroom. Bless my naive little heart, I honestly thought everyone in committed relationships was having mind-blowing sex on the regular.

Turns out, I was gravely mistaken.

It was a rude awakening the first time I slept with someone else. My first boyfriend after, Jay, wasn't well-acquainted with the clitoris. Or foreplay. And he'd definitely never found the G-spot. Oral was a one-way street and trying to discuss my sexual satisfaction or lack thereof went over like a lead balloon.

That's when I invested in several battery-operated boyfriends and readjusted my expectations to more accurately reflect the grim reality of college dating. It's a brutal landscape, marred with guys who either don't know what they are doing; don't care; or for whatever reason, can't get your engine revving.

At the end of the day, I don't want the guy who's going to ask if he can hold my hand. I want the one who's going to tear off my underwear, grab my wrists, and pin me to the wall. Preferably while whispering filthy things in my ear about what he's going to do to me next.

It's a bit of a problem.

Especially when Nash is the wrist-grabbing, wall-pinning, dirty-talking type.

"Violet?" a girl's voice asks.

"Huh?" I blink rapid-fire, and the library slowly comes back into focus. Fluorescent lighting buzzes overhead, illuminating the floor-to-ceiling shelves filled with worn books. The scent of old paper permeates the air, and there's a wicked cramp in my right hand. I set down my pen, which I've been clutching like my life depended on it.

Julianna gives me an imploring look. "You completely zoned out there."

"I'm tired, that's all. Didn't sleep much."

Offering her a weak smile, I shift my weight and try to ignore the liquid heat that's pooled between my legs. It's impossible. My black cotton thong is soaked.

In my Psychology of Human Sexuality class last year, we learned that men think about sex approximately twice as often as women—and ever since that toe-curling kiss with Nash, I've been giving even the horniest man a run for his money in that department. My daydreams about him have been constant, vivid, and filthy.

"Want to take a coffee break?" Julianna offers. "We could order it to go and take a walk around campus. It's gorgeous outside."

"Yes!" My voice comes out several times louder than is appropriate for the library, eliciting a glare from a blonde girl with oversized glasses seated at a nearby table. I lower my voice, leaning closer to Julianna. "That sounds great."

We make our way across campus to The Beanery, and 15 minutes later, I have a pumpkin pie latte in hand. It's The Beanery's version of the Starbucks staple, but it's superior to the original. It's also dessert in a disposable paper cup, but if I can't indulge in other vices like Nash, sugar and caffeine will have to suffice.

Afternoon autumn sun filters through the half-bare trees as we enjoy a leisurely stroll through campus, making small talk about school and our internship. It should be relaxing, yet it is decidedly not what I need. I won't be getting what I need any time soon, though, because that would be a Very Bad Idea.

"How are things with Marcus?" I ask Julianna.

The other night, I tried to broach about my misgivings regarding Marcus with her, but it was not well-received. To be fair, I don't have much to go off other than a gut feeling and belief that he exaggerates his hockey achievements. Neither is all that incriminating. She seems to really like him, so for now, I'm opting to be supportive while praying my intuition is wrong.

"Good." A smile plays on her lips, and she tips back her fall-themed cup, taking another sip of her white chocolate mocha. "We're going out again this Friday."

"That's exciting."

She steals a glance around us before replying, lowering her voice to a hush. Her hazel eyes scan across my face worriedly. "But don't you think it's unethical? It's a conflict of interest for me to date him, right?"

Unease settles in at her reminder, and I tamp down on it. "Marcus is with Preston. You're not training him. The rules only say you can't date your own athletes."

I feel like I'm calling myself out because unlike her situation, I am training Nash.

That's why nothing will happen.

Nothing can.

———

In the middle of nacho night, I finally decide to fess up to Claire and Jules about The Kiss.

Why, I'm not sure. Blame the carbs.

"Nash and I kissed," I blurt. "At Marcus's party last weekend."

Julianna whips her head in my direction, and the salsa heaped on her tortilla chip drips onto her lap. "That was two entire days ago. You're telling us this now?"

Next to me, Claire heaves a long-suffering sigh, biting into her cheese-covered nacho without a single word. It's a better reception than I'd expected, honestly.

Julianna busies herself wiping the salsa from her leggings for a few seconds, and then her gaze snaps up to me again, her hazel eyes wider than a hockey puck. "Oh my God. *That's* why you've been so spaced out lately."

I hug my knees into my chest, half-hiding my face. "I didn't know how to tell you guys. I didn't want you to be mad at me." Or to judge me for being an idiot.

"I'm not mad, I'm concerned," Claire says evenly. She pushes her plate aside, tucking her long legs beneath her. "Details, please. Who kissed who?"

"He hit on me in the training room one morning, so I pulled him aside at the party to talk about it. My intention was to give him shit but then it turned all flirty and hot, and he kissed me." I pile an aggressive amount of guacamole onto my tortilla chip, nibbling at it while they process my confession.

"Did you kiss him back?" Julianna presses.

"What do you think?" My cheeks burn hotter than a fireplace, and I bury my face in my palms. "Of course, I did. It's Nash. He's my own personal brand of heroin."

Ice cubes clink as Claire takes another sip. "I don't know what to say. I want to be supportive, but I don't want to see you get hurt again."

Her words strike a chord within me. Nash is the only guy who's ever truly hurt me, and here I am, putting myself out there for it to potentially happen all over again. It is uncomfortably close to the definition of insanity and yet, knowing that doesn't lessen the draw I feel to him.

"I'm neutral like Switzerland on this one," Julianna says, holding up her hands. "I don't know enough of the backstory to have an opinion or offer you advice. I just want you to be happy."

Dropping my hands into my lap, I look up at them. "Maybe he's changed."

"What if he hasn't?" Claire counters.

"I want to believe he has." Pushing my plate aside, I reach for a gingersnap from the Cookietopia box Julianna picked up on the way home. I bite into the spicy-sweet cookie, savoring the warm ginger and molasses flavors. It's soft and perfectly chewy, the way a cookie should be.

Swallowing, I add, "My brain is saying one thing, but my heart is saying something else."

"Just to clarify," Claire says, "is it your heart or your vagina talking?"

Good question. Based on my daydreams lately, maybe I'm being controlled by the wrong impulses. I would be lying if I said our chemistry wasn't clouding my judgment.

Then again, I know there's more to it than that. While spending time with him again has dredged up old feelings, there are new ones on top of those. I see that softer side to him that's always been there. Often well hidden, but there, nonetheless. That's the Nash I loved.

The one who held my hand all over campus even though the guys on the team gave him shit for being whipped. Who bought me a necklace with an amethyst pendant from Tiffany's while he was away for a tournament in New York City because it reminded him of me. Who used to sit and play with my hair, reserving all the yellow Skittles for me while we watched cheesy movies.

The one I made plans for the future with, who once promised me forever.

That Nash could be worth taking another chance on—especially if he's matured since then and his priorities are more in order. If he's ready to put the work into a relationship and all that it entails, it could be worth it. The problem is, he's always been a wildcard.

Nash will never be the safe choice.

"I don't know." I finish the last of my gingersnap, flopping against the massive heap of turquoise and lime throw cushions, contemplating Claire's question. "Maybe it's both. But they've got some strong opinions."

Claire leans over and grabs a dark chocolate-white chocolate chip cookie, waving it at me. "If you ask me, this is the equivalent of a dude thinking with the wrong head, Violet. Eyes on the prize. Think about your internship. Your career."

My heart does a slow descent, splattering at my feet. "You're right."

CHAPTER 23
APPLE CIDER AND STOLEN DANCES
VIOLET

FALL FEST IS a paramount LSU tradition held during the second weekend in October. It's a massive event boasting live music, fair food, and midway games, with all the proceeds going to the local children's hospital. Classes are canceled Friday, and everything on campus comes to a halt. With the exception of hockey. The team still had on-ice practice and dryland training this morning.

As Julianna and I walk through the gates, the scent of greasy fair food greets us. Guitar chords carry through the air from a local band playing on stage in the center of the grounds while people mill about with corn dogs, funnel cakes, and stuffed animal prizes.

"Spiked apple cider?" Julianna nudges me, pointing to the booth.

"Do you even need to ask?"

Drinks in hand, complete with caramel sauce, whipped cream, and a healthy dose of rum, we do a loop of the festivities. We grab some cotton candy before trying our hands at the cornhole competition, balloon pop, and pick a duck, but only Julianna wins a tiny giraffe. Although she kindly tries to console me by saying the games are rigged, we both know my hand-eye coordination leaves much to be desired.

When we turn the corner, we stumble upon the Mini-Grizzlies booth where kids get to play against 'the team' and get a stuffed

Griswold the Grizzly prize after. Nash and Vaughn are wearing their jerseys over jeans, playing ball hockey with two little boys who can't be much older than six or seven. Vaughn takes a shot on net, clearly not trying very hard, and the first boy blocks it. Then Nash lets the other boy get past him with the ball, pretending that he tricked him, while the kids howl with laughter.

It's adorable.

"This is pretty cute," Jules admits as we come to a stop, watching. I think Vaughn and Nash might be having as much fun as the kids. Meanwhile, I'm swooning over how cute Nash is. I've never seen him interact with children, and he's a complete natural. Between this and seeing him take care of a puppy, my ovaries are in overdrive.

A few shots later, the game wraps up with the Grizzlies 'losing' six to two. Julianna looks down at her phone and grimaces. "Oh, uh…Preston just texted to let me know he's here. Sorry, Violet. We'd been talking about attending this together for ages as the three of us, and I couldn't un-invite him. I'm going to go meet him at the front gates and then we'll see you at the stage?"

"Sounds good. I want to say hi to Nash first." Even though I probably shouldn't, especially after my talk with her and Claire last night. But we still have to see each other, so we can be civil, right? Friendly?

Fine. Not even I believe that, but I can't stay away from him. Especially after the heart-exploding cuteness I just witnessed.

Vaughn hands both of the boys their stuffed Griswolds while Nash saunters over to where I'm standing.

"Didn't expect to see you here," I tell him. He neglected to mention he'd be doing this, probably because he knew I'd come watch and see him being all soft.

"Voluntold." Nash props his stick upright, leaning against it, and his face brightens with a smile, like the sun peeking through the clouds. "It's for a good cause, so I don't mind."

"When are you done?"

He checks his black Apple watch. "About half an hour. Are you sticking around?"

"We're going to go watch the bands for a while. Reaping Glory is playing later."

"Nice. We'll stop by after Grant and Hanson show up for their shift." Nash nods to the spiked apple cider in my hand, forking a hand through his dark hair. "Just stay away from—"

"The basketball team," I finish, rolling my eyes and fighting a smile at the same time. Butterfly wings stir in my stomach. Despite my better judgment, I like his protective act a little too much. "Better yet, guys in general. Except for you, right?"

He grins. "Exactly."

———

By the time I arrive at center stage, several other hockey players have joined Julianna and Preston, including Marcus, who's standing with Jules, as well as Connor and Drew. I'd like to say things aren't awkward between me and Preston, but for some reason, tonight, they are. Maybe it's because of the kiss with Nash. Now that it's happened, I know there's no going back with Preston. Ever.

I'm forced to confront this head-on when I end up dancing with him. While he danced with Julianna for the song before ours, and our dance is perfectly platonic from an objective point of view, somehow the intent feels different when it comes to me. He doesn't say anything, doesn't do anything, but there is an undercurrent of something else; something more. A sickly guilt looms in my belly, because hurting him is the last thing I wanted to do.

Notes of the song die down, and we pull apart, stepping off to the side. I don't know if this is the right time or place to be doing this, but I don't want to lead him on, either. I'm trying to be fair to him, or as fair as I can be, considering what already happened.

"Pres," I start. "I'm not ready for anything serious right now."

As soon as the words leave my mouth, I silently kick myself. This is my way of breaking it to him? It's ineffective at best, and dishonest at worst. Sadly, I'm terrible with confrontation and will do anything to avoid it. The only person I have experience arguing with is Nash, and he's so infuriating that it's an entirely different ballgame. Nash could goad the Dalai Lama into a fight.

"I'm not trying to pressure you into anything." Preston frowns, running a hand through his dark blond hair. God, he's handsome. Normal. Nice. Why don't I like him?

And the fact that he's trying to be understanding only makes me feel worse.

"Yeah, but—"

"Hey, Vi." Nash strolls up, clutching a green glass bottle of beer in his large hand, and shoots Preston a look so hostile, you'd think they were enemy combatants on the battlefield.

Preston clears his throat. "We were in the middle of something, Richards."

"It's almost like that's the point, huh?" Nash smirks, but there's malice behind it.

I elbow him in the ribs. He remains undeterred. There's a lull, and an uncomfortable silence hangs between the three of us for several seconds too long. My life has officially reached peak awkwardness.

Preston glares at Nash before turning his gaze to me. "I'll talk to you later, Violet."

"Yeah, sounds good. Sorry about him." I jerk my thumb at Nash, though I can't decide whether I'm annoyed or relieved at the interruption. Either way, I feel bad about him being a jerk to Preston. While I'm used to Nash's prickly ways, most other people are not.

Nash steps closer, giving me an appraising once-over. "What was that about?"

"Nothing," I tell him. "Don't worry about it."

"Uh-huh." His jaw works for a beat, and then he sighs as if deciding to let it go. He inclines his head to the dance floor. "If you danced with Mr. Rogers over there, you definitely have to dance with me."

Heat laces my cheeks, and I blink at him blankly. Not because I don't want to dance with him, but because I'm not sure it's a good idea in front of so many people. How I feel is sure to be written all over my face. It probably already is.

Not one to be easily deterred, Nash doesn't wait for a response before he sets down his empty beer and takes me by the arm, steering me out onto the dance floor. His large, rough hand envelops mine, and his other hand slides to my lower back, exuding warmth through my thin fall jacket. I drape my left arm on his shoulder, lightly gripping as he leads.

With the sun rapidly setting, the lanterns strung around the perimeter have switched on, bathing the makeshift dance floor in dim, ambient light. It'd be romantic under different circumstances. As it is, something about it makes my chest ache.

A few steps in, his palm against my back slips a little lower, evoking a dull throb of longing between my thighs and a lightheadedness I can't blame on one spiked cider. The way he smells isn't helping, either. Clean and masculine, like temptation and everything I shouldn't want.

"Careful where you put that hand. I don't want people to think we're being inappropriate." I'm saying it for my benefit as much as his. The chemistry between us is so enchanting, his presence so overpowering that it eclipses nearly everything else, including my ability to think. If I let myself, it would be all too easy to forget we have an audience and nestle into the crook of his arm where I already know I fit perfectly.

"It's just a dance."

I glance up at him, and when our eyes lock, my pulse stutters like a polygraph. We both know there is no scenario where we are "just" dancing. I'm excruciatingly aware of how close we are, of the heat of his body against mine while we move together with such ease, it's like we were never apart.

The music winds down, but Nash doesn't let me go. I look up at him, questioning.

"That was less than half a song," he says simply. "Doesn't count."

When the band plays the next few notes, I immediately recognize it: it's a cover of The Dance, by Garth Brooks. The theme of the lyrics could not be more serendipitous. If the universe is sending us a sign, it's being awfully heavy-handed.

"My dad always used to play this song on his guitar when I was little," I tell Nash, trying to distract myself from the topic of us. "Before his arthritis got bad, anyway."

Sadness tugs in my stomach at the recollection. My father's rheumatoid arthritis isn't debilitating by any means; he still works as an accountant and has a normal level of functionality in most senses of the word. But when I was growing up, one of his favorite things to do was play the guitar for us after dinner, and I hate that he had that ripped away from him.

"Believe it or not," Nash says quietly, "I remember you telling me that before."

An avalanche of emotions crashes over me, stealing the air from my lungs. "You do?" It's a small detail, not one that I'd expect him to remember.

He expertly guides me in a turn. "We were in my dorm room, right before winter break."

"In the blanket fort."

It's one of my favorite memories from our relationship. We'd both finished our winter exams and his dormmate left for break early, granting us two rare, full days alone together before we had to split up and go to our respective families for Christmas. When I came over, Nash surprised me with a blanket fort constructed from artfully draped sheets and clothespins, decorated with soft twinkle lights and extra pillows that he'd bought. To this day, it's still the best blanket fort I've ever seen. Maybe that's the engineer in him.

We snuggled inside and streamed Netflix on his laptop while sharing Skittles and popcorn, making out so much that we missed half of what we were supposed to be watching. There was some sex thrown in there too, obviously, but it was more about the closeness and cuddling.

In addition to kissing for hours at a time tucked away in the fort, he took me skating beneath the stars the first night. Out to dinner at my favorite restaurant the second, and then to the see Christmas lights display downtown with hot chocolate for dessert.

That was when I knew I loved him.

And after he came back from winter break, there was a distance between us that never quite went away.

The bitter overtakes the sweet, sadness clawing at my throat. Snapping back to the present moment, I swallow hard, finding him watching me with his dark green eyes clouded over.

Nash's brow creases, something unreadable stretching across his face. "I'm sorry, Vi."

"For what?" I whisper.

"Everything." A terse frown brackets his mouth. "For how things ended. All of it."

The stitches holding my heart together split open at the words I've been waiting so long to hear. Truth is, I wasn't sure I'd ever get an apology, and it's validating and excruciating all at once. I loved him. Furiously, madly, passionately. And while he never said it, I'm pretty sure he loved me, too, which is why I still don't understand where things went wrong.

"You mean when you bailed on our plans for Easter to go on a road trip with your buddies?" My tone is sharper than I intend because it's still a sore spot, and it probably always will be. Breaking up would have hurt no matter what, but what he did at the end really twisted the knife.

"God, I was such a dick." Nash removes his hand from my back, running a hand along his square jawline before replacing it. His face tightens, his features imprinted with regret. "This probably won't make sense, but nothing I ever did was a reflection of how I felt for you or meant that I didn't care."

"Uh-huh." I huff to hide a sob that's threatening to wrench free, torn between hearing him out and resenting the message—because how much could he have possibly cared when he walked away so callously?

"I know this will sound like a cop-out, but the parent thing is… it's hard for me."

My breath sticks in my throat. He's never said anything like this before. Getting him to talk about his family is almost impossible. I could list what I know on one hand: he's an only child, his mother died of cancer when he was four, and he's not close to his father. The rest is a mystery.

"You mean because of your mom?" I ask softly.

Nash shrugs, breaking away from my gaze, and pulls me closer to him again. His lack of confirmation leaves me wondering what part of meeting my family was such an issue, and why. While he's hinted at not getting along with his father, I'm starting to think it might be worse than I realized. I know better than to pry, though. Slow progress is better than no progress.

Something in his demeanor shifts, and his grip on me tightens, deep voice turning gruff. "While we're on the subject of the past, why did you end up with Jay so quickly after we broke up?"

Beyond the predictable ire in his eyes, there's pain I don't expect to see. While I knew he was pissed about this, because that's his MO, I'd chalked it up to jealousy. I truly didn't realize it had hurt him. By the end, things were so hot and cold that it was difficult to tell whether he cared much about me in general.

Hesitating, I sink my teeth into my bottom lip. "It was a distraction, I guess, which was crappy of me." I'd feel guiltier about this if not for the fact that Jay turned out to be a raging asshole. Guess it's no big surprise my judgement wasn't stellar given my poor state of mind, still reeling and heartbroken. "But I couldn't take the back and forth with you anymore, so I decided to try to force myself to move on. Didn't work, though."

"It stung, Vi. I mean…I know I drove you away, but you were never replaceable to me."

My lower lip wobbles, my chest burning. That's it. I'm going to start crying in the middle of the dance floor.

"Trust me, you weren't replaceable to me, either."

He still isn't.

And that's the problem.

The last chords of the song fade out, leaving us standing on the periphery of the dance floor with unspoken questions and unknown answers. Off to the side, nearly all the team has gathered along with Julianna and Preston. Like I predicted, I'd all but forgotten where we are and what we were doing.

"We should get back."

His fingers circle my wrist, tugging. "Let's get a drink first."

As much as I want to be alone with him, I know I shouldn't.

"I can't ditch Julianna and Preston." It's a flimsy excuse when their backs are turned and they're immersed in conversation with the rest of the team. No one seems to notice or particularly care that we're missing. Preston probably isn't too thrilled with either one of us at the moment, anyway.

"It won't take long. My treat." He's already guiding me through the crowd because my protest is bullshit, and we both know it.

We reach the outskirts of the concert area, and I come to a screeching halt. "Only if you do your stretching and rehab for another month."

"A week," he counters.

"A month or no deal."

Nash's mouth tugs. "You drive a hard bargain. Deal."

A gust of chilly autumn air passes by, laced with the scent of smoke from the bonfire, and leaves on the ground in front of us swirl as the wind kicks up. I shiver and hug my wool coat tighter, but it does little to combat the bite in the air. Without missing a beat, Nash throws an arm over my shoulders, immediately warming me. While he's a good source of body heat, I'm burning up on the inside for another reason entirely.

We pass a group of sorority girls dressed in pink house tees, loudly chattering away. Three of them blatantly check out Nash, one of whom practically eye-fucks him, but his attention is focused on me. He has a way of making me feel like I'm the only girl he sees. Probably not the case, but it's fun to let myself pretend.

Then I wonder if that girl was one of the—allegedly many— girls he's slept with since we've been apart. While we both moved on, it sounds like one of us had a lot more moving on than the other. He's clearly been embracing the fringe benefits associated with being a high-level athlete for a long time.

It's not that I hold it against him, it's that it makes me nervous. I'm still not entirely sure what his intentions are when it comes to me, and with so much on the line this time, I would be risking a lot more than just my heart.

CHAPTER 24

WITH ALL DUE RESPECT

DRINKS IN HAND, I steer Violet in the opposite direction of the crowded stage. "Detour."

She huffs a soft laugh but doesn't protest. Probably because she knows me well enough to expect it by now.

Pumpkin-shaped lanterns light the path as we weave through the thinning fairgrounds, where vendor booths are closing up for the night and cornhole sets sit abandoned in the dark. Groups of rowdy students pass by, the foot traffic heading toward the sound of the live band playing.

"Where are we going?"

"For a walk," I say. "It's a nice night out."

"Uh-huh," Violet says, biting back a smile.

It's completely dark by the time we step out of the part of campus reserved for Fall Fest. I guide her over to a bench tucked away in the alcove of the library building, partially hidden by some trees. A streetlight shines through the branches above us, casting us in a pale circle of light.

I don't know what my plan is; don't have a real plan other than trying to get her alone.

"You didn't have to be so mean to Preston." She sinks onto the bench, angling her body to face me, and gives me her famous,

'you're an asshole' face. I'm on the receiving end of it a lot, generally warranted.

"Someone has to send him the message, and it doesn't seem like
you're going to be the one to do it," I say pointedly, setting down
our drinks. "But can we not talk about him? I've barely seen you
alone since..."

"...the bedroom incident?" she finishes, arching a blonde
eyebrow.

"You weren't complaining at the time."

"I'm not complaining now." Violet's wide eyes search my face,
her full lips slightly parted. I used to be able to read her so easily
but I can't right now, and I hate it. "It's just a lot. You're a lot."

"Not trying to be, Vi. I just fucking missed you."

Over two years later, I still haven't been able to replicate the
chemistry I have with her. With every other girl, there's always the
ever-present knowledge in the back of my mind that I'm not as into
it as they are. A looming sense that something is off, a pervasive
need to escape. My mind inevitably starts to wander, and I find
myself thinking about hockey or school or a million things other
than what I should be focused on.

I never lose my focus on Violet.

"You're beautiful." I brush a lock of hair off her forehead, and a
soft smile forms on her lips, her expression shifting into one that I
know well. Cupping her chin, I bring my mouth to hers. Her long,
dark lashes lower, her breath a gentle puff of air against my skin. I
pause, savoring the moment between the kiss and the before.

Anticipation wracks my body from head to toe until my hands
nearly tremble with need. As if drawn by magnetism, our lips crash
together and my entire world lights up, a rush of desire surging
through my veins. Violet lets out a little sigh, parting her lips, and
my tongue sweeps against hers, our mouths moving in perfect
synchrony. She tastes fucking delicious, like spiked apple cider and
traces of cotton candy. But there's an undercurrent of bittersweet, of
lost chances and wasted time, and I only have myself to blame for
that.

Emotions engulf me like tidal waves, overpowering and unrelenting. Desire, need, longing...Fear. But I have too much on the line to let that win. Two years is a long time to live in denial, and she's erased it in a matter of weeks.

She shifts her weight and leans in, pressing her chest against mine. The contact sends my body from zero to one hundred in a heartbeat, an effect only she's ever had. My hand slips beneath her coat, landing over her knit sweater, and she draws in a soft breath as I caress the familiar contour where her waist curves into her hip. It's like it was created specifically for me to hold her right there.

My body says, *her. This is the one, right here.*

My brain says, *you don't deserve her.*

And something clicks.

I know what's been nagging at me lately.

This is it. I'm in. I don't know how I'm going to do it, but I'll get her to give me another chance.

When we break apart, Violet's a little glassy-eyed. Dazed, like she always gets when she's aroused. From out of nowhere, her expression shifts into one of panic, sending me into it right along with her. What the hell?

Before I can ask her what's wrong, her brows draw together, and she shakes her head.

"No, no, no." She waves her hands, verging on frantic for reasons I still don't understand. Safe to say, this is not a reaction any girl has ever had to kissing me before. "I can't do this with you again."

I rest my hand on her knee, trying to calm her. "Can we rewind for a second? Where is this coming from?"

"This is a bad idea. You, me...Us." Her swallow is audible, and even in the low light, I can tell she's fighting back tears.

If this is cold feet, I'm not having it.

"Look me in the eye and tell me you don't feel anything for me."

Violet's eyes flick up to mine, her face stricken. "I can't lie, Nash. You know I do. But I'm not even allowed to be involved with you." She pushes to stand and begins to head back in the direction we came.

Adrenaline coursing and frustration simmering, I grab our drinks and catch up with her in two strides, working to stay calm because a fight isn't going to help my cause. That, and I've vowed never to be like *him*—to never lose control of my temper with someone I care about. For all our many arguments, I've never raised my voice to Violet, and I never will.

"Ward gave us the same spiel," I tell her. "Doesn't mean anything. They just want to make sure we don't act like idiots and cause problems at school."

She keeps walking, looking straight ahead, refusing to meet my eyes. "It's still a rule."

Dread grips me as the Fall Fest grounds come back into view, chords of music echoing in the distance. She's traveling at an impressive clip given her short stature, and I'm nowhere near ready to go back and face everyone with this hanging unresolved.

"With all due respect, Vi, fuck that. Are you going to let some arbitrary rule dictate how you live your life?"

Her voice climbs. "It's not arbitrary, it's meant to keep things professional."

"You and I know we crossed that line the day you started."

"It's not the same for me and you." She throws up her hands. "You'd get a slap on the wrist; a talking-to at most. I could be disciplined, lose my internship credit, or worse."

This is news to me. Violet has alluded to the rules here and there, but I assumed it was the same as it was for the team; window-dressing, a way to keep us in line without much teeth.

"Shit," I mutter, scrubbing my jaw. "I'm sorry. I had no idea they took it that seriously for the interns."

"Of course, you didn't. You're a hockey god. You could burn down the dining hall in broad daylight and the school would pretend it was an accident."

It's a little snarky, but in light of the situation, I choose to let it slide.

"There's nothing you can do? You can't ask to have me moved to someone else? Or I could, if you think that would play out better for you. I don't care if I catch some shit on my end as long as you're okay." That's my number one priority at this point: protecting her. I'm more than willing to take any blowback that could fall to me.

Besides, what are they going to do, suspend me from playing? Doubtful. Short of her "burning down the dining hall" scenario, the team needs me too much to do that.

Violet slows to a stop and takes a step back, keeping me more than an arm's length away. I want nothing more than to reach out and touch her, but I don't. My breath grows shallow, forcing me to consciously deepen it.

"I don't know," she admits quietly. Glancing down, she zips up her jacket, but I'm pretty sure it's an excuse to avoid meeting my eyes. "It's a bad look, at best. I'll seem unprofessional for getting involved with one of the athletes. Or for wanting to, depending on what I tell them."

"You're telling me you can't get involved with me because of this rule, even though there's a simple solution staring you in the face? This feels like an excuse."

"Look…" Violet trails off, looking behind me, and I know something bad is coming. "I can't upend my reputation for nothing."

The words hit me so hard, I feel like I just got blindsided with a check against the boards. By far, this is the harshest thing she's ever said to me. My natural instinct is to be harsh back, and it's taking serious self-control not to.

I huff, taking a sip of my beer. "Nothing? Damn, tell me how you really feel."

"Can you really blame me?" her voice climbs. "After everything that's happened, getting involved with you again is a gamble. The semester is only two more months. I just need some space until it ends."

This sounds suspiciously similar to "taking a break." No fucking thanks.

"Is that it?" I press, stepping closer and handing Violet her drink. She clutches it tightly, expression to match. "Or are you going to have a different reason then?"

Her lack of response says it all. I can't believe this is happening. How the hell did we do a complete one-eighty in the span of ten seconds? My frustration reaches a boiling point and despite my best efforts, some of it still escapes.

"I'm sure this rule doesn't apply to Preston, does it?"

Violet fidgets with the sleeve of her coat. "Nash. That's not it. Preston and I are just friends."

Are they? And does *he* know that?

I snort. "What kind of friend is he when he clearly has ulterior motives? Nothing you can say will change the fact that he wants to fuck you."

She props a hand on her hip, now in full-on defensive mode after my attack. "Kind of like you?"

It's no big secret that I'm crazy attracted to Violet, but that isn't the point at hand. I'm not in this to get laid; I could easily do that with someone else.

I resume walking, nodding for her to follow. Pissed as I am, the last thing I'm going to do is walk away and leave her standing here alone in the dark. Once I get her back to Julianna, though, I need to go take a long walk alone. Or go break something. Probably both.

"Difference is," I say slowly, "I'm not going to pretend to be okay with being friends. Unlike Preston, I care about you too much to lie about what I want."

"What is it that you want from me, Nash? Sex?"

It's a slap in the face. I just told her I cared about her, and this is the response I get?

My shoulders stiffen, mouth opening and closing. Drawing in a slow breath, I exhale to the count of five, and swallow words that are better left unsaid.

I realize that I hurt her—and on some level, I know that's where this is coming from—but it doesn't make it sting any less. She can blame the internship all she wants, but when it comes down to it, she doesn't think we're worth the risk. And I'm not talking academically.

With a few more wordless steps, we reach the edge of the crowd, and Julianna throws Violet a wave.

"Forget it, Vi. It's fine. You want space? You got it." I turn and walk away before saying something I'll regret.

CHAPTER 25

UNPLEASANT BY DEFAULT
NASH

THE BUS RIDE to our road game is misery on wheels.

Violet is sitting with Preston, Julianna is with Christina, and I want to punch both Preston and myself squarely in the face. In that order.

Instead, I pull out my phone to check in with Savannah about how puppy-sitting duty is going. I'm not sure why I'm so worried. He's an animal; he's going to be fine without me. And I'll be fine without him. Even if I might kind of, sort of miss his furry paws and smelly breath.

> Me: All good?

> Savannah: Yup. Thanks to your 100 page owners manual.

> Savannah: Just kidding, big guy. He's in good hands.

She's exaggerating; my instructions were only two pages. In my defense, Biscuit is particular about the cleanliness of his water bowl and deviating from his bathroom schedule can have disastrous consequences. Plus, I needed to make sure Sav knew about his fear of the vacuum cleaner. We have to store it in the closet when it's not being used, or he'll sit and howl at it.

Maybe I'm trying to cling to the only piece of my life within my control. Because everything else for the last week has been utter shit. Classes have been unbearable, training with Violet has been fucking miserable, and my game is off to the point where several guys have commented. I've been attending therapy like it's my part-time job, trying to untangle everything inside my head. Marie thinks I need to "put myself out there more" with Violet, but how am I supposed to do that when I tried and got blown to pieces?

Across the aisle from me, obnoxious pop music pours out of Connor's AirPods, volume turned up so high I can hear every lyric of his Justin Bieber song as clearly as if I were wearing them myself.

"Will you turn that fucking music down?" I swat his arm with my Hockey Today magazine. I thought sitting with Vaughn would buy me some peace and quiet, but that only works if everyone else exercises basic common sense.

Connor makes a face, pulling an earphone out and hitting pause on his phone. "You're miserable, you fucker. Do you need to get laid, or what? I mean, you're unpleasant by default but you're really taking it to a new level lately."

Vaughn leans over, voice low. "It's not really a sex thing, Haas. Cut the guy some slack."

"He's caught feelings," Drew adds solemnly. "Four-letter feelings."

I don't even bother protesting. Maybe he's right. Whatever it is, something is seriously wrong with me. I can't focus on hockey, I can't focus on school, and I can't focus on anything *but* Violet when she's around. Because I enjoy mind-fucking myself, I've still been driving her home. She even came over to visit Biscuit once. It was about as tense as one could imagine.

"Damn." Connor studies my face. "If this is what love does to you, consider it a hard fucking pass for me."

He's got a point there. This seems like a whole lot more trouble than it's worth. Too late for that now, though. Can't just turn off these feelings, however inconvenient they may be.

"Can you please turn it down before I flush those AirPods down the bus's toilet?"

"I will if you figure your shit out."

I lean back in my seat, closing my eyes. "I don't even know where to begin."

———

Our Friday evening game goes well, at least. I utilize a few strategies Coach Ward taught us recently to keep my head straight and experience a good degree of success. With my mind focused on the game, I put in a solid effort that contributes to our win despite the situation with Violet. I also somehow manage to avoid breaking Preston's kneecaps with my stick, which takes some serious self-control after the bus ride down.

When we return to the hotel, Coach Ward holds a miniature team meeting, reminding us about curfew before dismissing us. All the guys head to the hotel lounge to hang out until then, leaving me to linger in the lobby while I try to sneak back up to my room unnoticed.

"Come on," Connor prods, jerking his thumb to the bar behind us. "Come for a drink."

"Not in the mood. Gonna call it early."

His eyes land on a pretty brunette headed to the lounge, her curvy hips swaying as she walks by, and he loses his will to argue with me. "Fine. Suit yourself."

Relieved, I walk over to the bank of elevators and head up to my floor. And as luck would have it, Violet is standing in the hallway when I step out. Because, why not?

Unfortunately, my hotel room is down at the far end, which means I have to pass her.

"How's your shoulder doing?" she asks quietly, shutting the door to her room. While the team has to double-up, the athletic trainers got singles—probably because Preston can't share with the girls, and they're trying to make it fair.

I reluctantly come to a stop, wishing we hadn't crossed paths.

Talking to her like this hurts too much. It's easier to ignore each other, and even that's brutal.

"Slightly better." It's the truth. I've been doing more stretching and rehab like she said to, and it's mitigating my issues. I'm not sure it's making huge leaps forward, but at least it isn't getting worse. "The rehab exercises you told me to do seem to be helping."

She flashes me a nervous half-smile. "Good. Are you going to keep up with it?"

"I told you I would, didn't I?"

Confusion blinks across her face, like she doesn't know what I'm referring to. I said I'd do it for a month when I made her come get a drink with me. Regardless of how poorly that turned out, I'll keep my word.

"Fall Fest," I remind her.

Realization dawns in her eyes, along with something I can't place. One of the worst parts of this situation is, I can't seem to gauge what's going on in her head. Does she hate this space bullshit as much as I do? Then again, that's probably wishful thinking. It was *her* idea.

"Nash, I'm sorry—"

My shoulders go rigid, throat closing. The only thing worse than Violet's rejection is her pity.

"Let's not get into this again, okay?" I hold up my hand to cut her off. "I got the message the first time."

She opens her mouth to respond and then closes it again, her lips pressing into a thin line. Silence floods the hall, neither of us speaking. Thoughts and emotions war in my brain, a brutal battle with no clear winner. There are so many things I'd like to say; things I wish I *could* say, but I don't know if she wants to hear.

Finally, she nods. "Okay."

I have a split second-urge to apologize to her, too. To tell her she's all I've been able to think about ever since I saw her that day in the training room. To try to convince her we're a risk worth taking, even with the department's bullshit rules. But it's followed by an even stronger urge to self-preserve. If she doesn't want this, I can't force her to change her mind, and I don't think I can take it if she shoots me down again.

"I should go," I tell Violet.

Stepping past her, I continue to my room. She watches me retreat, and I can't shake the feeling I'm fucking everything up with her for a second time.

CHAPTER 26

VANILLA SUGAR
VIOLET

THE ROAD TRIP has been a success. It's Saturday evening, the team has won both games, and no one has been injured. Everything has been running smoothly. Everything except for my relationship with Nash, which is going as smoothly as a spike belt.

To celebrate the team's winning streak, Coach Ward and Christina take everyone out for a team dinner. I have no appetite, but it didn't seem possible to decline without seeming rude or raising a red flag. Reluctantly, I sit near the head of the table with Preston and Julianna; as strained as things may be between me and Preston, they're a million times better than they are with Nash. Even seated on opposite ends it's impossible to completely ignore each other. He keeps catching me looking at him, and I keep catching him looking at me.

As we're ordering our main courses, Nash pulls out his phone and checks the screen with a frown, evidently declining a call. He does the same moments later. A few seconds tick by, and he glances down at his phone again. His entire body visibly tenses, and he gives a near-imperceptible shake of his head. He snatches his phone off the table and pushes his chair back, wordlessly stalking out of the dining room.

"Violet," Christina says, leaning closer. My attention snaps over to her and concern overtakes me. Did she notice me staring at him?

"You did a great job assisting Coach Ward with the dynamic warm-up this morning."

I force a smile, reaching for my glass of ice water. "Thank you."

We discuss shop talk while we wait for our main courses to arrive, including a new ACL rehab protocol Christina learned about at a conference, but it's only a partially effective distraction. Worry swirls in me, growing heavier the longer Nash is gone. He doesn't return until well into our meal; my steak is half-eaten, stuffed potato nearly finished. Was it a girl? Who else would be calling him over and over like that? I hate that I don't know. I hate that I *want* to know. I hate this situation, period.

———

When we get back to the hotel, there's a team bonding event at the hotel pool. Should be easy enough to avoid Nash doing that. Jules and I change in our rooms and meet at the elevator to head down-stairs together.

The only snag? In addition to our team, the hotel is hosting several groups attending a cheerleading convention nearby, and they've also opted to make use of the pool facilities. I like to think I'm reasonably comfortable with my body, but sporting a string bikini in a room full of toned, perky competitive cheer-leaders would give most women at least some degree of insecurity.

Coach Ward stands off to the corner, talking to Christina while they supervise the raucous scene. Along the periphery, the enor-mous pool deck is surrounded by lounge chairs and tables with umbrellas, people lounging about. The aqua-tiled pool is filled with athletic bikini- and board-short-clad bodies playing beach ball, tag, and other thinly disguised excuses to flirt. Our team is in heaven. The ratio is heavily in their favor.

"Come on," Julianna says. "I see a free table we can put our stuff at."

Trailing beside her, I scan the festivities, covertly looking for Nash. I come up empty-handed until my eyes land on the hot tub, and my stomach implodes. There he is, sitting with Connor—and four drop-dead gorgeous girls.

One downside of having dated Nash before is that I know exactly what most of the single (and some of the not-so-single) guys do when they're on the road: hook up. And I'm scared I might be looking at it right now.

I avert my eyes and return my attention to Jules. "Want to swim, or just relax?"

"Let's go swim with Marcus and Preston." She juts her chin to the far corner of the pool. "They're over there by the waterslide."

Preston greets us with a warm grin, utterly oblivious to my fragile state of mind. For a while, I manage to fake having fun to a convincing degree, playing keepaway with him and some of the other guys. But he ducks out early to discuss tomorrow's off-ice warmup plan with Christina and Coach Ward, leaving me with a bunch of athletes I don't know very well while Jules and Marcus are caught up in their own world.

My attention keeps swinging back to the hot tub like some form of twisted self-torture. One girl in particular seems to have taken an interest in Nash. A blonde; she's pretty, with bigger boobs and a whole lot less cellulite than I'm sporting. Every time I glance over, she's moved a little bit closer. Now, she's nearly sitting in his lap, batting her eyelashes up at him. When she throws back her head, laughing, and touches his forearm, nausea mows me over, followed by a sudden desperation to escape. I can't be here. Can't watch this. Can't pretend everything is okay.

"Jules?" I catch her eye, fighting to steady the wobble in my voice. "I'm going to call it a night. I was up super early to go for a run with Claire yesterday, and I'm still feeling it."

She throws me a wave, squealing as Marcus scoops her up and hoists her onto his shoulders. It seems like nearly everyone in the pool is paired up or pairing up, which cements my decision to leave.

My pulse thunders in my ears as I dry off and wrap the towel around my chest, stepping into my sandals. I yank open the glass door without looking back, a little afraid of what I might see if I do. Flip-flops slapping my heels noisily, I stalk over to the bay of elevators and hit the 'up' button. To my relief, the metal door springs open with a cheerful ding. I press '4' for my floor, then jab the 'door close' button repeatedly to move it along.

In the mirrored wall next to me, my hair is wet, bare face tired. I look reasonably composed, but my mental state is hanging by a thread. Luckily, in a minute or two, I can have a breakdown in the privacy of my hotel room. Maybe I'll hit up the vending machine on my way so I can cry into a bag of potato chips and chase them with some chocolate.

Just before the door shuts, a large hand reaches out and trips the sensor, forcing it to slide back open. My inhale catches when Nash appears in the doorway, his dark hair wet and muscled torso bare, a black t-shirt and white hotel towel slung over one shoulder. A fire ignites in his dark green eyes when they lock onto me, and he storms inside, smashing the close button on his way by.

He continues forward, forcing me to shuffle back to keep a buffer between us. I bump into the handrail along the wall, and he takes another step, eliminating the cushion of space. Behind him, the door slides shut again at a glacial pace. My heart hammers, striking my ribcage so hard with every beat that I'm certain he can hear.

The instant the elevator car jerks upward, his hands land on my bare waist. He yanks me against him, a shocked gasp slipping through my lips.

"There could be cameras in here," I remind him breathlessly, skin heating beneath his claiming grip. I wish being in his arms didn't feel so good.

He gives me a dark grin. "Do you think I give a fuck what the front desk sees?"

From experience, I know the answer to that is no. Nash isn't an exhibitionist, per se; he doesn't get off on the idea of being seen, he just doesn't care.

"What if someone we know is waiting at the top?"

"Everyone's still at the pool."

I shoot him a warning look. With a sigh, he releases his grip, but he doesn't step back.

"Fine." He prods his cheek with his tongue as he considers me. "But we need to talk, and I'm not taking no for an answer."

The angel on my shoulder says I shouldn't do this. But the devil on the other side knocks her right off with a hockey stick, and I nod. "Okay."

While I go to my hotel room, Nash hangs back under the pretense of going to his, making sure the coast is clear. I use the alone time to quickly comb out my hair, which is tangled and knotted from being in the pool. As I'm working out the last knot, there's a quiet knock. Comb in one hand, I hesitate for a split-second. I don't know what I'm doing, but leaving him to stand out there and potentially be seen is not an option, so I snap to my senses and rush over to open the door.

Nash brushes past me in a wave of chlorine, much like I imagine I also smell. His broad upper half is still bare, taut muscles on full display, V-cuts leading to his deep blue board shorts. I linger in the doorway, momentarily incapacitated by his closeness and his near state of undress. His fingers wrap around mine and gently pry my hand off the door handle, pushing it closed.

He tosses his towel and shirt aside, pivoting to face me. Despite the gentleness of his touch a moment earlier, he's clearly pissed. What's his deal? Why is he mad when he's the one who's been ignoring me for the past week?

"Why did you just bolt out of there?" His dark eyes spear me, refusing to let me evade the question.

I shuffle away from him, and my heel hits the wall behind me. "Other than the fact that you won't even look at me?" It's a fumbled answer, the best I can land on with emotions running so high.

"Are you serious?" He takes a wide step back, incredulity stretching across his face. "I'm trying to stay away from you like you asked."

"That's not—"

"That's exactly what you said."

But it isn't what I want. Seeing another girl all over him made that crystal clear. Maybe I'm the one playing games. That wasn't my intention; I didn't expect to get so tangled up in my feelings for him. Now that he's standing in front of me, I want him more than ever.

"What's the real problem?" Nash places a hand on the wall above my head, peering down at me with a knowing look. A welcome contrast to the chill from my damp bathing suit, waves of warmth roll off his body, urging me to nestle in the crook of his neck. I catch myself about to lean in, and stop before I do.

"Violet." An edge creeps into his voice.

My cheeks flare with heat, a byproduct of frustration and embarrassment. I've cornered myself and I don't know how to get out, short of telling him the truth.

"You were flirting..." *with that girl downstairs.* The words wither on my tongue, an admission that I care more than I want to let on.

A smirk plays on his lips. "You know, I don't think I've ever seen you get jealous before. It's hot, for the record."

"I'm not jealous."

"You're a bad liar, Vi. Always have been." His pupils dilate as he traces the string of my turquoise halter top with his finger, leisurely traveling back and forth from my shoulder to my neck. "We can set aside the fact that I had to put up with Preston drooling all over you in this bikini. I wasn't interested in that girl. I was playing wingman for Connor so he could hit on her friend."

I know he's telling the truth—and I feel stupid for it.

"Then why did you leave?" I ask, trying to ignore my nipples hardening beneath my bikini in response to his touch.

"Because you looked upset, and I was worried about you."

A boulder forms in my chest, climbing into my throat. "After the way we left things between us last time we talked, I thought you might be moving on."

His hungry gaze rakes over my body before lifting to meet my eyes. The tension between us winds tight, binding our bodies closer together until he's sandwiched me flush against the wall. Liquid heat pools between my legs, my breaths coming out in shallow pants. With only my tiny bathing suit and his thin board shorts between us, I can feel everything; every sculpted muscle, every hard angle, and every thick inch of his erection pressing into my bare stomach.

"I said I was giving you space. Not that I was giving up."

"I don't like space," I whisper.

"I fucking hate it." His large hand slips around the small of my back, and he ducks his head, lowering his mouth until it's hovering above my own. My pulse careens as our breaths mingle, anticipation surging to a new high. Instead of his lips finding mine like I expect, he hangs back. The kiss I'm waiting for never comes.

His eyelids hood. "You come to me, Vi."

I already know this is more than just a kiss; this is everything.

And when it comes down to it, I would risk a hundred heartbreaks to have him again.

I rock onto my toes and place my hands on his broad shoulders, pressing my lips to his. Nash draws in a jagged breath, wrapping his arms around my body as his tongue slides against mine. Beneath the desire, there's an undercurrent of relief. We're finally giving in to what we both want.

Cupping my ass, he lifts me up against the wall with a thump. My arms circle his neck, legs wrapping around his waist. He kisses me until I lose my breath, my bearings, and my awareness of anything other than the two of us.

"Fuck, I want you." He palms the flesh of my backside, pulling me against him in perfect rhythm with the sway of his hips. Energy thrums between us, growing by the second as barely tethered power courses beneath the surface of his skin. "Need you."

My head falls back against the wall, and my eyes drift shut. "I need you, too."

Need isn't a strong enough word to describe it.

Slowly, he eases me onto my feet. Dark hair tumbles over his forehead as he snags the tip of his tongue between his canine teeth, studying me with pure, unadulterated desire across his face. Nothing compares to the way he looks at me. It's raw and feral, passionate and filthy.

Nash angles his head, and his gaze coasts down my body,

lingering on every dip and curve. A blaze ignites in his dark eyes. "Four bows."

"Four what?"

His gaze snaps up to mine. "That's the only thing standing between me and your naked body. Two bows on the top, two on the bottom."

My breath stills as he reaches up, playing with the tie at my neck, but he doesn't undo it like I'm expecting. Sliding across my shoulder blade, his rough fingertips land on the tie at my back, gently snapping it against my skin. His rough palm surfs down the side of my ribcage, sending a thrill through my entire body. A single finger slides between my bare left hip and the bow, dipping beneath the waistband of my bikini. Goosebumps erupt on my skin as he leisurely drags his fingertip along my lower stomach, all the way to the bow at my right hip.

I'm so turned on, it's a miracle my bikini doesn't take itself off.

Mesmerized, I watch him, waiting for him to continue and untie them, but he doesn't.

Nash brackets my face with his hand, his grasp firmer than I'm expecting. "What's our word, Vi?"

It takes a second to register what he's asking. It's been a long time since we used it. Since I used one, period. No one else I've been with shared the same proclivities, and even if they had, I wouldn't have trusted them enough to try.

My pulse goes haywire. "Vanilla."

"Good girl." He releases my face, stroking my damp hair. "And if your mouth is full?"

"Tap three times," I whisper, wondering what exactly he has in store for me.

"I'm in charge unless you safeword me, agreed?" Nash raises his eyebrows, eyes searching mine for confirmation.

The thrill this gives me is out of this world.

"Agreed."

From top to bottom, the ties go one by one, until I'm standing naked in front of him. Dipping his head, he lavishes my breasts while he glides a fingertip across my soaking folds, cursing softly about how wet I am. He thrusts a thick finger inside, followed by another, sending off fireworks in my core, and we both groan.

His thumb presses my sensitive bundle of nerves, delivering a sudden overdose of pleasure. I whimper, shamelessly writhing against his hand as the pressure in my core builds. He works me like an instrument he's played his entire life until I'm overheating, completely at his mercy. I can't see straight, can't think straight, can't focus on anything but what he's doing to me.

When I can't take it anymore, his touch idles, keeping me right on the precipice. Nimble fingers stroke me again, teasing me until I beg. I'm close, but we both know he's not letting me get off yet. He's just getting me so hot that my judgment is absolutely inciner- ated before he gets me near the bed. And it's working.

"Please," I whimper. My back arches off the wall, hips pressing into him needily.

He tsks, slowing his caresses even more. "When do you get to come, Violet?"

"When you say so."

"That's right."

Nash withdraws his fingers, leaving me achingly empty. Grab- bing me by the waist with a sudden ferocity, he hoists me up, effort- lessly tossing me over his shoulder. The wind knocks of my lungs, and the hotel room turns upside down.

"Put me down." It's a breathy, half-hearted demand, one that we both know I don't really mean.

"Will do." In a few long strides, he covers the distance to the bed. His large hand slides between my shoulder blades, supporting my upper body, and he flips me right-side-up. Setting me down, he places an elbow on either side of my head, hovering over me.

His green eyes lock onto mine, dark with desire and sinful promises, but his mouth tugs into a playful half-smile. He's always been a study in contradiction. Rough but gentle; hard but soft; hot but cold.

I regain my ability to breathe normally. "You still like throwing me around."

"You still like it when I throw you around."

I try to shift beneath him, but he's got me fenced in, pinned between a mattress and a wall of solid muscle. "I forgot you were big enough to crush me."

His expression softens. "I won't."

Maybe not my body; my heart is a different story. It's about to get steamrolled. Again.

Burying his face in my neck, he trails his nose along my skin, sending a wave of goosebumps cascading down my arms. He inhales deeply like he's trying to savor me, letting out a growly exhalation.

"What's wrong?" I comb my fingers through his damp hair, confused by the way he's suddenly come to a halt.

"I'm a mess over you," he murmurs. "You don't even seem to realize it."

My throat pulls tight at his unexpected confession. "Based on how I rushed out of the pool earlier, I'm not exactly the picture of stability."

Nash lifts his head, and when our gazes meet, my heart thumps against my ribs. "You don't need to worry about other girls, Vi. I want you so bad I can't fucking see straight."

"You've got me now." In truth, he's had me all along.

"Yeah." He grins, lowering his mouth to mine. "I do."

CHAPTER 27

CINNAMON SPICE
VIOLET

HOT, wet kisses circle the base of my throat while my fingers explore every sculpted inch of Nash's body above me. Mapping, reminiscing, savoring. I'm shocked by how much I remember. The scar on his back from a bike accident when he was a kid. The tiny birthmark on his shoulder. The inked, intricate tattoos along his right shoulder, which now extend the full length of his arm.

Fumbling, I untie the string closure of his board shorts, yanking them down his hips. He slips them off before kneeling between my legs again, heavy erection digging into my lower stomach as he covers my lips with his. I'm soaking and aching, expecting him to take me. Instead, he breaks away and presses his mouth to my neck, then my collarbone, leisurely working down to the swell of my breasts.

Soft, dark hair brushes my bare skin as he travels lower, worshipping every inch of my bare torso before landing on my hip. Nibbling and biting, he soothes away the sting with his tongue, marking my skin with his kisses.

Moving inward, his stubble scratches my upper thighs, then my lower stomach. The pulse between my legs flutters as I squirm beneath him, desperately waiting and wanting, nearly out of my mind with need. His tongue drags along the sensitive skin of my inner leg, nearly reaching the apex of my thighs, and reality comes crashing back down.

"I was in the pool," I protest, sitting up on my elbows and scooting back slightly. "I haven't even showered."

Then again, this is the guy who used to feast on me like a five-course meal after I came home from the gym, sweaty Lululemon gear and all. He also regularly went down on me after sex without a second thought.

Nash cocks an eyebrow, a glint of reprimand in his eyes. "Are you safewording me?"

"No." I fall back against the pillow, breath snagging as he dips a finger into my soaking heat, dragging it across my clit. *Oh, that's good.* My toes curl with ecstasy, all thoughts vacating my brain. The next words come out on a sigh of pleasure. "Not—at all."

"Then give me your pussy, Violet."

Eyes locked onto his, I nod slowly, too consumed by the heavy ache low in my belly to argue any further. His strong hands grip my thighs, parting my legs to him, and heated, primal desire stretches across his face.

"So perfect." He traces my slit, watching my pelvis tilt, greedily seeking more.

My self-consciousness melts away as he teases me with soft kisses and not-so-soft scrapes of his teeth, grazing my pubic bone and outer edges, deliberately avoiding where I want him most. Heated breath rolls across my skin, promising of more without delivering. Each additional second is torture, my core throbbing with need until it's almost too much to bear.

Finally, his mouth closes over my swollen bundle of nerves and I jolt, crying out. He dives in, caressing me in a decadent pattern of swipes and flicks, taking me higher and easing me down like an endless rollercoaster of pleasure. He isn't doing this because he thinks he should. This is a man devouring me because he gets off on getting me off—and it shows.

My hands sink into his damp hair, tugging at the roots to pull him against me, and a low, primal hum of approval vibrates in his chest as he continues to ravage me with precise, skillful strokes of his tongue. Needy whimpers escape the back of my throat, and I clamp a hand over my mouth to stifle them. I can't remember whose hotel room is next door to mine. Hell, I don't know my own name. All I can do is try to be quiet, but he's not making it easy. He's relentless and demanding, somehow dominating me even with his face buried between my legs.

In no time at all, I'm hovering on the brink and desperate for release. My hips begin to sway instinctively, and he plunges two fingers inside my soaking entrance, demolishing me with a renewed intensity. His fingers curl up and press against the perfect spot, sending me through the stratosphere. Overcome by the sensation, my back arches, and the movement pulls my body away from him. He growls and roughly yanks me back down, wrapping his other arm around my thigh to lock me in place against his face.

Incandescent pleasure ebbs and flows, each peak higher than the last, until I reach the summit and fall to pieces. A sob slips through my lips, my body trembling beneath him. Just when I think it's too much, he wrenches another wave of euphoria out of me with his mouth, wringing me out until I'm completely spent.

Nash eases me down slowly, kissing back up my body and trailing his lips along my neck, smiling against my shoulder. "Your pussy tastes even better than I remembered, especially when you come. You should sit on my face next time, though. I miss that view."

"You have such a dirty mouth."

"That's not new." A cocky smirk plays on his lips. "And you like it."

"Maybe." I shift, widening my legs so he can settle between them, desperate for our bodies to connect. Frantic need thrums through my veins, heating my skin. All I want is to have him inside me, filling me, stretching me, pounding me until he's so deep I feel him everywhere.

He kneels between my parted thighs, gripping my upper leg in one hand and fisting the base of his thick shaft with the other. "Did you miss my cock?"

"You know I did."

Brow furrowed in concentration, he presses the tip against my slick entrance, watching my reaction. I fist the sheets and squirm against him, trying to meet him halfway, but he pulls back. A low rumble reverberates in his chest as he rubs my clit with the head of his cock, sending another tremor through my core.

"Condom," he murmurs, watching himself push inside the slightest fraction of an inch. My body begs for him to keep going, but he stops.

"I don't have any," I admit. This wasn't exactly planned. "I'm still on birth control, but…"

Nash leans on one forearm and hovers over me, his expression sobering. His fingertip ghosts across my cheek, brushing my lips. There are a million things written across his face: fondness and admiration, desire and lust, even a hint of protectiveness.

"I've never done that with anyone else, Vi. And I haven't been with anyone since we got tested during our physicals at the start of the season, so I know I'm clean. But I'm not going to pressure you into anything."

"I haven't done that with anyone else, either. I trust you."

He glances up at the ceiling like he's praying. "Thank fuck." His gaze lands back on me with a wicked grin, and my heart skips with anticipation.

Our eyes stay locked as he slams inside me in a single, brutal thrust. My nails bite into his shoulders, and I cry out at the sudden loss of space, pleasure mingling with a hint of pain. He's not small —in any department—and I'm not used to his size anymore.

"Sorry, Petal." Forehead pressed to mine, he stills, buried inside of me from base to tip, his girth stretching me even more than I remembered. It's a snug fit that fills me completely, bringing us skin to skin, as close as we can possibly be.

"Ease me in a little before you rail me."

"I will." Nash claims my lips with another kiss, his tongue sliding into my mouth, coaxing the tension from my body. My walls relax around him, and we both groan as he starts to rock against me, the head of his cock nudging that perfect spot. This time, it's all pleasure, no pain.

Wave after wave of sheer bliss crashes over my body, slowly melding together into a blur of euphoria. This. This is all I want. In this moment, I don't care about the past, the future, or what I'm risking. If it means having him, I'll do it ten times over.

He pulls out slowly, driving back in with a thrust that's expertly angled to hit exactly where I need him. My eyelids flutter shut, head tipping back against the pillow. I haven't been properly fucked in as long as I can remember. Actually, I can remember—it was the last time I was with him.

"Christ, Vi. Has your pussy always felt this good?" He clenches his jaw, watching himself sink inside, abdominal muscles rippling with each thrust. "I think it was made for my cock."

Too overwhelmed by another rapidly approaching climax, my only reply is a breathy moan.

When he kisses me again, it's needy; rough. I meet his every thrust, nails raking down his back while he angles his mouth against mine, biting and tasting. He palms my thighs and lifts me off the bed, plowing into me, rubbing against my clit with every undulation.

I cinch my calves around his waist, frenzied with need. "Oh, God."

His palm connects against my ass with a smack, strong hand kneading away the sting before gripping me even harder, guiding me up and down on him. "God's not here."

It's too much, not enough, and everything I need all at once. My eyes squeeze shut, fingertips digging into his shoulders. Pleasure swells in my center, expanding until it explodes into shards of brilliant ecstasy, and I unravel beneath him for a second time, whimpering and pulling the sheets clean off the bed.

Nash clamps his hand over my mouth with a low chuckle, muffling my cries. "We need to work on your volume control."

I barely have time to recover before another knot forms in my center, pulling tighter with his every plunge. Animalistic ferocity gleams in his eyes as he pins my arms over my head with one hand, circling both of my wrists between his fingers in a bruising grip. He works me with savage determination, pummeling me with a punishing pace. Each drive of his hips charges the electricity pulsing in my core, voltage growing brighter and brighter.

"That's it, Vi." He fists my hair at the roots with his free hand, and my walls flutter around him. "Come again for me like a good girl."

The combination of his filthy encouragement and divine pain is like touching a live wire, and everything detonates again. A sob wrenches from my lips, followed by a string of unintelligible whimpers begging or thanking him or some combination of both, and I lose myself in him completely.

I'm still in the throes of my own orgasm when he slams into me with such force that it steals the breath from my lungs, driving the headboard of the bed into the wall.

"Dammit. Why do you have to be so—" With another snap of his hips, the headboard hits the wall again. "Fucking." He pulls back, plunging into me with another crash of the furniture. "Hot."

Releasing my wrists, his mouth crashes down on mine and he grabs my hips, holding me down. We both cry out as he drives into me one final time. A tremor runs through his body, and he buries his face in my neck with a low groan, throbbing between my legs with release.

Nash half-collapses over me, supporting his weight. "Holy shit." His mouth slides along my jaw. "I missed that."

"I did, too."

I have never been so thoroughly fucked in my life. In more ways than one.

Still buried inside of me, he wraps an arm beneath my waist and rolls us over, facing each other. Intertwining our top hands, he kisses the side of my wrist, emerald eyes tracing my face.

Something unspoken passes between us, but I'm afraid to let myself believe it.

He hauls me even closer, and I nestle in the crook of his neck, savoring the warmth of his smooth skin against mine, the steady thud of his heart against my cheek. As much as it might surprise other people, Nash is world-class at cuddling.

After a few more minutes of sweaty snuggling, he presses a kiss to my temple and shifts, reluctantly separating our bodies. "Hang tight, beautiful."

Nash rolls out of bed, striding into the bathroom without a single shred of self-consciousness. My eyes stay glued to him the entire time because his sculpted ass and hamstrings are a work of art, the broad taper of his torso geometric perfection. There should be a marble statue of him in a museum.

The tap switches on in the bathroom, and he returns a moment later with a warm washcloth, carefully wiping my inner thighs. When he dips between my legs, I draw in a soft breath at the stimulation from the terrycloth where I'm still sensitive and now a little sore, and his touch gentles even more.

My hands sink into his thick hair, playing with it affectionately. "You're still sweet, you know that?"

"Just cleaning up the mess I made." He sets the damp cloth aside, brushing his lips against my neck, right below my ear. Warm breath fans my skin, sending tingles down my spine. "But I like knowing you'll have a reminder of me between your legs for a while."

His gaze drops to my lower body again, and he sucks in a breath, gently tracing the red hickey blooming on the outside of my hip. "Damn, I marked you good. Does that hurt?"

"No. At least it's where nobody can see."

Nash quirks a brow. "Maybe I should put some where they can."

"Better not," I whisper. "We aren't even supposed to be doing this."

Pulling me into him again, he growls in frustration and rolls onto his back, staring at the roof. He's quiet for a moment, his chest falling with a long, slow exhale. "I know what I said before, but I didn't mean it, Vi. I'll respect your wishes if you want to wait until the semester ends. I'm not going anywhere. Or with anyone, if that's what you're worried about."

There's a pang in my heart because despite what I said to him at Fall Fest, that isn't what I want. I know that's not what he wants, either. After so much time apart, I can't imagine letting more slip away.

"I don't want to wait. We just need to be careful." At least, going forward. What we just did is the very definition of "not careful."

Nash's fingertips trace my upper arm, lightly tickling my skin in the best way. "I'll do everything I can to make sure you don't get in trouble. Promise. And if it ever comes down to it, I'll take the heat so you don't."

Tiny half-moon divots marking his upper arms catch my eye, raised red scratch marks along his shoulder. "Uh-oh. Think I got payback for that hickey you left behind."

"Huh?" He cranes his neck, his mouth pulling into a smug grin. "Nice. I didn't even feel that."

I drag the tip of my finger along his tattoos, studying the artfully shaded pictures and intricate designs. Some of them make sense to me, like his hockey number; a stick; and a pair of skates. Others I have to ask him to explain because the significance is less clear. I bypass a set of numbers that I'm fairly certain is the date his mother died without mentioning it.

Then I spot writing incorporated along his bicep, tracing the letters with my fingers. "Memento mori, amor fati," I read aloud. "Latin, right? What does that mean?"

"Remember death, love your fate."

"That's a little bleak." Yet oddly fitting, for him. He's one of the most unafraid people I know.

"I think it helps me keep my priorities straight." His hand glides along my belly, cupping possessively between my legs. "Like right now, my priority is your tight little pussy."

I giggle. "How are you still horny?" His refractory period is nearly non-existent; maybe it's an athlete thing.

"I'm always horny for you. Especially when you're laying here, freshly fucked, with me dripping down your legs." He fills me with a finger, followed by another. My mouth falls open on a whimper as my core flutters, thighs clenching. "There's nothing hotter."

CHAPTER 28
AFTERSHOCKS
NASH

IT'S 1:42 A.M., and Violet is curled up on her side facing me. Her smooth, bare curves are pressed against my body, and her top hand is still intertwined in mine, the way she fell asleep. The hotel room is silent aside from her hushed inhales and exhales, punctuated by the odd burst of noise from out in the hall. She's been asleep for a while, but I've been lying awake in the dark with my thoughts.

I should be happy right now.

I *want* to be happy.

But I'm not wired to be happy. And sometimes, getting what you want is the scariest thing of all—because I'm afraid I'm going to lose it again.

Which is one reason I haven't let myself doze off, even for a minute. I'm trying to soak up every single second of this time with her. Still, I have a game tomorrow and much as I don't want to drag myself out of this bed, I know I need to sleep at some point.

"Vi? I've gotta go." I untangle our hands and give her a gentle shake, trying to rouse her. The last thing I want to do is leave and have her think I ghosted. But unlike me, she sleeps like the dead. One time, the fire alarm went off in my dorm and she slept right through it. I had to wake her up, which was no easy feat.

"Hmph?" Violet mumbles groggily, hand landing on mine in the dark. "No, don't go."

I gently rub her upper arm, wishing more than anything I didn't have to. "Trust me, Petal. I don't want to, but I have to get back. Coach will kill me if I get caught staying out overnight, and I don't want you to get in trouble, either."

She yawns. "'Kay."

The bed shifts beneath my weight as I slide out, pushing to stand. I want to get right back underneath the covers with her but instead, I pull up the blankets and tuck her in, planting a kiss on her forehead. Already asleep again, she doesn't even stir.

Using only the sliver of light pouring beneath the door as a guide, I locate my board shorts and T-shirt on the floor, tugging them on. After giving the hall a once-over, I quietly slip out, heart pummeling against my ribs.

If I get busted, I'm screwed.

Several of the longest seconds of my life later, I slip back into my room. Vaughn is out cold in the bed next to the window, oblivious to my entry. He's nearly as heavy of a sleeper as Violet. Still surfing on adrenaline from the fear of getting caught, I climb under the covers and lie awake in the dark, worrying about all the ways this could go wrong.

———

Once I finally crash, I crash hard. Despite two alarms and Vaughn's attempts to wake me, I sleep until the last possible minute. If we didn't have another game scheduled, I'd skip breakfast to stay in bed longer, but there's no way I can power through three periods on an empty stomach.

When I head down to the hotel restaurant, I'm one of the last on the team to show. Violet is in line at the buffet and unsurprisingly, Preston is standing way too close to her. Fucking guy. She and I exchange a silent glance, which is all we can do. Then I shoot daggers at Preston with my eyes while I demolish two plates of food, wishing I could stab him with my fork instead of my breakfast sausage. He, of course, remains blissfully oblivious.

On the bus home after our final game, Julianna immediately

goes and sits with Christina, which leaves Violet with Preston again. Is Julianna on Team Preston or something? What the fuck? Either way, I'm sure he doesn't exactly mind. If he were any closer to Violet, he'd be sitting in her goddamn lap.

I wish he knew she was straddling me naked less than twelve hours ago.

My mind flashes back to her lips. Her moans. Her breathy pleas. Every part of my body is screaming, *mine*. But I don't know if that's true. I don't know where we stand. In the heat of the moment, we did a little too much fucking and not enough talking. Sure, we agreed to keep things between us discreet, but we never defined anything beyond that. While I may not be able to tell the world she's mine, I still need to know she is.

Unfortunately, Violet has a paper due at midnight. It'll be tomorrow night before we even have the chance to talk.

Due to an accident on the main highway, our bus takes an unplanned detour, turning onto a secondary road full of curves and bends. A few minutes into the route, I steal a glance at Violet because she gets motion sickness sometimes. She's doubled over in her seat, and her fair skin has taken on a ghastly pallor. Worry shoots through me, compounded by massive frustration with the situation. The fact that I can't go over there and take care of her fucking blows.

Connor leans over the aisle, poking me with a pen. "Richards? Hello?"

"What?" I swivel to look at him.

"I said, thanks for playing wingman last night. You did me a solid. Brandi took me back to her room and let me nail her with her uniform on. It was fucking hot."

"Sweet," I mutter.

He tilts his head. "What's your issue now?"

"Nothing. I'm just tired. That hotel mattress was trash." Slouching in my seat, I continue to keep an eye on Violet, who looks like she might throw up any minute. Preston leans in closer, rubbing her lower back as he says something to her, and I have the urge to rip the armrest off my chair. I should be the one helping her.

"No shit, Vaughn said you were late as hell. Where did you disappear to, anyw—oh." Connor's eyes track over to where I'm looking, and he laughs. "You were with her, weren't you?"

"Zip it, you dick." I try to punch him in the ribs from across the aisle, and he dodges me.

We're in the back row. Vaughn is napping, Drew is reading, and the row directly in front of us is filled with freshmen absorbed in Dungeons and Dragons or some similar kind of game. Even if they did overhear, they would have to be incredibly stupid to repeat anything. Still, I don't need that risk.

The nail marks down my back attracted a side-eye or two in the showers after the game this morning, though. I'm not the only guy who got laid last night, so it's not like that sticks out in isolation, but my previous threat to maim anyone who looks at Violet makes those dots a little too easy to connect.

Connor nods to Violet, lowering his voice. "You're jealous over our country club friend over there. Nice to see that you have feelings like the rest of us."

"No."

"You tell me how it is, then."

I draw in a slow breath and exhale, balling and unballing my fists. Not sure what it says about me, but I don't want to tell anyone what happened with Violet, high level version or otherwise. And I am definitely jealous of Preston.

"Why are you worried about him?" Connor asks. "You don't actually think he's hitting that, do you?"

At the start of the semester, I wasn't too sure. Now? Not a chance. Preston definitely has a thing for her, but I don't think Violet feels the same way. After last night, I'm more sure of that than ever. So why doesn't she tell him to get lost?

"No," I admit, craning my neck to check on her again. The bus has been on a straight stretch of road for a minute or so, and she looks slightly better. "I don't. But I still want him to take a fucking hike."

Connor and I are interrupted when my phone vibrates in my

pocket. Apprehension washes over me. Anyone I would want to text with is sitting on this bus.

I'm pleasantly surprised to find a video from Savannah of Biscuit living his best puppy life romping in the backyard, diving into a pile of fallen leaves. And eating them because, well, that's how he rolls. She also reports that he made a "girlfriend" at the dog park—Coach Ward's dog, Moose, who was there with his wife. Pretty fucking random but hey, maybe our dogs being friends can score me brownie points.

Wait. Not that Biscuit is my dog. My foster dog, I mean. Because like I told Violet, it's temporary. Though I have to say, nearly all of the potential adoption candidates have been abysmal. I wouldn't give those people a cactus, let alone a puppy.

Another message preview pops up while Savannah and I are texting, and my pleasant surprise takes an unpleasant turn.

> Doug: Remember that Russell will be attending the Ice Cup.

> Me: Already made note of it.

> Doug: Graham, Benson, and Smyth attending also. The more eyes on you, the better.

Graham, Benson, and Smyth are my father's friends. Don't ask me how he has any. Graham and Benson are pro scouts for Florida and St. Louis, respectively, and Smyth is a freelance hockey writer for all the major industry publications. He also writes independent consultancy reports on prospects for the league.

In a vacuum, my father wanting "eyes on me" could be construed as a well-intentioned parent looking out for their child to ensure they have a backup plan. In reality, it's because he has no faith in me. He is convinced my contract with Chicago will fall through. Getting dropped is always a big worry for players who've been drafted and having him reinforce that fear doesn't help.

A shadow blocks the sunlight, and Coach Ward appears in the aisle between me and Connor, catching my eye. "Richards. Let's go have a chat."

A chat? I rarely worry, but right now, I'm pretty fucking worried. Even Connor looks worried.

Pushing to stand, I grab my water bottle and follow him to the front of the bus, past the other athletes and athletic trainers. I try to steal a glimpse of Violet as I pass, but Preston is blocking my line of sight. There are four vacant rows in front of them, and Coach Ward leads me to the very front, gesturing for me to sit first. I take the window seat and brace myself for the worst possible scenario.

He eases down next to me, keeping his voice low. "So, Violet."

And we have hit the worst possible scenario squarely on the head.

"What about her?" I give him a blank look.

The only silver lining to this exchange is Coach has a whole lot more discretion than Connor, and between that and the noise of the engine up front, no one else can overhear. Still, that won't be of much comfort if I've ruined Violet's entire academic career. Maybe there's some way to throw myself under the bus while saving her.

"You dated before, didn't you?" Coach Ward asks.

I get the sense he's giving me just enough rope to hang myself with, so I opt to be truthful rather than tighten the noose with a lie. "Yes."

He nods thoughtfully. "I thought she looked familiar, but I couldn't place it at first. You two were inseparable freshman year."

This reminder hurts in a way I'm not expecting. In light of what happened last night, I'm not sure why I still have so much regret over the past. Maybe because I'm not sure I can forgive myself until Violet forgives me first.

I take a sip of my water to buy myself some time. "I didn't think—we didn't think it was going to be an issue."

"Is it an issue?" His dark brows lift.

"No," I say. "It's totally fine."

As if calling me out on my lie, the bus hits a bump in the road, violently jostling us both. My water bottle falls out of my hand, rolling under the seat.

"But you're involved again," he observes. "You followed her out of the pool last night."

Fuck me.

My blood pressure must set a new world record while I sit there, looking at him like a dumbass, completely lost for words.

"I don't know how to answer that," I admit, reaching down and fumbling for my water bottle, my fingers finally landing on it.

"Look, Richards." Coach Ward scans our surroundings, his voice stern but not severe. "I like Violet, and I'm not here to ruin anyone's internship or chances at graduation, nor am I going to tell you what to do on your own time. But make sure you keep it professional on the clock going forward, okay? My discretion ends if it becomes a problem."

A slight sense of relief sinks in. Ultimately, Coach Ward is a stand-up guy. I do believe that he won't say anything as long as I don't fuck up. And with the stakes this high, I won't.

"Thank you, Coach. I will. You have my word."

He dismisses me, sending me back to my seat. Violet, who looks much healthier than before, throws me a questioning look on my way by. I try to nonverbally reassure her. In truth, I'm not sure I should even tell her Coach knows. Christina doesn't seem to, and if he's not going to tell her, then it will only stress out Violet for nothing.

Guess I'd better keep my hands to myself in the training room, though. And on the road, if they travel with us again.

When I ease back into my seat, Vaughn turns to me. "What the hell was that?"

He's the only person I trust with the truth on this one. Fortunately, Connor is arguing with Drew over whether Vegas or Seattle is a better expansion team. This one is a no-brainer, but trust Connor to pick a losing argument. Sometimes I think he enjoys playing Devil's advocate just for kicks.

"Coach knows," I say tersely.

He ducks closer, his worry shifting to alarm. "Seriously? Are you fucked?"

"No, not as long as we keep it professional on school time."

"Phew." His shoulders sag. "Close call, though."

"Tell me about it."

Because I can't catch a goddamn break, Doug texts me again.

Doug: Speaking of the Ice Cup, make sure you show up in top form.

Me: Don't worry, I will.

Doug: You'd better. I don't need you embarrassing me.

I grip my phone harder, wishing I could toss it out the window. Better yet, at his head. Telling me to show up in top form? What the hell is that about? With Russell—the guy who could singlehandedly make or break my career—in attendance, does he think I'd decide to fucking phone it in? Thanks, Doug, I was planning to be a total pylon, but now I'll make sure I try.

Hands down, I would take an utter absence of interest in me over his constant lack of faith.

CHAPTER 29

GIVE ME A CHANCE
VIOLET

"NEW PERSONAL RECORD for both of us." Claire high-fives me as we climb the stairs to our place, sweaty and short of breath from our training run. "I'll shower quickly so you can get in there."

With one full bathroom between the three girls, we're forced to prioritize. Claire has an evening class, which takes precedence over my plans with Nash. I'm not sure she's thrilled that I'm seeing him, but she seems to have accepted it for now. She's even dropping me off at his place on her way to campus.

While Claire and I stumble through the door still blotchy-faced from our run, Julianna is also blotchy-faced—wearing head-to-toe ratty sweats, surrounded by junk food and a mountain of tissues on the couch. It's her version of my bathrobe mode, and something is seriously wrong. Claire heads directly down the hall to the shower, so she doesn't notice.

"Jules?" I slip off my running shoes, sitting beside her on the couch. "What's going on?"

She lifts her chin, hazel eyes reset and bloodshot. "It's M —Marcus."

Oh, no.

"What about him?" I ask carefully.

"We fooled around on Saturday night, and now he's acting like I don't exist." Her voice cracks, turning squeaky. "He went from texting me every day to completely blowing me off. Total radio silence."

Irritation ripples through me, along with a sickening confirmation. I knew I didn't like him.

She didn't tell me about this over the weekend, though it's not a huge surprise—on either front. I tried to warn her about Marcus, but I didn't have anything solid to go on other than a gut feeling and some heavy hints to offer, which didn't have much convincing power.

Still, I feel bad for leaving the pool when I was upset about Nash. Maybe if I had been there, this wouldn't have happened.

Jules doesn't have any experience with casual hook-ups, either. She's a serial monogamist to the core, and probably thought she and Marcus were going somewhere more serious, which means she is going to take this extra hard.

Julianna reaches for a fresh tissue and blows her nose. She grabs the fuzzy pink blanket off the back of the couch, cocooning herself in it. "I hate men."

Sympathy floods my veins, because I know that feeling all too well.

"Me, too, Jules." I rub her upper back, trying to think of what to say. I don't have a lot of personal experience with being blindsided like this early on. I've hooked up with a few guys casually, but I was never all that into it or desiring a repeat performance, so the outcome didn't matter. Maybe Nash was a good security system for my heart that way. One big break instead of several small ones.

Still, what she's feeling is totally valid. Marcus is a dick.

"It's Marcus's loss. You're a catch, even if he's too stupid to see it."

Julianna giggle-hiccups. "The sex wasn't even that good. He was counting his thrusts like they were reps in the gym."

Despite the situation, I snort a laugh. "Seriously?"

"Like, *one*." She grunts, imitating him. "*Two*." She grunts again, cracking up as she does.

"Oh my God, Violet. It was awful."

"Did he keep track of sets, too, or did he just keep a running total?" I can barely breathe, I'm laughing so hard.

Jules guffaws through her tears. "He didn't last long enough for me to find out."

We both collapse into a fit of laughter and she wipes away another tear with the corner of her hand. Random hookups are never worth it, in my limited experience. It's not that I think they're wrong on a moral level, it's that the sex tends to suck. Then again, I guess this kind of thing could happen with a new boyfriend, too. How disappointing would it be to really like a guy, only to find out he treats sex like a set of bicep curls? Would it be a dealbreaker? I could never take that seriously.

"And get this. Then he argued with me over whether I finished." Her voice climbs, and she waves a tissue in exasperation. "Like I wouldn't *know* if I had an orgasm?"

Guessing that means Marcus hasn't seen enough real orgasms to know the difference.

"You dodged a bullet, Jules."

"I know you're right, but it still hurts. I had this big, stupid crush on him and now he's completely blowing me off. I should be the one blowing *him* off." She sniffles, reaching for the open bag of mini-Reese's Peanut Butter Cups on the couch beside her, offering it to me. "How did you do it?"

"Do what?" I unwrap a tiny chocolate cup, popping it into my mouth. After a long run, the sugary peanut butter hit is so good, it practically makes my eyes roll into the back of my head. Probably not the ideal post-workout fuel, but that's what makes it taste so good.

Julianna eats three chocolates before responding, unwrapping a fourth. "Handle seeing Nash. I mean, I know things are different now, but at the start of the semester when things were tense between you two, how did you act like everything was okay? You seemed totally fine in training, even though I know you weren't."

Funny, because I was falling apart on the inside.

"Did I? Because I sure as hell didn't feel it." I pause, trying to remember. "I guess I just faked it."

"I don't know how to do that."

"I'm not saying it's super healthy, but I crammed my feelings down, ignored them as best I could, and cried when I got home. We also went through a lot of wine at the start of the semester," I point out. "Like, several bottles."

Her forehead furrows. "Okay. I can do that. Minus the alcohol intake."

"Good call." It's an admittedly unhealthy strategy. "Maybe you can get Preston to give Marcus an extra-grueling training plan as punishment. Burpees until he throws up, something like that."

Julianna laughs. "I totally should."

———

I'm not entirely sure whether I'm coming to Nash's for movie night or "movie night."

I'm not sure what we're doing, period.

Claire's white sedan pulls away from the curb as I draw in a breath, pressing the doorbell to Nash's house. While I know we need to discuss things, part of me is afraid to. Is he even looking for something serious? He hasn't exactly been relationship-minded since we broke up.

Nash opens the front door a minute later, interrupting my thoughts, and a tiny ball of fur launches itself at my legs.

"Look at you!" I bend down, scratching Biscuit's velvety ears. "You've gotten so big."

Biscuit stands on his hind legs, hopping and trying to lick my face. I scoop him into my arms, noting the weight he's gained already. Nash took him for a round of immunizations before the road trip, and the vet estimated he'd reach eighty to ninety pounds when he's fully grown, possibly more. At the rate he's going, it won't be long until he's too big for me to pick up.

I kiss the top of Biscuit's furry little head before I set him down, and he scampers inside the house. His stride is a little clumsy, almost like he hasn't yet grown into his gigantic paws. Cutest puppy in the world, hands down.

"He's grown so much."

"Because he eats everything in sight," Nash says, shutting the door behind me. "Even if it isn't food."

Stepping closer, he wraps his arms around my waist and picks me up. The warm cotton of his sweatshirt surrounds me, his cologne going straight to my head. Our lips collide, and his tongue sweeps into my mouth. A thrill runs through my entire body as our embrace escalates from gentle to heated, carrying on far longer than a simple hello kiss.

Breaking away, he squeezes me tighter, a satisfied hum resounding in his chest. "Missed you," he murmurs, kissing me again.

I smile against his lips. "It's only been one day."

He sets me back down. "Two days since I was able to kiss you."

True. We couldn't say a proper goodbye in the middle of the parking lot with the team yesterday.

"We have the place to ourselves," he adds, taking my coat and bag, hanging them on a hook by the door. "Vaughn's babysitting. I told Connor and Drew to make themselves scarce for the night."

His large hand wraps around mine as he leads me down the hall, and his expression shifts into something I can't quite read. The muscles in his jaw are tense, the cords in his neck tight. It's almost like he's nervous, which is incredibly rare for him. I can count the number of times I've seen him anxious on one hand.

Before I have the chance to ask him if something is wrong, we round the corner and my gaze lands on a huge structure in the middle of the living room.

Every single wall around my heart crumbles to dust.

"Oh my gosh." I step closer, admiring his handiwork. "You made us a pillow fort?"

A pillow fort on steroids might be more accurate. It's a work of art. White sheets draped atop a furniture frame form the walls and roof, with one side left open to the flat-screen TV. Inside, there are twinkle lights strung around the top and flameless candles on the floor, both casting the space in a warm glow. The floor is covered with stacks of pillows, a tray filled with all of my favorite snacks off to the side. It's dim and cozy, not to mention incredibly romantic.

It says more than a million words ever could.

"If I can't take you on a date in public, I figured I should do something else." A lingering hint of nervousness beneath his half-smile endears him to me even more. "Though it took twice as long as it should have because *someone* kept destroying it."

As if on cue, Biscuit trots into the fort with a stuffed monkey in his mouth.

"Thank you." I swallow, blinking back the moisture pooling behind my eyelids. "This is so sweet. I love it."

He rubs my lower back tenderly, dropping his forehead to mine. "Gotta say, tears aren't quite what I was going for."

"They're happy tears." I bury my face in his chest, circling my arms around his waist for a hug. He plants a kiss on the crown of my head as he squeezes me back. Once the urge to cry has passed, I add, "Let's go snuggle."

We duck beneath the sheet, and Nash lowers to sit on the floor, widening his legs. His arms wrap around my waist, hauling me down with my back against his chest. He rests his chin on my shoulder, his temple pressed to mine, and I get butterflies without a single kiss.

Underneath this canopy, closed off from the rest of the world, it feels like nothing else matters. For a few moments, neither of us speaks. I shut my eyes, reveling in the way we fit together, snug and secure, perfectly matched.

Nash nuzzles my cheek. "What do you want to watch?"

"You can choose." Truth be told, I'm so happy curled up like this together that I could watch paint dry and love every minute.

"No, you pick."

I hesitate briefly because I want to see a new romantic comedy that came out on Netflix last week, but I know it's not his thing. "Trapped in Heaven?"

"Done," he says, reaching for the remote.

An hour and a half later, Biscuit is asleep at our feet while we cuddle beneath a fuzzy white blanket atop a pile of pillows. We've finished our popcorn and have moved on to the jumbo bag of Skittles. Nash pours a handful into his palm, fishing out the yellow Skittles and handing them to me. I eagerly accept them because they're the superior flavor. Anyone who says otherwise is crazy.

The movie credits roll across the screen, and he closes Netflix, switching back to cable. It's tuned to a hockey game midway through the first period. New York is playing Chicago—the team that drafted him—but he doesn't comment on it, so I don't, either.

"I can't believe you don't like yellow Skittles," I tell him, popping them into my mouth. "They're the best kind."

Nash utters a sound of disgust. "They taste like Lemon Pledge."

"When did you eat furniture polish? And they taste like lemony sunshine, thank you very much."

"Whatever you say, Vi." He grins down at me, his emerald eyes dancing playfully. "We both know you have questionable taste in candy and movies. Don't even get me started on your music."

He's got me there. Even I know my taste in music is bad.

"Admit it. You were totally invested in that movie. You wanted Elle and Ryder to end up together, too."

"Maybe a little," he admits, rubbing the back of my hand with his calloused thumb. "It was better than some of the action movies Connor and Drew make me sit through. Those are nothing but three hours' worth of explosions and gunfire with zero plot."

"There's always the hot girl consolation prize, at least. You know, with the obligatory shot of them running in a tight white tank top during an action scene to show off their boobs."

"The only tits I'm interested in seeing are yours."

I laugh because it's kind of sweet. In Nash's way, at least.

He groans, surfing his palm down my thigh. "Speaking of that, these fucking yoga pants make your ass look unreal. I want to bite it." His fingers trace the inner hem at my knee, desire stirring in my core as he inches upward. My leggings are so thin, it's almost like he's touching my bare skin. When he's halfway up my thigh, a frown overtakes his face, and he stops abruptly. "On second thought, come here."

Shifting his weight, he pulls my legs into his lap, readjusting us both so we're facing each other. The energy in the dimly lit tent transforms, taking on a sudden weightiness. He cups my face, and his eyes bounce between mine, filled with uncertainty. I can tell he's trying to build up to saying something, but I don't know what.

"What's wrong?"

"Not a single thing." The uncertainty across his face vanishes, replaced by determination. His dark brows knit together. "Give me another chance, Vi. A real chance. No more one foot in, one foot out."

My teeth sink into my bottom lip, and my eyes well up again. His words hit hard because that's exactly what I've been doing— holding back to protect myself, although it hasn't been working. There is no playing it safe when it comes to love; it's a contact sport for your heart.

Falling for him again is a foregone conclusion.

I'm so head over heels that I think I might be permanently upside down.

CHAPTER 30

I'M SURE
NASH

TALKING about my feelings has got me so far out of my comfort zone that I can't even fucking see it. I feel like I'm on the edge of a cliff, about to do an epic faceplant onto the ground. But the only way out is through, and it's on me to get us there. I can man up and give Violet what she needs. What she deserves, frankly.

Violet blinks up at me, her blue eyes glistening. A lone tear slips out, rolling down her cheek, and I brush it away with my thumb.

"Good tears or not, I wish I could stop making you cry so much."

She sniffles, looking away as she pulls the blanket higher around her waist. "It's nice to know the other night wasn't just about sex to you, that's all. It meant something to me, but I wasn't sure…"

"For the record, it has *never* been 'just sex' with you," I tell her, gently angling her face back up to mine. "Sex makes me feel closer to you, sure. But you could remove it from the equation, and I would still want to be around you all the time."

"You would?"

"Of course." I love spending time with Violet. She's one of the only people on the planet who doesn't annoy the shit out of me.

She studies me, and her forehead crinkles like she's searching for an answer to something she hasn't yet asked. Her pink tongue darts out, moistening her lips, but she doesn't say anything. My heart clenches until my ribs ache, praying this doesn't turn into a repeat of what happened at Fall Fest. If she bails on me again, I'll be fucking gutted.

"Talk to me, Vi," I say hoarsely.

Her throat bobs with a swallow. "I want to be with you, but I'm afraid you're going to pull back like you did last time."

Even though I know that won't happen, I can understand why she's worried. Difference is, I'm better at compartmentalizing Doug now. Not perfect, but I won't let him fuck with my head when it comes to Violet again.

My father chuckled, pushing away his empty dinner plate. "You have a girlfriend? You can't be that stupid."

"What's the issue?" I asked, fighting to keep my voice level. Coming home for Winter break was a mistake. Should have taken Grant up on his offer to hit up his parents' cabin in Aspen. Snowboarding and chilling in a hot tub would have been better than dealing with Doug for five days. But he'd cut me off in a heartbeat if I even seriously considered doing that, so here I was.

"You need to focus on hockey, not some puck bunny."

My hands clenched into fists beneath the wooden table. "Violet isn't a puck bunny." This was why I didn't want to tell him. And I didn't—but privacy wasn't a thing in this house, and he overheard me talking to her on the phone.

"You don't think she actually likes you, do you? Don't be naïve, Nash." He tsked behind his glass of whiskey. "What have I always taught you? Women look at hockey players and see fame and dollar signs."

There was a kernel of truth to this. At eighteen, I'd already been surrounded by fake friends and jersey chasers for several years. That's how I knew Violet wasn't one of them.

"I get your concern," I said evenly, "but she isn't like that."

His expression hardened as he assessed me. Not like a parent looking at their child, but like someone evaluating a defective product.

"Guess this explains how poorly you've been showing up in your games. I thought you were serious about making it, but apparently not."

"I am serious." Why else would I have made hockey my entire life? Ever since I got to college, I'd been killing myself on the ice. While Coach Ward was thrilled with my progress, Doug was impossible to please.

He pushed his chair back, shaking his head. "Your priorities are out of order, son. No wonder you got passed up in the draft."

After five days of being torn down from morning until midnight, I arrived back at college in a full-on tailspin. Then, stupidly, I sabotaged myself until I ran our relationship right into the ground. But I won't fuck this up twice. I won't let myself.

Shoving down the bitter memory, I take Violet's hand and press a kiss to the heel of her palm. "Let me caveat this by saying, this isn't an excuse. What I did was shitty, but things were different back then. I was young and immature. And honestly, I got scared."

"Scared of what?"

"Lots of things. Fucking it up. Not living up to what you needed. Losing you." Her expression remains curious, lacking any judgment, and it gives me the courage I need to keep talking. "I know none of this makes sense when I say it out loud because it was a self-fulfilling prophecy. I'm working on it. Not saying it's fixed, but I understand it a little better now, and that's the first step."

Surprise flickers across her face. "Working on it? What do you mean?"

An imaginary fist winds around my throat, constricting my airway until I can barely breathe.

"In therapy," I finally force out. It's amazing how uttering a few simple words can be more difficult than any physical feat. "Coach sent me after my injury because I wasn't coping well. Hockey is my outlet for things, and I was a little lost without it."

We may never touch on the parts of therapy that involve Doug. I try to shelter Violet from his existence as much as humanly possible.

Violet nods slowly. "How do you know you're not going to get scared again?" Her voice is so gentle, it almost hurts. She's always been good to me, even when I don't deserve it.

"I'm scared now," I admit. "But I'm here, and that part won't change."

Scooting closer, she presses a soft kiss to my cheek. This time, she turns my face to hers, her expression uncharacteristically stern. "If this is going to work, I need you to be honest with me and tell me if there's a problem instead of withdrawing."

"I will. But speaking of problems, I need you to handle something for me."

"What's that?"

An undercurrent of irritation flickers within me at the memory of the bus ride home. "You need to deal with Preston because if he touches you like that again, I'm going to break his fingers, and that might interfere with his career plans."

"Touches me?" Her forehead crinkles in confusion. "You mean, on the bus? Preston was trying to make me feel better so I didn't throw up all over the aisle. For everyone's sake. He wasn't doing anything different than Claire or Julianna would have."

Cute that she thinks that, but I know how guys operate. He saw an opening, and he took it.

"I'm serious, Vi. Dude needs to be set straight. If you won't, I will, and I won't be nearly as nice as you."

It isn't that I think he has a shot. It's the fact that *he* thinks he has a shot that bothers me.

Violet gives me a withering look. "I assure you, it's not a thing. But if it makes you feel better, I'll talk to him. In fact, I *was* trying to talk to him at Fall Fest until someone interrupted us."

"Don't regret it, and I'd do it again."

"I know." She laughs. "That's the problem."

I trace her bottom lip with my index finger. "To be fair, I really wanted to dance with you."

Placing a hand on her upper back, I ease her down against the pillows. Her blonde hair spills across the white fabric as she looks up at me, her pink lips slightly parted. While sex wasn't my goal tonight, I can't stop myself from leaning in for a brief, candy-flavored kiss.

When we pull apart, vulnerability gleams in her blue eyes.

"Are you sure this is what you want?"

"Never been more sure of anything in my life," I tell her.

CHAPTER 31
MORNING RULES
NASH

THANKS to our hectic and wildly incompatible schedules, my quality time with Violet over the past few days has been limited to driving her home. While it hasn't been ideal, at least I get to kiss her when I drop her off now. That's been enough to keep me flying high until I get to see her later tonight.

It's had a spillover effect into the rest of my life, too. I've been crushing it on the ice all week. Classes are suddenly far more tolerable. Even my shoulder feels better than it has in months.

"'Sup." Connor strolls into the kitchen wearing nothing but a pair of navy boxer briefs. Frankly, I'm just thankful he's wearing those. It's been harder to housetrain him than Biscuit.

I hit send on a good morning text to Vi and lock my phone, returning to my half-eaten bowl of oatmeal. "Not much. You?"

"Got laid again, huh?" He pulls out a container of Greek yogurt from the fridge and peels off the lid, turning back to face me with a smirk.

"What are you talking about?"

Connor leans against the counter, pointing at me with his yogurt-covered spoon. "Are you fucking kidding me? You *never* talk to me in the morning."

Fair point. With the exception of practice and dryland, I have a strict no-talking, leave-me-the-fuck-alone policy in effect prior to nine a.m. on weekdays. Noon on weekends. Given that it's seven-forty-five a.m. on a Friday, I would normally level a death glare at anyone who dared to attempt conversation.

He adds, "You've been downright nice lately. Pleasant, even. The only logical conclusion is that you're getting some on the regular."

Vaughn appears with a silver travel mug in one hand, giving Connor a shove as he walks over to the coffee maker. "Told you, Haas. It's not a sex thing."

Getting laid last weekend certainly didn't hurt my mood. But Vaughn is right; in this case, it's not a sex thing. Violet and I didn't even fool around when she slept over Monday night. After seeing how insecure she felt, I wanted to prove that wasn't what mattered to me. It was nice, in a way—reminded me of when we started dating.

Don't get me wrong. Nostalgia is great and all, but I'm definitely hoping to fuck her tonight.

"Is Violet coming over later?" Vaughn turns away, popping a slice of bread into the toaster.

I scrape up the last bite of oatmeal in my bowl. "Yeah. Just remember, you guys need to keep the whole 'us' thing on the down low while there are other people here."

It pisses me off that we have to hide our relationship, but at least it isn't forever. By next semester, this secrecy bullshit will be in the dim and distant past.

"Wait. What are you going to do with the mutt?" Connor nods at Biscuit, who wags his tail eagerly and trots over to sit at his feet, watching him adoringly. He loves Connor, even if it's unrequited. Then again, Biscuit loves everybody. It's a good thing we don't need a guard dog. He'd bring the burglars his squeaky toy to play fetch with instead of chasing them away.

"He can stay locked up in my room."

Drew stumbles into the kitchen, bleary-eyed and rocking massive bedhead. His LSU athletics shorts are on backwards and I'm pretty sure he's wearing the same t-shirt he did yesterday. He's

usually impeccably groomed, which makes his current state especially jarring.

Connor gestures to him with a banana. "What the fuck happened
to you?"

"You okay?" Vaughn steps aside so Drew can access the coffee
maker, eyeing him with concern.

"I was up late talking to Savannah," he says, pulling out the
biggest coffee mug we own and filling it to the brim. "She had some
shit going on. She's okay now."

None of us bother to pry. Not because we don't care, but
because we already know he won't spill. Drew is like a vault with
secrets, especially when it comes to Sav.

"Who's coming over tonight for your birthday, anyway?"
Connor asks, tossing his dirty spoon into the sink instead of putting
it into the dishwasher beside him. You know, the one I emptied half
an hour ago. I'd chew him out, but I've given up at this point.

Drew rattles off the guest list. Savannah—obviously—plus a
chunk of the guys from the team, and a handful from his poli sci
program. Enough that we'll definitely have an audience.

I'll have to be on my best behavior tonight around Violet.

Somehow.

CHAPTER 32

STOLEN MOMENTS
VIOLET

"DID YOU TALK TO PRESTON?" Claire leans across the coffee table to grab the sweet chili dipping sauce, pouring some on her plate. After a taxing week of classes, we've done the only logical thing: ordered a boatload of Thai delivery. I figure it'll make for a nice, hearty pre-gaming meal to soak up whatever we drink at Drew's birthday party.

We're in various states of readiness, with Claire's hair tucked into a towel turban and Julianna's makeup half-finished. I'm in the black dress I'm wearing tonight with an old, ratty sweatshirt thrown on top to help protect it from any food spills.

I clear my throat. "Yeah. You could say that…"

After driving her and Julianna crazy all week, rehearsing speeches and opening lines, I finally did what Nash asked and let Preston down easy. Or tried to. I went into it thinking Preston and I were on the same page and that it was going to be redundant. But based on his reaction, I guess it was a necessary conversation.

Looking down, I drag my fork through the pile of coconut rice on my plate. "I told him I valued him as a friend but I didn't see him as anything more and I didn't want to give him the wrong idea."

Claire's eyebrows lift because being so direct isn't my usual MO. Maybe Nash is rubbing off on me. "Good on you for being honest. How did he take that?"

"Uh, not great. Not sure if it was my delivery or the message itself." I seize a forkful of green curry. "Why isn't it socially acceptable to have talks like that in writing? I'm certain it would go better if I did."

Julianna gives me a sympathetic look. "He's probably just hurt, Violet. It seems like he took that one kiss and got carried away with it in his head."

"Maybe so," I say. "Preston seemed pretty pissed. Then he asked if it was because of Nash, which I obviously couldn't answer. He topped it all off by calling Nash toxic and said I deserved better."

That part irked me. Other than the rumors floating around school, many of which I now know aren't true, Preston hardly knows Nash. But I didn't argue with him because I wasn't keen to twist the knife in an already painfully awkward conversation. I also didn't want to inadvertently own up to our relationship when it's against the rules.

"Ouch." Claire grimaces. "What are you going to do?"

"Not much I can do. He's been freezing me out ever since we spoke, so I guess I'll give it some time."

Next to me on the couch, Julianna waves her spring roll. "Speaking of freezing people out, guess who tried to apologize?"

"Marcus?" I offer. Not a huge surprise. It seems like guys usually come crawling back after they wrong you. Most of them should stay gone. Nash's redemption was an exception, not the rule.

"What a dick," Claire mutters, stabbing her Pad Thai with a fork.

"Yup." Julianna pops the 'p'. "He's been texting me for two days straight saying he's sorry. After blowing me off for nearly a week. I think he's just trying to keep me on the back burner."

I think she's right, and I'm glad I didn't have to be the one to say it.

"Fuck him." I shovel a bite of green curry and coconut rice into my mouth, immediately realizing the possible double entendre. "Wait. Not literally. You know what I mean."

Jules makes a face, heaping a pile of noodles onto her plate.

"Please. I'm not interested in a second round of disappointing sex. If I wanted to be depressed, I'd go watch a re-run of Grey's Anatomy. Just wish I didn't have to see him all the time."

"I vote you act like nothing even happened," I tell her. "Don't ignore him, just pretend he's some random guy on the team. Acting like you're not fazed will bother him more than you being angry." Speaking from experience, because it drove me crazy when Nash did it to me at the start of the semester.

Claire holds up her fork in assent. "Seconded."

"Good news is, Marcus won't be there tonight." I lean forward, nabbing the last spring roll. "You can go out and forget all about him."

"Are you staying over?" Jules nudges me with a grin.

"Yeah," I tell her, butterfly wings taking flight. "I am."

"Full house," Claire murmurs as we squeeze through Nash's front door. Bodies clutter the entrance, bass thumping in the background.

"No kidding." I scan the crowd for familiar faces, coming up short. There are a lot more people here than I'd been expecting.

We shuffle past groups of partygoers huddled in the hallway, dodging and maneuvering en route to the living room. I spot Nash the instant we step past the threshold. Hulking size aside, his enigmatic presence is impossible to miss. Our eyes meet, and invisible sparks fly between us. His lips curl as his gaze slowly rakes down my body, so heated that I can practically feel it on my skin. My black dress is short, hitting at mid-thigh, and the look on his face tells me it's a win.

We exchange a meaningful glance for a few more seconds until we're interrupted by a black-haired guy I don't recognize. He looks like a freshman, but he isn't on the team.

"Hey, blondie." His swagger tells me he's significantly drunker than we are. He gives me an air pistol. "Looking good."

Ryder, one of the athletes in my training group, pushes through the crowd to get to us. "Dude." His expression can only be described as terrified. He grabs his protesting friend by the arm and starts dragging him away. "Do you want to leave here in one piece?"

Claire and Jules shoot me bemused looks. I, on the other hand, am not even a little surprised. Nash lifts a shoulder, but his smirk is evident even from across the room.

"Violet!" Savannah rushes up, clutching a mango White Claw. She's rocking a floral minidress with her long, coppery hair in loose waves, and it's the epitome of boho chic. "I'm so glad you guys came. Want to play Up and Down the River with us?"

We join her and a handful of other people around the coffee table, more for the social aspect than the alcohol itself. Nash hangs back in the periphery, talking to Drew, both of whom occasionally glance over like they're checking on us. While hovering is part of Nash's playbook, Drew's glance lingers on Savannah more than I'd expect.

Spending time around Nash without being able to be with him is strange. It's one thing to remain apart at school, in a professional environment. It's another when I slept over here earlier this week and now I can't even give him a kiss.

My phone vibrates as I raise my drink to my lips. I check it beneath the table, because I have a hunch it isn't something I want everyone else to see.

> Nash: I'm going to put that pretty little mouth to good use later.

"Violet?" Claire nudges me. "It's your turn."

"Huh? Oh, sorry."

I lock the screen without replying so I don't hold up the game even more. My gaze flits over to Nash, and he flashes me a filthy grin that transports my mind to an equally filthy place. While being forced to stay apart in public is far from ideal, he's leveraging the situation to his fullest advantage.

One vodka cooler later, I decide to switch to water. I don't want to get sloppy if I'm staying over. With my nonexistent alcohol tolerance, I'd end up falling asleep on Nash before midnight, and neither of us wants that.

I push back my chair as I stand, and my cell hums in my hand.

> Nash: Then I'm going to fuck you so hard you can't walk tomorrow.

Fighting the rush of heat to my cheeks, I excuse myself from the game and set off for the kitchen. As I do, Nash cuts across the room and follows me. I tug on the faucet, running the water until it's cold while he prowls closer, stopping further away than I'd like due to the partygoers scattered around the room.

He leans a hip against the counter and juts his chin at me. "Nice necklace. Are you wearing it because it goes with your outfit?" His voice drops, sinfully deep and laden with innuendo only I understand. "Or for another reason?"

Shutting off the tap, I turn to face him. "The second one." My fingertips land on the amethyst pendant, caressing the stone between my index finger and thumb, and his pupils dilate.

This necklace is our 'game on' symbol from before—an invitation to grab me, take me, bend me over the nearest couch. Of course, that won't be happening since the couch is occupied by a handful of his friends. But it's still a green light for Nash to come up with something else.

Desire gleams in his eyes. "Noted."

When I return to the game, my phone vibrates again.

> Nash: Where do you want me to come tonight? On those perfect tits, or on your face?

> Me: Both.

> Nash: Good girl.

The rest of the night carries on without incident. Everyone else is drunk enough to be happy but not sloppy to the point that there are problems. Everyone but Nash, who's barely touched his drink. I haven't been drinking much, either. Sex is better sober. So is snuggling.

Just before midnight, I'm getting another glass of water when another text comes through. This time, Nash is nowhere to be seen.

Nash: Upstairs. Now.

Upstairs as in, come to his bedroom? I frown at the screen briefly. Isn't Biscuit locked up in there? He isn't exactly known for respecting personal space. Maybe Nash relocated him to another room.

Loud music throbs in the background as I scan the crowd, verifying that no one is watching. Julianna and Claire are talking with Silas and a cute friend he brought who's been making eyes at Jules all night. There's a heated game of beer pong at the kitchen table, and several of Nash's teammates are playing a first-person shooting game on the Xbox.

With all of the action going on, I'm easily able to slip away unnoticed. A buzz thrums through me that I can't attribute to alcohol, intensifying with every step I climb. I missed this more than I can possibly explain. It isn't even about the sex. It's about the way we get each other.

I reach the shadowy landing at the top of the staircase and a large hand clamps over my mouth, startling me.

"Shh." A strong arm locks around my waist, yanking me into the pitch-black bathroom. The door clicks shut behind me in the dark, sending a shiver of excitement down my spine. Nash's cologne envelops me, firm planes of muscle pressing into my back. I wriggle in his grip, making a half-hearted attempt to break free. His husky laugh echoes off the bathroom walls, and his hold on me tightens, securing me against him with no possibility of escape.

My breaths turn erratic as heated, open-mouthed kisses glide along the curve of my neck, up to my jaw. His hand skims beneath the hem of my dress, and he cups between my legs with a groan. "Not touching you all night has been fucking torture."

"What if someone comes upstairs?" I ask, keeping my voice low.

"No one is allowed upstairs." He tugs my neckline down off my shoulder, and his teeth scrape my bare skin. "Everyone knows that. It's the first rule of our parties."

The bathroom lights flick on, dimmed halfway, illuminating the two of us in the mirror. He towers over me, all height and brawn, an intimidating form compared to mine. Our gazes lock, and the devilish glint in his eyes tells me I'm in trouble.

Still watching our reflection, he yanks up my dress, bunching it around my waist. My lacy white underwear come into view, eliciting a rumble of approval.

"These are pretty." An ache throbs in my core as he leisurely traces the thin fabric covering my center. Tugging my underwear aside, he drags a fingertip along my slick folds. I'm soaked with need, completely entranced by him. "You look so innocent, Vi. But you want to be fucked like a bad girl, don't you?"

His thick fingers spear me, and the sudden fullness deploys a shockwave of pleasure through my body, stealing the air from my lungs. When I don't answer because I'm still catching my breath, his thumb presses my swollen bundle of nerves in an unspoken demand for a response.

"Yes," I moan as he strokes me again.

Heated breath skirts the shell of my ear. "Yes, what?"

His other hand glides between the valley of my breasts, gripping the side of my throat. My heartbeat dances beneath his fingertips, and his grip tightens, sending a rush of adrenaline coursing through my veins. He could close his fist and crush me, but I know he won't.

"Yes, please."

"Right answer." Nash releases his hold on my neck and wraps his fist in my hair, pulling it taut to angle my neck. His mouth descends, covering my lips with his with a sudden ferocity. Our kiss takes me to a new high, every sweep of his tongue reminding me that I'm his.

Working masterfully with his fingers, he brings me to the edge almost instantly. My back arches, swaying in tempo with his touch. Euphoria ignites in my core, burning brighter with every passing second. He can get me off with his hands even better than I can, and he's taking full advantage of that.

When he bites the sweet spot above my shoulder, my mouth falls open with a cry, and he clamps his palm over it again.

"Quiet, Vi, or I'll stuff those pretty panties in your mouth." Lost in the sensation, I swallow my next moan, grabbing his hand to urge him on. A dark, wolffish grin appears on his face in the mirror. "Actually, I have a better idea. Don't move."

My pulse careens as I hold still, facing the bathroom counter with my dress still hiked up and my lower half exposed. He removes his fingers, leaving my core empty and cramping with need. His hands land on my bare waist, and he presses a feather light kiss to my cheek.

He guides my underwear down my hips, gently helping me step out of them. Suddenly, he switches gears and grabs my arms, roughly pinning them together behind my back. Lacy fabric winds around my wrists, twisting and pulling taut until they're firmly bound together. A thrill runs through me as I writhe against the restraint, testing its strength. It's stretchy enough that I have some wiggle room, but tight enough that I can't escape. Not that I'd want to.

"Clever," I say, breathless.

Behind me, Nash shoves down his jeans and boxers in one fell swoop. "I thought so."

In a blur, he spins me around and sets me on the edge of the counter, spreading my legs. With my hands bound together, unable to hold onto him or the countertop securely, I'm a little wobbly. Which I suppose is his intention because it leaves him in control.

His gaze drops to the space between my legs, and he strokes my tight, aching bundle of nerves, making my hips jolt. I teeter to the side with a gasp, nearly losing my balance. Nash lets out a low chuckle, catching me before I even come close to falling.

"I've got you." His large hand slides under my dress and braces my bare lower back, steadying me in a way that's both affectionate and dominating. He studies me with fondness across his face, dragging his thumb along my bottom lip and pushing it into my mouth. I gently bite down, and he groans.

Dipping his head, he brushes his lips against mine, plying them open. Our tongues tangle as he teases me with the head of his cock without entering. Raw desire surges through me, verging on desperation. My back arches, my body greedily seeking his. He pulls away, and my thighs clench around his waist with need. My first instinct is to reach for him, but fabric cinches my wrists together, stopping me. The lack of control is both frustrating and exhilarating.

"Who do you belong to, Violet?" Nash lines up with my entrance again, barely pushing inside. It's delicious agony, so close but so far from what I want.

A needy whimper slips through my lips. "You."

"That's right." In one fluid motion, he thrusts so deep inside of me that I see stars. "Don't fucking forget it."

He captures my cries with his mouth as his hips move slowly, each plunge deeper than the last. Immediately, I rocket right back to the cusp of a climax. Ecstasy overtakes me, and my eyes drift shut. I'm drunk with pleasure, reveling in how we fit perfectly together.

CHAPTER 33
IN THE DRIVER'S SEAT
VIOLET

IF EVERY SLEEPOVER involves waking up to mind-blowing sex followed by Nash making me breakfast, I'm going to start spending the night way more often.

The only catch? Puppy dog eyes are hard to say no to. Scratch that, impossible.

"Can't I give him a little piece?" I ask Nash, holding up my strip of bacon.

Biscuit whines, his tail thumping against the hardwood floor. He's sitting on his haunches next to the table, waiting patiently while we eat and trying to guilt me into giving him scraps. Unfortunately, watching us dive into our big homemade breakfast of bacon, scrambled eggs, toast, and orange juice equates to puppy torture. If Nash weren't here, I'd probably have given him my whole plate by now.

"You already did," Nash points out, scooping up his last bite of eggs. "Any more and he's going to bring the term 'puppy fat' to life."

"He'll burn it off." Biscuit is like the dog version of the Energizer Bunny; he never sits still. Surely, that must consume a lot of calories.

Nash gives me a look but says nothing, setting down his fork. "Do you have anything to do after I drive you home?"

"Not really. I have to complete those training plans for Christina I told you about, but it shouldn't take too long. How come?"

"When was the last time someone drove your car?" He grabs his orange juice, looking at me over the rim. It's a bit off the cuff, but Nash is the king of random questions. I think it's because he has a tendency to ruminate inside his head. By the time he speaks up, he's already been thinking about something for a while. I'm used to it by now.

"Um, a few months ago? I guess it's been closer to almost a year." When my dad helped me bring it home from the dealer, specifically. He may or may not think I've eased back into driving since then. Grace picks me up and brings me to our parents' place, and they're none the wiser. It's a little white lie that hurts no one.

He sets down his glass, dragging a hand down his face. "Vi, that's bad for the vehicle. Even if you're not using it, someone's got to drive it now and then to keep it running properly. Otherwise, it'll deteriorate. And rust."

Oops. This makes sense, but it didn't occur to me before. My vehicle isn't something I give much thought to in general. It's just sort of there. I even considered selling it at one point but realized I'd probably regret it later.

"I...did not know that. But I will make a note of it for the future." I polish off the last bite of my buttered whole wheat toast.

"No, let's go by your place after we eat so I can check it out."

"You don't have to—"

He pushes back his chair, collecting our empty plates. "It's been sitting since last winter, right? You got it back in February and haven't driven it since?"

"Right," I admit.

"Battery's probably dead. I'll grab my booster cables. I have a hunch I'm going to need them."

———

After significant effort on Nash's part, my car is up and running again, and he informs me that we need to go for a drive to charge the battery. I don't really understand why, nor do I care as long as I'm not driving, so he takes us on a coffee run.

Instead of making a left-hand turn to head back to my place after we hit the Starbucks drive-through, Nash signals and takes a right, pulling into the deserted parking lot of the local mall. Aside from three parked cars scattered randomly, it's empty, probably because there are more than two hours until it opens.

Needless to say, I'm confused. It's a little exposed for public sex, even for his tastes.

"Are we going shopping?" I crane my neck, searching for signs of life in the deserted mall. Maybe there's a special event or something. Though, Nash has never been much for retail therapy.

"No." He eases my car to a stop in the middle of a vacant row of stalls and shifts the transmission into park, leaving the ignition idling. Reaching over, he unbuckles his seatbelt, jutting his chin at me. "Switch seats with me."

Panic shoots through me like a bolt of lightning. "Oh, no. I'm not driv—"

"You don't have to," he says gently. "Switch seats with me for a couple of minutes, that's all. Then we can swap back, and I'll drive us home."

I chew my bottom lip, biting it until it nearly bleeds while I debate the merits of his offer. On its face, this sounds like a perfectly reasonable request. Put my butt in the driver's seat for a couple of minutes, no additional action required. Easy enough, except it isn't. I haven't been in the driver's seat of my car, or any car, since the day of the accident.

Nash waits patiently for me to respond. With an exceptional amount of patience, actually, considering his default setting.

Okay. I can do this…I think.

I unfasten my seatbelt and reach for the door handle, but the instant my fingers land on it, everything comes rushing back to me. That awful feeling in the pit of your stomach as you slide toward an imminent collision you can't do anything to stop. That even worse feeling when you finally do. Impact. Then, waiting. Stuck. Helpless.

My mouth turns desert dry, and I remain frozen, one hand on the lever. As irrational as it may be, I can't shake the mental association between me driving and the accident itself. Can't shake the deeply ingrained belief that if someone else had been driving, all of it could have been avoided. Not just my accident, the entire pileup itself. Logically, I know this is one-hundred-percent magical thinking, but that doesn't make it feel less true.

Nash places a broad palm on my knee, regarding me with such tenderness it nearly renders me breathless. "It's okay, Vi. You don't have to drive anywhere. Just sit. Keep the car in park. Get used to being in the driver's seat again."

"Okay." Drawing in a breath, I fling open the door and force myself out of the vehicle, one foot in front of the other. Chill morning air greets me, the hum of traffic in the distance. My pulse climbs with every step until I'm certain it must exceed two hundred beats per minute.

Nash meets me at the driver's side door, placing a hand along my lower back, and kisses the crown of my head. "You got this."

One thing neither of us factored in? He's a giant. When I climb into the driver's seat, I nearly disappear. I can't reach the pedals, nor can I see over the steering wheel. I'm also reclined so far back that I might as well be horizontal. It's comical, and it brings a bit of welcome levity to an otherwise tense situation.

"I feel like I shrunk."

He gives me a wry smile. "If I adjusted it for you before I got out, I'd never be able to get out. My knees would be around my ears."

"Fair enough." Reaching down, I adjust the power seat controls, bringing myself up several inches, forward several more, and to a vertical position. Finally, I'm upright, able to see over the steering wheel, and can reach the gas and brake pedals. Not that I intend to drive anywhere, but it seems like it should somewhat replicate what it would be like if I were.

Then it comes rushing back to me again. Crunching metal. Shattering glass. Car horns blaring. I wrap my fingers around the steering wheel to steady myself, resting my forehead against it, and close my eyes, trying to push out the sounds.

"You okay?" Nash's broad hand lands on my shoulder, stroking back and forth. It helps ground me back into the present.

"It feels weird."

"That's normal. It's been a while."

Nausea bubbles up in the pit of my belly and I purse my lips, blowing out a breath. My grip on the leather-wrapped steering wheel tightens. "Distract me, please."

"Biscuit ate Connor's new Golden Goose shoes the other day." There's an unmistakable grin in Nash's voice.

Despite the situation, I can't help but laugh. I reopen my eyes, turning to face him. "Again? Did you tell him he was a bad dog?"

"Fuck no, I gave him a belly rub and extra treats." Nash tips back his coffee, pausing. "Honestly, it's kind of funny. Connor never puts his shit away, and now he's learning lessons the hard way. Had I known it would work out like this, I'd have gotten a dog years ago. Biscuit is parenting more than his parents ever did, and Connor resents the shit out of it."

"How could anyone resent him?" I ask. "Biscuit is the bestest boy."

I might be a little biased, but he's impossible not to love. Big, puppy eyes, big puppy paws, and an incredibly goofy personality. His attempt to "play dead" is also so dramatic, it's nearly Oscar-worthy.

"He may be cute, but he also shits on the floor occasionally," Nash points out.

I giggle again, shaking my head. That one, while funny, also makes me feel bad. Since I don't live there, I legitimately can't be around enough to clean up Biscuit's messes. Though I'm told his house training has improved markedly since Nash first took him home.

"Drew and Vaughn like Biscuit, though, don't they?" I ask, grabbing my vanilla latte from the center console and taking a sip. It's cooled to the perfect temperature, not too hot but not too warm.

"Yeah, especially Vaughn. He's always wanted a dog. Was never able to have one growing up. We call him Biscuit's dogfather now."

My cheeks tug into a grin. "Dogfather?" I can't decide whether this is nerdy or adorable. Maybe both. Once in a while, Nash still surprises me.

He shrugs. "If I'm going to keep him, at least I have some help."

"If you're going to—" my jaw drops, hand flying to my mouth. I shove my coffee back into the holder and grab his arm. "What?! Are you seriously thinking about keeping Biscuit? And you didn't tell me?"

Joy blooms in my chest, spreading out to my whole body. I'm so happy, I could cry. While it hasn't been that long, I've gotten attached to Biscuit, and the idea of saying goodbye to him was more than a little upsetting.

"I think we can both agree that the adoption candidates have been underwhelming," he says. "I can't pawn him off on just anyone, and it doesn't seem fair to keep him for months and then give him away later."

While this warms my heart, I know I have to ask the unspoken question that looms overhead. Regardless of whether Chicago sends Nash up to play professionally or puts him in the AHL, things will change a lot by next year.

"What about after graduation? You'll be traveling even more than you do right now."

Nash's expression sobers. "That depends, I guess."

"On what?"

"Lots of things, like where I'm living, and who I'm living with."

His last few words linger in the air between us. We haven't really discussed the future since getting back together, and we probably should because that future is hurtling towards us. This isn't freshman year when it seemed like we had all the time in the world. In less than six months, we'll be finished with our degrees and moving on.

But will we be doing that together? I have no idea.

"Worst case," he adds, "I figured you wouldn't be living with Claire anymore by then and you could take Biscuit. You're his favorite, anyway. Though, you'd have to watch his bacon intake."

"Or…"

He takes another sip of coffee, mouth tugging behind the white plastic rim. "Or what, Vi?"

"I don't know," I lie, suddenly having lost all courage to broach the subject.

Nash places his cup back in the holder and angles his body to face me, taking both of my hands in his. His thumb slowly strokes my skin. "I know I'm not in a position to ask you to change your plans or give things up, especially when I'm not entirely sure where I'll end up myself. If there's any way we can end up in the same place, I am fully for it. I didn't know if that was something you would even want."

"I would," I tell him honestly. "Under the right circumstances. But if we can't make that happen, at least not right away, what then?"

In other words, does this have an expiration date?

My question is followed by a pause that does nothing to assuage my worries. Am I risking everything for something fleeting? Another one-way flight to Heartbreak Town?

He squeezes my hands, his green eyes filled with affection and a glimmer of what I almost want to call worry. "Vi, I don't care if I have to fly out just so I can see you for an hour at a time. It would be fully worth it. Whatever I have to do to make it work, I will. If you will."

Butterflies cascade through my body. "I will."

The undercurrent of worry in his expression fades, replaced with a broad grin, the kind so rarely seen on his face it's like spotting a shooting star in the night sky. He leans closer and brackets my jaw with his fingers as his lips find mine, tongue sliding inside my mouth for a coffee-tinged kiss. It's brief; gentle; but it says everything he doesn't.

In this moment, I know. He may not say those three little words, but I know how much he cares about me.

Between us in the console, my phone vibrates with a text from Jules, and I glance down at the time. "Holy cow. We've been sitting here for like, fifteen minutes."

"See?" he kisses the tip of my nose. "I know you could do it. Let's switch back so I can drive us home."

CHAPTER 34

TO-DO LIST
VIOLET

SOMETIMES, I wish I had a good luck charm. I could use sure one right now.

After suggesting we order pizza from Gino's, I let Nash turn on the St. Louis versus Minnesota game in hopes of buttering him up, instead of angling to watch another episode of Bridgerton like I really want. Who knows, maybe a commercial for something Thanksgiving-related will pop up, and I can use that as a springboard into what I want to say.

Our pizza arrives before a good opportunity does. We eat dinner on the couch while I wrack my brain, trying to find a natural way to broach the subject. Three slices of cheese pizza later, I'm still empty-handed. Because of this, I stress eat an entire package of Skittles for dessert.

Several more minutes crawl by while I twist the knit gray blanket we're snuggled beneath in my hands, wringing the fabric over and over. We're well into the third period of the game, and I still haven't pulled the trigger.

"Vi," Nash says gently, covering my hands with his. "What's with the fidgeting? Is something wrong?"

"Are you going home for Thanksgiving?" I blurt.

So much for finding a low-pressure way to bring it up.

Something indecipherable flashes across his face. "No, not until Christmas."

If I'm reading him correctly, I'd wager he isn't happy about going home then, either. It's difficult not knowing anything about such a big part of his life—like this big, blank piece in the puzzle of who he is. Even the first time we dated, it seemed like he went out of his way to keep me away from his father. I wish he'd tell me more so I understood why.

Temptation to press the issue grips me, but I force myself to let it go. Overloading him won't help my case.

"My parents asked me if you'd like to come to Thanksgiving at their house," I tell him. "I'd like it if you came. But you don't have to if you don't want to."

While it would mean a lot to me if he did, I want to avoid a repeat of the Easter debacle. If Nash genuinely doesn't want to come, I'm not going to force the issue. Though it won't bode well for our future if he says no. At some point, he has to meet my family.

"Don't they hate me?" Nash raises his eyebrows. "They should, anyway. Then again, you should, too."

"No, they don't know about any of...that." Time for more candy. Reaching over, I tear open a package of Skittles, pouring it directly into my mouth. My stress level is at a twelve out of ten. While I tried to tell myself it wasn't a big deal, I'll be crushed if he says no.

Skepticism stretches across his face. "They don't? From everything you've told me, you're incredibly close to them. I was sure they'd heard all the gory details and constructed voodoo dolls of me."

My parents have no idea. Grace knows what went down, but she's open-minded enough not to hold it against Nash. When I gave her an update the last time we hung out, including the truth about my feelings for him and how deep they run, she was supportive of me giving him a second chance. I guess I'm not the only hopeless romantic in our family, after all.

"I lied for you that day. Told them you had food poisoning." My voice cracks. "Then I went home and cried into my pillow for a week, but I like to think I sold it in front of them."

He tsks, corners of his mouth tugging down. "I'm sorry, Petal."

"I've forgiven you. I don't think you'd do that now."

"I would never." He cups my face, brushing a kiss against my lips. "And I'd love to come."

My cheeks tug into a massive grin. "You would?"

"Yeah. It'll be good to meet them."

I nearly do a happy dance on the spot, but I refrain. Barely. Thanksgiving is one of my favorite holidays, and having Nash there with my family is everything I could have wanted.

"Oh my gosh, I'm so excited. Willow and Lincoln are going to love you. Everyone will, I know it."

"I think it would be good practice if you drove there, though."

My knee-jerk reaction to this is, heck no. But if Nash is willing to step out of his comfort zone, then I suppose I should, too. Plus, I've been making steady progress with driving. The first time I left the parking lot was a little shaky, but he helped me get through it. I even drove home from the mall with him a few days ago. It's still scary, but it's getting easier. And the idea of having my independence back is appealing.

"I will if you drive back," I offer. "Not sure I'm ready to drive that far in the dark."

Nash smirks. "I assumed that was a given. I don't get drunk off a single glass of wine with dinner like you do."

"I'm half your size, what do you expect?"

"It's cute, Vi."

I harrumph, poking his ribcage because he knows how I feel about the c-word. Being short, people throw that term at me a lot, and not always in a complimentary way—in a patronizing way like, "Oh, aren't you *cute*?" Almost as if I'm not a fully-grown adult.

"You're sexy," he amends, his lips drifting along the curve of my neck. His teeth sink into my earlobe, and my whole body comes alive. "And beautiful. So fucking beautiful it blows my mind."

CHAPTER 35

THANKFUL
NASH

VIOLET and I have been going to the mall before and after closing a couple times a week, making steady progress. Last week, she drove a lap around the parking lot. A few days ago, she drove home from the mall. And yesterday, she drove to school and back with me. Needless to say, that was pretty huge.

Today is the final hurdle: driving to her parents', which is over thirty minutes away.

She pulls into the merge lane and gasps, panic shooting across her face. "Nash. I haven't been on the freeway in over a year." Her slender fingers curl around the leather steering wheel, knuckles blanching.

"You're doing great." I'm not nervous because I know she can handle this; she just needs to have faith in herself. "All you need to do now is get up to speed and shoulder check before you move over. It's no different than merging onto McLaren Drive to get to school, only with a slightly faster speed limit."

"Okay." Her voice is shaky.

Accelerating, she matches the speed of the freeway traffic and signals, shoulder-checking three times before she moves over. Once she gathers her bearings, the rest of the drive goes perfectly aside from one asshole who cuts her off for absolutely no reason. She handles it surprisingly well, though I sorely wish I could run the guy off the road.

Half an hour later, she shifts the car into park in front of a sprawling white two-story house and lets out a long exhalation, killing the ignition. "I haven't driven here in nearly a year."

"But you did it." Pride swells in my chest, even though it's her accomplishment and not mine.

"Yeah. I guess I did."

"Knew you could." I unbuckle my seatbelt and lean across the console, pressing my lips to her smooth cheek. God, she smells fucking edible. Think I'll skip dessert and have her later instead.

Violet shifts in the driver's seat, pulling me back over to her, and levels me with a bruising kiss. "I would never have done that without you. Thank you."

"Proud of you, Vi. You're a fucking rockstar."

Hand in hand, we stroll up the sidewalk to the painted red door, empty-handed despite my multiple protests. In addition to being intimidated as fuck about being here, it feels wrong not to bring wine or something as a gift, especially the first time I'm meeting her parents. But she insisted her parents didn't want us to, and I have to assume she knows best.

We climb the front steps, and my pulse follows suit. While I wasn't nervous about the drive, I'd be lying if I said I wasn't nervous about meeting her family. However, she seems to have much stronger relationship with them than I do with Doug, so I'm cautiously optimistic.

Violet pulls out her keys and unlocks the door, pushing it open. "Knock knock!"

I follow her inside, greeted by the warm scent of pumpkin pie mingled with something savory, like turkey and other Thanksgiving foods. The white-painted walls are bright, hardwood floors gleaming, and a gallery of photos next to the door catches my eye. I make a note to check it out later and find some of Violet when she was little.

"Auntie Violet!" A chubby little girl runs up to Violet and throws her arms around her legs. Behind her, a toddler boy scoots up on a ride-on Thomas the Tank Engine, giving us both a shy smile.

"Hi guys! I missed you both so much." Violet bends down, embracing the little girl and smooching both of her cheeks at least a dozen times. She does the same to the little boy, tousling his fine blond hair as she pushes to stand.

"Pick me up?" she asks Violet, who complies, hoisting her up on one hip. Her niece is nearly five and not overly small, so it takes considerable effort on Violet's part.

"Oh my goodness, Willow. You're getting so big. Pretty soon, you'll have to carry me around instead."

"Nooooo." Willow giggles and shakes her head, chestnut ringlets bouncing.

Violet turns to face me. "Nash, this is Willow and Lincoln." She points to each of them. "Guys, this is Nash."

Lincoln studies me with big blue eyes the same color as Violet's and crams a thumb in his mouth, saying nothing. Slowly, he scoots back, putting more distance between us.

"Is he your boyfriend?" Willow eyes me suspiciously.

Violet grins. "Yes, he is."

Willow's suspicion increases and she gives me the side-eye, twirling a lock of violet's hair.

"Tough crowd," I say.

Violet laughs, setting Willow back down. A woman who appears to be a few years older than Violet comes around the corner holding a baby wearing a pink sleeper. I'm pretty sure this is Grace, Violet's oldest sister.

"There you two are."

Violet quickly introduces us, and then she leads me into the kitchen to introduce me to her parents, both of whom are wearing matching aprons. As we step through the doorway, my nerves skyrocket. In truth, I'm not sure how either of them is going to receive me.

Her father's eyes crinkle at the corner with a smile when he sees her, and her mother rushes up, wrapping her in a huge hug.

Everyone is so happy, I almost don't know what to make of it. It's foreign to me, like I'm watching a family sitcom.

"This is Nash," she tells them. "Nash, these are my parents, Rachel and Chris."

Chris shakes my hand enthusiastically, regarding me with more warmth than I was expecting, and Rachel wraps me in a hug that catches me totally off guard.

"We're so happy to finally meet you," she says, giving me another squeeze before she releases me.

"We have to finish preparing dinner," Chris tells us. "It'll be about half an hour."

"Anything we can do to help?" Violet asks.

Her mother shakes her head, wiping her hands on her blue checkered apron. "No, no. You two get a glass of wine and sit down with Gracie. Relax."

Violet protests, but they hold firm on not needing any help. I follow Violet into the living room, where Grace is holding Abigail on the couch. Next to the coffee table, Willow and Lincoln are locked in a fiery battle over a doll.

"Uh, Gracie?" Violet gingerly picks up a section of her sister's curly blonde hair, which is matted with something whiteish at the ends. "You've got a…situation."

Grace holds out the strands to examine them, making a face. "Oh, shoot. Abigail spat up in my hair again. I have to go wash this out in the sink. Can you take her for a minute?" She offers the baby to Violet, who takes her, cradling her in her arms.

Abigail starts to fuss, escalating from whimpers into full-blown crying in a matter of seconds. Her face reddens, tears falling down her chubby cheeks. If it were me holding a screaming infant, I would panic and hand it right back, but Violet simply stands up and starts patting her back, swaying on the spot. When that doesn't work, she offers her a pacifier and begins to gently shush her. After a minute or so, the combination does the trick and Abigail settles against her shoulder, eyelids growing heavy.

"I didn't know you were a baby whisperer."

Violet turns to me, her expression verging on bashful. "I'm not,

I just babysit for my sister a lot. With Michael in the military, he's gone for long stretches at a time."

"Sounds like it would be hard." There's a laundry list of reasons I don't think having kids is a good idea, and this is one—I'll be on the road for games half the time. Sticking someone else with that much of the workload doesn't seem fair.

The reasons extend far beyond that, though.

"Yes and no." Violet lifts her shoulder, a subtle half-shrug so she doesn't jostle Abigail. "I'm sure it isn't easy, but Grace is basically Wonder Woman. Plus, she's got me and my parents. We make sure she gets a break so she doesn't get too burnt out."

I wonder what it's like to have family that actually gives a shit. It seems nice.

Grace breezes back into the room, her light blonde curls pulled back in a low ponytail. "Thanks, Vi. I can take her if you want."

"Are you kidding me?" Violet clutches Abigail dramatically, pivoting out of reach. "No way. I'm going to soak up all the new baby smell I can."

"Suit yourself," Grace says. "Mom said she needs help with the salad, so if you'll excuse me, I'm going to drown myself in a giant glass of Rose with her in the kitchen."

The sight of Violet holding the baby does something to me. She looks so natural with her, so caring and maternal.

What the fuck is wrong with me? I'm twenty-one. I don't want a baby any time soon, if ever. Probably never. I'm sure that would be for the best for all parties involved. I didn't exactly have a shining example in my own father. While I like to think I don't take after him, I'm pretty sure I'd manage to screw up my kid like he did.

Violet notices me watching her and catches my eye. She crosses the room to me, still holding the baby nestled against her chest.

"Sleepy baby snuggles are the best kind." She leans her cheek against Abby's downy hair, exhaling and closing her eyes. For a minute, she looks completely blissed out. She reopens her eyes, fixing me with a hopeful look. "Want to hold her?"

"I've never held a baby." Kids and I get along great, but babies are like alien creatures to me. I have zero experience with them.

She smiles and shifts Abby in her arms, offering her to me. "It's pretty easy. Just support her head and the neck like I did."

Abby stirs in the transfer process and low-level panic rises within me. If she starts crying again, she's going straight back to Violet. But instead, her tiny fingers bunch up the fabric of my shirt, making a fist, and she lets out a little sigh, turning her head toward my chest. Violet's right, new babies do smell good.

Okay, fine. I don't completely hate it.

The baby-holding goes well for about ten minutes, at which point she starts to fuss again, and Violet deems her hungry based on the way she's sucking fervently on her tiny little fist. Giving her a bottle is way above my paygrade, so I pass her back to Violet. It turns out to be good timing, because my phone vibrates with a text from Doug a split second later. The timing leaves much to be desired, but at least he isn't calling.

Excusing myself, I slip into the bathroom to reply. He immediately writes back criticizing me for not coming home for Thanksgiving. I clench my phone, jaw following suit until my teeth grind together so hard I think my molars might crack. Really? He's in the middle of Thanksgiving with his girlfriend Shannon's family, and this is what he's doing? Even holidays aren't sacred. Then again, he's probably several drinks deep.

We go back and forth for a few minutes until I finally manage to shut him down, but not before he gets into my head about the game next weekend. I know the stakes are high; I don't need to be reminded of that.

When I walk back into the living room, Violet pulls me aside, her eyes searching my face. "Are you okay?"

"Yeah, I'm good. My dad texted me Happy Thanksgiving, that's all."

Her mouth tugs into a slight frown, seemingly unconvinced. "All right. Dinner's ready."

CHAPTER 36

MR. NASH
VIOLET

NASH IS a great sport during dinner. He politely answers my parents' million questions about NCAA hockey and his engineering program. He asks Grace about Michael's deployment, listens to Willow rank the best Disney princesses, and feigns interest in Lincoln's train collection that he drags to the table. And he's gracious when my dad tows him into the den after to show him all of his signed hockey paraphernalia—even when Willow tags along to "help explain."

Grace and I hang back in the kitchen, helping with the dishes while our mother prepares dessert. But when Nash doesn't return after a couple of minutes, I start to grow a little worried. I crane my neck and peer down the hall, envisioning Nash being bored to death by my father's stories about getting Mario Lemieux's autograph at an airport in Dallas and the year our favorite team made it to the Cup finals only to be "robbed." My father is very sweet, but he likes to talk. A lot.

"So, Vi." Grace lowers her voice, her blue eyes shining with affection as she dries a porcelain serving dish next to me. "Did you find your butterflies?"

"And then some." Warmth floods my cheeks as I rinse the final pan beneath the faucet and hand it to her.

"Good," she says. "I really like him."

My heart soars. "You do?"

"He's a little quiet, but I can tell he's crazy about you. I think Mom and Dad like him, too."

"Let's hope. He's been in there with Dad for a while." Another peek down the hallway reveals they're still in the den. Setting down my checkered dish towel, I tell her, "I'm going to go check on them."

I poke my head into the den to find Nash playing Mario Kart with Willow on my parents' oversized flatscreen TV. He's Toad, she's Princess Peach, and it's one of the cutest things I've ever seen. My dad is in the plaid armchair across from them, cheering Willow on. Due to his arthritis, he can't keep up with video games.

"What do we have here?" I ask, leaning against the wooden doorframe.

Willow's attention doesn't deviate from the screen. "I'm beating Mr. Nash!" She leans over, angling her entire body as she rounds a bend in the course.

Nash steals a glance at me over his shoulder, his expression slightly sheepish. "It was her idea."

I grin. "Sure it was."

After they finish the Mushroom Cup, we visit over coffee and dessert until it's time to leave. Fortunately, my parents are early risers and Grace goes to bed when her kids do, which means we won't be staying too late. Nash has been a trooper, but I don't want to push my luck.

"So, Nash." My father sets down his fork next to his half-eaten slice of pumpkin pie. "Violet tells us you've been drafted by Chicago. That's an impressive accomplishment."

"It must've taken a lot of dedication and hard work to reach that level," my mother adds.

"Er, yeah." Nash rubs the back of his neck, evidently unsure of how to accept the compliment. "I guess it did."

I finish my last bite of pie, swallowing. "He's being modest. Nash is one of the hardest working athletes on the team. And he's a force to be reckoned with on the ice. You guys will have to come to watch one of their games."

Nash squeezes my hand beneath the table, looking both slightly embarrassed and flattered. I wish he knew he deserved to hear things like that all the time.

"We absolutely will," my father agrees. "Maybe we could bring Willow and Linc, too."

We're interrupted by a huge crash, followed by Willow wailing for her mommy. Grace thrusts Abigail into my arms and dashes into the kitchen. She returns a moment later, letting us know that Willow was attempting to serve herself seconds of pie, the remainder of which is now on the floor. It's both cute and sad because Willow is always trying to do "grown up" things.

It's also sad because I love pumpkin pie, and now there are no leftovers to take home.

Everyone exchanges hugs at the front door and my parents fawn all over Nash, insisting he come back for Christmas. As much as I would love that, I assume he has to go home to his own family eventually. Even if he doesn't seem happy about it.

My car has been idling for a few minutes, thanks to Nash sneaking out to start it, and the interior is warm and cozy when we climb in. Good thing, too, because it feels like winter in the air and I have a wicked chill.

"My parents liked you," I tell Nash, fastening my seatbelt.

Ignition still in park, he turns to look at me with genuine worry across his face. "You sure? Your mom seemed to, but I couldn't get a read on your dad."

"I think my dad was a little star-struck. I told you, we're a big hockey family." I tried to prepare him for this. In their eyes, he's a sports hero. The good news is, I can tell that they liked him beyond just that. But I knew they would.

"Hope so," he mutters, shoulder-checking as he eases out of the street parking spot. "Dads are tricky."

And there it is. I know there's more to the father thing than he lets on.

"You were a big hit with Lincoln and Willow, too, Mr. Nash."

I don't mention Abigail, even though seeing him hold her gave me instant baby fever. I get the sense that holding her was a big enough step for him, and I don't want to freak him out by sounding too baby crazed. I mean, I kind of am—I love babies and I always have. But I know I'm not having one of my own any time soon.

Maybe in five more years or so. Before thirty, I hope.

"I still can't believe Willow kicked my ass at Mario Kart. I was trying, too."

"Ooh, is your fragile male ego bruised?"

"A little." He laughs, easing the car to a halt at a four-way stop. "In my defense, we only have an Xbox. I haven't played Nintendo since I was a kid."

"I hope you didn't mind them following you around like lost puppies. I think they miss having Michael around. My dad tries to play with them, but he can't really keep up. They're too full of beans."

"Nah, it was fun. I like kids..." Nash trails off, a crease forming in his forehead. "I'm not sure I want my own, though."

Disappointment slams into me like a wrecking ball to the stomach. If Nash doesn't want to have kids, that means we could never have a real future. I can't believe we've never discussed this before.

"But you're so good with them." I bite the inside of my cheek, regretting the words as soon as I blurt them out. Pushing Nash is a surefire way to get him to clam up.

He keeps his eyes focused on the road, saying nothing. I can't read his expression. My regret increases with every second that passes, and I desperately wish I could take back what I said. Heavy silence fills the vehicle while the heater whirs away, blowing air that suddenly feels ten degrees too hot even though I was chilly mere moments ago.

"Not sure it's a good idea," he says.

The rest of the drive home is quiet.

———

Nash's house is deserted when we arrive, unusually silent in the absence of boisterous roommates and skittering puppy paws. Connor flew home for Thanksgiving, Drew and Savannah reportedly go see each other's families together, and Vaughn took Biscuit to his mom's, where I was assured he'd be spoiled rotten.

Mind spinning, I grab my overnight bag and head into the bathroom, washing off my makeup and brushing my teeth. Then I change into a skimpy pink pajama set with a strappy tank top and tiny shorts that I bought specifically for tonight. I skip underwear, like I'd planned, but my brain isn't even remotely in seduction mode.

There's no way we could make it this far only to fail over something so fundamental, so impossibly irreconcilable.

I've just finished brushing my hair when Nash strolls out of the bathroom and comes up behind me, cinching his forearms around my waist. He's wearing nothing but black boxer briefs, his heated skin pressing against mine. Setting down the hairbrush, I let my eyes drift shut for a brief moment while I memorize the way it feels to be in his arms.

"You've been quiet. Is something wrong?" His grip is firm and steadying, spearmint toothpaste breath warm against my cheek.

Pausing, I summon the strength to say what I need to—even knowing I might break us in the process.

My bottom lip wobbles. "I really want a future with you. And I would never want to force you into having kids if that isn't something you want. But having a family someday is important to me, and I don't know where that leaves us."

"It's not that I don't like kids. It's that—" He cuts off abruptly.

Anxious to hear what he has to say, I wait for him to finish but he doesn't.

"That what?" I ask.

His chest rises against my back and falls with a sigh, but he doesn't respond. My skin turns cold as he releases me, walking away to sit on the edge of the bed, resting his corded forearms on his thick, hockey thighs. A hairline crack forms in my heart. This is all too familiar, and it hurts even worse the second time around.

"Don't do this again." My voice wavers, a lone tear spilling down my cheek. "You always used to shut down on me."

Nash's face falls. "Please don't cry. Not because of me. I promise you, I'm not worth it."

"Then stop pushing me away and talk to me like you promised. I know there's a lot you aren't telling me, but what I don't know is why." I feel like I'm begging but I see a gap in his armor, and I desperately want to get beneath it. "What goes on in your head that always makes you want to bail?"

Frustration creeps into his tone. "I don't know how to stay, Vi."

"What do you mean?"

The emotional walls shoot right back up and he goes blank again.

"Nash." I ease onto the black comforter beside him and splay my hand across his bare chest, feeling the steady rhythm of his heartbeat against my palm. Call it naïve, call it denial, but I refuse to give up on him. He's come so far with letting me in. Something tells me we can work through this.

He looks down at my hand and swallows hard, his Adam's apple dipping. "Like I said, I don't know how to stay. I don't want to lose my temper with you."

The words stop me cold. Nash did lots of not-so-great things near the end, like not prioritizing me and taking me for granted. But he's never lost his temper with me; he's never even raised his voice. Even when we argue, he's in control—until he walks away, at least.

And the closer we got last time, the more he walked away. That doesn't feel like a coincidence.

"You never have. Why do you think you would?"

His gaze stays aimed down, fixed on the floor at our feet. "It's all I ever knew growing up."

My stomach turns because I'm starting to get an idea of what he's been hiding—and why he's been hiding it. I reach up, gently stroking his stubbled jawline, and his eyes drift shut.

He grabs hold of my fingers, pressing them to his cheek. "I don't want to be like that, especially when it comes to you."

"You're not," I insist. "Not even a little."

"I don't know," he says quietly, his eyes still closed. "Sometimes I feel like that inside."

Now my heart is breaking for another reason entirely.

"Everyone gets mad, Nash. It's how you handle it that counts."

"I guess."

A chill in the air runs over my skin. I shiver, goosebumps popping up along my arms. Nash reaches over and grabs the blanket folded at the foot of his bed, draping it over my bare shoulders. His heavy arm curls around me, tucking me against him.

"Can you please tell me what you were going to say before?"

Several heartbeats pass before he answers. "I was going to say, I like kids. But I don't know if I'd be a good dad."

More pieces of the puzzle click together. I want to ask him to elaborate but get the sense I shouldn't. Instead, I lean my head on his shoulder and place a hand on his muscular thigh. His rough hand covers mine, squeezing it in response.

"I think you would be," I tell him gently. "I mean, if you wanted to. Someday." While I don't want to be pushy, I get the sense his reservations are coming from a place of fear and not a true aversion.

"I didn't have the best example. I don't want to repeat his mistakes."

CHAPTER 37

STAY WITH ME
NASH

IT'S like there are a million radio stations blaring inside my head, and they're all saying different things. I don't know which ones to listen to and which ones to tune out.

"Whether or not you realize it, you have a good heart." Violet climbs on top of me and straddles my thighs, gently stroking my jaw. Her touch is so soothing, so loving, that some of the turmoil in me dissipates. "An amazing heart, in fact."

"You're saying that because you see the good in everyone," I point out. "Even if they don't deserve it." Sometimes, I think Violet could find redeeming qualities in a serial killer.

She tilts her head, bringing her lips to hover above mine. "I see the good in you because it's there. Lots of it."

Her words do something to me I can't explain, and all I know is that I need her closer.

My hand slides up to the nape of her neck, pulling her to me and eliminating the distance between our lips. Violet sighs, gripping my shoulders as my tongue slips into her mouth. Everything clicks into place, the way it always does when I'm with her, and suddenly, nothing else in the world matters.

Mouths still sealed together, I lower onto my back with her straddling my hips. Her full breasts press against my pecs through the thin fabric of her tank top as I palm her perfect, round ass. My fingers slip beneath the hem of her shorts, finding an expanse of soft, smooth skin, and I let out a tortured groan when I discover that she isn't wearing any underwear. She laughs softly, deepening our kiss and rolling her hips, teasing us both.

I love the way she feels pressed up against me.

Fuck, I love *her*.

I wrap arms around her narrow waist and flip us so I'm on top between her legs with my erection straining through the fabric of my boxer briefs. Violet reaches down and I help her tug them off, tossing them aside. With a few more heated kisses, I guide her pajama shorts down her hips and pull her tank top off overhead, finding her completely naked and ready for me.

My mouth crashes against hers for another kiss while I stroke the cleft of her thighs, barely grazing where she's most sensitive, eliciting a needy whimper from her. My cock twitches in response to the sound, my spine tingling as the urge to rail her sets in. All I want is to be buried inside her to the hilt while she's wrapped around me, moaning my name. To be close to her. To lose myself in her.

Before our bodies connect, Violet breaks apart from my lips. She presses my hipbone with one hand, holding me off. I stop in response to her nonverbal cue, waiting with the head of my cock pressed up against her slick entrance. Her other hand lifts to my face, cool fingertips stroking my cheek.

"Nash." Her voice is hushed. "Look at me."

When my eyes lift to hers, there's a pang in my gut that I can't explain.

"Don't go somewhere else in your head. Stay here. Just you, just me. Let me have you."

"Okay." My gaze drops to her body beneath me, tracing her supple breasts, the curve of her hips, the tiny dip of her navel. She's the opposite of me in every way. Small, soft, gentle. All curves, all woman.

And on the inside, she's the most beautiful person I know.

"I—" the words stick in my throat. I draw in a breath and try again, but I can't seem to say it. Fuck. Some kind of deep-rooted error in my operating system prevents me from uttering three simple words.

I lower onto my forearms above her, running my fingers through her silky hair. "You're beautiful."

"So are you." Her pale blue eyes trace my face, her bare lips pulled into a soft smile. "I love you. Even if you won't say it back."

Another pang. It's not that I won't—it's that I can't. I want to.

I don't deserve her. Never have.

But I want to believe that I can grow into someone who does.

"You're all I think about, Vi. I'm fucking crazy about you." I hope I demonstrate it enough to compensate for my emotional shortcomings. Maybe someday, I'll overcome all that other shit weighing me down.

A soft smile plays on her lips. "Can you show me?"

I think I know what she's asking, and it feels scarier than anything I've ever done.

"I can try."

Grabbing her wrists, I pin them above her head against the mattress using one hand. Violet pretends to resist me, playfully pushing back, and I shake my head, holding her in place.

Stay with me.

Still restraining her, I bring my mouth to hers. She smiles against my lips as I slide my other arm beneath her body, holding her against me. This time, I kiss her like she might vanish at any moment. Like she's the air I need to keep breathing. Because she is.

I need you.

With my erection pressing into the apex of her thighs, I tilt my hips, channeling every ounce of strength I have to hold off until her cue. Violet opens her legs wider and hooks a calf around my waist to urge me on. My cock slides against her, drenched with her arousal. She draws in a breath as I slowly push inside, going inch by inch until I've claimed her completely.

Our eyes lock.

I love you.

Her soft breaths mingle with mine in the silent room.

I've never been so present in the moment. Not anticipating

what's happening next, not worrying about what just happened. Right here, right now, she's the only thing that matters.

Bringing my lips to that sweet spot along her neck, I start to thrust. At first, it takes self-restraint for me to go slow, but we quickly fall into a perfect, unhurried rhythm. When I drive deeper, my name falls from Violet's lips, and her head lolls back against the pillow. Releasing her wrists, I cup her face and kiss her again. Sometimes I get caught up and don't appreciate her fully, but in this moment, I'm savoring her. Every nerve in my body is alight. Every part of me is tuned in.

It's quiet and gentle, but it's big and significant somehow.

Intentionally, deliberately, I keep going until she's right at the edge and I'm right there with her. I keep us both there and it's like a drug, high on the pleasure and high on her. Nothing else comes close.

I slip a palm under her backside, pumping into her again, hitting exactly where I know she needs it.

"Nash." Her eyes squeeze shut, teeth snagging her lower lip as her nails bite into my lower back. "Please. There."

With a few more movements, she falls apart beneath me. Somehow, I manage to hold off, wanting to watch her face. Her cheeks flush scarlet and she cries out, legs trembling. She's the most beautiful thing I've ever seen.

Sensing that she needs a short break because I know she gets too sensitive after an orgasm, I slow to a stop, resting my lips against her forehead.

Violet's eyelids flutter open, and she looks at me curiously. "You didn't—"

"Not yet. Come here." Shifting, I pull us upright and set her on top of me while I lean back against the headboard. Violet sighs as she rises up on her knees, sinking back down and taking me fully. Tingling forms in the base of my spine, a pent-up need for release threatening to burst.

Her hands sink into my hair, tugging at the roots as she grinds against me. "You feel so good." Soft lips find mine, then my cheek, my neck, and my earlobe.

"Fuck." I cup her breasts, savoring the weight of them in my hands. "You do, too."

She moves slowly, sensually, bringing us both closer to the peak. Her breathing grows ragged as she gets clenches around my cock, getting even wetter, and the pressure in my pelvis builds. I'm buried so deep in her that it feels like she's part of me.

"Oh, God." Violet whimpers, digging her fingers into my back. I know she's on the brink of a huge climax.

I grip her hips, pulling her down and meeting her halfway. "I got you, Vi."

This time, when she tumbles over the edge again, I fall right behind her. Everything plows me over, the intensity of coming inside her, the intensity of my feelings, the closeness to her in this moment. It's the single greatest feeling I've ever had, and not because of the physicality of it.

When we're both spent, Violet sags against me, dropping her head to rest on my shoulder. I hug her close, waiting until my strength returns before even attempting to reposition us in the bed.

"How's that for showing you?" I ask, pressing my lips to her cheek.

She sighs. "Perfect."

CHAPTER 38

GAME NIGHT
VIOLET

WAKING up beside Nash is one of my favorite things in the world.

Following it with dirty shower sex is even better. Well, except for the part where we ran out of hot water and had to get clean afterwards beneath an arctic blast. Nash is used to cold water because he takes ice baths for recovery. Me, not so much. I've dried off and gotten dressed, and my teeth are still chattering. Nash even turned up the thermostat a couple of degrees to help warm me.

"Let me help you with breakfast," I insist, squeezing the moisture out of my hair with a towel.

"Nope." He sets down a steaming mug of coffee with cream and sugar for me on his desk, smacking my butt on his way by. "I'll call you when it's done."

When I come downstairs after blow drying my hair, Nash shoos me into the living room with my coffee and my book, plus one furry little companion who seems to think he should be the focus of my attention and not my novel. I curl up on the couch with a blanket, stroking Biscuit's head while I lose myself in the pages.

It's a picture-perfect morning. But when Nash tells me breakfast is ready a few chapters later, I can't help but notice he seems a little quiet while I'm fixing my plate.

I ease into my chair, pulling it closer to the table, and nudge him with my bare foot. "Are you okay?"

"Not looking forward to tonight," he confesses, setting down a plate piled with a mountain of food next to me. Pancakes, eggs, bacon, strawberries, and blueberries. Enough to feed at least three regular people. "I hate playing MSU. They're such shady assholes."

It's the last game before the guys get several days off to prepare for the Ice Cup tournament. It's also the third time we've faced MSU this season, and games against them are always contentious. Suddenly, I remember the verbal altercation he got into when I was on the bench the last time we played against them. It nearly escalated into a full-blown fight, and Nash never told me why.

I swallow a bite of my pancake. "What was the deal last game, anyway? Why did that guy from MSU try to fight you?"

Let's be real, Nash isn't exactly well-liked among the other teams in general, but this one in particular appears to be nurturing a serious grudge against him.

"Eriksen?" He leans back in his chair, scrubbing a hand across his jaw. "It's a long story."

Why is he dodging the question? Usually, Nash is more than happy to share hockey stories with me, both the good and the bad.

"I have time. And I'm curious."

Nash avoids meeting my eyes, inhaling slowly, and exhaling even slower. He pushes his cut-up pancake around his plate with his fork. "Over the summer, I slept with his ex. Or his girlfriend. Or something. I don't really know what she was to him at the time. I didn't even know who she was, but he's been pissed about it ever since."

"Oof." Part of me wishes I hadn't asked, but too late now.

Worry crosses his face. "I was going to make up another explanation to tell you that didn't make me look so bad, but I didn't want to lie."

"No, I'd rather have the truth." I squeeze his hand from across the table. "Besides, it's not like you slept with her after we started talking again. That'd be a different story."

"You know I'd never do that. Still didn't think you'd like hearing about it, though."

I don't love it, but what can you do? We both have pasts, and our relationship right now is what matters. Plus, Nash has always had a one-track mind when it comes to me. His fidelity was never something I've questioned, and I love that about him.

"So now Eriksen has it out for you on the ice?"

"Big time," he says, biting into a piece of bacon. "Which would be fine if he wasn't such a cheap motherfucker. He's always pulling sneaky shit and getting away with it."

"I saw him slash you during the last game, and the refs didn't even call it." Though the brutal hit Nash leveled against Eriksen shortly after that was probably punishment enough.

"They seem to look the other way with certain players." He gives me a wry smile. "I'm not one of them, obviously."

Footsteps thunder down the stairs. Connor strolls into the kitchen wearing nothing but a pair of bright blue athletic shorts with his broad, toned torso on display. It's barely above freezing outside, and the house isn't overly warm, but Nash tells me this is their compromise between him walking around naked. And for that, I am relieved.

Connor gives us a nod and pats Biscuit's head on his way to the stove, snagging a piece of bacon from the pan. "Yo, Bitty." He tosses Biscuit a scrap, which he catches mid-air.

"No more, Haas," Nash warns him. "Vet said he can't have too much people food."

"He can work it off later when I take him to the dog park." Connor winks at us, turning away to throw some bread into the toaster.

"Bitty? Dog park?" I mouth to Nash. He shakes his head, rolling his eyes, which I interpret to mean, "long story."

Connor saunters out of earshot, clutching a bacon sandwich and a glass of orange juice. I scoot closer to Nash, lowering my voice. "Okay, you have to fill me in. I thought Connor wasn't a fan of Bitty. Er, Biscuit."

"Remember how I said Connor was pissed because Biscuit kept eating his shoes? Once Connor finally mastered the preschool-level skill of putting away his shit, that improved. Then, Vaughn managed to talk him into taking Biscuit for a walk with him one day. When

Connor realized how easy it was to strike up conversations with other dog owners—including *attractive* dog owners—he became an overnight fan."

My jaw drops. "He's using my sweet, innocent puppy to pick up women."

"Pretty much." Nash shrugs. "But whatever keeps the peace around the house. Plus, Biscuit needs the exercise."

―――――

The athletic training interns are required to arrive early for games, albeit not as early as the team. When I pull into the parking lot an hour before puck drop, it's already swamped. Due to the close geographic proximity and the intensity of the rivalry, games against MSU attract a lot of spectators supporting the away team. Allegedly, there are even fights in the stands from time to time.

While warm-up goes according to plan, something about what Nash said this morning has put me on edge, and I'm oddly nervous as Vaughn skates over to center ice for the first faceoff. Our team comes out strong, but so does MSU. As much as I hate to admit it, we're pretty evenly matched.

Like always, the game is heated. Thanks to a defensive error on our part, MSU scores a goal three minutes in. Nash is on the bench when it happens, and he lets out a string of curses, slamming the butt end of his hockey stick into the ground. Irritation etches into his features, and he leans in to say something to Vaughn while the play continues. Giving up a goal so early sets a dangerous tone for the rest of the game

We manage to tie up the score with one minute left in the first, thanks to a slapshot by Connor, with assists from Marcus and Vaughn. But we lose two valuable players to injury during the second, and the loss of depth on our bench means the remaining players have to put in even more ice time. By the end of the second, Nash is clearly exhausted. All of them are.

It's a nerve-wracking match heading into the third period tied, one that could go either way at any moment. Penalties fly on both sides—some called, others not—with physical gameplay, and a rowdy arena filled with screaming fans. Both teams are playing an aggressive offense strategy, and both goalies are practically standing on their heads to save the puck.

The clock runs out with the score still tied one-one, sending the game into sudden death overtime. From the other end of the bench, Coach Ward watches like a hawk, his posture stiff. All the players are dead on their feet from working at full tilt for over sixty minutes and counting.

MSU's shot pings off the crossbar, sailing wide across our zone. Eriksen takes possession and apprehension grips me as Nash speeds for him, preparing to issue a check. While I love watching him play, I always worry about him taking and delivering hits because of the impact. Especially when he's tired like he is right now and more prone to potentially making an error.

He closes the distance before Eriksen can maneuver out of the way, crashing into him with a perfect, clean hit. The puck goes loose, sailing across the blue line. Vaughn pivots, beating everyone else to it, rocketing down to their end on a breakaway. Shouts and applause erupt throughout the arena, spectators on their feet. Everyone is focused on the scoring opportunity that could determine the outcome of the entire game, but I'm still watching Nash, like I always do.

Nash pivots to rejoin the play, and Eriksen jams his stick between Nash's skates, sending him off balance with his next stride. I gasp, and my hand flies to my mouth. Icy fear grips me as he staggers, his arms flailing. *Please don't fall.* He tries to regain his footing, and his large body smashes into the boards before crashing to the ice.

Nausea barrels into me, and my belly cramps with fear.

"No," I whisper. "No, no, no."

He stays face down, and his gloved head slides up to grip his helmet. Moving is a positive sign, but I need him to get up.

Down on the other end, the Grizzlies cycle the puck while MSU tries to fend them off. Ear-splitting yells and whistles rattle the rink. I step around one of the players on the bench to get a better view.

Get up.

Acid climbs the back of my throat as I hold my breath, watching. Nash pushes to standing, and his next few strides are unsteady. With a shaky exhale, I scan the bench, checking for Christina or Coach Ward's reaction, but nether noticed. Julianna or Preston didn't, either. They're all too wrapped up in cheering for the game-winning goal Vaughn just scored.

The buzzer sounds, marking the end of the game.

LSU won.

And no one else knows Nash got hurt.

CHAPTER 39
AGREE TO DISAGREE
NASH

I SURE DIDN'T APPRECIATE that cheap bullshit at the end of the game. Fucking Eriksen. As per usual, the refs had their heads up their asses tonight. He got away without a call, and now I have a killer headache to show for it. I'm going to pulverize him next time we cross paths on the ice.

Drew signals left, turning onto our street. "I know you were down at the other end, but I wish you could have seen the look on McLennan's face when Vaughn was barreling for him with that puck in OT. Pure terror. That was a beaut of a shot, too. Right through the five hole."

My phone buzzes in my suit pocket. I pull it out, hoping for a sext from Violet so we can pick up from where we left off earlier. Instead, it's another message from Doug about the Ice Cup. The cell starts to ring in my hand, and his name appears on the caller ID.

Nausea crashes over me, and not just because I'm vaguely dizzy. Between my father's constant harassment lately and Chicago's assistant general manager flying down to see me play next weekend, it's like the walls are closing in on me from all sides.

"Couldn't have done it without that hit you delivered," Drew adds. "Perfectly timed."

"Huh?" Locking my phone, I switch off the ringer. I'll pay for it later, but I'm too tired to care. "Oh, yeah."

Violet's CRV is already parked in front of our house when Drew pulls in, parking behind her. Sadly, there's no sense in her waiting for me at the arena when we can't be seen leaving together. I climb out of the passenger side of his truck and meet her halfway on the sidewalk. Unlike most game nights, she's still wearing her training uniform. She usually changes before she leaves the arena because she claims the polo is "frumpy," whatever the fuck that means. I think she looks hot in anything.

When I lean down for a kiss, Violet gives me a quick peck and wordlessly yanks me up the path to the house. A few more cars pull up behind Drew's truck, people pouring out. We step through the front door to find a small impromptu party in our living room. Thanks to Connor, no doubt.

"Come on." Ignoring the fact that there are people other than my roommates present, she takes me by the arm and hauls me straight upstairs.

"You in a hurry to get me alone?" I ask, stepping into my bedroom. Before we get any farther, I need to go find Biscuit and lock him up. But he's a furry little cockblock, so I'll stick him in Vaughn's room for now.

She slams the door behind her, whirling around to face me. "You're dizzy."

This is a disappointment, to say the least. I was expecting victory sex. Or a victory blowjob. Preferably both.

"A little." No point in lying. I'm not quite one hundred percent, but it's not dire. A bit like the spins after slightly too much to drink. I've taken harder hits, though this one knocked me for a loop more than most.

Violet clasps her hands, pacing in a small circle in front of me. Without stopping, she unzips her long-sleeved training jacket, shrugging it off and tossing it onto my desk chair. "You know the concussion safety protocol," she says, almost as if she's talking to herself instead of me. "You need to stop playing until your symptoms are fully resolved and then you can follow a stepwise return-to-sport plan. But you need to sit out for a few games, at least."

Oh, we're doing this, now? Great.

"Not gonna happen, Vi." I slip out of my navy suit jacket and begin to unfasten the buttons of my dress shirt, working my way down. If we aren't going to fool around, I'm changing out of this fucking suit.

Violet comes to a screeching halt, her eyes wide. "What? You can't play like this."

"It was one hit." Turning away, I rifle through my closet for something to wear, grabbing a pair of jeans and a long-sleeved black t-shirt. "Wasn't even that bad."

To some extent, I understand why she feels this way. But by the time the tournament rolls around next weekend, I'll be back to normal.

"It was one thing when it was your knee or your shoulder, but this is your brain we're talking about. Does second impact syndrome ring a bell?"

"I'm fine." Or at least, I will be soon. Especially once I get some painkillers and food. I'm fucking starving, and it isn't helping my patience level. If we could put a pin in this fight until later, that would be great. Better yet, until never.

"You are *not* fine." She throws up her hands, making another loop at the foot of my bed. "I have no idea how everyone else failed to notice that you couldn't skate a straight line to get off the ice. I looked the other way with your shoulder more than I should have, because it's ultimately your career to burn. I won't look the other way with your life."

I tug on my jeans, glancing back up at her. "Would you give it a rest already?"

Violet stops short, and her big blue eyes regard me uncertainly. My irritation wanes, replaced with guilt. I hate the way she's looking at me right now. I never raise my voice at her.

"I'll be okay by next weekend." I soften my tone.

"And if you're not?"

"I have to be. I need to play in that tournament. My stats have already suffered enough because of all my time off last year. Plus, Russell is going to be there."

My father is coming to the game, too, but I can't use that to support my case. Bringing him up will raise questions I don't want to answer. Besides, he's not the biggest reason I need to put in ice time. I don't need Chicago thinking I'm a bad investment. I know guys who've been drafted and dropped, and it decimated their careers. I haven't worked this hard, sacrificed this much, and gotten this far only to let it all slip away.

Her forehead furrows. "Russell?"

"Chicago's AGM, Vi." I tug my shirt on overhead, running a hand through my hair to smooth it. "They want to see how I've grown this year. I can't be sidelined again. Being injury prone is a massive liability."

"You know what else is a massive liability?" she asks. "Permanent brain damage."

Head pounding, I perch on the end of my bed, debating how to handle her. What I really need is some Advil, but getting that right now will only add fuel to the fire.

Violet steps closer and gently massages my scalp with her fingertips. Some of the tension I'm holding melts. Her touch is a welcome distraction from the throbbing in my skull.

"Besides, maybe this will give your shoulder a chance to rest without having to draw attention to that."

Another rush of frustration creeps in. She has no idea how much pressure I'm under. One wrong move could blow my career to smithereens.

I draw in a deep breath, slowly emptying my lungs before I reply. "Why can't you trust my judgement?"

Violet is a worrier through and through, and she's overstating things. Yes, I have a headache, but it'll be gone by tomorrow. I'm sure the dizziness won't last, either. It's not like I got knocked out or something. My concussion last year was worse than this, and it still resolved quickly.

"Because your criteria for being fit to play appears to begin and end with 'being conscious.' If you think—" A loud knock startles us both, cutting off Violet mid-sentence.

"Yo, I hate to interrupt your victory sex but I think there's something wrong with Bitty," Connor calls through the door. "He seemed kinda out of it when we got home. Vaughn and I tried feeding him, but he won't eat."

Fuck. Biscuit is a four-legged garbage disposal. Refusing to eat is unheard of for him.

"Give me a sec, Haas. We'll be right down." I shoot Violet an apologetic look. "I should go check on him. He might need to be checked out."

"If he does, I'm driving. Not you. And we're not done talking about this."

———

One three-hundred-dollar veterinary bill later, diagnosis: kennel cough.

According to the vet, Biscuit probably picked it up from the dog park. It usually resolves on its own, but because he's so young, he prescribed antibiotics to treat any potential secondary bacterial infections. He also gave me a cough suppressant. How the hell I'm supposed to get cough syrup into a puppy is anyone's guess, but his coughing is downright pitiful, so I guess I'll have to try.

I pay the bill at reception while Violet gathers Biscuit in her arms, cooing at him. He gazes up at her adoringly, working his puppy dog eyes to the max. While I know he's sick, he definitely doesn't mind all the extra attention. I wait as the receptionist tries my card once, twice, then a third time with a frown. I hope we can hurry this the fuck up, because the fluorescent lighting in this office isn't helping my headache.

Squinting, she quickly taps on the keyboard, then glances back up at me. "I'm sorry, sir. I'm not sure if there's some kind of error, but it says this credit card has been reported as stolen."

"Stolen?" I repeat.

"Maybe you should call your credit card company," she suggests, handing my Mastercard back.

Oh, of course. This is payback for ignoring those calls earlier. Well played, Doug. Escalating after only two hours is a new record for him.

"Yeah." Working my jaw, I strive to keep my voice level while Violet's gaze weighs down on me. "I will."

What the hell am I supposed to do now?

Over the past few years, I've stashed away a decent chunk of change in a separate account only held in my name. Not sufficient to live on long-term, but enough to get me by temporarily should things really hit the fan. But in my rush to leave the house, I didn't grab any cash or my other bank card. Now I can't pay this bill. Not a great look in front of my girlfriend.

Violet sets Biscuit on the tiled floor. "It's okay. I've got it, Nash." She pulls out her wallet and grabs her Visa, passing it over the counter to the receptionist.

"I can pay you back. I just didn't bring anything else with me." While I know she isn't exactly strapped for cash, that isn't the point. I feel like a fucking deadbeat.

I'll be making three-quarters of a million dollars by this time next year, but the gap between here and there is a chasm.

"Don't you dare. I talked you into taking care of him, and you've covered all of his other expenses so far."

I hold Biscuit while she signs the receipt, and then I carry him out to her car. He's even needier than usual, so I let him curl up on my lap while Violet drives. Neither of us speaks, probably because we know it'll escalate right back into another disagreement.

Ten minutes into the drive home, Violet breaks the silence at a red light.

"Why would your card have been reported as stolen?"

"Can we not get into this right now?" I still have a headache, still haven't eaten, and I'm worried my phone service will be the next thing to go. I can replace it, if it comes to that, but getting a new number would be a huge pain in the ass—not to mention, one more thing I'd have to explain to her. "I told you I can pay you back."

Her gaze darts over to me, then back to the road ahead. "It's not about the money. I was wondering if it was fraud or something you should be worried about. Maybe you should call your credit card company, like she said."

"Not fraud." I adjust the passenger seat, reclining it, and close my eyes in hopes it will put the subject to rest.

"How do you know?"

"I just do, okay?" Bad enough this happened in front of her. The last thing I'm going to do is let her know how much of a tire fire it really is behind the scenes. Graduation and financial independence can't come soon enough.

When I start to think she's dropped it, she asks, "Does this have something to do with your father?"

Fucking Christ.

Why can't she see that I'm trying to protect her from the shit-storm that is my life?

"Drop it, Vi." The words burst from my mouth, my tone harsher than I intend.

Violet's lips press into a line, but she says nothing. She shakes her head, heaving a small sigh, and returns her attention to the road. Her disappointment with me is so palpable I can feel it, like a rusty blade sawing the two of us apart.

The longer she remains quiet, the larger the gash grows. All the progress we've made, the trust I've earned, bleeds onto the floor of the car. I want to mend it, but I don't know how.

When she pulls up to the curb in front of my house, she shifts the car into park, leaving the ignition running. The party has continued in our absence, and there are people milling about in the living room window visible from the front street.

"Are you coming in?" I unbuckle my seatbelt, glancing over at her.

"I don't think that's a good idea."

Panic rises in my stomach, flooding the rest of my body. I can't handle yet another thing going wrong right now, especially not the most important one of all.

"Don't be like that."

"Be like what?" Her voice climbs, waking Biscuit in my lap with a start. "Don't expect you to respect and listen to me when I feel strongly about something? Or don't expect you to let me in and tell me about your life? Tell me, where am I being unreasonable?"

I don't know what to say to that, because she isn't. But how can I be honest with her when there are so many ugly truths I need to shelter her from?

Would she even want me if she knew them all?

We look at each other in the darkened interior of the car, neither of us saying anything. She looks more sad than mad, and I hate that it's because of me. More than anything, I want to make things better, but I don't see a way to do that. Not without telling her everything, and that isn't an option.

Violet unbuckles her seatbelt and leans over the center console, wrapping her arms around my neck and catching me by surprise. I hug her back with my one free arm while I bury my face in her hair, inhaling her scent. Time slows, everything fades, and I never want to let her go.

But she pulls away all too soon.

Disappointment washes over me as she refastens her seatbelt, and her gaze drops to the steering wheel. She stares at it, and her bottom lip quivers. "I'm trying to be patient with you, Nash, but you make it so damn difficult sometimes."

CHAPTER 40

HOLE IN MY HEART

VIOLET

NASH and I have barely spoken in two days.

Over forty-eight hours of hardly sleeping, over-eating, and constant worrying.

He insists he's okay in the few, sparse texts we've exchanged, but it's little consolation. Then again, I'm sure he *is* okay in terms of day-to-day functioning. His symptoms were mild, and if he were at any imminent risk, I'd have been forced to act already. But it's his determination to return to hockey this weekend that concerns me.

"Ready, Violet?" Claire stretches out her quad next to me, switching legs and grabbing her other ankle.

After weeks' worth of training, we're standing at the starting line for our 10K Turkey Trot, surrounded by dozens of other runners donning race bibs. It's a cool, clear day outside without a cloud in sight. A bit brisk while we're standing around, but it should be ideal once we start to sweat.

"Ready as I'll ever be," I tell her. "I'm sure you're about to kick my butt."

With the starting signal, Claire quickly pulls ahead. I don't even attempt to keep pace with her. She's faster than me at the best of times, and I'm not well rested after two nights of tossing and turning. Before long, I've lost sight of her completely and I'm still struggling to find my groove.

Sometimes, running is meditative for me. I get into the zone where my breath and pace seem to align perfectly. My mind turns calm; clear; almost empty, in a peaceful way.

This race isn't one of those times.

I try to focus on my form. On my foot strike, posture, and cadence. But it's easier said than done when it feels like the world is crashing down around me. I miss Nash, I'm mad at him, and I'm concerned about him. I'm a barrel of mixed emotions that only he can ever evoke.

He's all I can think about. And even though the course is mostly flat, it feels as though I'm running uphill for the entire ten kilometers.

———

When Claire and I get home, exhausted and triumphant, there's a huge bouquet of flowers sitting on our counter. A gorgeous, vibrant purple blend of roses and Calla Lilies, with a few other flowers I don't recognize mixed in. Maybe they're for Claire, or from someone new for Jules.

"The delivery guy just dropped them off for you..." Julianna tells me, grimacing slightly.

Oh. They're from Nash.

I pull out the card, reading it, and I don't know whether I want to smile or cry.

Proud of you, Vi.
- Nash

———

Three more days pass without any progress on the Nash front.

I go through the motions, but it feels like I'm walking around with a gaping hole in my heart. Now that I've been driving myself to and from school, Nash and I have little excuse to see each other alone and making plans doesn't seem to be a viable option when we both know it will inevitably lead to yet another argument.

Dryland training on Wednesday is the first time we see each other face-to-face since the party. Unlike his ill-advised determination to return to impact sports, light exercise can be okay with a mild concussion—and may even be beneficial, since aerobic exercise increases blood flow to the brain. But if he pushes himself too hard, he'll experience setbacks and prolong his recovery. I quietly remind him to pace himself several times, but it's difficult to gauge whether he listens. Although he seems to manage, he's slightly off. He's a little less coordinated in the agility drills, a little slower to recover from intervals. It isn't obvious enough that you'd notice unless you were watching closely for it, which is probably why no one else seems to.

After my last class on Thursday, I find Nash waiting for me in the hall. All the wind knocks out of me, and I tell Jules I'll see her at home. He pushes off the wall, meeting me halfway in a few long strides. The air between us is laden with tension in a way that reminds me of the start of the semester, and I hate it.

Shifting his bag on his shoulder, his eyes bounce between mine. "Can I walk you to your car?"

"Of course."

He falls into step beside me as we navigate the corridor. "How have you been?"

"Fine." The lie is bitter and hard to force out. "How about you?"

"I miss you." His words slip beneath my defenses, hitting where I'm vulnerable. In my peripheral vision, Nash's brow lowers, and he hesitates before he speaks again. "Can you come over so we can talk?"

"Okay."

We make small talk until we reach my vehicle, and a moment passes where neither of us is sure what to do. Since we're in public, we can't exactly hug or kiss anyway, but there's a definite awkwardness between us that isn't usually present.

"I'll meet you at my place?" He seems uncertain, like he's not sure whether I'm going to show.

"I have to run home first, and then I'll come by."

Maybe I can talk some sense into him.

———

A little under an hour later, I'm standing at Nash's front door. I square my shoulders and draw in a breath, trying to feign confidence. This is my last-ditch effort before I deploy the nuclear option.

The doorbell barely finishes chiming before Nash answers, almost like he'd been lurking in wait. Maybe he's as nervous about this as I am.

"Hi." His eyes crinkle at the corners, but there's a sadness behind them.

Stepping aside, he lets me enter and closes the door behind me. I want to reach out and touch him, but I don't want to be the first one to bridge that gap. He turns and wraps me in a gigantic hug, picking me up off the ground like always. But he doesn't try to kiss me, and I'm not sure whether it's because he doesn't want to or doesn't think I want him to.

When sets me back down, his arms linger around my waist so briefly I think I might have imagined it.

Nash leads me down the hall to the living room, where we find Biscuit laying in a heap on the floor, curled up with his favorite stuffed monkey toy. It's a pathetic, though adorable, sight.

I scurry over, kneeling at his side. "You poor baby."

He nudges my hand with his wet nose, letting out a whimper. I scratch behind his ears, and his tail thumps against the hardwood, his eyes drifting shut.

"I know he's sick," Nash says, his mouth hinting at a smile, "but I think he might be playing it up a little for your sake."

After another minute of puppy snuggles, I stand back up, going to sit next to Nash on the couch. His large hand grabs hold of mine, interlacing our fingers. My stomach flip-flops, because being with him feels so right even when things between us are going terribly wrong.

"I don't want to fight with you, Petal." His voice is quiet, regretful in a way that gives me hope.

"Are you still having symptoms?"

"Barely," he says. "It's nothing."

My hopes come crashing down. "If it's even borderline, you can't play tomorrow night."

"You should trust me when I tell you I'm fine."

"But you just admitted you're still having symptoms." Tears prick at my eyes, my breath turning jagged. I've never been so frustrated with someone else in my entire life. "Second impact syndrome is serious, Nash. One hit is all it takes, and you could be critically injured. Not to mention, I'm violating a million rules by not telling anyone when I know you shouldn't be playing."

For the life of me, I can't understand why he'd put his health—and possibly even his own life—at risk for this tournament. I understand that it's important and, to some extent, I understand the pressures he's facing. But those things can be dealt with later. A brain injury can't.

Nash withdraws his hand from mine, and it hurts more than a simple action should. "Go ahead, then. Tell them."

A freight train of grief slams into me at full speed. He's going to force me to pull the pin on a grenade that will blow up our relationship?

"I don't want to be the one who does—"

He cuts me off. "I'm not benching myself. Do what you need to do, and I'll do the same."

Suddenly, it clicks. It's a bluff. Nash doesn't think I'll tell Coach Ward and Christina.

He's wrong.

I push to my feet and begin to pace around the coffee table. The air in the room feels too thick, too heavy, and the ache that's been in my chest since last weekend has grown into a stabbing pain.

How is this happening? This can't be happening.

Maybe part of the problem is that it's difficult to love someone who doesn't seem to love themselves. I'm trying to love him enough for the both of us, but I'm not sure it's working.

"You're doing it again," I tell him, trying to appeal to whatever shred of sense he has left. "Just like last time."

"Doing what?" He rests his corded forearms on his thighs, dark green eyes watching me as I continue to pace around the living room.

"Breaking us." A tear lands on my arm, and only then do I realize I'm crying. Nash watches me, a helpless expression on his face. But it only frustrates me more, because he's not helpless; he could fix this right now. He could do the right thing, pull himself from the lineup, and salvage the wreckage of whatever we've become.

Instead, he's sitting there watching my heart break at his feet. Again.

"This has nothing to do with us," he says. "This is about me and my career."

The worst part of what he's saying is, he actually seems to believe it.

"This has *everything* to do with us. How can you stand there and say you care about me when you'd be risking both of our futures by playing? You're forcing me to make an impossible choice." My voice fractures. "I don't want anything to happen to you."

"I'll be fine, Vi."

"This is the concussion talking. You're not thinking clearly."

He doesn't respond.

A sinking sense of defeat settles in my gut, and my chest rises with an inhale, the air fueling words I don't want to have to say.

"If you don't pull yourself," I tell him, "I will. But I'm asking you to do the right thing, so it doesn't come to that. If you won't do it for yourself, do it for me."

Weariness grips me, and I march past the couch, heading for the hall. I linger in the doorway for a few seconds, waiting for Nash to come after me. To apologize, to ask me to stay, even to keep fighting. Waiting for him to do something—anything—but he doesn't.

CHAPTER 41

GUT, HEART, HEAD
NASH

IF FUCKING things up were an Olympic sport, I'd be a gold medalist.

Things have been strained with Violet all week. While we've still been texting and talking, it isn't the same. The distance between us is slowly killing me, like there's a piece of myself missing.

I've lived without her before, and I don't want to do it again.

Not only am I stressed as fuck about her, but I'm also worried about the game—and starting to think she might be right. My symptoms haven't improved nearly as much as I'd expected.

Vaughn drops his towel and sinks into the cold tub next to me, grimacing as the ice water envelops him. "What's going on with you and Violet? Didn't mean to eavesdrop on your fight last night, but it was kind of hard not to."

"She doesn't think I should play tonight," I mutter.

Thing is, even if I wanted to pull myself from tonight's lineup, it's terrible timing now. Everything has already been set in motion, and I'd be letting a ton of people down by bailing on such short notice. Russell, my father, the scouts my father is sending, the team, Coach Ward. Not to mention, I'd look like an idiot for not speaking up sooner.

But it tears me apart to see how upset Violet is over this. If she wasn't in the picture, this would be a much easier call.

No matter what I do, someone is going to be disappointed in me.

Vaughn scans the room like he's checking to make sure anyone is around. "Maybe you shouldn't."

"Not you, too. It's not that bad." It really isn't. Some mild dizziness here and there when I get my heart rate up, nothing I can't deal with.

"You know I'm the last person to interfere with other people's lives, but if there's any doubt, you shouldn't get on that ice. A minor concussion is still a concussion..." Vaughn trails off. "Besides, I need you to stay healthy so I can kick your ass when we play each other in the big leagues."

"You mean, so I can crush your ass into the boards?"

"Gonna have to get faster before next season if you want to do that." He smirks, but his expression quickly turns serious. "Real talk, Russell is a professional. I'm sure he'll understand. Coach and the team, too. As for Doug, fuck him."

I want to believe Vaughn, but what if Russell doesn't? What if this is the final nail in my career coffin, burying it before it even begins?

Maybe Doug was right about Chicago dropping me eventually. I'm sure no one else will be chomping at the bit to pick up an injury-prone free agent once they do.

After a few more minutes, we get out and hit the showers, changing in the locker room. We head across campus together, splitting off as Vaughn heads to the Center for Management Studies. I continue to the parking lot, skipping my afternoon classes. I have somewhere else I need to be.

———

The wind howls as I slowly walk up to the gravesite, pulling up my hood. My dad used to bring me here several times a year. He stopped when he started dating Shannon. It was a slow fade-out at first. We used to go on major holidays, and then we started to go less and less often until we were down to only my mother's birthday. Finally, when I was about twelve, we stopped going completely.

Once I got my driver's license, I started going again alone.

"I don't know what I'm doing, Mom." I shove my hands into my pockets, staring at the engraved marble headstone. Wishing I could remember her face; her voice; her laugh. What she smelled like. What her cooking tasted like. What she liked to do. All I have is a handful of shitty home videos from my first four birthdays. It's not like Doug is much use for retelling stories.

"I know I'm fucking everything up." Easing myself down to the frozen ground, I sit, leaning against the frigid slab of rock. I sit until the sun disappears behind a veil of gray clouds without returning. I sit until big, thick flakes of snow start to fall, flitting through the air on the breeze. I sit until my ears turn numb and my hands grow stiff from the cold.

I don't know what I'm waiting for—what I think I'll get out of sitting here like this. It's not like she can answer me, and I've never been a big believer in signs.

There are a few things I remember. Being at a park with her when she was pushing me on the swing. Waking up from a nightmare in the middle of the night and being comforted by her. Decorating the Christmas tree with her and crying because I broke an ornament, and her telling me it was okay.

I close my eyes, trying to turn down all of the outside noise inside my brain. Pushing out all the other voices. Doug, Coach Ward, my friends, even Violet.

In my gut, in my heart, in my head, I know what the right choice is.

It's just not the easy one.

LESS THAN ONE hour until puck drop.

Every minute that passes is a new heartache, like watching a clock slowly tick down to the end of our relationship.

I still believe Nash will do the right thing, but he's running out of time to do it. And if he doesn't, I will—even if it means he never forgives me. I'd rather he live to be angry with me than end up in a hospital bed with permanent brain damage, or worse.

My mind races as I pace in small circles in front of the Grizzlies' locker room entrance, making lap after lap. Team members filter by, greeting me as they pass, but none of them are the one I'm looking for. Where's Nash?

Turning, I start lap number forty-one. And that's when I see his large figure standing at the other end of the hall. My breath catches, and I swallow a sob of relief. He's wearing street clothes, with his puffy black winter jacket and a beanie on his head.

Cautious hope blooms within me as I rush over to him. When I draw closer, I see that his cheeks and nose are red and chapped-looking, like he's been outside. He looks positively frozen. Where was he?

We step to the side, partially sheltered by a wall. Early evening sun pours through the windows beside us, highlighting his tired-looking features. Dark circles line his eyes like he hasn't slept in several days.

"You're not dressed," I whisper.

He rubs his forehead, tension stretching across his face. "Just talked to Coach. I pulled myself."

Tears spring to my eyes, and I blink rapidly, trying to hold them back. It takes every shred of self-control I have not to wrap him in an enormous hug. I knew he'd do the right thing, and I'm so thankful I was right.

"Don't worry," he adds. "I made sure you won't get any blow-back from it."

I'd been so concerned about him, that had been the last thing on my mind.

My throat clogs with emotion. "Are you okay?"

"I'm fine." His gaze drops to the floor. "I mean, it obviously fucking sucks, but I know it was the correct call."

When he glances back up, sadness gleams in his green eyes. I knew he'd be disappointed, but he's taking it harder than I thought. Probably because of the Chicago factor, although I'd hope a professional team would commend him for doing the right thing, not punish him for it.

"How are you feeling?" I ask carefully.

He blows out a breath. "Fine, right now. It's only when I get my heart rate up."

"Like in dryland," I murmur. "I could tell you were struggling."

His lips press into a grim line. "Yeah. Coach and Christina said we can meet on Monday to discuss a return to sport plan."

A weight lifts off my shoulders. Having this out in the open means one less secret to keep.

"I'm glad you decided not to play."

"Me, too. You were right. I'm sorry, Vi." Stepping forward, he reaches for me and catches himself, stuffing his hands in his pockets instead because we're in public. "Can we talk at my place after the game?"

"Sure. Are you staying to watch?"

Nash shakes his head. "Too hard when I can't be out there.

Makes me feel frustrated as hell. Think I'm gonna go hang out with Biscuit for a while."

His gaze darts over to the doors, and he blanches. I follow his line of sight, but I can't make out what he's looking at. Maybe he spotted Chicago's AGM. With the way he's acting, I'm afraid to ask. I don't want to rub salt in a fresh wound.

"I don't want to make you late," he says, shooting another nervous glance in that direction. "Come by after?"

"I'll come over as soon as it's done."

We linger for a few more seconds. I desperately wish I could close the distance between us. Put us back together. Be in his arms for a brief, blessed moment.

"I'm proud of you for doing the right thing," I tell him. "I know it can't have been easy."

"If I'm being honest, I'm not sure I would have done it without you." He takes a small step closer, pushing the envelope with respect to what a platonic buffer between us would be. Our gazes meet, and he pauses. "If there's one thing this week taught me, it's that I need you. More than you know."

My heart cracks open. "You shouldn't say things like that when I can't kiss you," I whisper.

One corner of his mouth lifts. "Save it for later, so we can make up properly."

———

Nash isn't responding to my texts.

Logically, I'm sure he's okay. I saw him less than half an hour ago. But after seeing how crestfallen he was about pulling himself from the lineup, I need confirmation. A response. Something to tell me he got home safely and that he's all right.

Like he always says, I'm a worrier.

A few minutes into the first period, I excuse myself from the game under the guise of needing to use the bathroom. As soon as I step into the hall, I check my phone for the millionth time in the past twenty minutes, but Nash still hasn't replied.

Something compels me to go check the parking lot for his car, and my worry skyrockets when I spot it parked off to the side. If his vehicle is still here and he's not watching the game with the team, then where is he? Is he okay?

I'm composing another text to him when voices echo in the distance, startling me. Not just voices—raised voices, clearly in the midst of a confrontation. They're both male, albeit too muffled for me to discern whether one of them belongs to Nash. Heart in my throat, I creep down the hall, following the direction of the commotion. Down at the end, the black-painted door to one of the meeting rooms is half-open, an argument tumbling out.

"...if you're going to choke when it counts?" the first guy snarls.

This voice, I don't recognize.

"You think I don't want to be out there? It's killing me not to play."

My breath seizes in my lungs, because this one, I do. It's definitely Nash.

"Russell is sitting out there in the stands as we speak, along with Graham, Benson, and Smyth. I vouched for you. I put my reputation on the line to get them out here tonight, and you didn't even have the courtesy to let me know you weren't in the fucking line-up."

"I'm sorry, okay? I wanted to, but I knew you'd be disappointed in me."

"That's the least of my issues. You're an embarrassment."

"Dad." Nash sounds choked up.

My gut wrenches, and everything comes together in a blink.

I get it. I finally get it now.

His father continues to berate him, laying into his supposed lack of work ethic and a million other alleged shortcomings that are patently false. My hands tremble as I stay frozen to the spot, wracked with indecision. Leaving feels wrong, but so does intervening. Nash obviously didn't want me to know, and I don't want to make things worse. But how could I ever pretend I never overheard this? If it hurts for me to hear, I can only imagine what it feels like for him.

"This is a critical time in your career, and you're slacking off now?"

Red-hot anger blooms in my stomach, flooding the rest of my body. There is no one—literally no one—I know who's more dedicated to hockey than Nash. To the point where he's been hell-bent on risking his health and safety because of it. And clearly, that traces back to his upbringing. He's been brainwashed into not taking his own needs seriously. Into not trusting himself. Into not *valuing* himself. I'm sure that's a difficult pattern to break, which is why he felt pressured to play.

"It's a good thing your mother isn't here to see what a disappointment you've become," his father adds.

I gasp and clamp my hand over my mouth. If I thought my heart was broken before, it shatters when I hear this. What parent says that to their child?

My phone slips through my fingers and lands on the floor with a clatter, echoing in the empty hall.

Everything falls silent.

Nash and his father both turn to look at me standing in the doorway.

CHAPTER 43

INEVITABLE

I HAD CONVINCED myself this day would never come.

Maybe it was inevitable.

"I-I'm sorry," Violet stammers, bending to pick up her phone. "I didn't mean to—you weren't answering my texts, and I was worried. When I saw that your car was still here, I went looking for you to make sure you were okay."

There are so many things written across her face. Concern, anger, sadness. . . love. But most of all, she looks fucking terrified, and I hate him even more for it.

My heart roars in my ears as I walk over to her, ducking to catch her gaze. "It's okay, Vi."

Her big blue eyes fix on mine, shining with compassion. Shame simmers in my gut, acrid and bitter. Because I know she heard it; she heard it all.

Interlacing my fingers with hers, I give her hand a squeeze and lower my voice. "Let me finish handling this—"

"Who the hell is this?" My father barks, nodding at her.

"This is my girlfriend, Violet." Not particularly eager to drag her into this, but it's a little late for that now. I suck in a breath, bracing for the worst. "Vi, this is my dad, Doug."

He waves me off, suddenly disinterested in the answer despite his question. "Are you going to man up and get out there tonight, or not?"

"Why are you pressuring him to play?" Violet snaps. Her cheeks are flushed scarlet with anger, her voice shaky. "He's injured. Playing could put him at risk of serious harm. Permanent harm."

"This is a family matter, Violet." He rolls his eyes. "We don't need jersey chasers getting involved."

My blood pressure shoots through the roof. Jersey chaser? Who the fuck does he think he's speaking to?

I whirl around to face him. "Don't talk to her that way."

Violet is more like family to me than he's ever been. My friends, too. Hell, even Coach Ward. At least he cares enough to listen and to help me when I need it.

"Back to the point." The scorn in his voice is venomous. "It's easier to explain you showing up late than not showing up at all."

Right. That's all he cares about—his reputation. Not my health or safety, and sure as hell not my happiness.

"Like I said, I'm out. Already told Coach Ward I have a concussion, and our team's doctor checked me over before the game. They both agreed that pulling myself was the right call."

He assesses me with cold, flinty eyes. "Never thought I'd raise a quitter. But I guess it makes sense. You're too distracted by your little puck bunny these days to focus on what matters."

My free hand clenches into a fist, and the thin tether holding me in line strains until it nearly snaps. If there's one person who knows how to trigger me, it's him.

"Quit fucking calling her names," I grit.

"Don't disrespect me over some little bitch."

Violet flinches, and my entire body coils like a spring. An unprecedented level of fury ignites within me, threatening to incinerate my fragile self-restraint. The temptation to knock him out is almost too much to resist. It's a good thing she's standing beside me, because I'm not sure what I would do if she wasn't.

"Say that one more time, and I'll throw you outside myself." My tone sharpens until it's skate-edge sharp. "Leave Violet out of this. Last warning."

"You ungrateful little shit. You don't appreciate a single thing I've done for you."

Which part should I be grateful for? The parts where he tore me down and told me I wasn't good enough my whole life, or the perpetually moving goalposts? Or maybe the time he dislocated my shoulder when I was ten? Footing the bill for a couple of years doesn't even remotely compensate for that upbringing.

Everything he's instilled in me for so many years reaches a boiling point. All of the guilt, the shame, and the unworthiness condenses, distilling into something else.

And all I'm left with is pure, unadulterated rage.

"It's not my fault you didn't have what it takes to make it," I tell Doug.

On some level, I'm aware that provoking him will make it worse, but I've lost control of my mouth. Better than the alternative.

"What did you say?" He's eerily calm in a way that's scarier than yelling could ever be. Or at least, it would be if I were still afraid of him. But he hasn't laid a finger on me in over five years, and for good fucking reason.

"You're a washed-up never-was who didn't even make it to the league," I add. "I've already accomplished more than you ever will. It kills you, doesn't it?"

My father steps closer, and I pivot, putting myself between him and Violet.

"Who do you think you're talking to? After the sacrifices I've made for you, you'd better show some goddamn respect. You didn't get here all alone, son."

Oh, that's rich. Now he's trying to take credit for my hard work.

"I got here by freezing my ass off hiding at the rink down the street, deking the puck and working on my wrist shot for hours on end all winter long. Because I'd rather do that than be trapped inside our miserable excuse for a home with you!"

Violet clutches my hand harder, and I realize I'm nearly shouting. Swallowing, I fight to keep my anger in check. I don't want to lose control in front of her. I refuse to.

"What the hell is the matter with you?" my father roars.

"What's the matter with me?" I laugh, but it's dark and mirthless. Fuck it. Violet has already seen all of the skeletons in my closet. What's the point in trying to shove them back in? "You're the one who beat the shit out of me every time we lost a game in the minors. I was a kid, Doug. Look in the mirror."

His face reddens, a telltale vein in his forehead bulging. "You're embarrassing yourself."

"The only one who should be embarrassed here is you. Don't expect me to keep your secrets anymore. I don't owe you shit."

I steer Violet over to the door, gripping her more tightly than I should. The minute we step out into the hall, I'll have to let her go.

"If you walk away right now, you can consider yourself cut off," he calls. "That includes your vehicle."

A nauseating amount of adrenaline courses through me. I'm done. So fucking done.

"Good thing I have a full ride then, huh? You can keep the car." I yank my keys from my pocket and disconnect the key fob, tossing it underhand to him. It lands at his feet with a clink, but he doesn't move to pick it up. "Go fuck yourself."

For the first time in my life, he has nothing to say.

***

I'm dizzy with overwhelm as Violet and I step out into the hall, hands breaking apart. An older, grey-haired man in a navy suit stands at the other end looking at his phone, an arena guest pass lanyard around his neck. Even from a distance, I recognize him instantly.

Russell Peters. The AGM for Chicago.

Fuck my life.

He glances up from the screen and his eyes widen in recognition. "Nash," he says, strolling toward us. "I stepped out to give you a call. Coach Ward told me about your concussion, and I wanted to see how you were doing."

My concussion is the least of my concerns. Did he just overhear all that?

"I'm sure it's okay," Violet murmurs under her breath.

"Russell." My father appears behind us, striding up to him.

Perfectly on cue to steamroll me like always. Dread consumes me as he continues, "I'm so sorry about all of this. My son should never have—"

"Why don't you let me worry about my prospect, Doug?" Russell says coolly.

He blinks, rapid-fire. "But I'm the one you've been dealing—"

Russell cuts him off again. "Do you mind if I have a word with you in private, Nash?"

While I'm still in shock and not fully in my right mind, I know I need to say yes. Not having my father acting as the go-between with Chicago means there's one less thing he can hold over my head.

"Sure. I'd like to walk her back to the bench first, though." I nod to Violet standing next to me. No way am I leaving her to head back by herself with Doug around. I've never seen him get violent with his girlfriend, but I still don't trust him.

"That's fine." Russell returns his attention to my father, leveling him with an icy look. "I'll be speaking to the board at Copperhill Academy about my concerns with respect to your behavior and your lack of suitability for overseeing minors."

"It's not—come on, Russell. You know me." Doug starts to ramble, grasping at straws, alternating between blaming me and minimizing what just happened.

Russell turns away, evidently uninterested in his excuses, and we leave him glued to the spot, glowering with incandescent rage. I'm sure there are a million threats he'd like to make, but he can't say shit with Russell present.

It's never felt better to walk away from him.

***

Once Violet steps onto the bench with the rest of the team, Russell and I head into the concession area and grab drinks, then sit down at a table off to the side. He's got a coffee, while I'm nursing a hot chocolate. It seemed like I should order something, and beer was obviously out. Though I could sure as hell use one right now.

Russell leans back in his seat, draping his arm along the back of his chair. "I was speaking with your coach before the game, and we both agreed that it shows a lot of maturity to pull yourself like that, knowing you weren't fit to play. I know it can be hard when you're hoping an issue will resolve itself in time, and it doesn't."

"It was hard," I admit, clutching my hot chocolate like my life depends on it. My hands are still shaking from the adrenaline rush of quarreling with Doug.

"In the long run, you'll be better for it. The league takes concussions very seriously these days. If it's even borderline, we don't want you to get out on that ice. But make sure you tell your training team right after a hit like that next time, okay?" His graying eyebrows lift. "Don't try to wait it out on your own. They're there to support you."

"Understood." I do see that now. Maybe it was hard for me to trust that they were on my side when Doug never was. I've played with bruises, cuts, sprains, you name it. He always told me to suck it up, shake it off, and get back out there.

Russell nods at me. "Speaking of that, how's your shoulder been?"

My relief wanes at the topic, but I know I should be honest. "I've been consistent with my rehab. Still have some twinges here and there, but it's doing okay."

"You're in great hands with your athletic training team. After school wraps up, we'll send you to Chicago to work with our staff over the summer to make sure you're ready for the season."

A wave of gratitude engulfs me. Most of the time, rookies are on the hook for their own training during the gap between their college graduation and their rookie season. While I would easily be able to afford that with my signing bonus, working with the team is infinitely better. In addition to receiving world-class coaching and rehab, it's an opportunity to get to know the staff and some of the team, as well as to familiarize myself with the facility.

It's a huge honor—coming on the heels of one of the worst moments of my life.

"That would be great." I swallow another sip of hot chocolate, my brain working overtime to process everything. Too much has happened in a short span of time, and I suspect it'll be several days before it does.

"We can help set you up with accommodations if you don't have time to arrange for that while you're still in school," he adds. "Coach Ward tells me you're one of the hardest workers on the team. We're committed to helping you grow as an athlete, and we're investing in you for the long-term."

I nearly choke up on the spot, but I manage to keep it in check. After working for as long as I can remember, this is what I've always wanted to hear.

Russell asks me about school and my classes before jumping into discussing my game. He walks me through an honest assessment of my strengths and weaknesses, what they'd like me to work on, and where I fit in with respect to their roster. I learn multiple things Doug withheld from me, which is no surprise. Up until now, he was always the point of contact between me and Chicago.

"I'll come back in the new year to watch you play once you're ready, but it's important not to push it. Take the time you need to heal fully before you return to the ice." Russell pushes his chair back, gathering our empty cups.

We walk through the empty concourse and back to the spectator area while I debate whether to stick around and watch the game. Then I realize I don't have a choice, because I no longer have a car.

Or any money.

My scholarship takes care of tuition, but I still need to cover everything else. I'll have to stretch my rainy-day fund paper-thin to get it to last until graduation.

"Why don't you stick around and watch the rest of the game?" Russell asks, nodding to the seating area. "Last I saw, the Grizzlies were handing the Vulcans' asses to them."

Good. The only thing worse than losing is losing while I'm benched. I always feel at least somewhat responsible.

I follow Russell into the viewing suite he's been given access to, and we sit down, watching the rest of the second period. With three minutes to go, Vaughn scores a killer goal with an assist from Connor, and the crowd erupts into booming cheers.

Once it dies down, I force myself to ask the question that's been haunting me.

"About my dad," I begin. "How much of that did you hear, exactly?"

Russell steals a glance at me, sympathy across his face. "Enough to pretend that I didn't hear any of it, if that's what you'd prefer."

"Not sure there's any point in that. I think everyone in the entire arena may have heard."

"There's nothing to be ashamed of, Nash." His lips press into a grim line. "There are a lot of athletes in the hockey world who grew up in similar situations. I'm just sorry to see that you're one of them."

CHAPTER 44

BIG SPOON, LITTLE SPOON
VIOLET

THOSE PHONE CALLS. The issue with his credit card. Nash's caginess about his family—and mine. It all makes sense now that I know the truth.

While I had some suspicions about his home life, never in a million years would I have guessed it was so bad. It crushes me to know it's something he felt like he had to hide. There are so many things I want to ask, but I don't want to bombard him with questions.

Nash is quiet as we weave through the mobbed corridors and out into the parking lot after the game. It's swarming with people, so I'm not worried about being seen leaving together. Without a word, he opens the passenger side door for me, taking my keys and walking around to the driver's side. He starts the ignition and rests his forearm along the door, looking out the window. In his side profile, his jaw is rigid, the cords in his neck strained.

I don't know what to say, so I wait until he's ready to talk.

He runs a hand along his jaw, turning back to face me. "Vi, I know you're probably horrified by the shit show you just witnessed, but that's basically just an average Friday in the Richards family. It's not the first time he's said those things to me, and I'm sure it won't be the last." A rueful smile plays on his lips. "It's the first time I've told him to go fuck himself, though."

Queasiness brews in the pit of my stomach. That's how he was raised. His entire childhood. Growing up without his mother, and having to handle all of that abuse on top of it? It's gutting.

"You don't deserve to be treated that way, Nash. And I'm sorry if I made it worse with what I said. I didn't mean to intrude. Hearing him talk to you that way just made me so upset."

"You were trying to stand up for me, Vi, and that means a lot." A line forms between his brows. "But I'm sorry for the way he spoke to you. That was completely uncalled for."

When I glance down, I realize that he's shaking, and I take his hand in mine. Even in the parking lot, no one is going to get close enough to see that. I probably can't risk hugging him, though, which I hate. He looks like he needs it.

"His behavior isn't your fault." I hate that he's apologizing for that vile man, especially when he's done so much worse to Nash.

"He's my dad."

My eyes brim with tears and I bite the inside my cheek, willing them away. This is why he never told me. He felt ashamed. He's been mistreated for God knows how long by a monster of a father, and he's spent all this time trying to hide it. Carrying the burden alone, hiding someone else's secret.

"You can't control him," I say. "You're not responsible for what he does, either."

Nash opens his mouth and closes it, wagging his head like he's having a silent argument with himself. "I should have told you." His throat bobs. "I just—I wanted to protect you. I thought if I held on a little longer, he'd be out of my life forever and I could keep you from ever having to meet him."

A sob bubbles up in my chest. Knowing that he thought he was protecting me makes it hurt that much more.

"I wish you'd told me, but I understand why you didn't."

"I realize it seems fucked up." His free hand grips the leather steering wheel, his knuckles turning white. "It's not straightforward. Due to the demands of hockey and school, I've never been able to work consistently, which means I have no personal credit history. I couldn't get private loans, and Doug earns too much money for me to qualify for student aid or government loans."

He exhales, and his shoulders sag as he stares ahead blankly. "So, I made a deal with the Devil. I told myself I'd get through the four years. That it wouldn't be as bad once I was no longer living under his roof. That I could take his help temporarily so I could be free of him forever later. You know, short-term pain, long-term gain. But it got worse and worse as college went on, until he was breathing down my neck so much this year that I couldn't even blink without him knowing it."

My stomach twists. "That sounds awful." It must have added an insurmountable amount of stress to what is already a highly stressful hockey career.

"It is what it is." His brow lowers, still looking straight out the window. "I'll have to figure out something else. I don't want another dime of his money."

Beyond the financial component, I know there's more. I heard firsthand how choked up he got when his father called him a disappointment. Like anyone, he wants his father's love and approval. He deserves it, too, even if he might not get it.

"I'll support you no matter what you do."

"I know, Vi." He squeezes my hand before he untangles our fingers, reaching for the gearshift. Putting the car into reverse, he watches the rearview camera as he eases out of the stall. People mill around the parking lot, forcing us to crawl at a painfully slow pace.

"My talk with Russell went well," he says, brightening slightly. "They want to send me to Chicago after graduation to train with the team."

Oh, thank God. He needed a win today after everything that's happened. From what he's told me, being offered something like that is a huge deal.

I place my palm on his knee. "That's amazing. I know how hard you've worked for that. You deserve it."

Maybe one day, he'll finally believe that.

***

Biscuit greets us at the door, grunting with excitement after being without human companionship for all of three hours. Nash grabs his leash off the stand then turns back to face me, waves of agitation rolling off of him.

"Mind if I take him for a walk solo? Nothing against you, Vi, I just need a few minutes to get my head straight."

At hearing the W-word, Biscuit snorts and prances in circles, a blur of black and tan-colored fur.

"Take as long as you need. I'll be here."

While I wait, I curl up on the couch and turn on an episode of Gilmore Girls on Netflix to distract myself. Much as I try to focus on the show, it's impossible. Sadness and anger claw at my chest relentlessly, determined to break free. All I want is for him to get home so I can give him a giant hug and tell him how much I love him.

A few minutes later, the door opens. I glance up, expecting it to be Nash, but it's Vaughn. He greets me with a nod, his expression laden with concern.

"Drove past Nash walking Biscuit," he says quietly, easing onto the couch opposite me. "When I saw him after the game, he told me what happened, but he couldn't get into details at the rink. Is he okay? Are you okay?"

Vaughn is obviously one of the few people who knows the full situation with his father. At least Nash had someone supporting him all this time we've been apart, so he wasn't facing that alone.

"I'm fine. I want to say he is, but I don't know." I ball my hands into fists, trying to quell the flashbacks from earlier tonight. It felt surreal; like something out of a movie, not someone's life. "I can't believe I didn't know how bad it was with his father."

Vaughn's chest rises beneath his white T-shirt with a deep breath, and he raises a tattooed arm, raking his hand through his dark hair. "When you grow up that way, sometimes things like that start to feel normal. I mean, on a deeper level you know it isn't, but you've never known anything else so it's still your normal."

My heart hurts in a way it never has before, because what I witnessed is anything but normal.

"It was awful," I whisper. "I feel so bad for him."

He nods, staring at the floor. "Me, too. I'm glad he has you looking out for him. Even if he's stubborn as hell sometimes."

All the time might be more accurate. But I love the total package, stubbornness and all.

"You made the right call by telling him to pull himself," Vaughn adds, his ice-blue eyes lifting to mine. "I would've told Coach myself, if it had come down to it. Would have asked him to keep it anonymous, though."

Can't blame Vaughn for the anonymous part. Nash has been known to hold grudges.

The door slams, and Biscuit sprints into the room, leaping over the couch to Vaughn. He picks up Biscuit as he pushes to stand, starting for the hall. "Haas and Parsons went to Overtime, so they'll be out for a while. I'll get out of the way and head over there."

"I'm not trying to kick you out of your own—"

He offers me a half-smile. "All good, Violet. You guys need some time alone."

Vaughn and Nash talk quietly in the other room for a few minutes, and I return my attention back to my phone while I wait.

Finally, Nash appears in the living room doorway. "What do you say we go to bed? I know it's only ten, but I'm fucking wiped."

He follows me upstairs as Biscuit squeezes past, leaping onto the foot of the bed and settling in. Like always, Nash lets me get ready first, and I read while I wait for him to come out. Once he does, he lowers down next to me, mattress sinking beneath his weight, but he stays facing away with his elbows on his thighs. His posture is rigid, the stacked muscles in his upper body stiff, like the weight of everything has caught up to him—the weight of what he's been carrying around nearly his entire life.

I lower myself to the floor, scooting forward until I'm kneeling between his legs. He lifts his chin slightly, his green eyes stormy beneath his thick lashes. Sympathy swells in my stomach, and another wave of tears threatens to burst free.

"Are you okay?" I ask softly, resting my hands on his bare thighs.

Nash shakes his head and reaches down, pulling me into his lap.

He loops his muscular arms around my torso, burying his face in my hair as he draws in a jagged breath. "I don't want to be like him, Vi."

There's so much pain in his voice that it makes me ache down to my bones.

Beneath the anguish in his voice, there's something else I rarely detect in Nash—fear. I always thought his biggest worry was getting dropped and losing his career, but it's not. It's the idea of turning out like his father.

"You're nothing like him." My fingertips rest on his cheek. "Sure, you're a little guarded at times. But like I said, you have a big heart. You're caring and thoughtful with me in so many ways."

He huffs. "I almost ruined the best thing that ever happened to me for a second time. Sounds exactly like something he'd do."

"I'm still here. And like you said to me, that won't change." I shift in his lap, turning so we're facing each other. There's a wariness across his face, like he doesn't quite believe me. Like he thinks I'm going to cut and run after what I saw tonight, which couldn't be further from the truth. If anything, we'll be stronger for it with everything out in the open.

"You don't have to earn being loved, Nash. I know hockey is a huge part of your identity, but it isn't all of you. You could hang up your skates tomorrow and I'd still be just as crazy about you."

Nash pauses, and his brows knit together like he's taking in what I said. A smile forms on his lips; it's a smile that he reserves only for me. "I'm so fucking lucky to have you. I think about that every day."

Then his focus drops to my mouth, and his gaze darkens until it smolders. The ever-present magnetism between us intensifies as he cups my cheek, unleashing a flock of butterflies in my belly. We both let out a sigh as our lips meet, instantly parting. Everything else vanishes, and I melt into him. It never ceases to amaze me how it feels like the first time and forever, every single time.

His hand slides to grip the back of my neck, holding me in place and deepening the kiss. This one says a thousand things all at once, even words he's never voiced out loud. I feel them every time we touch.

He pulls back, studying me with a mixture of reverence and desire, awe and adoration. "I love you, Vi. I never stopped."

"I love you." My voice breaks, along with my composure. Tears begin to stream down my cheeks, complete with huge, wracking sobs. I want to kiss him, but I'm bawling too hard. Gulping for air, I press my face into his bare shoulder while he strokes my back.

He plants a kiss on the crown of my head, holding me tighter. "Thank you for not giving up on me. I promise I'll never give up on us."

This only makes me cry harder, because it's something I needed to hear without even knowing it.

Eventually, my breath steadies, and the tears slow to a halt. Nash presses his lips to my forehead and scoops me up, setting me beside him at the head of the bed. He arranges the covers over both of us and drapes his large, heavy frame around mine, intertwining our hands.

"I love when you're big spoon," I murmur, savoring the closeness between us.

He hums. "Me too."

For a few heartbeats, we lay in silence. It feels like we've been broken apart and now, the pieces are mending back together. Only this time, it's for good.

Nash rises onto one elbow and pushes my hair to the side, exposing my neck. A warm kiss lands below my ear, and his palm slips beneath my tank top as his hand drifts lower, past my navel.

"I thought you said you were tired," I tease, rolling onto my back to look up at him.

He grins down at me, his chestnut hair tumbling down his forehead. "Never too tired for you." Dark green eyes study me playfully as he shifts against me, his thick length pressing into my thigh as proof. "I love you, and I'm going to spend all night showing you just how much."

EPILOGUE
NASH

Six months later
Chicago, Illinois

TONIGHT MARKS GAME four in the second round of the playoffs—otherwise known as the first time I'll step out onto the ice professionally.

No pressure or anything.

I wasn't supposed to play this post-season, but that changed on short notice after a torn hip flexor took out one of our key D-men for the foreseeable future. Since I was already in Chicago working with the team, calling me up was the logical move. It's more than a little ironic that someone else's injury propelled me up into the league. But Baxter should be back in top shape next season, and we'll be playing right alongside each other.

At any rate, I might not get a whole lot of ice time tonight, but I'll definitely be out there.

Thoughts about hockey swim in my head as I place an empty glass in the dishwasher and hit the controls to start it, shutting the stainless steel panel. We already had our morning skate, game tape review, and team lunch. Now that I'm back home, I should nap, but I'm too wired.

Only eight hours to go until puck drop.

I head into the living room, and Violet bumps me with her hip on her way to the coffee maker for a refill. She's barefoot, in yoga pants and a tank top with her blonde hair piled on top of her head and no makeup. My gaze follows her, lingering for a beat. Sometimes I catch myself staring at her, wondering how she could possibly be real. Wondering how she's with me. Wondering how the hell I got so lucky.

Right now is one of those moments.

Snapping back to reality, I lower onto the sectional and unlock my phone, scrolling to the game plan for tonight. It's hard to believe that after working so hard for so long to make it to the league, it's finally coming to fruition.

Some days, my life feels like a dream even beyond my career. Violet and I have a huge townhouse in the heart of Chicago close to shopping, dining, and most importantly, dog parks. Last week, she got hired as an assistant athletic trainer at a local university. And we're still within driving distance to her parents and sister. I mean, it's three hours, but it's doable for a weekend trip.

Granted, I miss my college friends, but I'll see some of them when we play against each other next season. And living with Vi— waking up next to her every day and going to sleep with her every night—more than makes up for that. Plus, I'll bond with the guys on the team soon enough. Teams are always close-knit.

"Just talked to Gracie, and she said yes," Violet says, strolling into the room and coming to stand in front of me, bouncing on her heels excitedly. "Though she's a little afraid to have an adult weekend away because she apparently gets knocked up every time Michael is home from tour." She laughs, taking a sip from the over-sized pink mug in her hands.

I lock my phone, glancing up at her. "Sounds great."

"Are you sure you're ready for a full house of kids next month? With Abigail crawling, I'm told she's into everything."

"I like to think of it as good practice." I wink, and Violet practically swoons on the spot. If there's a way into her heart—and her pants—it's talking about having babies. But I mean it. I can't wait to do those things with her. We agreed to wait a few more years, but it's not too far off.

Plus, her nieces and nephew are cute. I always have fun with them. Though we'll have to do some major childproofing before they come over. We have a lot of breakable shit.

"Yeah?" She sets her coffee on the end table and steps closer, straddling my thighs. Her breasts heave with a breath beneath the thin fabric of her pink tank top, the outline of her pert nipples visible. "We could go upstairs and practice some of that right now."

"We definitely should." I wrap my arms around her tiny waist, meeting her for a kiss.

Biscuit starts barking like it's the apocalypse, interrupting us. Our front door has frosted glass panes, and he considers anyone who walks by to be an intruder on his territory. Mental note to look into those obedience classes again.

I bring my mouth to hers again, and the doorbell rings.

For fuck's sake.

"I can get it," I offer.

"No, it's just, er, something from Sephora." Violet climbs off me and rushes away with a guilty look on her face. She gets weird about her online shopping, even though I never give her a hard time about it. With both of us working, money isn't an issue, and she doesn't buy all that much.

She quietly thanks the delivery person, closing the front door. "I'm going to put this away," she calls, and footfalls sound as she runs upstairs.

Unlocking my phone, I return my attention to the game plan for tonight. My phone pings with a barrage of good luck texts from Vaughn, Connor, Drew, and a handful of my other former teammates. I write them back in between reviewing my notes.

A few minutes later, I hear Violet walk back downstairs behind me, followed by puppy paws clicking on the hardwood.

"Close your eyes," she says, a hint of shyness in her voice. "Don't reopen them until I say you can."

"Okay." I close my eyes, waiting for her to give me the word. I like surprises. They're usually sexy surprises. Maybe it's lingerie…

There's some shuffling as she steps closer.

"All right. Open them."

I reopen my eyes and find Violet standing before me in a red Chicago jersey with my name and number on it.

Nothing *but* a red Chicago jersey with my name and number on it.

It's slightly oversized, hitting at mid-thigh. Her legs are bare and I'm betting there's no underwear beneath, either.

I toss my phone aside without looking, staring at her as all the blood leaves my brain. Perfect face, perfect body, my jersey. It's too much for me to process. How the hell is she mine? I must have been a fucking saint in a former life.

"Do you like it?" She bites back a smile, doing a little twirl to show me the back where it says RICHARDS over the large number twenty-two.

Instead of answering, I push off the couch and circle her legs with one arm, tossing her over my shoulder. In a few, purposeful steps, I cover the distance to the staircase and begin to ascend.

"Is that a yes?" she asks, giggling.

"It's a fuck yes. Sexiest thing ever. How'd you get that made so quickly?" As a rookie who's not due to join the roster until the fall, my jersey isn't exactly something stores have sitting around in stock, and we didn't have a lot of notice about me getting called up.

"Can't tell you all my secrets," Violet says into my T-shirt covered back, still face down. "But I was thinking. Biscuit and I will be awfully lonely with you gone during the season. What do you think about getting another puppy? Maybe he needs a brother."

A deep chuckle rumbles in my chest as I climb another stair. "Don't push your luck."

"So what you're saying is, you want to get a girl dog this time?"

"Feeling sassy today, huh? I can fix that." My palm connects with her backside, and she lets out a yelp. I keep my hand planted on the curve of her ass, gripping her as I continue down the hall to our bedroom.

I reach the edge of our bed and place Violet down onto the plush mattress more gently than I normally would. She leans on her elbows, pale blue eyes peering up at me, waiting for my next move. I can almost see up the jersey, but not quite. I'll get there soon enough.

Instead of ambushing her, I lower onto my side next to her and drink in every inch of her face. Full lips, big eyes, perfect nose. She's so fucking pretty; I'll never get over it.

"I love that smile," she says softly, her fingers skimming my mouth. "I feel like I'm the only one who gets it."

"That's because you are." I kiss her fingertips one at a time. "I'm going to miss the fuck out of you while I'm away next season. Especially after getting spoiled from seeing you every day right now."

She makes a sad face. "I'll miss you, too."

While it isn't the end of the world, it'll be an adjustment for both of us. Since we moved in together two months ago, I've only taken a few short overnight trips for training. We've spent all our free time together hitting up bookstores and bars and everything in between.

My hand slides up to her bare hip, gently stroking her skin. "I love you, Vi. So much."

"I love you." She tilts her head, pressing her soft lips to mine, and her hand sinks into my hair at the nape, tugging hard. My cock jumps, eager to be inside her even though it's been less than twelve hours since I was.

With a low groan, I push her onto her back, hiking up the scarlet jersey halfway to grant me access to her body. Perfect, smooth skin surrounds her perfect, pink pussy. Fuck, she's so hot.

And she's all mine, which makes it even better.

Bracketing her jaw between my thumb and index finger, I sink my teeth into her lush bottom lip, releasing it. "These lips are mine," I tell her. "They always taste so sweet."

I let go of her face and cup her supple breasts beneath the red fabric. "These tits are mine, too."

"What else?" Her eyes are smokey, her voice husky.

Moving lower, I drag my tongue down her flat stomach, digging my teeth into her hipbone and sucking hard enough to leave a mark.

Violet whimpers, and her back arches off the bed. I push her legs apart, kissing and nibbling her inner thighs. She squirms beneath me, trying to urge me on while I continue to tease her.

I dip one finger inside her, using the slickness of her arousal to circle her clit as I watch her hips sway. "This pussy is definitely mine."

I'm tempted to faceplant between her legs and stay there for the next three hours until I need to leave. Still might happen. But before I let myself get too carried away, I need to address the most important part of all.

Sliding back up her body, I place my palm on her chest. "And this heart is mine. At least, I hope it is, because you have my heart, and you always will."

Violet gives me a soft smile and covers my hand with hers. "You've had my heart all along."

***

It's game time.

After warm-up and an impassioned pep talk from Coach Jacobs, I follow the rest of the team out of the dressing room. As we walk through the grey-painted tunnel, the clamor from the crowd grows even louder. Shouts and whistles practically shake the walls of the arena. While I'm used to playing in front of a crowd, this is next level.

It's a home game, so at least they're cheering for us. Next game, we won't be so lucky.

I step out into the players' area, scanning the rows of seating. It's a sea of red from wall to wall, with nearly all of the fans decked out in Chicago gear. My eyes land on Violet and her parents in the section reserved for team families, and I momentarily forget the nerves that have set in. They wave at me excitedly, and Violet blows me a kiss. I throw them a wave back before going to sit on the bench next to Coleman, another defenseman.

He was a rookie last year, so this is his first playoff rodeo, too. While I like him, he reminds me a lot of Connor—which is to say, he's a hot mess off the ice.

Coleman nudges me with a grin. "Ready?"

"Fuck yeah," I say, adrenaline kicking in.

The series is sitting at one win for us and two wins for New York. Despite the incredibly high stakes, I'm not as anxious as I was before games in my college days. While I'm keyed up, there's no underlying sense of dread. No looming worry about what's to come later. My coach and my team have my back. As for who's watching, Violet and her parents are the only familiar faces I see, and they're the only ones I need.

For all I know, Doug could be here—he could be one of the faces in a sea of nineteen thousand people. We haven't spoken since the Ice Cup tournament. Last I heard, he had gotten fired from Copperhill Academy after Russell spoke to the school. I have no idea if he found another job. I don't really care. My life has been a thousand times better without him in it.

Everything kicks into warp speed, and the national anthem speeds by like it's being sung on fast-forward. Before I know it, the puck drops, and the game begins. New York comes out hot, but we come out even hotter, almost instantly taking three shots on net.

A few shifts later, it's my turn. I hop the boards to join the play in progress, and my skates hit the ice with a familiar jolt. Heart galloping, I dig in my blades and barrel into position, trying to keep up with the breakneck pace. Despite the team practices I've attended, the learning curve is steep. Playing at the college level is entirely different than facing seasoned, fully-grown athletes in the midst of a playoff game. It's fast-paced, it's exhilarating, and it's everything I trained nearly two decades for.

It's one of my biggest dreams coming true.

But when my shift ends and I climb back onto the bench, I know one thing for certain. The most important part of my life isn't hockey or my career. She's sitting in section 106, row 5, and she's my whole fucking world.

THE END

ABOUT THE AUTHOR

Avery Keelan is an award-winning author of sports romance and contemporary romance, a lifelong hockey fan, and a diehard coffee lover. She writes swoon-worthy happily ever afters with hot hockey heroes, snarky banter, and enough steam to fog up a mirror.

With undergraduate degrees in Commerce and Psychology, Avery specialized in government policy and legislation in a previous life. She lives in Canada with her husband and their two children, along with two spoiled rescue cats who like to sit on her keyboard at inopportune times.

ALSO BY AVERY KEELAN

Rules of the Game Series

Offside (Chase and Bailey)

Shutout (Tyler and Sera)

Lakeside University Series

The Enforcer (Nash & Vi)

Standalone Novels

Otherwise Engaged

Made in United States
Troutdale, OR
05/01/2024

19583923R00213